When the snow
begins to fall,
that's when
he strikes...

WATCHING JENNA

Tonight, with the snow so heavy, he was forced inside, to watch Jenna via monitor, and as he did, he felt nausea attack. He was hot, itching from the inside out. Furious, he kicked a paint can and sent it reeling, the red color splashing the walls. He barely noticed.

She was with another man.

Kissing.

Touching.

His pulse pounded, throbbed through his brain, and he felt betrayal of the worst kind. Didn't she know that only *he* could satisfy her? His shrine to her was nearly complete— and this was how she repaid him, by acting like a common tramp for the sheriff.

Shane Carter, a man who had vowed to uphold the law— and there he was, stripping off her clothes, running his tongue and hands over her skin. And she let him.

His Jenna.

She let him!

Rage burned through him, and he plotted all kinds of satisfying revenge, but he could not abandon his plan. Not now. Precision was key.

He watched them make love, and his rage grew cold as the night. How long had he worked for this? For years.

He and Jenna were meant to be together. There were no coincidences. His life was meant to be entwined with hers, and everything he did was for Jenna.

Always for Jenna . . .

Books by Lisa Jackson

SEE HOW SHE DIES

INTIMACIES

WISHES

WHISPERS

TWICE KISSED

UNSPOKEN

IF SHE ONLY KNEW

HOT BLOODED

COLD BLOODED

THE NIGHT BEFORE

THE MORNING AFTER

DEEP FREEZE

Published by Zebra Books

LISA JACKSON

DEEP FREEZE

ZEBRA BOOKS
KENSINGTON PUBLISHING CORP.
http://www.kensingtonbooks.com

ACKNOWLEDGMENTS

There are tons of people who helped me with this book. They range from agents and editors to researchers and proofreaders, and friends and family who have offered their support. These people were all instrumental in getting this book published:

In New York, thanks to John Scognamiglio, my editor, and Robin Rue, my agent, who are both incredibly smart, hilarious, and patient. On the West Coast, thanks to Nancy Bush, Ken Bush, Matthew Crose, Michael Crose, Ken Melum, Sally Peters, Marilyn Katcher, Linda Sparks, Larry Sparks, Carol Maloy, Celia Stinson, Danielle Katcher, Kathy Okano, Ari Okano, Jack Pederson, Betty Pederson, and Samantha Santistevan, and anyone else I may have inadvertently missed.

PROLOGUE

Last Winter

Unmoving, she waited.

As if she sensed he was near.

He could feel it—that throb of desire between them as he looked across a dimly illuminated expanse to the bed where she lay in semidarkness. Jenna Hughes. The woman of his dreams. The single female he'd lived his life for. So close. And in his bed. Finally in his bed.

And he was ready. Oh God, he was ready. Sweat began to bead on his upper lip and forehead. His cock was stiffening, his nerve endings dancing.

The lamps were turned low, a few night-lights giving the large room an intimate atmosphere of shadows and fuzzy, muted corners. Soft music, the romantic score from the movie *Beneath the Shadows,* whispered through the cold, cavernous room. His breath fogged as he stared at her in the sexy black teddy he'd bought for her. So nice that she'd decided to wear it for this special tryst. Their first.

Good girl.

The silk and lace had fit perfectly, sculpting her body. Just as he'd known it would.

He caught a glimpse of her breasts through the sheer fabric. Dark nipples looked nearly wet as they peeked through the lace. Had she moistened them for him? In eager expectation?

Beautiful.

He smiled inwardly, knowing that she was as eager as he was.

How long had he anticipated this moment? He couldn't remember. It didn't matter. The time was now. The pills and vodka he'd swallowed had kicked in and he was working on the perfect buzz—just enough chemicals to make this moment even better.

"I'm here," he told her quietly, expecting her to turn her head, arch one of those delicate black eyebrows, and cast him a come-hither look. Or perhaps she would rise on one elbow and slowly crook a finger toward him, silently drawing him closer, her silvery-green gaze holding his.

But she didn't move. Not one strand of ebony-colored hair shifted. She just lay on the bed and stared upward.

That was wrong.

He froze.

She should look his way. That was what he wanted.

"Jenna?" he called quietly.

Nothing. Not so much as a flicker of a glance in his direction.

What was the matter with her? Dressed like a damned harlot, she acted as if she didn't care that he was near, that this night was special to her. To him. To *them*.

Not again!

His back teeth ground together in frustration at her cool disinterest. Was it a game? Was she teasing him? Just what the hell was going on here?

"Jenna, look at me," he commanded in a near-whisper.

But as he edged closer, he realized that she wasn't as perfect as he'd thought. No . . . her makeup wasn't quite right. Her lipstick was too pale, her eyeshadow barely visible. He'd wanted her to look more like a whore. That was the plan. Hadn't he told her to play the part of a prostitute? *Isn't she dressed as a prostitute? Isn't this part of your fantasy?*

Damn, he couldn't think straight. His mind wasn't as clear as he'd hoped. Probably the drugs . . . or was it something else? Something vital? Jenna wasn't responding the way he'd hoped.

She knew what he liked.

But then, she'd always been defiant. Always aloof. Icily so. That was part of his attraction to her.

"Come on, baby," he whispered, deciding to give her another chance, though he was having trouble focusing. Maybe he was a little too high and he wasn't seeing those little nuances of lust that she was known for. That was it. His mind was a little too cloudy, his thoughts not quite joined, his lust overtaking reason. He was quivering inside, and his lungs felt constricted. His erection was rock-hard, straining against his fly, but the images in his mind were a little blurry.

He licked his lips. No more waiting.

He placed a knee on the bed beside her, and the mattress creaked loudly.

Still she refused to look at him.

"Jenna!" he said more sharply than he'd intended, his temper catching fire, his tongue a little thick.

Take it easy. She's here, isn't she?

"Jenna, look at me!"

Not so much as a flinch.

Stubborn, thankless woman! After all he'd done for her! All the years he'd thought of no one but her! Rage burned through his blood, and his hands began to shake.

Calm down! You can still have her. In your bed. She hasn't moved away, has she?

"Jenna, I'm here," he said.

She ignored him.

Fury blazed white-hot, but he tried to fight his anger. This was her game, that was all. She knew that the more she pretended disinterest, the more he would want her, the higher the erotic stakes. And that was all the better.

Wasn't it?

He didn't know. Couldn't really remember.

He was sweating though it was cold in here, the tempera-

ture hovering only a few degrees above freezing. And yet he
was hot inside, a fire raging through his blood.

*Didn't she feel it—the intimate bond that tethered them
together?*

He leaned closer, and with a trembling finger traced the
outline of her cheek. It was warm to his touch.

Then he understood. This was all part of *her* fantasy. She
wanted him to think of her not as Jenna Hughes, but as one of
the roles she'd played on the big screen. Wasn't she dressed
as Paris Knowlton, a New Orleans prostitute in *Beneath the
Shadows*? Hadn't he wanted Jenna to act like Paris tonight?
Isn't that exactly what she was doing? Suddenly he felt better, the warmth running through his veins due to lust and
drugs rather than rage.

"Paris," he cooed, touching her dark hair lovingly. It
shimmered a blue-black in the shadowy lights. "I've been
searching for you."

Still no response.

Jesus, what did she want? He was playing *his* part . . . or
was he?

"Jenna?"

Not so much as a glance his way. Anger sparked. It tore
through him, his blood suddenly thundering in his ears. "Oh,
I get it," he snarled, his fingers roughly grazing her neck.
"You're really into this, aren't you? You *like* acting like a
whore."

He heard a gasp.

Finally!

His fingers surrounded her throat. It was warm to his
touch. Pliant. He tried to feel her pulse as his hands pressed
against her skin.

A groan.

Pain or desire?

"That's it, isn't it? You like it when I'm rough, don't you?"

"Oh God, no!" Her voice seemed to come from a distance, echoing in his head, bouncing off the walls. "Don't!"

His grip tightened, sinking into her nearly hot flesh.

"Stop! Please! What are you doing?"

He was so hard he was trembling, but he couldn't take his hands from her neck, couldn't unzip his fly. He shook her then and her head wobbled wildly, beautiful green eyes fixed straight at him.

A terrified scream ripped through the room.

Jenna's head fell backward.

Her neck wobbled in his hands.

Another horrified, panicked shriek ricocheted off the rafters, the sound echoing through his brain.

"Bitch!" He slapped her hard.

Smack! Her face twisted hard to one side.

"Oh God!" There was crying now. Sobbing. "No, no, no!"

Her makeup began to run, her perfect features distorting from the blow. Her hair came loose, the thick black wig falling onto the rumpled mattress, her bald pate visible in the dusky room.

A gasp.

Her head twisted to one side.

That was better.

He raised his hand again.

"Don't . . . oh God, please don't!" she pled from immobile lips. "What're you doing?" She was wailing violently, nearly incoherently, panic stretching her vocal cords. But her shoulders remained stiff. Inflexible. Her face without any passion.

Something was wrong here, very wrong . . .

"Oh God, oh God, oh God . . . please stop."

The sound of fear, the gulping, gasping sobs, reverberated through the room, yet no tears fell from Jenna's eyes, nor did they blink. Her lips didn't tremble. Her shoulders didn't shake. Her body didn't convulse . . .

He blinked. Cleared his head. His erection softened as he realized where he was and realized what he was doing.

Hell!

He stared down at Jenna Hughes, and as if his hands were burned, dropped her onto the mussed silk sheets.

Crack!

Her head hit the bed frame.

A shriek of pure terror ripped through the room.

Jenna's neck snapped.

Her bald head fell away from her body.

"Oh God, noooooooooooo!"

Eyes wide, the head rolled off the mattress.

With a dull thud, her skull landed on the concrete floor of this, his sanctuary.

The screams became hysterical, violent, horrible sobs that tore through the chamber, bouncing off the walls and climbing up his spine.

"Oh God! Please, don't!" Her voice seemed to echo to the rooftop. So she *could* feel. And yet she wasn't looking at him. Something was wrong here . . . very wrong.

On the floor, Jenna's features compressed and flattened in the ooze that had once been her face.

His mind cleared.

He realized that his near-perfect creation, his waxen mask of Jenna Hughes's gorgeous face, was destroyed.

Because he hadn't been able to wait.

Because he'd taken too many pills.

Because he wanted her so badly that he'd lost his judgment and slapped her. Long before her likeness had hardened.

"Fool," he ground out and slapped himself alongside the head. "Idiot!" All that work for nothing. The beautiful face— could it be reconstructed? Where once it had been nearly lifelike, now it was goo; once a Michelangelo, now a Picasso, her beautiful features distorted as they pooled around sightless eyes that were glassy and stark.

He leaned back, away from the mess on the bed. There was no blood. No flesh and bone. Not from this lifeless form. Swiping the sweat away from his forehead, he glanced across the shadowed expanse to his darkened stage, already set, where several near-perfect mannequins stood silently waiting in the gloom. They were beautiful, if not alive. Replicas of Jenna Hughes.

But this one! He looked again at what had once been his

masterpiece and frowned. A pathetic imitation! He'd been distracted lately.

"Please . . . let me go."

He rocked back onto his feet and looked over his shoulder to the murky corner. His eyes focused on the live woman, bound and naked, just waking up from a drug-induced slumber. Hers had been the voice he'd heard. Her terror was the emotion that had rippled through the room.

"Please . . ." she mewled again softly, and he smiled, feeling a renewed hope as he surveyed her musculature and facial features. The width of the forehead, the straight nose, the high cheekbones beneath big, frightened eyes. She was a dirty blond, but hair color was the least of his worries. Facially she was a near-match. His grin stretched wide, and the mess on the floor was instantly forgotten.

His next replica of Jenna Hughes would be perfect.

This pathetic creature, bound and begging for her life, was anatomically correct.

His anger subsided in an instant as he glanced to one window, where the barest hint of moonlight slipped through the panes. Snow was melting on the outer sill.

Winter was slipping away.

The spring thaw was already in the air.

He'd have to work fast.

CHAPTER 1

This Winter

"So you're concerned about the coming storm," Dr. Randall said calmly from the chair near his desk. He'd positioned his body so that there was nothing between himself and his client but an imported rug covering the polished wooden floor of his office.

"I'm concerned about the winter." The response was angry, but coldly so. The man, tall and taciturn, sat near the window on a padded leather chair. He stared straight at Randall with a hard, unforgiving gaze.

Randall nodded, as if he understood. "You're concerned, because—?"

"You know why. It seems that things always get worse when the temperature drops."

"At least for you."

"Right. For me. Isn't that why I'm here?" Tension was evident in the stiffness of his neck and the bleached knuckles of his clasped hands.

"Why are you here?"

"Don't patronize me. None of that psychobabble doubletalk."

"Do you hate the winter?"

A beat. A second's hesitation. The client blinked. "Not at all. Hate's a pretty strong word."

"What would you say? What would be the right word?"

"It's not the season I don't like. It's what happens."

"Maybe your concern about things being worse at this time of year is just your perception."

"Do you deny that bad things happen in the winter?"

"Of course not, but sometimes accidents or tragedies can occur in other months. People drown while swimming in the summer, or fall off cliffs while hiking in the mountains, or become ill from parasites that only breed in the heat. Bad things can happen at any time."

His client's jaw became solid granite as he seemed to struggle silently with the concept. He was a very intelligent man, his IQ near genius level, but he was struggling to make sense of the tragedy that had scarred his life. "I do *know* that intellectually, but personally, it's always worse in the winter." He glanced to the window, where gray clouds were muddying the sky.

"Because of what happened when you were a child?"

"You tell me. You're the shrink." He cut a harsh glance at the psychologist before offering a bit of a smile, a quick flash of teeth that Dr. Randall supposed would be considered a killer smile by most women. This man was an interesting case, made more so by the pact that they had agreed upon: There would be no notes, no recording, not so much as a memo about the appointment in Randall's date book to indicate that the two had ever met. The appointment was cloaked in the deepest secrecy.

His client glanced at the clock, reached into his back pocket, and pulled out his wallet. He didn't count out the bills. They were already neatly folded and tucked into a special compartment.

"We should meet again soon," Dr. Randall suggested as the money was left on a corner of his desk.

The tall man nodded sharply. "I'll call."

And he would, Dr. Randall thought, idly pressing the fold from the crisp twenties as his patient's boots rang down the steps of the back staircase. For no matter how hard the man tried to convince himself he didn't need counseling, he was smart enough to realize that the demons he was trying to exorcise had burrowed deep into the darkest parts of his soul and wouldn't be released without the proper coaxing, the treatment he so abhorred.

Pride goeth before a fall, Randall thought as he slipped the bills into his own worn wallet. He'd seen it time and time again. This man, though he didn't know it, was about to tumble.

"Dad-gum dog—where the hell did ya run off ta now?" Charley Perry said around a wad of chewing tobacco. He was tramping through the wilderness, high above the Columbia, through old-growth timber and little else as the first light of dawn splintered through the trees. Winter was chasing down the gorge, and his stupid, two-bit spaniel had taken off again. He considered leaving her out here—she'd probably find her way back to his cabin—but a bit of guilt nagged at him, and truth to tell, she was all he really had in the world. Tanzy had once been a helluva huntin' dog, Charley mused, but like himself, she was half-deaf now and more than a little crippled with arthritis.

Squinting through the sparse brush, he whistled sharply, the sound piercing its way through the forest as branches rattled overhead. His gloved hands tightened over the barrel of his rifle, a Winchester that his daddy had bestowed upon him over half a century earlier when he'd returned from the war. He had newer weapons, a lot of them, but this one, like the tired old dog, was his favorite.

Damn, he thought, but he was gettin' nostalgic in his old age.

"Tanzy?" he called, knowing that he was chasing off any chance of prey. *Stupid bitch of a dog!*

He stomped up a familiar trail, his gaze scanning the ground for signs of deer, or elk, or even a bear, though they'd already gone into their dens for the winter. There had been talk in town of a mountain lion that had been seen near the falls this summer, but Charley hadn't come across any spoor that indicated the big cat was prowling these slopes. Charley didn't really know what cougars did in the winter but he didn't think they hibernated. Not that it mattered. Never, in all his seventy-two years of living in these mountains, had he ever seen one. He didn't figure today would be his unlucky day.

His feet ached from the cold, even in his wool socks and hunting boots. The shrapnel still embedded in his hip pained him. Still he hunted, searching these woods as he had as a kid with his pa. He'd nailed his first buck up on Settler's Bluff when he was fourteen. Hell, that was a long time ago.

A blast of wind hit him hard in his face and he swore. "Come on, Tanzy! Let's go, girl!" It was time to drive his battered Ford truck into town, pick up a paper, and drink coffee at the Canyon Café with the few of his friends who were still alive and healthy enough to leave their wives for an hour or two. Later, he'd do the crossword puzzle and stoke the fire in his woodstove.

Where the hell was that mutt?

He whistled again and heard a whimper, then a bark.

At last! He turned and walked down a sharp gully where Tanzy was suddenly going ape-shit, her nose to the ground around a decaying log. "Whaddaya got, girl?" Charley asked, as he stepped over a bleached-out snag and into a scattering of brush. His boots snapped small twigs as he inched his way down to the dog, bracing himself for a squirrel or weasel to dart out from what appeared to be a hollow log. He sure as hell hoped it wasn't a porcupine or skunk holed up in there.

A breeze stirred the branches overhead and he smelled it then—the rank odor of decaying flesh. Whatever was inside was already dead. No worry about it dashing out and scaring the bejeezus out of him.

Tanzy was barking her fool head off, jumping at the log and leaping back, the bristles of her spotted coat standing on end, her tail swatting the air.

"Okay, okay, just let me have a look-see," Charley said,

lowering himself on one knee and hearing it pop. He bent
down and peered into the cavity of the log. "Can't really
tell." But something was wedged inside and it smelled bad.
Curiosity got the better of him, and he shifted the log a bit,
allowing the wintry sunlight a chance to permeate the darkness. As he did, he got a good glimpse of what was inside.

A human skull stared back at him.

Charley's blood turned to ice. He yelped and dropped the
log.

It splintered against the forest floor.

The skull, with tiny, sharp teeth, strings of blond hair, and
bits of rotting flesh attached to the bone, rolled into the pine
needles and dry leaves.

"Jesus H. Christ!" he whispered, and it was a prayer. The
wind seemed to pick up, shaking the snow from the trees,
skittering across the back of his neck. Charley took a step
back and sensed evil—from the darkest part of Lucifer's heart—
lurking in the gloom of this forest.

"Charley Perry's a crackpot," Sheriff Shane Carter groused
as he poured himself a cup of coffee from the carafe that
simmered for hours on end in the kitchen of the sheriff's department. As soon as the last cup was poured from the glass
pot, another was made.

"Yeah, but this time he's claiming he found a human skull
up near Catwalk Point. We can't ignore that," BJ Stevens
said. She was a short woman, a little on the hippy side, with
three men's names. Billie Jo Stevens. She didn't seem to
mind.

"Send two men up there."

"Already have. Donaldson and Montinello."

"Charley claimed to have seen Bigfoot a couple of times
before," Carter reminded her as he headed through the break
room toward his office near the rear of the Lewis County
Courthouse. "And then there was the incident where he was
certain a UFO had hovered over the Bridge of the Gods, remember that?"

"Okay, so he's eccentric."

"Nutcase," Carter reminded her. "Full-blown."

"Harmless."

"Let's just hope this is another one of his wild-goose chases."

"But you're going up to investigate," she said, knowing him better than he wanted her to.

"Yeah." Carter made his way past glowing computer monitors, jangling phones, cubicles, old desks, and filing cabinets to his office, a glassed-in room with miniblinds he could lower for privacy. His two outside windows overlooked the courthouse parking lot and Danby's Furniture Store across the street. If he craned his neck, he was able to peer down Main Street. He rarely bothered.

He set his cup on his desk and checked his e-mail, but he couldn't quite shake the feeling that there was more to Charley Perry's story than they knew. It was true Charley was over the top, an eccentric loner who lived by his own rules, especially when it came to poaching game, but he was essentially harmless and, Carter suspected, a decent enough guy. But every once in a while he seemed to freak out, or need attention or something. The Bigfoot fiasco had gotten him some press. Two years later he claimed he'd spotted a UFO and had been beamed aboard so that aliens who looked humanoid with huge heads could study him. Well, if the poor aliens had thought Charley was a prime specimen of the human race, they were probably sorely disappointed in humankind. No wonder they hadn't been back.

The phone rang and he answered automatically, managing to drink from his cup as he turned from the computer screen.

"Carter."

"Montinello, Sheriff," Deputy Lanny Montinello said, his voice barely audible for the bad cell phone connection. "I think you might want to come up to Catwalk Point. It looks like old Charley is right. We've got ourselves a body. Or, at least, most of one."

"Damn," Carter muttered, asking a few more questions

before ordering Montinello to seal off the crime scene and keep Charley on ice. As soon as he hung up, he called the state crime scene lab, grabbed his jacket, hat, and weapon, then collected BJ. On the way he left messages with the Medical Examiner and D.A.'s office.

"What did I tell you?" BJ asked as he drove his Blazer up the winding logging road to Catwalk Point, a mountain that rose three thousand feet from the Columbia River basin floor. They'd been delayed, called to an injury-accident on a county road just south of town that had held them up for nearly two hours.

By the time they reached the end of the gravel-and-mud road, yellow crime scene tape had been strung around the area. Not that there was much chance of rubberneckers up here. Sooner or later the press would hear of it and converge, but not for a while. Carter pulled the hood of his insulated jacket over his head as he stepped out of his rig.

It was cold with the promise of winter, a snowstorm having been predicted for the next few days. The ground was nearly frozen, the tall fir trees shivering and dancing in the icy blasts of an east wind that roared down the gorge.

Carefully he and BJ picked their way down a sharp ravine where detectives from the Oregon State Crime Lab were already at work.

Pictures were being snapped by one photographer while another aimed a video camera at the ground. A grid had already been established over a wide area, the scene secured. Through the snow, soil samples were being collected, debris sorted through, a hollow log tagged. Bones had been carefully laid upon a plastic tarp. The skeleton was small, but incomplete. And the skull was odd, its teeth too tiny and sharp.

"What've we got?" Carter asked Merline Jacobosky, a reed-thin investigator with sharp features and an even sharper mind. Her eyebrows were slammed together over the tops of rimless glasses and her lips, devoid of any color, pinched together as she stopped writing on the pages attached to her clipboard and again surveyed the human remains.

"Off the top? White female, mid-twenties to thirties, I'd guess, but don't quote me until the M.E. releases her to the lab and there's a full autopsy. She'd been stuffed into that log over there." With her pen, Merline pointed to the hollowed-out cedar. "We're missing a few bones, probably because an animal or two dragged off parts of her corpse, but we're still looking. Already found an ulna and tarsal that were missing at first. Maybe we'll get lucky with the rest."

"Maybe," Carter said without much enthusiasm as he surveyed the forest floor and the craggy hillside that dropped steeply toward the Columbia River. The terrain was rugged, the forest dense, the river wide and wild as it carved a wide trench between the states of Oregon and Washington. Even tamed by a series of dams, it raged westward, whitecaps visible through the trees. If a body were ever dumped in the Columbia, there wasn't a whole lot of chance of it ever being recovered.

He heard the whine of an engine struggling up the hillside and glimpsed the M.E.'s van through the trees. Not far behind was another rig, one belonging to one of the Assistant District Attorneys.

Merline wasn't finished. She said, "Here's what I think is really odd. Check out her teeth." Jacobosky knelt and pointed with the end of her pen. "See the incisors and molars? That isn't a natural rot . . . I think they've been filed."

Carter felt a whisper of dread touch the base of his spine. Who would file someone's teeth? And why? "To keep the body from being identified?" he asked.

"Maybe, but why not just pull the teeth or break them? Why go to all the trouble of filing them to tiny points?" She rocked back on her heels and tapped her pen to her lips as she studied the skull. "It doesn't make any sense."

"Maybe our guy is a dentist with a sick sense of humor."

"The sick part is right."

"Any ID?" he asked, but assumed the answer.

"Nothing yet." She shook her head and flipped over a page of her clipboard. "No clothes or personal effects, either. But we'll keep looking, under the snow, through the ice and into the soil. If there's evidence, we'll locate it." She squinted up at Carter as gray clouds scudded overhead.

"What's this?" Carter bent down and studied the skull with its grotesque teeth and gaping eye sockets. He indicated her hair. There was something clinging to the strands that were visible. A pinkish substance that he didn't think was flesh. It reminded him of eraser residue.

"Don't know. Yet. But some kind of manmade substance. We'll have the lab check it out."

"Good." He straightened and noticed BJ talking with one of the photographers as Luke Messenger, the M.E. arrived. Tall and rangy, with curly red hair and freckles, he made his way to the crime scene and frowned at the body.

"Only a partial?" he asked Jacobosky.

"So far." He knelt beside the bones as Amanda Pratt, the Assistant D.A. lucky enough to be assigned this frigid job, picked her way down the hillside. She was bundled in layers of down and wool and smelled of cigarette smoke.

"God, this is miserable weather," she said, her pert nose wrinkling at the partial body. "Jesus, would you look at that? Found in a hollowed-out log?"

"So Charley says."

"You can't believe a word out of his mouth," she said flatly, but eyed the scene.

"Maybe this time he's telling the truth."

Her eyes flashed behind thin, plastic-rimmed glasses. "Yeah, right. And I'm the friggin' queen of England. No, make that Spain. England's too damned cold. Jesus, we've got ourselves a regular party up here." She scanned the vehicles. "Is Charley still around?"

"In one of the pickups—over there." Jacobosky hitched her chin toward a white truck idling near the end of the road. Montinello was at the wheel. Charley Perry was huddled in the passenger seat. "He's not too happy about being kept up here," Jacobosky added. "Making a whole lotta noise about wanting to get home and warm up."

"Don't blame him. I'll talk to him."

"Good," Amanda said. "Be sure to have your bullshit meter with you."

Carter laughed, took another long look at the grid that was the crime scene, then said to the Medical Examiner, "Let me know what you find out."

"Soon as we sort it all out," Messenger replied. He was still crouched over the remains. Didn't bother looking up. "You'll be the first to know."

"Thanks." Carter headed up the hillside and found Charley as cranky as ever. He was cradling a cup of coffee someone had brought up, but he glared through the passenger window at Carter as if he held the sheriff personally responsible for ruining his day. Carter tapped on the glass, and Charley reluctantly lowered the window.

"Are you arrestin' me?" he demanded, short, silvery beard covering a strong, jutted chin. Angry eyes peered from behind thick glasses.

"No."

"Then have one of your boys take me home. I done my duty, didn't I? No need to treat me like some kind of damned prisoner." He spat a long stream of tobacco juice through the window to land on the snowy dirt and gravel. Fortunately for Charley, this area wasn't considered part of the crime scene.

"I just want to ask you some questions."

"I been answerin' 'em all mornin'!"

Carter smiled. "Just a few more, then I'll have Deputy Montinello take you home."

"Great," Charley muttered, folding his arms over a thin chest. He cooperated, if reluctantly, and was right; he didn't have any more information. He told Carter that he'd been out hunting, lost his dog, and found her down in the gully near the hollow log. He'd lifted the log and a skull had rolled out, nearly scaring him to death. ". . . and that's all I know," he added petulantly. "I half-ran home and called your office. And don't you give me no grief 'bout huntin' with Tanzy. I needed a trackin' dog to get me back home," he said, as if he realized he could be in trouble for hunting with a dog.

Hurriedly he added, "Two of your men hauled me back up here a few hours back and I'm still freezin' my butt off."

"We all are, Charley," Carter said, and slapped the door of the department's truck. "Take him back home," he said to Lanny Montinello before looking at Charley's grizzled face again. "If you think of anything else, you'll call, right?"

"'Course," Charley said, though he didn't meet Carter's eyes and the sheriff suspected that the loner was stretching the truth. They'd never gotten along, not since Carter had debunked Charley's Bigfoot story and had once threatened to call the game warden about Charley poaching deer. No, Charley Perry wasn't likely to call again, not if he had to speak to the sheriff. Carter glanced at Montinello and said, "Take him home." The interview was over.

"Will do." Montinello slid the pickup into gear, and Carter slapped the door a couple of times as Charley rolled up the window. Within seconds the truck disappeared around a stand of old growth that was as dense as it was tall. The firs loomed high, seeming to scrape the steel-colored bellies of the clouds just as the first drops of icy rain began to fall.

Carter shoved his hands deep into the pockets of his parka and looked down the hillside to the crime scene crawling with investigators. The unknown woman's partial skeleton was stretched out on the plastic sheet. Amanda Pratt was standing a few yards off, smoking a cigarette and hashing it out with Luke Messenger. In the midst of it all was the corpse, with her filed teeth and bits of pink gunk in her hair.

Who was she and what the hell was she doing up in this isolated part of no-damned-where?

CHAPTER 2

Click!

The French doors opened.

A gust of wind, cold as all of winter, swept inside the darkened house. Near-dead embers in the fireplace glowed a brighter red. The old dog lying on the rug near Jenna's chair lifted his head and let out a low, warning growl.

"Shh!" the intruder hissed.

Jenna's eyes narrowed as she squinted at the silhouette easing into the large great room. As dark as it was, she recognized her oldest daughter slinking toward the stairs. Just as she'd expected. Great. One more teenager sneaking home in the middle of the night.

"Hush, Critter!" Cassie whispered angrily, her voice sharp as she tiptoed to the stairs.

Jenna snapped on a nearby lamp.

Instantly the log house was illuminated. Cassie froze at the first step. "Damn," she muttered, her shoulders sagging as she slowly turned and faced her mother.

"You are *so* grounded," Jenna said from her favorite leather chair.

Instantly, Cassie was on the offensive. "What're you doing up?"

"Waiting for you." Jenna unfolded herself from the chair and met her daughter's sullen expression. Cassie, who so many people said was a carbon-copy of Jenna as a younger woman. Cassie was taller by an inch, but her high cheek-bones, dark lashes and brows, and pointed chin were nearly identical to Jenna's. "Where were you?"

"Out." She tossed her streaked hair over her shoulder.

"I *know* that. You were supposed to be in bed. As a matter of fact, I remember you saying something like ''Night, Mom' around eleven."

Jenna was rewarded with an exaggerated roll of Cassie's green eyes. "So who were you with? No, forget that—I figure you were with Josh."

Cassie didn't offer any information, but in Jenna's estimation, Josh Sykes was a foregone conclusion. Ever since Cassie had started dating the nineteen-year-old, she'd become secretive, sullen, and mutinous.

"So where did you go? Precisely."

Cassie folded her arms over her chest and leaned a shoulder against the yellowed log wall. Her makeup was smeared, her hair mussed, her clothes rumpled. Jenna didn't have to guess what her daughter had been doing, and it scared her to death. "We were just out driving around," Cassie said.

"At three in the morning?"

"Yeah." Cassie lifted a shoulder and yawned.

"It's freezing outside."

"So?"

"Look, Cassie, don't start with the attitude. I'm not in the mood."

"I don't see why you care."

"Don't you?" Jenna was standing now, advancing on her rebellious daughter, getting her first whiff of cigarette smoke and maybe something else. "Let's just start with I love you and I don't want to see you mess up your life."

"Like you did?" Cassie arched one brow cattily. "When you got pregnant with me?"

The barb hit its intended mark, but Jenna ignored it. "That was a little different. I was almost twenty-two. An adult. On my own. And we're not talking about me. You're the one who's been lying and sneaking out."

"I can take care of myself."

"You're sixteen, for crying out loud." And a woman. Cassie's figure was already enviable by Hollywood standards.

"I was just out with friends."

"'Driving around.'"

"Yeah."

"Right." Jenna wasn't buying it for a minute. "Haven't you heard the old axiom that 'nothing good happens after midnight?'"

Cassie just glared at her.

"Look, this isn't getting us anywhere now, so go on up to bed and we'll talk in the morning."

"There's nothing to talk about."

"Sure there is. We'll start with sneaking out and cruise right into the pitfalls of teen pregnancy and STDs. And that's just for starters."

"I can't wait," Cassie said, reminding Jenna of herself at the same age. "You just don't like Josh."

"I don't like that he seems to have some kind of control over you, that you'd do anything to be with him. That he talks you into lying to me."

"I don't—"

"Ah-ah. If I were you, Cassie, I'd quit while you're ahead, or at least while you're not too far behind."

But Cassie's temper had sparked and she was suddenly defiant. "You don't like any of my friends," she accused, "not since we moved up here, so it's your fault. I never wanted to come."

That much was true. Both of her daughters had had fits about her decision to leave L.A. behind and seek out some kind of peace and normalcy in this quiet little town perched on the rocky shores of the Columbia River in Oregon. Jenna had heard the complaints for a year and a half. "That's old news. We're here, Cassie, and we're all going to make the best of it."

"I'm trying."

"With Josh."

"Yeah. With Josh." Rebellion flashed in Cassie's eyes.

"To punish me."

"No," Cassie said slowly, her jaw setting. "Believe it or not, this isn't about you, for once. Okay? If I wanted to 'punish' you, I'd go back to California and live with Dad."

"Is that what you want?" Jenna felt as if she'd been sucker-punched, but she didn't show any emotion, didn't want to let Cassie know that she'd hit a very strong and painful nerve.

"I just want someone to trust me, okay?"

"Trust is earned, Cassie," she said, and inwardly cringed as she realized she was echoing words she'd heard from her own mother years before.

Jenna bit her tongue rather than start in on that one. "We'll talk about it tomorrow." She snapped off the lamp and heard Cassie's footsteps trudge up the stairs. *I'm turning into my mother*, she thought, and refused to let her mind wander too far in that frightening direction. "Come on, Critter," she said to the dog as she relocked the door and started up the flight of stairs to the second story. Her bedroom was halfway up the stairs, just off the landing, the girls' another half a flight higher. "Let's go to bed." The old dog padded behind, his gait slowed by arthritis. Jenna waited for him at the landing and heard Cassie's door shut with a quiet thud. "We're finally all safe and sound." *And you have to get up in two and a half hours.* Inwardly groaning at the thought, she turned the final set of stairs, but from the corner of her eye, through the landing's stained-glass window, she caught a glimpse of something.

Movement?

Her own pale reflection?

Critter growled softly, and Jenna's muscles went rigid. "Shh," she said, but squinted through the colored glass, searching the distorted image of the yard and outbuildings of her ranch—"the compound," as Cassie referred to it. Security lamps glowed an eerie blue, casting pools of light on the barn, stable, and sheds. The old windmill creaked, its blades turning slowly as it stood, a wooden skeleton, near the lane. The main gate gaped open, the result of the lock freezing and snow piling up around the gateposts. The lane leading to the gate was empty—no rumble of a car or truck engine cutting through the night.

Still, the forested hills and craggy banks of the river were dark and shrouded, the cloudy night a perfect cover . . .

For whom?

Don't be silly.

Surely no one was lurking in the wintry shadows.

Of course not.

The worst-case scenario would be that Josh Sykes was still hanging around, hiding behind the corner of the barn, maybe hoping to follow Cassie inside.

Right?

Nothing more sinister than a horny boyfriend hiding near the barn.

The old dog growled again.

"Hush," Jenna said as she turned into the double doors that opened to her master suite, a cozy set of rooms that she shared with no one.

She'd moved to this isolated spot on the Columbia River for peace of mind, so she'd ignore the knot of dread in her stomach. She was just edgy and out of sorts because her teenager was giving her fits. That's all.

And yet as she stepped into her darkened bedroom, she couldn't shake the sensation that something was about to happen.

Something she wouldn't like.

Something intimately evil.

CHAPTER 3

"Cassie!" Jenna yelled up the stairwell. "Allie! Breakfast. Get a move on! We have to be out of here in half an hour!" Listening for sounds of life coming from upstairs, she walked into the kitchen and glanced at the clock mounted over the stove. They were going to be late. There was just no two ways about it. They really should be at Allie's school in forty-five minutes and it would take at least twenty to get to the junior high. She flipped on the television, slammed two English muffins into the toaster, and yelled, "Come on, girls!"

She heard the thud and shuffle of footsteps overhead. *Thank God.*

She swallowed her second cup of coffee, nearly tripping over Critter, who was hovering near the counter, dropped her empty cup in the sink, and yanked open the refrigerator door. Still no sound of water running. Cassie was usually in the shower by this time. Yanking open the refrigerator door, she found a carton of orange juice and poured two glasses as the muffins popped up. From the television, the local weatherman was predicting the worst snow of the season so far, as temperatures had dropped far below freezing.

Slathering the first set of muffins with butter, she heard footsteps on the stairs. A few seconds later, Cassie appeared.

"There's no water," she said glumly.

"What do you mean?"

"I mean there's no friggin' water. I turned on the faucet and nothing!" To prove her point, she walked to the sink and twisted on the faucet. Nothing happened.

"No hot water?" Jenna said, hating the thoughts running through her mind. Better a problem with the water heater than the pipes.

"No cold, either." Cassie looked over at the coffeepot. "How did you . . . ?"

"Got it ready last night. It's on a timer." She was at the sink, trying to get the water to flow and failing miserably. "Damn. I guess you'll just have to get dressed without a shower."

"Are you out of your mind? I *can't* go to school without washing my hair."

"You'll survive. So will the school."

"But, Mom—"

"Just eat your breakfast and then change into something clean."

"No way. I'm not going to school." Cassie slumped into a chair in the nook. Dark smudges surrounded her eyes, and she couldn't keep from yawning from her tryst the night before.

"You're going. Remember the old saying, 'If you fly with the eagles, you have to rise with the sparrows?'"

"I don't get it."

"Sure you do."

"Well, it's dumb."

"Maybe so, but it's our credo for the morning."

Cassie rolled her eyes and took a swallow of her juice, but let the muffin sit untouched on her plate. Critter planted himself under the table, his head resting on Cassie's knee. She didn't seem to notice or care.

"You and I still need to talk. Last night isn't going to happen again. I don't want you sneaking out. Ever. It's just not safe."

"You just don't like Josh."

"We went over this last night. Josh is fine." *Even if his IQ was smaller than his shoe size.* "But I don't like him manipulating you."

"He doesn't."

"And, if you two are having sex—"

"Oh God. Save me."

"—I need to know about it."

"It's none of your business."

"Of course it is. You're a minor."

"Can we talk about this later? Or never?" She glared at her mom as if Jenna was soooo out of it, which, Jenna supposed, she was. But she had to tread softly or she'd do exactly the opposite of what she wanted and send Cassie reeling into Josh Sykes's ready and randy arms. Jenna glimpsed the kitchen clock counting off the seconds of her life. "Okay, later. After school, when we have more time."

"Great. Just what we need. *More* time," Cassie mumbled as Jenna, telling herself that timing is everything in life, stepped out of the kitchen and away from the confrontation they'd have this evening. She walked down a short hallway to the bottom of the stairs. "Allie? Are you up?"

She heard the shuffle of feet and Allie, still wearing her pajamas, inched her way into the kitchen. Her red-blond hair was a disaster, her pixie-like face pulled into a pained expression worthy of an Oscar. "I don't feel good."

"What's wrong?" Jenna said, though she suspected it was nothing. This was one of her twelve-year-old's favorite tricks these days. Allie had never liked school, still didn't. She was smart, but one of those kids who was a dreamer, the proverbial square peg that could no more fit into the round hole of student life than fly to the moon. But she had to try.

"Sore throat," Allie complained, doing her best to look miserable.

"Let me see."

Obediently, Allie opened her mouth and Jenna peered down what appeared to be a perfectly healthy throat. "Looks okay to me."

"But it hurts," Allie whined pathetically.

"It'll get better. Eat some breakfast."

"I *can't.*" She slumped into a chair and folded her arms over the table, burying her head in the crook of one elbow. "*Dad* wouldn't make me go to school if I was sick."

Neither would I, Jenna thought, but didn't take the bait and give a quick retort about Robert Kramer and his less-than-stellar performance as a father. Allie scowled at her mother and determinedly ignored her breakfast.

Perfect. Jenna glanced at the clock. The morning was disintegrating from bad to worse and it wasn't even eight yet. She hated to think what the rest of the day would bring.

Leaving the girls at the table, she tried the faucets in the rest of the house and realized that Cassie was right. Water was nonexistent. By the time she reached the kitchen, Allie had come to life, and, ignoring the English muffin Jenna had toasted, had found a box of frozen waffles and dropped two into the toaster. Apparently her sore throat hadn't gotten the better of her appetite.

Cassie, finishing her juice, was staring at the television. On the screen a woman reporter was standing in the darkened woods somewhere, in front of a crime scene if the yellow tape could be believed.

"What's this?" Jenna asked.

"They found some woman up at Catwalk Point," Cassie said, her gaze transfixed on the television. "I heard it on the radio."

"Who is it?"

"They're not saying."

As if to answer Jenna's question, the perky, red-haired reporter, wearing a coat and scarf, was saying, ". . . no word yet from the sheriff's department as to the identity of the woman who was found yesterday morning by Charley Perry, a man who lives not far from the crime scene." The screen flashed to an elderly man whom Jenna thought she'd seen in the local café, though she'd never met him. He was talking about discovering the body while hunting.

"Catwalk Point isn't very far from here," Allie said as her waffle popped up and she slid it onto the plate with her muffin. "That's kinda creepy."

"Real creepy," Jenna said, then changed her tune quickly. "The police are handling it. No need to worry."

Cassie sighed loudly, as if she couldn't believe what she

was hearing. Allie found the syrup bottle and squeezed a puddle large enough to cover ten pancakes. Her two small waffles were saturated and then some.

Jenna didn't comment. She was too busy staring at the small screen, watching as the image changed and the reporter was talking to Sheriff Carter, a tall, broad-shouldered man who dwarfed the woman. "It's too early to determine the cause of death," he was saying cautiously, his voice having the hint of a drawl. He was a rugged-looking man with chiseled features, suspicious deep-set eyes, and a dark brush moustache. His hair was straight, coffee-brown, and trimmed neatly. "We're still trying to identify the body."

"Are you treating this as a murder investigation?"

"We're leaving our options open. It's still too early to tell," he said firmly, ending the taped interview.

"Thank you, Sheriff Carter," the reporter said, rotating to face the camera again. "Karen Tyler reporting from Catwalk Point." The screen flipped to the anchor desk, where a clean-shaven man with receding hair said, "Thank you, Karen," then, with a smile, turned to the sports report.

Jenna snapped off the set. "Let's go," she said.

Cassie stared at her mother as if Jenna were out of her mind. "I told you I can't go to school like this."

"And you were wrong. Move it. I don't have time to argue."

Muttering under her breath, Cassie shoved her uneaten breakfast aside and banged up the stairs.

"You, too," Jenna said, pointing a finger at her youngest daughter. The waffles were nearly gone.

"My throat really, really hurts."

This was just Allie's most recent ploy to avoid going to Harrington Junior High. Jenna wasn't buying it. Especially when she saw how easily Allie swallowed her juice. "I think you'll live . . . but I'll call the school later and see how you're doing. Now, let's go."

Seeming to decide that her current strategy wasn't working, Allie crammed the last piece of waffle into her mouth and flew up the stairs while Jenna dialed Hans Dvorak, a retired horse trainer and now part-time foreman of her small ranch. Hans, like Critter, had come with the property. He picked up on the third ring, his voice deep and rattling from too many years of cigarettes. "Hello?"

"Hans, it's Jenna."

"Just on my way over," the older man said quickly, as if he were late.

"And I'm taking the kids to school now, but we've got a little problem here." As she heard one of her girls clomping down the stairs, she explained about the lack of water.

"Probably the pump," he said. "It's had an electrical problem. Happened before, 'bout five years back."

"Can you fix it?"

"I'm not sure, but I'll give it a try. You might need an electrician, though, or some kind of handyman who knows more about wiring than I do—possibly a plumber as well."

Jenna inwardly groaned at the thought, though she did know Wes Allen, an electrician and sometime artist who did work at Columbia Theater in the Gorge, the local theater where she volunteered. Then there was Scott Dalinsky, who, too, helped out with the lights and audio equipment at the theater, though Jenna wouldn't trust him with work at her house. Even though he was Wes's nephew and her friend Rinda's son, Jenna felt uncomfortable around Scott. She'd caught him staring at her one too many times to feel at ease with him.

"I'll be there in half an hour," Hans said.

"Thanks."

Hans was a godsend. At seventy-three, he still helped with the livestock and kept the place running. He'd been the caretaker for the previous owners and when Jenna had moved into the house, she'd nearly begged him to stay on. He'd agreed and she'd never regretted the decision for a second. Today was no exception. If Hans couldn't fix what was wrong, he'd find someone who could.

Allie, her wild hair somewhat tamed, walked into the room. She was already wearing a fleece jacket and had the strap of her backpack slung over one shoulder.

"Did you brush your teeth?" Jenna asked, then realized

what she was saying. "I know this isn't what the Dental Association would suggest, but chew some gum on the way to school if your teeth feel fuzzy."

"They're fine," Allie said in a weak voice, gently reminding her mother that she wasn't well.

"You've got a math test today, right? Ready for it?"

Frown lines drew Allie's eyebrows together, and for an instant she was the spitting image of her father. "I hate math."

"You've always been good at math."

"But it's pre-algebra." Allie's nose wrinkled in disgust.

"Yeah, well, we all suffered through it," Jenna said, then heard herself and thought better of her response. She pulled her jacket off a peg near the back door and slipped her arms through its sleeves. "Look, I'll try to help you with it tonight and if I can't, maybe Mr. Brennan can. He was an engineer and in the Air Force and—"

"No!" Allie said quickly, and Jenna backed off. Neither of her daughters was comfortable with their mother dating, even though since the divorce Robert had remarried twice. A record even by Hollywood standards. Harrison Brennan was their neighbor, ex-military, and a widower. He'd shown more than a passing interest in Jenna since she moved in and yet hadn't treated her with the kid gloves and awestruck attitude of many of the townspeople when she'd first moved to Falls Crossing.

"Okay, I'll see what I can do," she said, marching to the bottom of the stairs as she tugged on a pair of leather gloves. "Cassie, get a move on! We'll be in the car!"

"I'm coming, okay?"

"Yeah, right." Back in the kitchen, she said to Allie, "Let's go warm up the car," and was out the back door in a heartbeat. Outside, the air was cold as ice and just as brittle. It swept over the covered walkway and caught in her hair. As she unlocked the garage door, she caught a glimpse of the sky. Low, gunmetal gray clouds skimmed the surrounding hills and threatened snow, just as the weatherman had predicted. "Brrr," Jenna muttered, shivering and promising herself that next summer she would enclose this breezeway with triple-paned, insulated windows and add heat.

Critter and Allie followed her into the garage—another building that could use thick insulation and a new roof. They all piled into her Jeep, and Jenna rammed her key into the ignition.

Pumping the gas, she flicked her wrist.

The engine ground.

Didn't catch.

"Oh, come on," Jenna urged the SUV, then glanced at Allie, who was buckling her seat belt. "It's just cold," she said, as much to herself as her daughter. Determined, Jenna tried again. And again. And yet again, but the damned thing wouldn't start and she didn't have time to try to figure out what was wrong with it. Frustrated, she glanced to the next bay of the garage where an old Ford pickup that had come with the ranch was parked. "We'll take the truck."

"Really?"

"Yeah. Come on." Jenna was already out of the SUV and headed for the driver's side of the truck when Cassie, cell phone pressed to her ear, hurried into the garage.

She took one look at what was happening and stopped short. "I'll call you back," she said, and snapped her cell phone shut. Dropping the phone into her purse, she said to her mother, "You're kidding, right?"

"No."

"I can't be seen in this . . . wreck," she said, motioning to the truck's dented fender.

"Sure you can."

"But—"

"Keep complaining and I guarantee you, it'll soon be yours."

"Oh God!" Cassie's face was a mask of sheer horror.

"Get in. *Now*." Jenna was through with complaining teenagers. It was bad enough that Cassie was lobbying hard for her own set of wheels, but that she somehow thought she needed to drive a BMW or sporty Mercedes or the like really bugged Jenna. All those years of privilege in L.A. hadn't worn off. She climbed behind the wheel, inserted the key, and the truck roared to life on the first try. "Thank you, God," she said as her girls, subdued, squeezed in beside her and she started down the long lane leading out of her fifty acres.

Finally they were on the road, icy though it was.

Allie played with the radio, and between bouts of static finally found a station that she liked and Jenna could stand while Cassie groused about the weather, noting that she'd seen on the Internet that the temperature in L.A. was supposed to reach eighty-two degrees today. *Perfect,* Jenna thought sarcastically, and attempted to ignore her daughter's bad mood. She only hoped the last few hours weren't a precursor of things to come. But that was ridiculous, wasn't it? she silently asked herself as she glanced in her rearview mirror and saw her own worried green eyes.

What else could go wrong?

Another glance in the mirror and she had her answer.

Red and blue lights were flashing as a cop vehicle roared up behind her truck. She eased off the road, expecting him to fly by.

No such luck.

"What's going on?" Cassie demanded, and both girls swivelled their heads to look through the dirty back window. "Oh, shi–shoot!"

"Watch it!" Jenna warned, but her eyes were focused on the side-view mirror where she could see what was happening behind her. It wasn't good.

An SUV from the sheriff's department followed her onto the shoulder. A tall, broad-shouldered man in county-issued jacket and hat stretched out of his vehicle. Long legs moving swiftly, harsh expression fixed on her truck, a few flakes of snow catching in his thick moustache.

All business.

"It's that sheriff," Cassie whispered. "The one on the news."

"Our lucky day," Jenna said under her breath. Cassie was spot-on. Sheriff Carter himself was striding up to her pickup. The morning was going to hell in a handbasket at breakneck speed.

CHAPTER 4

"Was I speeding?" the woman asked as she rolled down her window. Carter recognized her in a second. Jenna Hughes. Falls Crossing's most famous citizen. Fresh out of Hollywood and squeezed into an ancient farm truck with bald tires, a few dents, and brake lights that weren't working. Sometime back, he'd heard she'd bought the old McReedy place and he'd seen her from a distance a few times, but they'd never met. Until today. Helluva way to introduce himself to a woman whose beauty was legendary, and, from what he could see of her, accurate. Her face was small, knotted now in concern, and she gazed at him with the famous green eyes that he'd seen in half a dozen of her films.

"No, speeding's not the problem," he said. "Your brake lights aren't working."

She winced. "Great," she muttered.

"Oh, God." This from the girl seated on the far side of the truck, a teenager whose features were a near match to Jenna's. Daughter number one, he guessed, while the kid in the middle of the bench seat was younger, with wild reddish hair poking out of her stocking cap and a mutt of a dog on the floor at her feet. The dog growled and was shushed quickly.

"Can I see your license and registration, please?"

"Of course." Jenna fumbled in her purse, then the glove

compartment that opened with a creak. "I'm sorry about this, Officer. I usually don't drive this truck, but my Jeep wouldn't start this morning and I had to get the girls to school and—"

"Mom! He doesn't want to hear your life story," the teenager cut in. She slid Carter a dark, surreptitious glance, then stared pointedly out the passenger-side window as if the frozen roadside sludge and snow were fascinating.

"I was just explaining," Jenna said, and managed a smile that, he supposed, was meant to melt his bad attitude. It didn't. Not when he had a decomposed, unidentified dead woman dumped in his jurisdiction. "This must be it," she said, pulling out a dusty envelope.

"I assume you have proof of insurance."

"It should be in here, too." She handed him the packet and stole a peek at her watch, reminding him that she was in a hurry.

"Look, I don't think you want to do this," she said.

He skewered her with a look.

"I mean, we both have better things to do."

Pampered princess. Probably never had a ticket in her life. Yeah, I have a lot better things to do than to freeze my butt off here and listen to you try to talk your way out of a ticket you damned well deserve. "This will just take a few minutes," he said, and was rewarded with a bored sigh from the far side of the truck.

"Good, because the girls are already late."

"They won't be the only ones," he said.

"Oh." Again the well-practiced, sexy Hollywood grin. As if she knew she could turn a man's head and probably change his mind, a subtle attempt to get her way. Her ploy had probably worked more times than not, but this wasn't Jenna Hughes's lucky day. Not when Carter was in a foul mood already.

He took the information to his vehicle, checked it, and started to write out a warning, then caught himself up short. The woman deserved a citation. No doubt she was used to privilege, to getting people to do her bidding, including starstruck officers to let her off easy. Well, this wasn't L.A., and he didn't give a damn who she was.

Even in the heated Blazer, his fingers were half frozen as he scribbled out the citation and heard the crackle of his radio barely audible over the howl of the wind. Man, it was blowing today. A few vehicles, seeing his lights flashing, braked quickly as they passed. Cowards. More afraid of getting ticketed than of being safe or legal.

Angry at the world, he tore off the citation and climbed out of his rig. As he approached through the blowing snow, he noticed Jenna Hughes's famous eyes watching him in the truck's side-view mirror. Lord, she was beautiful. Drop-dead gorgeous. Not that it mattered. This morning, on his watch, she was just Jane Citizen-With-Bad-Taillights.

"Here ya go, Ms. Hughes," he stated when she rolled down the window again and he handed her the citation. "You can go to court and they'll most likely reduce the fine. Meanwhile, get those taillights fixed pronto—and I mean while you're in town today. They're a hazard."

"I'll try," she said, her voice clipped, her full lips pinched at the corners.

So she was angry. Big deal. "Try real hard," he advised with a well-practiced, humorless grin. "Drive safely, ma'am."

She sent him a stare that had probably cut weaker men to the quick. He didn't give a damn what she thought. Turning, he fought the wind back to his Blazer. As he climbed inside, he watched as Jenna "Hollywood" Hughes eased onto the road, using her turn signal, careful to be the considerate, law-abiding driver.

They all turned into perfect drivers once they'd gotten spanked with a ticket. He figured her new cautiousness would last all of ten minutes.

Hey, she wasn't speeding. Wasn't driving erratically. She just had the bad luck to have her taillights out. Give the lady a break.

Carter would. As much of a break as he'd give anyone else. No more, no less. He slid into his vehicle, turned off the overhead lights, and followed her into town.

* * *

He sat in the Canyon Café, in a corner booth near the window, and cast a quick look over the top of the half-curtains. Through the ice-glazed panes, he caught a glimpse of the old church, a wreck of a building that had seen better days and several renovations, the most current being a local theater— The Columbia Theater in the Gorge—a pretentious name if he'd ever heard one.

His hot tea came and he poured it over a glass of ice, listening to the cubes crack, noticing how they melted as the amber liquid cooled quickly. There were few patrons this morning, only a few old coots chatting about the weather. Hash browns and bacon sizzled on a grill in the kitchen, country music was barely audible, and the waitress slipped from the tables to the booths and counter. Some of the regulars were huddled over papers or deep in discussion. He waved at a few, smiled up at the waitress, and kept one eye on the theater.

Stirring his tea, he stared through the slit in the lower curtains while pretending to pore over the sports page. He tried to appear calm but his nerve ends were strung tight as piano wire. Energized by the cold front. Enraged by the placard in front of the theater announcing the Christmas play.

It's a Wonderful Life.

Like hell.

He remembered seeing the movie in black and white. He'd shuddered at the scene where George Bailey's brother had fallen through the ice and had imagined all too vividly what the boy had felt . . . cold, cold water swirling, pulling him down, freezing his lungs as he gulped the frigid water, the entire world swimming, his heart pounding . . . the black terror that struck . . .

"Are you okay?"

His head snapped up and he looked at the waitress, a girl of about eighteen who held a carafe of coffee in one hand and a pitcher of ice water in the other.

Noticing the cubes floating in the water, chilling it, he managed a smile. "Yes . . . fine. Just not happy that the Trail Blazers lost again."

"Nobody is. Aside from the weather, it's all the talk this morning." She seemed mollified, managed a wide grin that showed off her braces. "More water or tea?"

"I'm fine." To prove it, he lifted his glass and took a long swallow.

Satisfied that her customer was content, she slid to the next table.

You idiot! he silently admonished. *Don't blow this! Not now. Be patient. Everything's working fine. Perfectly.*

Calming himself, he slowly picked up the paper and turned the page; then, through the slit in the café curtains, caught the image of an old, beat-up truck just outside the window. His heart jolted as he hazarded a closer look and recognized Jenna Hughes at the wheel.

It was fate. He was sure of it. She'd driven up solely to remind him of his purpose.

He trembled.

She was so close.

His breathing became shallow.

Her pickup was paused at a stoplight and she was looking straight ahead . . . no, she checked the rearview mirror, touched the corner of her perfect mouth as if to brush off a bit of errant lipstick, then focused on the street again.

His insides quivered and he licked the edge of his mouth, silently hoping that she would turn in his direction so he could get a glimpse of her incredible face. Her profile was regal. Classic. But he wanted desperately to stare into her eyes.

It was not to be.

Instead, she turned her head in the opposite direction, giving him a brief view of glossy black hair as she drove through the intersection. Immediately after the turn, she flipped on her blinker and rolled into the theater's parking lot.

He smiled inwardly, feeling a deep satisfaction.

He knew the remodeled church as well as he did his own home. As well as he knew hers.

His pulse was thrumming in his ears now . . . he hadn't expected to see her and usually he planned everything. But this . . . this sighting was so close it had to be fate. Kismet.

As she stepped out of the cab of the truck, she paused and looked up the street.

He couldn't resist. He left more than enough money on the counter, hurried outside, and bundled against the wind, walked toward the theater.

In an alley across the street, he stood in the shadow of a huge fir tree and watched her climb the steps to the double doors. She pulled one open. As she did, before she disappeared inside, he blew her a kiss.

"It won't be long," he promised, his voice the barest of whispers in the rush of icy wind.

"So what have we got?" Carter asked BJ as she settled into the side chair near his desk. He was just taking off his jacket and hadn't quite shaken off the encounter with Jenna Hughes, which bothered the hell out of him. It wasn't as if he didn't have more important things to think about.

"What have we got?" BJ repeated, shaking her head. "Not enough." BJ's hair was short and brown, shot with streaks of red. Her facial features were on the small side, except for her eyes, which were large, dark brown, and didn't miss much. "The M.E. is still working on Jane Doe. We're not certain of when Jane Doe died, but the M.E. thinks it's probably within the year—possibly last spring, because of the decay of the body, the insect larvae found around it, the fact that animals had dragged body parts away. You'll get a full report as soon as one's available."

Carter frowned and tapped the eraser end of his pencil on his cluttered desk. "I talked to Missing Persons in Salem. Nothing yet, but they're still working on trying to match Jane physically to someone who's been reported missing in the last couple of years."

"Just statewide?"

"More. West Coast for starters, and I've talked to the local jurisdictions, as well. Just to double-check. So far, nada." Carter fiddled with his pencil, wiggling it between his fingers, a nervous habit he'd taken up right after he quit smoking. It had worked for him except for that black time surrounding Carolyn's death. From the corner of his eye, he saw the last remaining picture he'd kept of her in the office, propped in a rosewood frame, a snapshot he'd taken of her on their last trip to the coast. "What about cause of death?"

"Unknown at this time, but the M.E.'s working on it."

"And the pink stuff on her hair?"

"I asked about that and they're still analyzing it." Her lips folded over her teeth as they often did when she was mentally working through some kind of puzzle. "It's probably some kind of synthetic, sort of like modeling clay made out of some rubbery substance. Kind of like . . . Silly String or Play-Doh, but not really . . ."

"Plastic?"

"I don't even think they can go that far. But the lab's working on it."

"And?" he encouraged, seeing her eyebrows knit.

"And?" she repeated.

"And you look like you have something more to say."

"Nothing concrete, but they found more of that pink stuff in the log. Quite a bit of it. They're trying to reconstruct the scene."

"So she had it on her body?"

"Maybe, but more likely *in* her body. The stuff was compacted, solid, in bigger chunks rather than a little bit that would have been smeared on her. They think it was either in her lungs or her stomach."

"She *ingested* it?"

"Maybe. Possibly drowned in it. That pink gunk, whatever it is, might well be the cause of death."

"Drowned in it?" His jaw clenched. He rubbed his moustache thoughtfully. "It was liquid?"

"I don't know. We'll have to wait for the report."

"Wait a minute. This is sounding like something that would be aired on the Sci-Fi channel. Why would anyone kill a person with pink crud?"

"We don't officially know it's a homicide yet."

He leveled a gaze at her. "You think suicide? By inhaling pink goo? And ending up at the top of a mountain in a hollowed-out log? What kind of weird ritual is that?"

"I'm just trying to stay rational."

"Forget rational. Because it's not. This isn't an accident, either. It's a homicide, I'm sure of it. But why all the mess? Why not just shoot the victim, or choke her, or slit her throat?"

"Who knows?" She lifted her shoulder. "If your theory's on the money, then we've got a psycho running loose, or maybe we had one who was just passing through last winter. He did his business, either around here or somewhere else, decided to dump the body, and took off. It's been a while since this girl was killed. Our guy could have moved on."

Carter wondered, his eyes narrowing. He looked through his window and saw the ominous gray skies surrounding this small town nestled deep in the foothills of the Cascade Mountains. It was isolated; the only serious connection to the rest of civilization was I-84, the interstate freeway that ran parallel to the Columbia River at this point on the map. He scanned the timber-covered ridges and thought, not for the first time, that the steep cliffs and dark forests surrounding Falls Crossing were the perfect place for a wanted man to hide. But a psychopath? The thought set his teeth on edge.

Maybe he was jumping to conclusions.

"We'll keep trying to find out who she is, but we'll work with the State Police, let them run this thing; they're gonna want to anyway, and they have more resources than we do." Scratching his chin, he added, "I'll talk to Larry Sparks in the local office—I'm sure he'll keep us informed."

"It's not like you to call in another agency."

"This case is different," he said, but didn't add that he had a bad feeling about it. Real bad. "Contact all the surrounding jurisdictions again—make that all of Oregon, Washington, Idaho, and California, even western Montana. See if we come up with any matches. Find out if there are any other cases of a woman found dead with some kind of unknown substance in her hair or body cavities."

BJ nodded. "Anything else?" she asked, slapping the folder of missing-person reports onto his desk.

"Yeah," he said, reaching for the phone to call Lieutenant Sparks. "Get me that autopsy report on the Jane Doe ASAP."

CHAPTER 5

Cassie had insisted on being let off two blocks from the school so that as few people as possible would see her being dropped off from a "dump of a truck" by her mother. She'd already been mortified by the sheriff pulling Jenna over. Jenna had been burned by the ticket, but hadn't wanted any more arguments with her daughter, so she'd complied, figuring if Cassie was half frozen by the time she made it to her geometry class, it was just too bad. Cassie hadn't seemed to mind the cold temperature and had strolled off, cell phone plastered to her ear, wind whipping her hair over her face and eyes. *Tonight,* Jenna had thought, *tonight we'll have a heart-to-heart, mother and daughter.* It sounded simple and yet her stomach was tight in anticipation.

She'd dropped Allie off at Harrington Junior High without incident and then driven straight to the theater, where, in a room that had once held the baptismal tank, Rinda Dalinsky was trying to keep warm in a turtlenecked sweater, down vest, and ski pants. Already sipping coffee from an oversized cup, she was making copies on an old Xerox machine. She was about Jenna's height, had an athletic build, and had been blessed with auburn hair, olive skin, and gold eyes that always seemed to catch the light.

"Is Oliver here? If so, watch out. I brought the dog,"

Jenna, with Critter padding happily after her, announced as she strode through what had once been the apse of the old church. Narrow stained-glass windows filtered in the daylight and a few Christian relics adorned the tall, clapboard walls.

"I'll tell him," Rinda yelled back, and Jenna laughed. Oliver was an ancient yellow tabby whom Rinda had found hiding under the porch of the church when she'd purchased it for stage productions. She hadn't had the heart to take the cat to the local animal shelter, and so she'd promptly adopted him and named him Oliver for her favorite Charles Dickens character. In the process, Oliver had become the theater troupe's unofficial mascot. Critter gave a quick bark and began wagging his tail wildly at the sight of Rinda.

At that moment the cat in question shot through the series of adjoining rooms behind what was now the stage. Hissing indignantly, he climbed up a pillar to hide on a crossbeam. Critter, still begging for Rinda's attention, hadn't noticed the cat at all.

Rinda chuckled at the dog's nonchalance. "I guess Oliver has a rather inflated image of himself."

"He's a male, isn't he?" Jenna said, and thought of the officer who'd pulled her over this morning. Rinda's friend. Sheriff Shane Carter, a man's man, with dark eyes, thick moustache, square jaw, and what appeared to be a very bad attitude.

"Oliver *was* a male. I had him neutered."

Again Jenna thought about Carter. Tough. Sexy. And a royal pain in the backside. "Let's not go there," Jenna warned before she said something she'd regret. Rinda seemed to think the local sheriff walked on water. "Critter's in the same nonsexual boat. What're you working on?" Jenna picked up one of the copies that the Xerox machine was spewing out. "Flyers?"

"Mmm. The first batch. We'll do something more detailed closer to the date, but we needed something to put around town now and add to the Web site. Scott did the art." Rinda's son, Scott, was a college dropout who worked part time for his mother designing sets, painting scenery, and sometimes working the lights with Rinda's brother, Wes Allen, during a production. A movie buff, Scott could quote dialogue from nearly every major motion picture since 1970. Rinda motioned toward the copy in Jenna's hand. "So, what do you think?"

"I like it." The flyer was reminiscent of a 1950s movie poster in faded red and green. "The nostalgia angle works."

"I think so, too," Rinda said, but there was a hint of hesitation in her voice as there always was when she talked about her only son, and her smile tightened a bit.

Jenna set the copy on the rapidly increasing stack, then reached for a thermos of coffee and poured herself a cup. The old church-cum-theater was in desperate need of insulation and a new heating system. As it was, the ancient furnace was blasting away, but the warm air seemed to seep right through the stained-glass windows and thin wooden siding of a building that was, despite all of Rinda's efforts, slowly deteriorating.

"So how's the production coming together?" Jenna asked. She had agreed to help coach some of the actors, but wasn't scheduled to start running lines with them until early next week.

"Working with kids is always . . . a challenge."

"Are adults a whole lot better?"

Rinda held up a thumb and index finger, showing very little space between them. "Marginally."

Jenna grinned as she found a packet of nondairy creamer and slapped it against the counter. "I predict it'll be a smash. Standing Room Only."

"It would be if you'd play Mary Bailey," Rinda wheedled, not for the first time.

"You've got Madge Quintanna." Jenna opened the little packet and poured in the white powder. Immediately clouds swirled upward in her cup. "Besides, I've already got a job. I'm Coach Hughes, remember?"

Rinda wasn't about to give up. "Madge is . . . how can I put this delicately? I guess I can't. Madge is awful. Stiff as a board and to say she's 'struggling' with her lines would be the understatement of the year."

"She'll improve." Jenna took an experimental sip of her coffee. "I told her to watch the movie before I start working with her next week. Donna Reed was incredible. Madge'll catch on."

"She isn't a natural. You are."

Jenna was unmoved by Rinda's pleas. "Didn't I tell you I'd gladly be a part of this as long as I didn't have to act for at least five years?"

"But you're a household name."

"Was," Jenna corrected as she set down the flyer. "That's the operative word. Was. And I'm not even sure about that. I'm sure in most Hollywood circles the term 'has been' is attached to me."

"You were an A-list Hollywood actress!"

Jenna laughed for the first time this morning. "That's stretching it."

"We could get some good press out of this."

Inwardly Jenna shuddered at the thought. She'd seen enough of what kind of damage the tabloids and rumors could do to a family. Ever since the accident during the filming of her last project she'd shrunk away from any kind of media event. But Rinda was in another time and place, trying everything she could think of to make the upcoming Christmas show a smash. At least by Falls Crossing's standards.

"Think what it would do for this production and for the theater troupe in general if you were on the stage! We could pay off some of the debt on this old place and jazz it up. Insulate it, for Pete's sake. Even put in a small wine bar. And that's just the start—think about computer-operated lighting and sound systems and new costumes and curtains that aren't in shreds after being mended and remended!"

"Whoa!" Jenna held up the flat of one hand. "Slow down. You're getting waaay ahead of yourself. I told you I'd help out around here, including some of the financing, but when it comes to acting or putting my name on anything, I said 'no' and I meant it. For now. I remember being very specific about wanting some time and space for myself and my kids, to get away from Robert and Tinseltown and just have the chance to be a regular mom."

"As if!" Rinda said, snapping up her copies from the shelf of the Xerox machine. "You'll never be a 'regular' mom."

"Okay, so that might not be possible, but I really want to avoid any kind of . . . hype."

"You mean you don't want your famous name and face exploited?"

"Thank you! Yes. Today I have to concentrate on such glamorous things as fixing my pump—we're out of water at the house and Hans thinks it's the electric pump. Then I'm hoping that my Jeep starts when I get home. Otherwise I'll have to have it towed to a garage." She crossed the fingers of her left hand and held them up. "Maybe it's just being ornery with all the bad weather."

"Or maybe you're just cursed by the gods of all things mechanical?"

Jenna groaned and thought of the things that had happened over the last week—her problems with her computer and connecting to the Internet, her cell phone that wouldn't hold a battery charge, the microwave that had recently given up the ghost, and now the frozen water pump and Jeep that wouldn't start. "Let's hope not. It could be a long winter if that's the case."

"It's gonna be, anyway. Haven't you heard? This is supposed to be the coldest winter in seventy or eighty years. They're takin' bets down at the lodge that the river will freeze over and that hasn't happened since the early 1930s, I think."

"By 'the river,' you mean the Columbia? It actually froze?" Jenna asked, thinking of the huge, swift channel of water that cut through the cliffs and flowed speedily to the Pacific Ocean. How cold would it have to be to freeze a river that size?

Rinda grinned and finished her coffee. "Yep. It was a solid, thick sheet of ice. People who had cars could drive across it."

"That's unbelievable," she said, looking out the iced-over windows.

"Are you having second thoughts about moving up here?"

"Second, third, twenty-seventh, you name it," Jenna joked.

"What's the temperature in L.A. today? Seventy? Eighty?"

"Eighty-two and balmy."

"Crank out the sunscreen!"

"Very funny," Jenna said, taking another long swallow from her cup and feeling the warm coffee slide down her throat. With all the problems she was having, she wondered again if she'd made a mistake in moving so far north. Though she'd denied it to herself, she second-guessed her plans. Had her exodus from L.A. actually been, as Cassie had often accused, an example of Jenna running away from her problems, rather than to solutions? Had she made a mess of things rather than found a better life for her little family?

The door to the theater banged open and along with a rush of frigid air, Wes Allen, Rinda's brother, strode in.

"Hey!" Rinda called, beaming.

"Hi, Rin. Jen." He nodded at Jenna, his gaze hesitating a beat too long on her face. As always. It was a little thing, but it bothered Jenna.

He was taller than his sister by nearly a foot and blessed with the same genes that gave them both thick, dark hair, trim bodies, and straight teeth. "Thought I'd come in and check out the lights one more time before I went to work. Maybe I can figure out where the short is."

"That would be a good idea," she said, giving him an older-sibling stare. "You know, I'd really hate to have this place go up in flames."

Jenna glanced around the hundred-year-old wooden building. A tinderbox by any insurance adjuster's standards.

"Have a little faith. I won't let that happen." Wes was nothing if not self-assured. He poured himself a cup of coffee, sat on the corner of her desk, and picked up the stack of copies she'd slipped into a folder. "Are these the flyers for the new production?"

"Yeah."

He slid one out and eyed it critically as he blew across his cup. "Not bad. Did Scott do 'em?"

"Mmm. My budding artist," Rinda said.

Wes slid the flyers back into the file and turned to Jenna. "Did you hear about the body they found up on Catwalk Point?"

"Just a little on the news this morning."

"Scary, isn't it?" Rinda said. "It's not something you'd expect to happen around here . . . I mean, this isn't the big city—everybody knows just about everybody."

Jenna said, "I don't think anyone really knows anyone else."

"*That's* because you're not from around here," Rinda said.

"No, I think she's right. I've heard there are public lives, personal lives, and private lives. The public life is the one everyone sees in your daily routine, the personal one you reveal to your family and closest friends, but your private life, that's just what you know about yourself, what you hide from everyone else." Wes drained his cup as the words sank in.

"You're saying that you really don't know me, even though we're brother and sister?"

"I don't know you privately. Your most intimate thoughts or actions. And neither of you," he moved his hand from Rinda to Jenna as he looked directly at Jenna, "has any idea of what I'm like. Privately."

"What are you trying to do, freak us out?" Rinda asked.

"Just tellin' it like it is." He winked at Jenna, left his cup on the edge of Rinda's desk, then hurried up the back stairs.

"Sometimes he can be so weird," Rinda whispered. "I don't believe we're really related."

"I heard that!" he said from somewhere overhead. "Remember, Big Brother is watching *and* listening."

"Then hear this—get to work."

"Yeah, yeah . . ."

Rinda rolled her eyes. "That's what I get for letting him and Scott wire the place."

Twenty minutes later the stairs creaked with the weight of Wes's footsteps. "I think I found the spot that needs repair," he announced, returning to Rinda's office. "I'll run a new wire and that should take care of the problem."

"I hope."

"Trust me," he said, and his gaze moved to Jenna's as he zipped his jacket. "Younger sister. As I said before, she has 'no faith.'"

"Limited faith. I have limited faith," Rinda countered.

He checked his watch and winced. "Gotta run." Flashing a smile at his sister and Jenna, he added, "Seems like you're on top of things."

"Don't bet on it," Rinda said as he lifted his hand and left, his boots ringing on the hardwood floor as he exited through the front. The double doors banged hard behind him.

Rinda shivered as a blast of cold air swept inside. "We've got to find a way to insulate this place." She walked to the thermostat and turned the heat up a few more degrees. "Can't have the paying customers freezing. By the way, there's something I've been meaning to ask you."

"Shoot."

"Did you take back the black silk dress—you know, the sheath with the beaded neckline? The one you wore in *Resurrection?*"

"Take it back? No. I donated it to the troupe. Why?"

Fine lines appeared between Rinda's eyebrows. "It's missing."

"Missing?"

"Yeah, Lynnetta came in over the weekend and was going to make a few alterations to it and she couldn't find it."

"But it was in the large stage closet."

"I know. I checked the closet."

"I saw it here last week." Convinced she could lay her hands on the garment in question, Jenna walked behind the stage to the area that had once housed the church's office and minister's quarters. Over the years it had been changed and remodeled to the point that it was a veritable rabbit warren cut into dressing rooms and closets. There were three makeup vanities with mirrors and a larger storage area for scenery and props. Old stairs led upward to a glassed-in office of sorts where the lighting and audio were controlled. The steep steps continued upward still and eventually opened onto the bell-tower which Rinda, who had bought the church, had never had the heart to tear down.

Jenna quickly flipped through the clothes on hangers in the main stage closet. Twice. The dress was definitely missing. "It's got to have been misplaced," she said, as much to convince herself as Rinda. She searched through a few smaller closets, hooks on the backs of doors, and large wicker hampers, but the sheath was nowhere to be found.

"How's that for a mystery?" Rinda grumbled.

"What about under the stage?"

"That dust hasn't been disturbed in years."

"Someone must have 'borrowed' it."

"Or stolen it."

"The dress? Why?" she asked, but knew the answer.

"Because it was yours. In a movie. You still have fans, you know. Just because you quit making films doesn't mean they all dried up and went away. I'm going to look on e-Bay. If someone isn't keeping it for their private collection, then they'll probably be trying to make some quick money off it."

"On e-Bay?"

Rinda nodded. "You wouldn't believe what people sell on there. I've heard of organ donations and one guy even tried to sell his soul, I think."

Jenna laughed. "Someone paid for it?"

"Mmm. A guy named Lucifer, I think."

"Give me a break!" She laughed, but felt a chill on the back of her arms, the premonition of something much worse than a missing costume.

Rinda must have had similar thoughts because her smile faded as they walked back to the office. "Some other things are missing, too. Things you donated. Remember I asked you about a bracelet and a pair of earrings a couple of weeks ago . . ."

"Yeah, but I figured they were just misplaced."

Rinda's scowl deepened.

Jenna cajoled, "Come on, you don't really think they were stolen, that we've got a thief running around here?"

"I hope not. God, I hope not. The worst thing is, if someone did take the dress and the bracelets and other stuff, it's someone we work with, someone who has a key to the theater."

"Now you're jumping off the deep end. It's just temporarily lost," Jenna insisted, trying not to let Rinda's concerns infect her. She had enough problems to solve without worrying about a dress and a couple of pieces of jewelry that were missing. They'd turn up.

But all the stuff is yours. Whoever is doing this is taking things because they belonged to you.

"Don't go there," she muttered to herself.

"What?"

"Nothing. Just talking to myself."

"Not a good sign. Anyway, I'm keeping a list of everything that's 'misplaced.' I think I'll talk to Shane about it."

"Shane? As in the sheriff?" Jenna flashed back to her confrontation with the man less than an hour earlier. She felt her cheeks burn. "I don't think so."

"Why not?"

She thought about fessing up, but said instead, "Get real. He has much bigger problems to solve, starting with the dead woman they found in the woods. Don't bother him with this."

"He'll want to know."

"Carter?" Was Rinda out of her mind? The sheriff was taciturn and gruff and no-nonsense. He wouldn't want to be bothered with anything so petty as the missing items at the theater. She could imagine the mockery in his dark eyes if she approached him with the thefts. It would seem frivolous to him, she was certain.

"He's an old friend of mine. Owes me a favor or two. I don't know why you don't like him."

"It's not a matter of liking him. I just don't know him."

"Because you haven't tried."

"Okay—if you have to know, he pulled me over this morning," Jenna admitted. "Wrote me a citation."

"For God's sake, why didn't you say so?"

"I didn't want to dwell on it, okay?" Jenna quickly explained about Carter busting her for the bad taillights. "He wasn't exactly happy with me this morning, so I don't think going to the sheriff's department and complaining about a few missing items will endear me to him."

"He was just doing his job."

"When women are found dead and half the county is without power and the roads are iced over, he busts me for bad taillights?" Jenna was still burned.

"You should have told him you were a friend of mine."

"Oh, yeah, that would have scored me major points," Jenna mocked, remembering Carter's stern countenance with the snow blowing all over him. "Let's just cross Carter off my dance card, okay? That should be easy, since I don't have one."

Her cell phone chirped and she flipped it open. "Hello?" she said a little sharply.

"Mom?" Allie said, her voice worried. Jenna's anger immediately dissipated. "Do you have my backpack?"

"No . . . well, maybe, I'm not in the truck. Did you leave it there?"

"I dunno, but could you bring it back to the school, *please*? It's got my math homework in it and if I don't turn it in today . . ."

"I'm on my way, Allie. Don't worry." She mentally crossed her fingers that the backpack was in the pickup and not left somewhere at home. "I'll find it and leave it at the office."

"Thanks, Mom."

"No problem," Jenna said, relieved that her younger daughter's sore throat seemed to have been forgotten. At least for the time being. "Gotta run," she called over her shoulder. "A mini-crisis at the junior high."

As she reached the door, it swung open and petite, lively Lynnetta Swaggert hurried inside. "Geez Louise! It's freezing out there," she complained, rubbing her hands together. Lynnetta, the wife of a local preacher, worked in an accounting office in town, but volunteered at the theater in her time off. Aside from keeping the books, she also altered and created costumes for the stage productions.

"It's only gonna get worse," Rinda predicted.

"Such happy news," Lynnetta tossed back at her, then took one look at Jenna. "Are you leaving?"

"Yeah. I'll see you later."

"She's on her way to be a 'normal mom,'" Rinda teased.

Lynnetta chuckled, her hazel eyes glinting mischievously. "Is there such a thing?"

Probably not, Jenna thought as she walked outside and hiked the collar of her jacket close to her neck. Lynnetta hadn't been kidding about the weather. If anything, the temperature seemed to have tumbled another ten degrees in the short time Jenna had been inside the theater.

She blew on her hands, then whistled to Critter and climbed into the truck. Sure enough, there was Allie's backpack, big as life and tucked behind the bench seat. "Ready for a little side trip?" she asked the dog. "Back to Harrington Junior High."

The dog whined and Jenna patted his graying head as she pulled out of the lot. "Yeah, I know. I feel the same way."

So she was finally leaving.

Good.

He was sitting in his truck, parked in a parking lot of the grocery store. Several other minivans, cars, and trucks were scattered over the snowy asphalt, but no one paid any attention to him. Through his windshield, he viewed the parking lot of the old church and watched as she maneuvered the old half-ton through the nearly empty city streets.

He didn't waste any time but fired up his rig and drove out of the lot just in time to see her veer off the main road a few blocks ahead of him. He followed at a safe distance, a Ford Explorer and a feed truck between his vehicle and hers.

Still he caught glimpses of her, and he felt a thrill being this close, knowing she didn't realize how near he was.

She doesn't even know who you really are.

"She will," he said aloud and felt the familiar thrill that came with winter trembling through his blood. Being this close was dangerous, though he had an alibi in place if anyone noticed him here. That was the convenient thing about this town; he could walk and talk with the townsfolk and no one knew who he really was or what he really did. He was everyone's friend and a stranger to them all. He watched as she drove into the parking lot of the junior high. He followed and slid into an empty space not too far away.

She didn't notice.

So focused was she on her mission that she dashed into the school and didn't realize he was nearby.

He licked his lips and caught the reflection of his eyes in the mirror.

Ice blue.

Intense.

Deadly.

But she didn't know that.

Yet.

CHAPTER 6

The school wasn't far from the middle of town. Jenna parked and attempted to ignore the cold air that rushed through the schoolyard as she carried Allie's backpack into the red-brick building. The first bell had already rung and kids who had clustered around the central commons area were shooting off in different directions, talking wildly, hurrying this way and that, laughing and teasing. Jenna didn't see Allie in the group, but she did notice a knot of girls near the doors to the gym. They were staring at her and one was actually pointing.

You should be used to this by now. As long as there are DVDs and videos, someone's going to realize who you are. She smiled right at the kid and waved. The blonde who was pointing immediately dropped her hand, her cheeks suddenly flooding with color.

"Fame," a male voice said, "a real pain sometimes, right?"

Jenna turned and found Travis Settler striding into the school. The father of Allie's friend Dani, Travis was a widower who'd shown mild interest in her. They'd met a couple of times for coffee and even sat together during Back to School Night, much to her daughter's dismay.

She remembered the conversation vividly.

"Mom, you *can't* date Mr. Settler," Allie had said, obviously mortified at the thought that her mother was seeing Dani's father. Dani had been the one to spill the beans that Jenna and Travis had met at the local espresso house earlier in the day, and Allie had let Jenna have it with both barrels as they'd driven home from her school.

"And I can't date Mr. Brennan, either," Jenna had clarified as they'd driven through town.

"Right! You *can't* date anyone. It's too embarrassing!"

"I do have a life, you know," Jenna had countered.

"But you're already famous . . . and . . . kids have seen you in the movies and . . . well," Allie had shrugged and blushed, then looked out the side window of the Jeep. "You know."

"They've seen me almost naked on the screen."

"Yeah!" Allie had said. "Do you know how weird that is?"

As a matter of fact, Jenna did. Every person she'd met in this small town had probably seen her in various states of undress either on the big screen or on televisions in the privacy of their living or bedrooms.

"So . . . you can't go out with . . . Mr. Settler," Allie, redfaced, had insisted. "He's seen those movies. I know. I saw DVDs on his shelf. *Resurrection, Summer's End, Beneath the Shadows, Bystander.* All of them! Even *Innocence Lost!* It was in the DVD player! How old were you when you were in that one, like fourteen?"

"Almost," Jenna had admitted.

"*My* age. That is *so* creepy."

Jenna hadn't been able to argue with Allie's logic.

Jenna had once been told by the owner of the local video store that any movies in which she had a part were impossible to keep on the shelves.

Allie had been right. It was creepy. Big-time creepy.

No matter how many times she rationalized that it was all part of what she'd done for a living, she'd never been comfortable with the fame and curiosity about her. Not here, at least. Every time she met a person in this town, whether it was the local bartender or the librarian, Jenna wondered what they were thinking and which, if any, of her movies they'd seen. In L.A. no one cared. Everyone was in the industry in one form or another. But here . . . in this tiny, provincial burg in Oregon, attitudes were different.

Now, staring up at Travis in the hallway of Harrington Junior High, Jenna said, "Believe me, fame's a pain *all* the time."

"And yet everyone tries to achieve it one way or another."

"I guess." They walked across the hallway to the glassed-in office. Travis held the door open for her. "Allie forget her backpack?" he asked. "Or is that yours?"

Jenna glanced down at the pack in question. It was unique—a canvas print in pink-and-purple camouflage and, in Jenna's estimation, ugly as sin. Allie loved the damned thing because Robert had sent it to Oregon last Christmas. It had been delivered in a huge box, no doubt packed by Robert's most recent wife, and filled with gifts Jenna suspected Robert had never seen. The backpack had been purchased at a spendy boutique on Rodeo Drive and probably had cost a small fortune. "No, this one isn't mine," Jenna said with a grin. "You were right on the first guess. This one belongs to my daughter. Mine is at home. It's similar—camouflage, but trimmed in gold lamé. It's for evening wear. I save it for important dates." She offered him a smile and noticed that his blue eyes crinkled at the corners.

"Maybe we should go to dinner sometime. A big date. You can bring it along."

"Wouldn't be caught dead without it," she said, handing Allie's backpack to the secretary. "Will you see that Allison Kramer gets this?" she asked.

"No problem," the secretary assured her as she took the pack and also an envelope Travis left for Dani. "Lunch money," he explained to Jenna as they walked outside together. "She left it on the counter, and I thought I should just let her go hungry. Maybe then she'd remember, but . . ." He lifted a shoulder.

"You couldn't do it."

"Nah! Maybe next time."

"Yeah, right," she mocked as the icy bite of the wind blew across the playground that connected the junior high to the elementary school. Empty swings swayed, chains rattling with the gusts.

"They're predicting the heaviest snow of the season tonight," Travis said.

Jenna glanced at the leaden sky as they hurried to the parking lot. "I believe it."

"Got time for a cup of coffee before the storm breaks?"

"I'd love one, but I'd better take a rain check. I've got some problems with my Jeep and pump and who-knows-what else."

"Something I could help you with?"

Jenna grinned. "Careful," she said, "you don't know what you're getting into." She yanked open the door of her truck and Critter started wagging his tail wildly as she hoisted herself up behind the steering wheel. "But I might just take you up on it if Hans can't fix the problem."

"Do. Really."

"Thanks. I will."

She pulled the door shut and forced the old truck into gear before she maneuvered the big rig out of the icy parking lot. She glanced in the rearview mirror and saw Travis, hands pushed deep into the pockets of his jacket, walking to his truck. He was fit and good-looking, with sharp features and eyes that didn't miss much. His hair was a warm brown that, she suspected, lightened in the summer, and whatever baggage he carried around about being a single father, he managed to stash away somewhere. Jenna had heard it rumored he'd lost his wife to some disease, but she wasn't sure if that was unfounded, small-town gossip or a hard-and-fast fact. Someday maybe he'd tell her.

If she gave him the chance.

"Come on, let's ditch." Josh's arm was around her shoulders and his face was only inches from hers as they sat, smoking, in his pickup, a relic from the 1970s that he'd "cherried-out" with huge tires, chrome rims, mag wheels, and a stereo system that could almost blow the roof off the cab. The body of the truck was lifted so high that Cassie had to use the running board to climb inside. Josh thought it was cool. Cassie thought it was kind of stupid. "We're already tardy," he was saying. "Why not make it a day?"

"Cuz my mom will kill me," Cassie argued. "I can explain why I'm late to class, come up with something, but if I miss the day, she'll ground me for life!"

"She's always grounding you," he grumbled.

That was true, Cassie thought, dragging hard on her cigarette and letting the smoke curl out of her nose.

"You'll talk your way out of it."

"I already have to deal with last night."

"Shit." He rolled down his window and flicked out the butt of his Marlboro. "You should have been more careful."

"*We*," she reminded him, trying to tamp down her anger. "*We* should have been more careful." She glanced out the side-view window to the park, empty now, the playground equipment vacant, the trees bare of any leaves. "I probably shouldn't have snuck out."

"You had a good time, didn't you?" He nuzzled her neck, lips brushing her nape, and she shrugged him off.

"It was all right."

"No, babe, it was great." He squeezed her to add emphasis to his position.

"Yeah," she said, without any enthusiasm. She had enjoyed herself, she supposed, parked far up on the mountain, getting a nice little buzz from the weed and beer, but she still had a bad feeling about it. Not because she'd gotten caught. Not because she'd snuck out. But because of Josh. Sometimes . . . sometimes he came off like a real hick, and she thought that he might be more interested in her famous mother than he was in her. Unlike the girls in her class, who were obviously jealous. She sighed. In the eighteen months she'd lived here, she hadn't made one single friend she could really count on. Aside from Josh. And sometimes he was questionable. In L.A. she'd had lots of girls she hung out with at the private school her father had insisted upon. Rich kids, some with famous families, most connected in some way to the film or music industry. Paige and Colby and Bella . . . real friends who understood. The yahoos in Falls Crossing all looked at her as if she were some kind of freak.

Maybe she was.

She shivered. Even though Josh had cranked the heat in the pickup to high, she was still cold. This damned weather and the stupid truck weren't part of her fantasy date. In L.A. it would be warm. Maybe even hot. And she'd be sitting in a BMW or Range Rover or Mercedes convertible. *New* cars that didn't need to be "tricked out." They came with all the bells and whistles.

"I think we should drive up to Catwalk Point," he said, and she felt her insides turn to ice.

"Why?"

"Haven't you heard? They found a body up there."

"And you want to go?"

"It's the most interesting thing that's happened around here in years. I think we should check it out."

"No way."

"Chicken?"

"There are cops up there, and we'd be caught for cutting class."

"Not if we're careful."

"Forget it."

"I can't," he said, and his eyes glinted with a bit of macabre excitement. She felt a frisson of fear—or was it intrigue?—skitter up her spine. But she couldn't risk it. Not today. "Look, I've really got to go." She squashed out her cigarette in the ashtray and pushed open the door.

"Oh, come *on*. Do you really want to go to chemistry and English?"

"No. I don't." Hopping onto the hard ground, she looked up at his hangdog expression. His hair was shaved nearly to his scalp, his sideburns pencil-thin, his goatee a shadow that was against school rules. He claimed his folks didn't care about him, that his stepdad thought school was "a waste of time." His mom, it seemed, had given up on her kids. College wasn't in his future. Unless he joined the military. "I've really got to go." Before he could argue, she walked briskly toward the school. She'd already missed the first class of the day, a fifteen-minute mini-period held for the express purpose of announcements and attendance, so she was screwed. The school would call her mother before noon. Great.

She cut through an alley and heard Josh's truck scrape into gear, then the engine roar as he gunned it. His big tires chirped as he angrily headed out of town.

Well, fine! She didn't look over her shoulder, just in case he could see her in his rearview mirror. No matter what her mother thought, Cassie didn't always do what Josh wanted. God, it wasn't as if she was under his spell or he was her Svengali or anything dumb like that. Sometimes her mom bugged the hell out of her.

She ran up the steps to the school.

Get a clue, Mom, she thought disgustedly. *And while you're at it, get a life!*

CHAPTER 7

"I know a helluva lot more about horses than I do about machines," Hans admitted as he wiped his hands and stared at the pump in the tiny pump house between the barn and garage. Hans Dvorak was a short, wiry man with silvery stubble on his chin and a flat nose that looked as if someone had punched it in years before. He'd worked outdoors with horses all his life and had the ruddy complexion to prove it. He'd managed to replace the taillight in the truck, but this pump was another story. "It's froze up solid." Red-faced, ski cap pulled over his ears, he'd bent onto one knee. "And here's the reason, I think. Check out this wire."

Using the beam of a flashlight, he pointed to the electrical connection in question. The wire had become loose, the ends ragged, as if they'd been chewed by an animal. "I can probably patch this up, but look around." He swept the beam across the interior of the old building, which was little more than a shed. It was dirty, dusty, lacked proper insulation, and was freezing inside. The single lightbulb in the ceiling was dim.

The pump house was one of the areas pointed out by the inspector who'd checked out the place before she'd bought it. Even though he'd suggested new wiring, updated plumbing, a new roof, improved security system, and countless other updates to the buildings, she'd had her heart set on moving to this remote spot and had promised herself to take care of all the needed repairs. She'd made a good start, but some of the old equipment—this pump, the electronic gates, the security system—seemed to have minds of their own. No matter how many times they were fixed, they continued to break down.

"You know, I told the McReedys for years that the place needed new wiring. Would Asa listen? Hell, no! And when he put it on the market, I was sure he'd fix things up, but you came along before he had to do anything."

"I should have taken care of everything the minute I moved in, but there was too much." She'd spent a lot of time and money replacing windows and doors, refinishing the wood floors, and attending to the wiring inside the house. She'd figured the outbuildings could wait. Apparently she'd been wrong. "I planned to do some more updating this coming spring. I guess I waited too long," Jenna said, her breath fogging. God, it was cold. And getting colder by the minute.

"Well, we'll figure something out," he said, rubbing his chin. "I've got enough water for the horses in the troughs, but that's gonna freeze tonight." Hans squinted and shook his head. "I should have come over last night and started a drip to keep the water flowing through the pipes. If I had, I might have noticed the wiring and we wouldn't be in this mess."

"It's not your fault, okay? I think I'd better get a plumber out here pronto."

"And an electrician."

"And a mechanic." They'd already looked at the Jeep and tried to jump it. The damned engine didn't so much as turn over.

"Isn't there anyone I can hire that can fix everything?"

"Maybe. Jim Klondike's a good all-around handyman but he's probably pretty busy." Hans lifted his hat and rubbed his near-bald head. "Then there's Seth Whitaker and . . . oh, what's his name, the guy that lives up the river—" He snapped his fingers. "Don Ramsby. Owns his own garage.

They all could be pretty busy. Other folks are probably in the same spot as you today."

"I imagine." As Hans turned to the stable where she housed the five horses Allie adored, Jenna walked into the house and hoped to find a local handyman who could help her. "Fat chance," she thought aloud. In the den, she opened the drawer where she kept her phone books and noticed the red light blinking on her answering machine. Crossing her fingers that Allie hadn't decided she was feeling worse or that she'd left something else in the truck, Jenna played the messages. The first was from the high school. Cassie, whom she'd dropped off a couple of blocks from the school, was officially AWOL. "Fabulous," Jenna muttered sarcastically, but refused to panic. Obviously Cassie was with Josh. A lot of good grounding did. The second call was from Harrison Brennan, her neighbor. He was nearly fifty, retired from the Air Force, single, and had intimated more than once that she needed a man to help her out with her place.

Today, she thought unhappily, he was right.

The problem was that Harrison considered himself a prime candidate for the job. They'd dated a few times and it was obvious that he was interested in her. She wasn't certain what she felt for him, but he certainly wasn't the love of her life, nor her "soul mate," a term she didn't understand nor really trust. He was a friend. She doubted he would ever be more.

"I'm sorry I missed you," Harrison had recorded. "I was just checkin' in. I hear we're in for one helluva storm and wondered if you needed a hand with anything. Give me a call when you get in."

She hesitated. She didn't want to depend on Harrison or let him know that some of his instincts were valid or that she couldn't handle these rugged acres on her own. When she'd moved to Falls Crossing, she'd been determined to make it on her own and didn't want to be beholden to anyone. If she'd learned anything from her marriage to Robert, it was that the only person on whom she could count was herself. So she'd better be strong.

Sighing, she wondered if everyone in California had been right. Maybe her move north had been a rash decision. It had seemed like a good idea to give up her cheating husband, stalled career, and glitzy life in Southern California. She'd opted for something more "real" for her two children and herself, and this large estate set in the mountainous terrain of the Columbia River had caught her attention when she'd been up visiting her friend Rinda and noticed the "For Sale" sign bolted onto the gate. She'd called a local realtor, been shown the ranch, and made an offer. Private, if isolated, her new home was close enough to I-84 that she envisioned herself popping onto the freeway and driving into Portland in a little over an hour.

The place had seemed perfect when she'd moved here. Set in the hills with oak, pine, and fir trees, a creek, five horses, and an old, half-blind dog that came with the rambling, three-storied log cabin, the hilly acres had appeared to be just what her splintered little family had needed. Charming paned windows, a sharply peaked roof, dormers, and French doors stained to match the rest of the wood interior were complemented by two massive stone fireplaces. Once owned by a timber baron, the house and acres were quaint. Bucolic. A refuge.

Jenna had fallen in love with the ranch.

Of course, she'd first seen the gated acres in the waning days of summer when the weather was dry and warm, the view of the swift, dark river spectacular. And it had been at a time when she'd needed to escape the nightmare that had become her life. This house was so roomy, yet cozy, with its north-woodsy, log-cabin charm, and it was only half an hour away from skiing on Mount Hood. The private log home had seemed custom-made for her and her kids.

But not today, she thought. With the wind whistling down the gorge, the impending threat of snow and ice, and no running water, the place wasn't quite so enchanting.

A second after she clicked off the recorder, the phone rang. Jenna picked up the receiver and before she could say a word, she heard, "Mom? It's Cassie. I missed first period, but I'm here at the school and I have to go or Mr. Rivers will mark me absent in Chemistry."

"Why were you late?"

"It's complicated. I'll tell you about it when I get home. I just wanted you to know I'm okay. 'Bye."

"Cassie, wait—" she said, but heard her daughter click off. "'Bye," she said to herself and sighed. "Fabulous." She glanced down at Critter, who thumped his tail against the floor obligingly. "Just damned fabulous."

"I called the Oregon Department of Transportation. ODOT's got sanding crews and plows ready. We could get freezing rain as well as snow. In that case we'll not only lose road service, but we'll have power outages and people will be stranded. So far, I-84 is clear and passable, but if it gets bad, the State Police will shut it down," Deputy Hixx was saying from his patrol car somewhere in the county. Carter had the guy on speaker phone in his office and while listening with half an ear, was also skimming his e-mail, hoping for something from the crime lab on the Jane Doe that Charley Perry had discovered.

"Just keep me posted on the road conditions. Maybe we'll get lucky and the storm won't hit."

"Yeah, right," Hixx said, without so much as a chuckle. "You know the old saying 'when hell freezes over?' Well, I think this is it."

Twenty-nine-year-old Bill Hixx was a glass-is-half-empty sort, but this time, Carter thought as he hung up, the kid was probably right. And the storm, if it was as bad as predicted, would make life hell for everyone, especially the electrical crews, road service people, and, of course, law enforcement. He looked through the window and noticed how the sky had darkened, the gray clouds burgeoning ominously, seeming to collect over this part of the Columbia Gorge.

The door to his office was ajar and he heard his secretary say, "Just a minute . . . I'll see if he's busy—"

Too late. Rinda Dalinsky suddenly appeared in his doorway.

"Are you?" she asked with a familiar smile. "Busy?"

"Always. Just ask Jerri."

His secretary had followed Rinda into the office, and it was evident from the glare she sent Rinda that Jerri was furious. "I tried to stop her," she explained, with a but-what-can-you-do frown pursing her lips.

Carter waved Jerri off. "It's all right. You know she's an old friend."

"Just don't put the emphasis on 'old,'" Rinda suggested. She seemed completely oblivious to the fact that Jerri was nearly spitting nails.

"Never." For the first time that day, Carter felt one side of his mouth lift into a smile. He'd known Rinda Allen since they were kids, lost touch with her when she got married and moved to California, reconnected when she'd returned to Falls Crossing, newly divorced, a kid in tow. There had never been any romantic connection between them, but a lifetime ago Rinda Allen had been Carolyn's best friend. She'd been the one who had set up the blind date where both Carolyn and Shane, both reluctantly, had met. And that counted. For that, and countless other favors over the years, Rinda Dalinsky could bend a few rules here and there.

"You're the one who suggested we stick to protocol," Jerri reminded him huffily. She had a temper that she was always trying to contain but she was hardworking and honest.

"That I did, and you, accordingly, did your duty."

"Her barging in here is *not* protocol."

"I know. But it's okay. Thanks." He winked at Jerri and noticed her cheeks begin to redden. "Would you mind shutting the door?"

"Not at all." Direct orders she understood.

As soon as the door clicked shut, Rinda groaned and rolled her huge eyes. "You're insufferable, Carter."

"So they claim."

"But she's a drill sergeant." Rinda flopped into a side chair and studied the single bloom on the Christmas cactus that rested on the corner of his desk, the only plant he hadn't killed. Yet. "Things a little tense around here lately?"

"I suppose."

"Have an ID on that woman up at Catwalk Point?"

"You came here to try and pry information out of me? What happened, did you give up the theater for the newspaper?"

"No—it's just on everyone's mind, I guess."

"Are you worried?"

"Are *you?*"

"Trying to keep things in perspective," he said, not ready to admit to anyone, not even Rinda, that the Jane Doe case bothered him on a lot of levels. There was something about it that gnawed at him. Yeah, he was worried. Big-time. "Look, I guess I'm here because we're friends."

"What's on your mind?" he asked, as the old heater kicked into overdrive and the sound of air being pushed through old ducts muted the hum of computers and ring of phones outside his office.

"Some things are missing from the theater," Rinda announced.

"What kind of things?"

"Props. Costumes. Fake jewelry. Nothing all that valuable."

"You're sure they're not misplaced?"

She shot him a look that reminded him she wasn't an idiot. "At first, I didn't know. But the last thing bothered me. It's a black dress that Jenna Hughes donated. It's probably only worth a couple of hundred dollars, except that it was a costume she'd worn in one of her movies. That ups the street value."

"You're here because a dress is missing?" he asked, unable to hide his surprise. "Really?"

Rinda shifted in her chair and avoided his gaze, instead staring through one of the windows in his office. Ice glazed the panes, blurring the lines of the buildings across the street.

"Or is there something else?" he prodded. He hoped to

hell she wasn't going to try to get him to do something about the damned citation.

"Okay . . . yeah," she admitted, finally looking directly at him again. "I don't know who else to tell, Shane. When I figured out what's been happening, it kinda freaked me out."

"And what is that?"

"That everything missing once belonged to Jenna Hughes, and not just that, but the items"—she opened her purse and pulled out a sheet of computer paper—"were from her movies. Two bracelets, a ring, a scarf, a pair of sunglasses, three pairs of shoes, all from different films. Now a black dress is missing. The one she wore in *Resurrection*." She handed the typed list to Carter. "I guess I should have been more on top of it, but I thought we'd misplaced some of the items, and I didn't really think that everything that was missing had been used in Jenna's movies. Today, after Jenna and I couldn't find the dress, I typed up the list. That's when it really hit home."

He studied the piece of paper. "You've looked everywhere for these things?"

"Of course!"

"And asked the staff and actors?"

"I spent all morning calling everyone who has access."

"You mean, all this stuff is locked up?"

"Locked in the theater. I don't have locks on the closets and wardrobes and cubbies."

"Maybe you should." He glanced down at the typed sheet.

"You're patronizing me."

"No, I'm not," he lied. "I just don't know what I can do about it."

"You mean, you're too busy."

"Right. Have you talked to the city police?"

"Not yet. I figured they'd just laugh at me."

"And I wouldn't?"

"You might, but I wouldn't lose any sleep over it."

"I get it—this is a personal matter, not really a police matter."

"At least for now. I just thought I should talk to someone

about it." She leaned forward in the chair. "Don't you think it's odd that everything that was taken came from Jenna Hughes?"

"Not really," Carter said. "She's the most famous person around these parts. It makes sense."

"In a sick sort of way."

"Right." He slid the list back to her and thought of the Jane Doe and the threat of the storm. There had been a break-in at the old logging camp in the forest just to the east. A hiker was missing in the foothills of Mount Hood, and a meth lab had been discovered at the south end of the county. Two drunks had plowed their SUV into the side of Grandy's store and were in the jail. A motorist had been robbed at a rest stop near Multnomah Falls. And a woman had been murdered. Carter's phone had been ringing all morning. "There's not much I can do, Rinda. We're swamped and it's only going to get worse with this weather. You might have better luck with the city guys."

"Never have so far. Keep that." She wouldn't pick up the paper lying between them. "It's a copy, and yes, I will go talk to Officer Twinkle, if that's what you want."

"It's Officer Winkle and with an attitude like that, you won't get far."

"Yeah, Rip Van. The guy's been asleep at the switch for years."

"You're talking about Falls Crossing's finest and another cop. We all watch out for each other."

"Then you're in trouble if Wade Winkle's got your back," she said, with more than a little acrimony as she climbed to her feet. "He's too busy hassling teenagers to do any real cop work."

Carter knew where this was coming from. A few years back, Rinda's son, Scott, had experienced a couple of run-ins with the local police. Rinda, who was a mother bear when it came to her only son, had asked Carter to intervene with Officer Winkle.

"Okay, so I'll keep the list, but I won't have any men to put on it, you know that," he said and scooted back his chair.

"Talk to Wade, file a theft report, and lock things up, okay? You could even get a guard dog to patrol the theater."

"So this isn't a big enough crime for you."

"It might not even be a crime."

"I'm telling you—"

"It's a matter of priorities, Rinda. You know that." He walked to the door and yanked it open, signifying that their time was over.

Standing, Rinda hiked the strap of her purse over her shoulder. "Okay, okay, I get it. I *know* you're busy. But this is really worrying me . . . it's just kind of creepy."

He didn't respond as she made her way to the door and the sounds of the office—computers humming, phones ringing, conversation buzzing—drifted inside. "But you know, Shane, you really should give Jenna a chance, rather than a ticket." She paused at the threshold, earning a dark look from Jerri.

"I figured that was coming," he said, bracing himself. "What'd she do, ask you to try and get me to void the citation?"

"Of course not. Look, forget the ticket. Who cares about it?"

"Jesus, Rinda, you never give up, do you?"

"You wouldn't love me if I did."

Again a look from Jerri. Jesus, they didn't need to be discussing his love life here!

"You should meet her," Rinda insisted as she paused in the doorway. "And not as the big, bad cop. I'm talking socially."

"I don't need to meet *any*one. Got it?" But in his mind's eye, he conjured up a vision of Jenna Hughes—not the small woman huddled behind the wheel of her beat-up Ford, but the Hollywood star. Every man's fantasy. Shiny black hair, large greenish eyes, big breasts, small waist, and a tight ass that she'd flaunted in all her movies. They were her trademarks. She had a heart-shaped face that could appear innocent one second and slyly sexual the next. The kind of face that made a man want to protect her, all the while hoping to get her into bed. And she had all that fame chasing her around. A celebrity from Tinseltown. Not his type. Not his type at all.

"I think you'd like her."

"You're always thinking I'll like someone."

"I was right about Carolyn."

"At first."

She pulled a face. "I don't think we should go there."

"Probably not."

"You could have made it work if you'd had enough time. I knew she was the right one for you."

He caught her gaze, decided she was right—no reason to rake up the muck. "Okay, so you're batting a thousand, so there's no need to spoil your record."

Little lines appeared across her forehead and she placed a hand over his sleeve. "You can't grieve forever."

"Is that what I'm doing?"

"I think so."

"Because I'm not in the dating scene?" he baited. "What about you?"

"We're not talking about me."

"Good. We're not talking about me, either."

"You'd like her, Shane," Rinda insisted as she finally made her way past Jerri's desk and through the rest of the department.

He didn't offer any protest as she left, but he knew she was wrong about his love life. Dead wrong. He suspected Rinda knew it, too. She just couldn't face the truth.

No more than he could.

CHAPTER 8

"I *hate* it here," Cassie said, sitting cross-legged on her unmade bed while glowering at her mother through a curtain of thick hair. Her earphones were dangling from her neck and she could still hear the lyrics of her favorite song, but couldn't concentrate, not with Jenna standing in the doorway like some kind of medieval sentry. "I never wanted to move here and neither did Allie, so you can't blame me if things aren't as perfect as you thought they'd be."

"I didn't expect them to be 'perfect,' Cassie. Nothing ever is."

"L.A. was." Cassie was boiling inside. She saw her mother wince and knew she'd hit a raw nerve.

"It wasn't."

"Not for you, maybe, but you did exactly what you tell Allie and me not to do. You ran away. Because of Dad and because of Aunt Jill."

Jenna's face turned ashen for a second and Cassie felt like she'd gone too far, but then, her mother deserved it. "I brought you girls up here because I thought it would be best for all of us."

"Yeah, right," Cassie snarled, furious. "It didn't have anything to do with *White Out?*"

"Oh God," Jenna whispered and leaned against the doorframe of the odd-shaped room with its dormers and bench seats.

Cassie felt like a heel but refused to show it.

"You're right, Cass. I did leave to get away from all that and I . . . I missed Jill so badly, felt so awful about what happened to her." Jenna's throat worked and Cassie turned away.

Cassie didn't want to see her mother hurt; she just wanted Jenna to back off. "Just leave me alone," she said angrily, though she wanted to break down in tears.

"Not until we get a few things straight."

"I thought we already did. You grounded me. I get it."

"I grounded you last night and you cut class today. I don't really think you do get it."

"God, Mom, give it up."

"You know, honey, I don't want to fight with you."

"Then get off my case."

"I can't. I'd love just to be your buddy, but I'm your mother and it's my responsibility to—"

Cassie groaned and didn't hear the rest. She replaced her earphones and tried to concentrate on the music. But Jenna didn't leave. She waltzed in and plopped down to sit uninvited on the corner of Cassie's bed. Like they really were "buddies." Jesus. Could she just get out? Cassie tried to ignore her, attempted to close her eyes and get lost in the music, but she couldn't. Not with her mom perched on the end of the bed. Didn't Jenna get it? Didn't she understand how hard it was to be Jenna Hughes's daughter? To look so much like her famous mother? *Everyone* she knew, either at school or in her dance classes, wanted to know what it was like to have a famous celebrity for a mother, a mother who looked more like an older, beautiful sister. How many times had Cassie witnessed astonished faces as she'd heard the same old line: "*This* is your daughter? No way! You couldn't possibly be old enough to be her mother!" Jenna had always been flattered and Cassie mortified. Cassie suspected that anyone who befriended her did it just to get close to Jenna Hughes, the once-upon-a-time actress, the beautiful woman whose life was marred by tragedy, the single mom striving to leave her glittery life behind for her kids. It was enough to gag Cassie.

Then there was Josh. *Her* boyfriend and quite possibly the worst of the lot. Though he'd never said it, Cassie suspected that Josh only hung out with her because of Jenna. Cassie had found his secret DVD collection, the one he'd hidden in the bottom drawer of his nightstand. And there were pictures of Jenna, too, prints he'd gotten off the Internet. Even more disgusting was the way he acted whenever they were around her mother. Josh had attempted to hide his fascination with Jenna Hughes but had failed. He hadn't been able to take his eyes off her. He'd stared at her in that certain way Cassie recognized as pure lust. Just the way all men did.

No, Josh didn't love Cassie because she was special, as he'd claimed a thousand times. She knew better. If he did love her, which she sometimes doubted, it was because she was Jenna Hughes's daughter. How sick was that? Cassie's throat thickened and got hot. Oh, crap, she was gonna cry! No way! No friggin' way! She squeezed her eyes tighter, determined not to shed one solitary tear over anything, or anyone, so stupid.

"Cassie?" Her mother's voice was gentle. She felt a hand on her jean-clad knee.

"Go away." Cassie upped the volume on her CD.

"We really do need to talk."

Was it impossible to drown out her mother's concerned voice? Damn it all! "Leave me alone, Mom. I got the message. Loud and clear." She refused to open her eyes, and cranked up the volume again, until the singer was screaming in her ear. The hand on her knee dropped and the mattress moved a bit as Jenna, presumably, got to her feet.

At the end of the song, Cassie barely lifted one eyelid. The room was empty, the door ajar. Finally Jenna had taken the hint and left. Cassie felt a jab of remorse. Deep down, she knew her mom really did care about her and Allie, but Jenna had made a colossal mistake uprooting them and hauling them to this podunk town in the middle of nowhere.

Cassie's social life had nose-dived and Allie had become

shyer than she'd been in L.A. Yeah, she had the horses and piano lessons, but other than that, the kid was always holed up in her room with her Game Boy.

Like you are with the TV and CD player?

She wouldn't think about that; wasn't a nerd like her little sister.

Angry with her mother, herself, and the whole damned world, Cassie scooted off the bed and crossed the room, quietly shutting the door. Then she let out a long breath and grabbed her remote control. She flipped on the TV, searching for a reality show when she caught a glimpse of the local news. The reporter was up in the mountains, at Catwalk Point where the dead woman had been found. Cassie let the image linger for a second. It was morbid. The word in school was that the remains had been beheaded and torn apart, maybe by animals . . . some of the stories she'd heard were pure gossip, but Cassie figured whatever had happened up in the mountains, it had been gruesome.

She shivered and flipped the channel until she found an ultimate dating challenge and, opening her chemistry book in case her mother barged in and invaded her space again, settled against the pillows.

Still stinging from Cassie's cruel words, Jenna made her way down the hall and told herself to be strong. Cassie was angry and had lashed out. She'd felt backed into a corner and probably hadn't meant all the hateful things she'd said. But it still hurt. It hurt like hell.

Because she was too close to the truth?

Jenna didn't want to go there. Didn't want to think about Jill and all those dark reasons she'd had to leave California. The divorce was bad enough, but she could have handled that. Jill's death was another matter altogether. Guilt gnawed at her as it had ever since the accident. Once again, Jenna attempted to ignore the overwhelming sense of responsibility as she made her way down the stairs and into the kitchen. *Don't let Cassie get to you. That's what she wants. Remember who's the mother and who's the daughter, Jenna. She's only trying to hurt you because she's hurting. Give her a couple of hours to cool off, then try again. You're the one in control here.*

Or was she? Sometimes it didn't seem like it at all.

She reheated coffee she'd made from the bottled water she'd bought in town, then checked on Allie and found her seated on the floor of the den, playing her Game Boy while watching television. "You have all your homework done?"

"Almost," Allie said, concentrating on the tiny screen.

"What does 'almost' mean?"

"That I don't have any. I did my math at school and I just have a book report." She finally looked up and added, "I'll do it after dinner."

"Okay." Jenna wasn't up for another fight. She blew across the top of her coffee cup and walked to the kitchen where she pulled out a phone book from a cupboard near the telephone, then scanned the yellow pages. She'd already called several handymen she'd found listed in the local paper, not reaching a single real person, just answering machines. So far, no one had responded. Time to call in the big guns. She leafed through the section on home repairs and scanned the names, some of whom she'd heard, others who were complete strangers; still others were yahoos, self-proclaimed handymen who hadn't known which end of a nail to hammer who had come out here in their own sweet time, sworn they'd fixed the alarm system, or the gate, or the stove, and left, only to have whatever it was go out a few days or weeks later. She avoided those flakes.

You could call Wes Allen.

She discarded that idea as quickly as it popped into her head. She didn't like the idea of being alone with him. At all.

She also planned to call a tow truck to have her Jeep taken to the dealer in Gresham, nearly fifty miles west, or she could try a local guy, the owner of one of the two gas stations in town. "Decisions, decisions," she said as she reached for the receiver.

As she waited for someone to answer, Cassie's accusations about why she'd left California echoed painfully through her mind. *It didn't have anything to do with* White Out?

She felt the old familiar ache deep in her center. Jenna still couldn't talk about the accident that had taken her sister's life. *White Out,* the movie that was never finished. *White Out*, a movie she hadn't wanted to make. *White Out*, Robert's pet project that seemed cursed from the get-go. *White Out*, the end of her career, her marriage, and life as she'd known it. *White Out*, the reason Jill had died.

"RS Plumbing," a cheery female voice said, breaking into Jenna's thoughts. She realized she was talking to a living, breathing person, not a voice mail machine with a series of prompts.

"Great." Jenna tried to put a smile into her voice and push all thoughts of the tragedy that had propelled her to Oregon out of her mind. "I'm hoping you can help me. I've got a problem with my pump and—"

"Can you hold?"

Before Jenna could respond, the woman clicked to another line and Jenna was left listening to silence. Hoping the woman on the other end of the line hadn't disconnected her, Jenna waited and nothing happened. The line seemed dead. She hung up and retried, but the phone line was then busy. Of course. Today nothing was going right. She tried again and got nowhere.

"Great," she said, and hung up feeling cursed. "Get over it," she told herself as she rested against the window ledge and glanced through the glass to the wintry twilight where the ranch's few security lights were blazing, giving an eerie blue glow to the grounds. The wind had finally died and with it came a stillness that seemed weird and out of place. Unearthly.

The calm before the storm, she thought, and felt a shiver as cold as death trickle down her spine. There was something about the coming night, something dark and lurking, something deadly. She could feel it.

Stop it! Don't do this to yourself, she silently admonished and noticed the first few flakes of snow beginning to fall from the sky.

She was there.

Inside.

Somewhere in the rambling log home.

No doubt Jenna Hughes felt secure. Safe.

But she was wrong.

Dead wrong.

As the flakes of winter snow drifted from the gray sky, he watched from his hiding spot, a blind he'd built high in the branches of an old-growth Douglas fir that towered from this high ridge. Her ranch stretched out below in frozen acres that abutted the Columbia River.

The rustic old house was the core of what he considered her compound. Graying logs and siding rising upward to peaked gables and dormers. From the ice-glazed windows, cozy patches of light glowed against the frozen ground, reminding him of his own past, of how often he'd been on the outside, in the freezing weather, teeth chattering as he stared at the smoke rising from the chimney of his mother's warm, forbidden house.

That was long ago.

Now, focusing the military glasses on the panes, he caught a glimpse of her moving through her house. But just a teaser, not much, not enough to focus on her. Her image disappeared as she turned down a hallway.

He refocused, caught a bit of movement in the den, but it was only the old dog, a broken-down German shepherd who slept most of the day.

Where was she?

Where the hell had she gone?

Be patient, his inner voice advised, trying to soothe him. *Soon you'll be able to do what you want.*

The snowflakes increased, powdering the branches, covering the ground far below, and he glanced down at the white frost. In his mind's eye he saw drops of blood in the icy crystals, warm as they hit the ground, giving off a puff of steam, then freezing slowly in splotches of dark red.

A thrill tingled up his spine just as a stiff breeze, cold as Lucifer's piss, screamed down the gorge, stinging the bit of skin above his ski mask. The branches above and around him danced wildly and beneath the mask, he smiled. He embraced the cold, felt it was a sign. An omen.

The snow was now falling in earnest. Icy crystals falling from the sky.

Now was the time.

He'd waited so long.

Too long.

A light flashed on in the master bedroom and he caught another glimpse of her, long hair braided into a rope that hung down her back, baggy sweatshirt covering her curves, no makeup enhancing an already beautiful face. His pulse accelerated as she walked past a bank of windows, then into a closet. His throat went dry. He refocused the glasses, zoomed in closer on the closet door. Maybe he'd catch a glimpse of her naked, her perfectly honed body, an athlete's body with large breasts and a nipped-in waist and muscles that were both feminine and strong. His crotch tightened.

He waited. Ignored a light being snapped on in another part of the house. Knew it was probably one of her kids.

Come on, come on, he thought impatiently. His mouth turned dry as sand and lust heated his chilled blood. The master bedroom with its yellowed-pine walls and softly burning fire remained empty. What the hell was taking her so long?

How he wanted her. He had for a long, long time.

He licked his lips against the cold as she reappeared, wearing a black bra and low-slung black jeans. She was beautiful. Nearly perfect in those tight pants.

"Strip 'em, Jenna," he muttered under breath that fogged through his insulated mask.

Her breasts nearly fell from the sexy black undergarment. But she headed into her bathroom and he readjusted the lens as she leaned over a sink and applied lipstick and mascara.

He saw her backside, that sweet, sweet ass, straining against the black denim as she leaned closer to the mirror; within that smooth glass surface, he stared at her wide eyes, silvery green and rimmed in thick black lashes. For a second she seemed to catch his eye, to look right at him, and she hesitated, mascara wand in hand. Little lines appeared between her arched eyebrows, a hint of worry. As if she knew. Her eyes narrowed, and his heart pounded hard against his ribs.

Turning quickly, she stared out the window, to the gathering darkness and the snow now falling steadily. Was it fear he saw in her green eyes? Premonition?

"Just you wait," he whispered, his voice soft in the deadly quiet forest, the snow becoming thick enough that her image was blurred, his erection suddenly rock-hard as he conjured up pictures of what he would do to her.

But that instant of fear was gone, and her lips pulled into a half smile, as if she'd been foolish. She flipped off the bathroom light, then headed back to her bedroom. Once in her cozy master suite, she yanked a sweater from her bed and pulled it over her head. For a few seconds he felt ecstasy, watching as her arms uplifted and for a heartbeat she was blindfolded and trapped in the garment, but then her head poked through a wide cowl neck and her arms slid through the sweater's sleeves. She pulled her rope of hair from the neckline and walked quickly out of view, snapping the lights off as she entered the hallway.

Hot desire zinged through his blood at the thought of her.

Beautiful.

Arrogant.

Proud.

And soon, very soon, to be brought to her knees.

CHAPTER 9

"Get this," BJ said, as Carter walked into the courthouse the next day. He'd spent the last three hours at the scene of an accident where a semi had jackknifed on I-84. The huge truck had hit a patch of black ice and slammed into an SUV filled with teenagers on their way to the mountain for night skiing. One kid had been treated by EMTs and released, two others had been sent by ambulance to local hospitals, and a third had been life-flighted to Portland. The driver of the eighteen-wheeler had escaped without injury except for the mental anguish he was putting himself through.

"Just don't tell me it's more bad news," Carter said, yanking off his gloves. He was cold, tired, and hungry, as he'd missed both breakfast and lunch. Freezing rain had snarled traffic, the schools had closed, and now a blizzard was blowing down the gorge.

BJ ignored his bad mood as he stopped in the small kitchen and poured himself a cup of coffee from the pot simmering in the coffeemaker. He took a long sip and felt the hot liquid splash against the bottom of his empty stomach. Finally, as they headed toward his office, she asked, "What is it you've been bugging me about for over twenty-four hours?"

"The autopsy on the Jane Doe."

"Bingo." She flashed him a smile. "Just ask and ye shall receive."

It was on his desk. He unzipped his coat and hung it on a peg, then picked up the computer pages and scanned them quickly. "Cause of death hasn't been determined."

"That's right, but check out the teeth. Definitely filed down. No dental work to be found, so we can't ID her that way. No flesh on her fingers, so no prints. Not enough left of her to identify her from physical marks. No tattoos or scars, none of her bones were ever broken, well, at least none of the ones we've discovered. But they did analyze the stuff in her hair."

Carter had already seen the note. "Latex?"

"Yep, but foam, not paint."

"Foam," he repeated. "Like the rubber stuff."

"Mmm. And some of it was *inside* her. Now, check the other stuff they found. Alginate."

"What the hell's that?"

"It's manufactured from a seaweed source, comes in a powder that, when added with water, creates the stuff that dentists use to make molds of teeth. Have you ever been fitted for a crown and had to bite into a mold filled with some cherry-flavored goop? That's alginate."

"How do you know that?" he asked. BJ always amazed him.

"I'm Internet-friendly."

"So while I'm out freezing my butt off in the worst storm of the century, you're surfing the Web," he accused, leaning one hip on the edge of his desk as he reread the report.

"And drinking hot cocoa and eating bonbons, while I'm at it." One reddish eyebrow arched impishly. "Isn't that the way it should be?"

"Absolutely," he said sarcastically as he tried to wrap his brain around this new information. "Why alginate and latex?"

"It might have something to do with why her teeth were filed down."

Looking up, he asked, "You think we've got a sado-masochistic dentist on the loose?"

"I don't know what we've got." Suddenly she wasn't kidding. Carter felt the humor disperse with the chill in the air. "But I don't like it."

"Neither do I."

"They think she's been dead nearly a year."

Carter nodded, reread the notes on the report.

"Any other information?"

"The crime lab's working on it, but they didn't find any tire tracks or footprints to cast and, so far, no other evidence in the surrounding area."

"She didn't crawl into the log by herself."

"No, but whoever did it covered his tracks, and it's been a long time, nearly a year. Seasons change, wild animals drag off body parts, soil erosion and rain wash away footprints. Any evidence that might have been left could be buried deep. So far, though, metal detectors have found nothing." BJ ran a hand through her short hair. "You know what bothers me? The teeth. I keep coming back to that. Why kill someone and take the time to file down her teeth?"

"Maybe he did it while she was still alive."

"Jesus. Don't even say it. I hate dentists and drills and . . . God, that's just so twisted."

"Maybe it's how he gets off."

"Then we've got to nail the bastard."

"If he's still around. A year's a long time. Maybe he's already slipped up and is serving time. The State Police are checking to see if there are any other cases, solved or unsolved, like this one."

"Nothing's like this one," she said. "At least I hope not."

"Me, too," he agreed as she headed down the hall and he settled into his chair. He checked with Missing Persons again, and finished a report on the accident on the freeway while taking calls and keeping one eye on the window where snow was piling against the icy panes.

Jenna pulled her ski mask over the lower half of her face and walked the three blocks from the garage to the post office. According to Skip Uhrig, the owner of the garage, her Jeep would be ready within the next couple of hours. All that was wrong with her rig was a faulty alternator.

One problem down, a few thousand to go, she thought as she crossed the street and tried to avoid slipping on the icy pavement. Snow was slanting from the gray sky, thick enough that it was impossible to see the length of the street; both her kids were at home, as the schools had let out early because of the weather, and so far, none of the repairmen she'd called had shown up. "It's still early," she told herself as she pushed her way past the glass door into the post office, a yellow-brick building that had been erected before the turn of the *last* century.

There was counter space for four clerks, but only one person was helping customers. Not that it mattered. Only two people were waiting and one, a tall woman bundled in parka, scarf, and ski pants, kept looking over her shoulder to eye Jenna as she opened her post office box and withdrew a stack of mail. Jenna didn't pay much attention. It happened all the time. Either people recognized her and were suddenly tongue-tied in the face of her celebrity, or they studied her surreptitiously, the wheels in their minds turning quickly to try and connect a face with a name. Those people didn't expect to see her in a small town, running the same errands they were.

Since she had some hours to kill, she decided to walk the few blocks to the theater and see if Rinda wanted to go to a late lunch or grab a cup of coffee at the local café. Stuffing the mail into her purse, she shouldered open the door and hustled down the street. Few people were on the sidewalks and the usual slow traffic had dwindled.

Think of it as an adventure, she told herself, as she made her way down an alley where trash bins, parked cars, and garages were covered in four inches of snow. She hurried briskly through a parking lot to the old theater. Its steeply pitched roof was covered in white, its belltower knifing upward to the dark sky, its stained-glass windows glowing from the lights within. The once-upon-a-time church appeared bucolic and had a Currier and Ives nostalgia, until you looked more closely and noticed the blistered and peeled paint, some rot in the siding, crumbling mortar on the brick walkways, and a dark spire that seemed incomplete and somewhat sinister without a cross mounted at its highest point.

Don't be ridiculous, she told herself, but had thought the old church was a little eerie, an odd choice for the theater, despite whatever tax breaks Rinda had received for restoring the historic building.

Rather than walk up the front steps, she cut around the back and stepped through a door that opened to a landing of a staircase. It wound up to the main part of the theater and curled down to the basement where the kitchen and dressing rooms were located in what had been Sunday-school classrooms fifty years earlier.

Voices echoed through the stairwell—one she recognized as Rinda's, the other she couldn't place other than it was male and, from the sounds of it, irritated.

". . . I told you to talk to Winkle," the man was saying.

"And I told you that would be a waste of time. He and I have a history."

"I know, but that wouldn't keep him from doing his job."

"Look, Shane, I've got a problem here."

"Because someone's stealing trinkets that belonged to a celebrity?" he replied gruffly, and Jenna realized Rinda was talking to the sheriff. Great. Jenna melted back into the shadowy staircase as the man behind the badge ranted on. "Is that really a surprise? What do you expect, Rinda? It doesn't matter if it's Jenna Hughes or Jennifer Lopez or Drew Barrymore or anyone with a face and name that people recognize—people are going to try and get close to her, either by asking for her autograph, or befriending her, or taking a little something that was once hers. Celebrities ask for this kind of thing to happen. It comes with the territory. The price of fame."

"That's a pile of garbage, Shane, and you know it. Thievery is thievery. It doesn't matter who you are."

"That's why I'm here."

"You could have sent one of the deputies."

"Not today," he shot back. "They're too busy. I'm here on my lunch hour as a personal favor to you, okay? Now, I'll look around, but you've already said there isn't any evidence of forced entry, that the only things missing were donated by Jenna Hughes, and that you've searched the entire premises. Have you asked the people that work here?"

"Most of them."

"*Most?*" he repeated, not hiding his sarcasm.

"Not everyone has been in since I discovered the dress was missing, and I called those I could, but I haven't reached a few."

"Keep trying," he advised. "And talk to Ms. Hughes. Maybe she decided she didn't want to donate the things after all."

Jenna bristled. Why would he think she'd take back her old costumes after giving them to the theater?

"She wouldn't do that," Rinda protested.

"Someone did."

"Not Jenna."

"Then who?"

"That's what I expect you to find out."

He swore under his breath and all Jenna could make out was ". . . the last time, okay? Damned Hollywood types . . . more trouble than they're worth . . . should stay in California where they belong."

Jenna had heard enough. She stomped her way up the half flight to what had been the apse, where she walked through the open door and found Rinda and the sheriff standing at the middle aisle between the first row of pews. *Here we go,* she thought, as she stepped out of the stairwell and faced the tall man. He was at least six-feet-two or three. Wide shoulders that tapered to a narrow waist and slim hips suggested he was either naturally athletic or that he worked out. Dressed in his uniform, but bareheaded, the brim of his hat twisting in the fingers of one large hand, he was a presence, a male presence. No two ways about it.

"I think I heard my name," she announced.

"Uh-oh." Rinda winced and leaned against the arm of one pew, but the sheriff, his rugged face a mask of indifference, merely looked over his shoulder.

Near-black eyes assessed her without the slightest bit of interest. "You did if you're Jenna Hughes." His gaze skated over her face and he nodded as if to confirm her identity to himself. "So, yeah, you did."

At least he wasn't pretending he didn't recognize her. "Thought so. And . . . from what I gather, you've already decided you don't trust me."

"I don't trust many people," he drawled. "Comes with the territory."

"I figured," she said as she walked in front of the first row of pews. "But that's too bad." Extending her hand, she stopped directly in front of him, the toes of her boots nearly touching his.

"I don't think so."

"Well . . ." She angled her face up to stare at him. ". . . Just for the record, Sheriff, I didn't steal my things, okay? Yes, I was driving an old truck with bad taillights, but this week, that's the extent of my failure to follow the letter of the law."

"Oh, God," Rinda whispered. She braced herself on her seat and turned paler with each exchange between her friends.

"Good to know." One thick brow lifted. The sheriff shook her hand in a firm, warm grip but didn't allow even the hint of a smile to change the contours of his face. Letting go of her fingers, he didn't seem the least embarrassed that she'd overheard any of the conversation.

"I told him you wouldn't take the dress," Rinda said, some of her color returning.

"That she did." His gaze was rock-steady, nearly harsh, dark brown eyes that, she guessed, didn't miss much. They were set deep in his skull, guarded by black eyebrows and placed above high cheekbones that hinted at a Native American ancestor not too many generations back. His hair was near-black and thick, only a few strands of silver daring to show. "As a matter of fact, Rinda's been singing your praises to me ever since you moved here."

Jenna shot her friend a look guaranteed to cut through stone. Lifting her palms, Rinda shrugged, acting as if the entire direction of the discussion was out of her hands.

Jenna said, "But you set her straight, right?" She was too tired to rein in her anger and she felt her cheeks flush. Why the hell was this bohunk of a lawman prejudging her? "You saw fit to let her"—Jenna hitched a thumb in Rinda's direction—"know that I wasn't all that great, that maybe I couldn't be trusted."

His dark eyes glinted, but beneath his moustache one corner of his mouth twitched as if he were amused at her bluster and bravado. She supposed if he smiled there was a chance he might be handsome. A slim chance. To another woman.

Carter nodded. "I just want her to remain objective."

"Hey!" Rinda cut in. "You don't have to talk about me as if I'm not here!"

"Wouldn't dream of it," Carter said.

Jenna almost grinned. So he did have a sense of humor. Not that it mattered. "Look, Sheriff, I know you're busy," Jenna said, angling her chin upward in order to study the man. "I think the easiest thing to do would be for me to replace the missing items with other things I've got at the house." Rinda seemed about to argue, but Jenna went on. "And this time we'll lock them in a closet and only Rinda will have the key."

"But the dress and bracelets and—"

"Maybe they'll turn up," Jenna said. "If not, we'll just make do. I've got another dress that will work and lots of costume jewelry."

Rinda shoved stiff fingers through her hair. "Oh God, Jenna, I feel awful about this."

"It's not life and death, though."

Carter's jaw hardened, as if somehow she'd insulted him. "Robbery is a crime just the same. I'll talk to Sergeant Winkle at the city. He'll send someone over. In the meantime, I'll look around." He turned back to Rinda. "Show me where the items were stowed."

Celebrities, he thought later as he crossed the street to the café. *Who needed them?* He'd done his duty for his friend and paid back one of a million favors he owed Rinda, but he was finished with *the case of Jenna Hughes's missing black sheath.* Damn, what a waste of time. And the "victim" didn't even seem to want his help. He'd seen her from a distance a few times in the past year and a half, but had never met her formally. He was surprised not so much at how petite she was, but that despite her small size, there was a presence to her—not what he'd expected.

In the theater she hadn't exhibited any of the creeping Hollywood paranoia or demanding-princess attitude that, he supposed, were stereotypes. From the few minutes he spoke with her, she seemed levelheaded, if a bit feisty, bullheaded, and unaware that even without any makeup he could see, she was drop-dead gorgeous. She hadn't even seemed too pissed off about the ticket. Not that he cared. He stepped over a pile of snow pockmarked with sand and gravel, a reminder that the snowplow had been through earlier. God, it was cold. With no end in sight. In fact, the weather service predicted things would get much worse. There was even talk of the falls freezing solid.

He didn't want to think about that, nor the last time the cascading sheets of water had turned to ice and the tragedy that had ensued. In his mind's eye, he saw David, noticed his feet slipping on the slick sheet of ice . . . Carter slammed his mind shut to the image and felt the same frozen fear that always accompanied the memory. He glanced up at the sky where snow was falling relentlessly and hoped the weather would break before all the ice-climbing idiots found a way to descend on this place and pull out their picks and ropes and crampons to scale the falls.

His cell phone blasted and he stepped under the awning of the Canyon Café to take the call, which happened to be about another report of a car sliding off the road. A state trooper was already on the scene and taking care of it. No injuries, just a frightened driver and a totaled Chevy Impala.

Carter snapped his phone shut. The good news was that while he was in the theater poking around, his cell phone had

rung three separate times and no doubt both Rinda and
Jenna Hughes had heard his side of the conversation about
the serious problems facing the department. Even bullheaded Rinda had seemed to understand that the missing
dress would have to wait. Carter had to focus his attention on
the life-threatening situations brought on by the storm. Jackknifed semis, kids life-flighted to hospitals, and an unidentified dead woman found up at Catwalk Point took precedence
over some ex-Hollywood star's missing costumes.

A couple of men in ski wear walked out of the café as
Shane strode in. The Canyon Café was small, with only a
few booths, a scattering of tables, and a long counter with
stools that were usually occupied by locals. The little restaurant had been an institution in Falls Crossing for over fifty
years and was known for all-day breakfast, large greasy
burgers, onion rings, and thick wedges of home-baked pie.

Shane ordered a cheeseburger basket and coffee to go, ignored the attempts of the waitress to flirt with him, and once
the order was filled, didn't waste any time, but headed outside where the temperature seemed to have plummeted
again. The wind was harsher, its screaming edge raw enough
to cut through leather and bone. Icicles hung from the eaves
of the buildings—long, clear daggers that reminded him of
the day David had suggested they climb the falls.

Carter had been sixteen at the time and a dumb-ass kid to
boot. Both of them had been stupid, full-of-themselves,
spot-on cretins, he thought angrily as he climbed the courthouse steps. Jaw tight, he made his way to his office, left his
door ajar, then dialed up the city police where he left Wade
Winkle a voice mail message about the "crime" at the theater. As he talked, he managed to slide out of his jacket and
shoulder holster.

He wondered what, if anything, Winkle would do.

Not his problem.

He'd had as much contact with Jenna Hughes as he
wanted.

After dropping into his chair, he opened the tiny ketchup
packets and drizzled ketchup over his small carton of French

fries. They were cold and limp, but he was so hungry he didn't mind. He'd managed to take three bites of his burger when BJ appeared and rapped on the edge of his door before striding in. "Isn't it a little late for lunch?" she asked, balancing a hip against his desk.

"I was busy." He leaned back in his chair, set the burger on its white paper bag in the middle of his desk. "Chasing crime at the Columbia Theater in the Gorge."

"At the theater?"

"Don't ask," he said, as an image of Jenna Hughes burned through his mind. Just as she had much too often in the last few hours. He swiped his mouth with the back of his hand and pushed the sack with its nest of fries toward BJ. "Help yourself. Anything new?"

"The State Police are checking with all the dental alginate and latex suppliers and widening the missing persons search. And there's talk of closing I-84 if there's not a break in the weather."

"I figured." Things just kept getting worse.

"A couple of snowboarders are missing up at Meadows Ski Resort," she said, mentioning the local ski resort as she picked up a fry and plopped it into her mouth.

He was attacking his burger again, but still listening.

"Ski patrol is looking, and there's already power outages in Hampton—the weight of ice on the branches is snapping limbs, taking down wires."

"Sounds like the fun is just beginning," he said, tucking a slice of escaping onion under the top bun.

"Oh, yeah . . . we're in for a blast." She straightened and stretched, rotating the kinks from her neck as she glanced out the window. "I wonder when this weather is gonna let up."

"Never."

"Yeah, right," she said with a mirthless chuckle. "The storm's gotta break soon." There was a note of desperation in her voice and Carter understood it. He had the unlikely sensation that until the temperature elevated, things around Falls Crossing were just going to get worse. A lot worse.

* * *

He closed his eyes, felt the tingle of snow against his bare skin. Tiny, frigid flakes that were meant to cool, but heated his blood. He was hard. Rigid. Standing naked in the small clearing, old-growth firs surrounding him, their needles coated in ice and snow, the wind whistling through their heavy branches, he felt the call. The need.

It was the killing time.

With each tiny touch of the snow, the ache grew stronger. Pumping through his blood, pounding in his brain, bloodlust that only came in the depths of winter.

This is my time, he thought, his mind racing ahead to all he'd planned. *I'm only really alive when the sheen of rime glazes the road and crystals of ice rain from the sky.*

It had been a long time since the last one, nearly a year. But now, the time was at hand.

In his mind's eye he saw her, Jenna Hughes. Remembered spying her in town earlier . . .

The woman of his dreams.

His obsession.

Oh, how he wanted her.

Tonight would be perfect.

He opened his eyes and stared upward, watching the snow fall, keeping his eyelids wide so that the icy little droplets would touch his bare eyeballs and sting just a bit.

Jenna—beautiful, beautiful woman.

But the timing wasn't right. For her. The cold not yet deep enough. The hoarfrost not covering the trees and shrubs and windows. No, he wasn't prepared for her.

There were others to be sacrificed for her. They had to come first.

Paris Knowlton.

Faye Tyler.

Marnie Sylvane.

Zoey Trammel.

A few of those who would precede her. No matter how much he ached for her, he would force himself to wait.

And he knew who would be next, he thought, his blood so cold it seemed to congeal in his veins.

He'd already found her.

She wasn't perfect.

Not like Jenna.

But she would do.

For now.

CHAPTER 10

"Okay, girls, we've got the Jeep back," Jenna sang as she walked into the kitchen, dropped three bags of groceries onto the counter, then peeled off her jacket. She didn't add that despite four-wheel drive, the trip home on the icy roads had been unnerving. "Girls?" she repeated when no one answered. She stopped in the center of the kitchen, feeling the snow melt in her hair. "Allie?"

Why did the house feel so empty?

She bounded up the stairs and expected to find Cassie, headphones covering her ears, in her room, but the bedroom was empty, the bed unmade. "Cassie? Allie?" She hurried past the bathroom and into Allie's bedroom, but it, too, was vacated, the television flickering, the volume on mute, her Game Boy left on her rumpled pillows.

Don't panic. They've got to be here. Where could they go? It's a blizzard outside.

"Hey, kids, this isn't funny!" she said, hurrying down the back stairs again and making a sweep of the den, dining area, and living room. "Allie! Cassie!"

She stopped near the fireplace and listened. All she heard was the moan of the wind and she wondered how long the lights would last.

Where's the dog?

The hairs on the back of her neck raised. "Critter?"

No response. The house was empty.

All the anxiety she'd experienced in the last two days gelled. Fear knotted her stomach. Hadn't she sensed something wasn't right? Hadn't she felt as if she was being watched, even followed? And now the girls . . . oh, God.

Get a grip, Jenna. They're here. Somewhere. Keep searching.

A truck's engine caught her attention and she felt a second's relief. Obviously they had left with someone, that was it, and whoever it was—probably Josh—was returning them. Cassie had probably thought they could come and go before Jenna returned and they would never be caught. They'd taken Allie along so she wouldn't blab.

And the dog? Why Critter? She was already hurrying outside.

Probably Cassie's doing, she thought, but then realized the truck plowing through the open gate didn't belong to Josh Sykes. She hurried outside as the big rig parked near the garage and a tall man climbed from behind the wheel. Harrison Brennan emerged from the passenger side. One side of his mouth lifted at the sight of her.

"Do you have the girls with you?" she asked breathlessly.

"No."

"Have you seen them?"

Harrison glanced over her shoulder and his smile was suddenly perplexed. "You're kidding, right?"

Then she knew. She heard the crunch of boots behind her and felt like a fool, an overprotective idiot of a mother.

"Mom!" Allie's voice called out, and she turned to find Cassie, Allie, and the dog, breaking a path through the snow from the stable. Allie started running, Critter bounding through the drifts behind her. "We were just checking on the horses."

"Are they okay?"

"They're fine," Cassie said as if she were disgusted. "Hans left plenty of water for them, but The Runt was worried."

From beneath the rim of her pink stocking cap, Allie shot her sister a warning glare. "Hans told me to check!"

"He only left two hours ago!"

"Hey, it's all right." Jenna felt like a fool. She should have seen her daughters' tracks leading to the stable. What had she been thinking? Why was she so on edge? "Sorry," she said to Harrison.

"No problem. This is Seth Whitaker." He indicated the tall man next to him. "Jenna Hughes."

"Glad to meet you," she said and shook his gloved hand.

"Seth's been over at my place working on my furnace and I twisted his arm to come down and check out your pump."

"Great." Jenna flashed him a smile. "So you're an electrician?"

Harrison said, "And plumber and regular handyman. A jack of all trades."

"And master of none," the guy said. He was pleasant-looking, a couple of inches taller than Harrison and a bit thicker around the middle. Harrison prided himself in keeping his body in strict military shape, his short, silvery hair not much longer than when he'd been with the Air Force.

"Between the two of us, we should be able to fix things," Harrison said.

"That would be great," she said. "Hans thinks it's faulty wiring in the pump house," she said, pointing in the direction of the small outbuilding.

"I know where it is." Harrison turned to Seth. "It's not locked."

"I'll get my tools." The taller man walked to the back of the truck and opened the canopy doors while Jenna stared at Harrison.

"How did you know I don't lock it?"

"Because I know you. You don't lock anything but your doors, your garage, and the front gate, and that's iffy." He scowled slightly. "I wish you would take more precautions. I worry about you." He glanced at the house. "And the girls."

"We're fine," she said and felt the muscles in the back of her neck tighten. She didn't need him to be acting the part of her father. "I close the gate when it's working. No one seems to be able to fix the lock."

"Maybe I could find someone."

"No!" she said, then heard the tension in her voice. "Look, I'll take care of it."

"Okay." He nodded, which surprised her. She half-expected him to argue. "I hope so, Jenna," he said, then added, "Go on inside and warm up—you're not even wearing a coat."

She'd forgotten to put her jacket on in her panic over her children.

As if he knew, he smiled kindly—or was he patronizing her? Treating her like a china doll? "We'll handle things from here."

"I could help."

"We'll be fine," he insisted, and she realized she was in no position to argue. The man was helping her, for crying out loud, and she was worried about his attitude. What was it they said about looking a gift horse in the mouth?

"Then I'll make us all some coffee," she said, telling herself she was being sensible and gracious, not a weak, man-dependent woman, like the housewives portrayed in black-and-white sitcoms from the fifties. June Cleaver she was *not!* "It's the least I can do." She nearly choked on the words.

"That would be great." Harrison's grin broadened as he headed toward the back of the truck where Whitaker was already pulling out a large toolbox.

Jenna suddenly felt the cold through her sweater and headed toward the house. Once inside, she discovered Allie's jacket and hat thrown over the back of one of the bar stools, the snow that had clung to the material beginning to melt and drip, a small puddle forming on the floor.

"Ron called," Cassie said as she came down the stairs. She'd changed into tight jeans and a sweater. "He said he couldn't make it because of the storm."

Jenna was wiping the water from the floor with a dishrag. "I'd forgotten about him," she said, disbelieving. Ron Falletti was Jenna's personal trainer. Recently he'd been working with Cassie as well. She tossed the rag through the open door to the laundry room.

"You?" Cassie asked in mock horror, her hand flying over her heart. "Forget a workout? I didn't think that was possible!"

"I've had a lot on my mind the last couple of days." Jenna ground her favorite Italian blend of coffee beans, then tossed the pulverized coffee into the basket of the coffeemaker and added bottled water she'd picked up at the store. But Cassie's remark had hit home. Jenna had rarely missed a workout session since moving up here after the divorce. Keeping in shape had become her obsession, had gotten her through the emotional pain, had kept a thirty-eight-year-old body as taut as it had been in her twenties.

As the coffee brewed and Jenna unpacked her grocery bags, Cassie walked to a window and stared at the pump house. "You know, Mom, you're always giving me advice about boys and dating." She drew on the condensation on a window with her fingernail.

"That's my job. I'm your mother."

"Maybe it's my turn to give you some."

"Oh. Okay." Jenna followed her daughter's gaze. Harrison had emerged from the small outbuilding and was staring at the main house, as if sizing up the place.

"I don't like him," Cassie said, pointing at Harrison.

Jenna wrapped her hand around Cassie's outstretched finger. She didn't want Harrison Brennan to see them gesturing toward him. "He's just trying to help out."

"I know that's what it appears, but . . ." Cassie worried her lower lip and turned to face her mother. "He tries to help out too much and tell you what to do. He's not really bossy, just seems to think that his way is the best way."

"Or that there is no other way."

"Exactly." Cassie nodded. "Like a really old guy."

"I know," Jenna admitted as she wiped off the counter. "He's not that old. Fifty-two or -three, I think."

"Oh God, Mom, that's ancient!" Cassie was appalled.

"To you."

"And to you, too."

"No, honey, not really." She opened the refrigerator and pulled out mustard, mayonnaise, and a jar of pickles. "It's just that he seems to be from another generation."

"He is! And Josh's dad says that he was in the CIA, not the Air Force like he told you. He was a spy or operative or whatever you call them."

"That's not a crime," Jenna pointed out, irritated that Josh and Cassie had obviously been discussing her relationship with Harrison.

"I know, but it's just kind of . . . weird. I mean, how many spies do you know?" Cassie opened the refrigerator and pulled out a carton of yogurt.

"Maybe more than I'd guess, if they're spies and sworn to secrecy," she teased.

"I'm serious, Mom."

"Okay, okay. I understand. Mr. Brennan's never mentioned being with the CIA to me."

"Even weirder." Cassie found a spoon and pulled off the seal to her yogurt.

"Maybe it's not true, Cassie," Jenna said, but realized how little she really knew about her overprotective neighbor. She looked out the back window to the pump house, but Harrison had either gone back inside or was somewhere else on the grounds. That thought should make her feel safer, she thought, but it had the opposite effect, made her a little edgy.

Oh, for God's sake! Now she was getting paranoid—make that *more* paranoid. What did she know of him she wondered as she slapped mustard on the bread she'd picked up at the bakery two days earlier. He'd told her he'd been married and had been divorced for quite a while, though she couldn't remember how long or why. At the time he'd mentioned it, over dinner and drinks in Portland, he'd been evasive, as if it was a subject too painful to confide. Or had it been a matter of pride?

Cassie, too, was staring thoughtfully at the pump house as she stirred the fruit into her yogurt.

Maybe it was his upbringing, or the military, or whatever,

but Harrison seemed too polite, almost as if he wanted to hold a woman high on a pedestal, but all the while keeping her directly under his thumb.

"Okay, I understand your point. But don't worry. I've had dinner with him a couple of times, yes, and I've let him fix things around here and hang out, but I'm not really interested in him."

"So you're just stringing him along?" Cassie spooned a bite of yogurt into her mouth.

"No . . . I was just waiting to sort out all my feelings." Again rummaging in the refrigerator, she found a package of sliced roast beef.

"And?"

"I really don't have any feelings for him. At least not of the romantic nature."

Cassie appeared relieved. "Are you going to tell him?" Another bite.

"Not today," Jenna said. "But, yeah, I will. Soon." She found a container of fat-free half-and-half in the refrigerator, sniffed it to make certain it was fresh, then poured it into a little pitcher. "So, Cassie, now that we've discussed the pros and cons of my love life, why don't we talk about yours?"

Cassie groaned. "I should never have said anything."

"No . . . I'm glad you did." At least her daughter was reaching out to her, communicating.

"Not now, okay?" Again Cassie glanced out the icy windowpane.

"Then later."

"How about never?" She scooped out the rest of her yogurt.

"No way. You're not getting off so easy."

"Give me a break," Cassie said as Allie, feet clomping wildly, barreled down the stairs. Behind her, taking the steps one at a time, Critter followed.

"We're not having school tomorrow!" Allie announced gleefully. The kid who so recently had sworn her sore throat was killing her was now nearly doing cartwheels across the kitchen floor.

"How do you know?" Cassie demanded.

"It was on the television!" Allie acted like a condemned man who'd just heard he'd gotten a stay of execution.

"High school, too?"

"*All* schools! Can Dani come spend the night?" she asked, just as the lights flickered.

"Oh, great," Cassie muttered under her breath and flipped on the small television in the built-in bookcase near the pantry, the set they watched at dinner.

Jenna walked to the pantry, pulled out a drawer, and started searching for a flashlight just in case they lost power. Oh God, what would that mean?

"I don't think having Dani over tonight would be such a good idea," Jenna said. She hated to burst Allie's bubble, as her younger daughter had made only a handful of friends since moving to Oregon. She'd become shyer and more withdrawn than she had been in L.A. "I'd love to have Dani over another time, but today's not that great. The reason school's been cancelled is because of the weather."

"But we could sled and build a snow fort."

"Are you out of your mind? It's going to be *below* freezing tonight," Cassie said, staring at the small screen where a newswoman dressed in a red parka was standing near the Interstate in what appeared to be a blizzard. Snow was blowing everywhere, and a long line of huge trucks had pulled over to chain up.

". . . and temperatures are predicted to keep plummeting, much to the dismay of some of these long-haul drivers . . ." she was saying, before attempting an interview with an unhappy trucker only slightly shielded from the elements by his eighteen-wheeler.

"It's really not safe to be driving," Jenna said.

"But Mr. Settler said he'd bring her over," Allie wheedled.

"And how do you know this?" Jenna was testing the first flashlight she located. Its beam was weak but steady.

"I already called."

The lights, television, and everything else electrical blinked off for several seconds before coming on again.

"This is getting creepy," Cassie said.

"I think it's cool." Allie was undeterred. "Can Dani come over Mom, pleeeease?"

The phone jangled and Allie snagged it from the receiver before the second ring. "Hello?" she said and waited. "Yeah . . . just a minute." She straight-armed the cordless to her mother. "It's Mr. Settler," she stage-whispered as Jenna took the phone. "Please, please, please." Now she was begging, her hands clasped desperately under her chin as if she were praying.

Cassie rolled her eyes and Jenna ignored her youngest's supplications. "Hello?"

"Hi." As expected, Travis Settler was on the other end of the call. "I imagine Allie told you the plan."

"For Dani to come over."

"Yeah. She's twisting my arm, but I said I'd have to check with you first."

"I think they're working us both, but if you can get her here, it's fine with me," Jenna said and heard Allie whoop behind her. "However, I was out about an hour ago. The roads are nearly impassable and my electricity's been flickering. Also, we don't have running water, at least not yet, but I've got a couple of men working on my pump and I did pick up some bottled water in town. It might be like camping over here."

"Which Dani will love," he said, a little bit of pride in his voice as he spoke of his athletic daughter. "But this is definitely your call," Travis said.

Jenna felt Allie's eyes boring into her back. "She's always welcome."

"Fair enough. Anything I can pick up for you on the way?"

"Thanks, but we're okay. I was at the store stocking up earlier. We're set for the next couple of days."

"Then if you're sure it's okay, I'll be over within the hour."

"Great. I'll tell Allie."

She hung up and found that her daughter was already bounding up the stairs. "Hey, wait, Allie, don't you want a sandwich?"

"Later!" Allie sang down the stairs.

Cassie announced, "I'm not hungry."

"Fine. They'll keep," Jenna decided and was glad that her youngest daughter was happy. For the moment. Which was more than Jenna could say for Cassie, who had finished her yogurt and dumped the container into the garbage can under the sink, then stood, arms folded under her chest, as she watched the news. "This is sooo lame," she muttered when the weatherman predicted subfreezing temperatures for the rest of the week.

"We'll survive."

"If this is surviving."

"Just wait until I have you splitting wood and stoking the fire and cooking in the cast iron skillet over the coals if we lose power. We'll all get to sleep down here in sleeping bags in front of the fireplace."

"Oh, save me," Cassie said.

"Think of it. No MTV, or hot showers or hair dryers or electricity for anything. Maybe, if we're lucky, the cell phones will work."

"You enjoy making me miserable, don't you?" her daughter accused.

"Just pointing out that things aren't so bad."

"Yeah, right." Cassie rolled her eyes and headed up the stairs. Jenna poured coffee into a thermos and was about to carry it out to the pump house, when she heard a rap on the back door. Half a second later, Harrison let himself inside. "You must've read my mind," he said as he spied the steaming canister. He called over his shoulder, "Seth! I told you she'd have coffee for us!"

Through the glass of the door, Jenna saw Whitaker wave as he carried tools to his truck.

"So tell me, do I have water?" she asked.

"Not yet. But soon. We started thawing out the pump and Seth fixed a couple of the loose wires. It'll take a little time. We've got a heater running in the pump house and have a drip pan and a hose that'll siphon the water out of the house, so it doesn't refreeze in there. While he was working on the pump, I put up some more insulation. It'll take a few hours, but before the night's over, everything should work and yes, you will have water again."

"Hallelujah!"

"You might consider building a more substantial pump house next summer." He settled into a chair at the table as Jenna poured him a cup of steaming coffee. "Until then, I'll help you get through the winter."

"Thanks," she said, though there was a part of her that objected to his proprietary tone. She ignored it. Right now she needed his help. A few minutes later, Seth appeared at the back door. She offered coffee, but the handyman declined as he stepped into the house and wiped his boots. "Too much caffeine," was his quick excuse. A quiet man, he glanced at his watch.

"You in a hurry?" Harrison asked.

"Another job."

"In that case, we'd better shove off."

"What do I owe you?" Jenna asked the handyman.

"I already paid him." Harrison was zipping up his coat.

"What? For me? No way." She was reaching for her purse.

"He did," Seth said.

"Wait a minute. I can't accept that. Harrison, really. Thanks for your help today, but I pay my own bills." She looked him steadily in the eye. "It's the way I want it."

Harrison's face turned red. "Then think of it as a favor. One neighbor to another."

"That's the problem. I don't like to be in debt. To anyone. Favors tend to mount up." She turned her attention to the handyman. "Business is business. I'll pay you for your time and any equipment you had to buy."

Seth shifted from one foot to the other, obviously embarrassed by the awkward scene. "Don't worry about it."

"But I do."

"This is how we do things up here," Harrison explained. "We take care of each other."

"Hey, no!" She held up both hands. "Wait a minute. This is not the way I run my life! I can't let you 'take care of me.'

No way. Believe it or not, Harrison, I can take care of myself, and that's the way I like it."

He was having none of it. "Like it or not, I'm concerned about you and your kids alone up here. I already talked to Seth, here, about helping install a new security system here at the house. And I don't like the way the main gate is froze open."

"*What*?" Jenna nearly came unglued. "I think this is my decision."

"Your old system is shot."

That much was true. "Then I'll get a new one. I planned on it. But right now, with the storm, it'll probably take time."

"Seth, can you set her up? Didn't you say you have connections with the local company."

Whitaker lifted his palms and backed up. "Hey, I don't want to get into this."

Jenna appreciated the man's response. She turned on Brennan. "Look, Harrison, the house *has* an alarm system already. It's sketchy—doesn't work all the time, even though I've tried to have it fixed. Even so, I try to remember to turn it on, and, if it makes you feel better, I'll try even harder."

He smiled disarmingly. Because he'd gotten his way. "It does."

"Fine!" she snapped, angry. Jesus, who did this guy think he was? "Now that we've settled that, you won't have to worry about me and the girls any longer. Really." She crossed her arms over her chest. "To tell you the truth, all your concern makes me extremely uncomfortable. I can take care of myself."

"All right, all right." He held his hands palms outward as if in surrender. "I'm sorry . . . I made a mistake."

Jenna was still seething, but nodded. "Okay. Just so we understand each other."

"I guess I'm too used to taking command of a situation and giving orders. Military training."

"I guess." She tried to rein in her temper. To his credit, the guy was giving his all to help her out. He was just a little heavy-handed.

He winked. "I'll try not to let it happen again."

"Good."

"It's just that I care, so I tend to worry about you and the girls."

"I already told you not to," she said firmly. "We're not your problem."

Seth, as if he couldn't stand the argument another second, ran a hand around his neck. "Look, I'd like to finish up in the pump house, double-check that it's all working." Before anyone could object, he walked out the back door, letting a blast of wintry air into the house. The door slammed shut behind him.

Jenna was left staring at Harrison Brennan. "Listen, I'm sorry if I flipped out. I know you're just trying to help, but I'm really trying to make it on my own. You're right—sometimes I do have to call in the reserves, and I appreciate everything you did for me."

"But," he said, a vein starting to throb in his forehead. "I sense a 'but' coming along."

She shoved an errant hair out of her eyes. "But I can't have you running my life or paying my bills, or—"

"The guy owed me," Harrison cut in. The remnants of his smile disappeared completely. He was suddenly stern. All business. Contained fury evident in his rigid stance. The muscles of his jaw worked involuntarily, and she sensed that she'd insulted his manhood. Which was ridiculous.

Men!

"If you want to pay Whitaker yourself, hire him another time," Harrison said. "But for today, we're even. All of us. That was the deal I had with him. Let's keep it neat and tidy. In the future, you can work out anything you want with him or me, but I'll never take any money from you for helping out."

"Fair enough," she said, surrendering. For the moment. She glanced at the counter and the half-made sandwiches her kids had rejected. She motioned to the cutting board. "Soooo . . . how about a roast beef on sourdough for all your trouble?"

"Deal," he said, and brightened as she finished placing slices of beef, dill pickles, and onion on the bread. An image of June Cleaver in pearls and a full skirt flitted through her mind, but she pushed it aside. For the moment there was peace in the house, and the promise of running water. Who could ask for anything more?

CHAPTER 11

Half an hour later, Harrison was setting his plate in the sink when he looked out the window. His silvery eyebrows slammed together, his face muscles tightened even more. "Looks like you've got company," he said.

"Oh, right," Jenna said. "Allie's having a girlfriend spend the night."

Harrison's lips compressed as he watched Travis Settler hop to the snow-crusted ground. A second later, his daughter, Dani, landed beside him.

"I'd better shove off." He was already slipping his arms into his jacket and making his way to the back door.

"Oh, well, thanks again," she said, as Harrison slid into his boots and started off to Seth Whitaker's truck. Jenna saw him nod curtly to Travis just as feet clattered on the stairs and Allie ran pell-mell out the back door. Without a coat.

Jenna snagged her ski jacket from the back of the kitchen chair just as Dani and Allie burst into the room. They were laughing and giggling and racing each other up the stairs. "Can we have nachos?" Allie called over her shoulder, but didn't wait for a response.

A second later, Travis slid through the open door. "You can tell that they're all broken up about not going to school tomorrow."

Jenna grinned. "I used to love it, too."

"You had snow days in L.A.?"

"No." She shook her head and laughed. "I grew up just outside of Seattle. I remember getting together with my girlfriends and sending up group prayers for snow."

"Did it work?"

"Rarely, and never when a major assignment that I'd forgotten was due." She heard the rumble of a truck's engine and saw Seth Whitaker's rig backing up.

"Did I chase away your company?"

"Nah," she said, but wondered if she were lying. The passenger side of the big rig was visible, and Harrison Brennan was sitting stiffly inside while staring straight ahead. Or was he? He was too far away to tell, but she thought she caught him watching the house from the side-view mirror. *Stop it! You're imagining things! He's just a nice neighbor trying to help out.*

"Something wrong?" Travis asked, and Jenna was suddenly aware that he was standing near the table and staring at her.

"No . . . sorry . . . I guess I've been caught up in my problems."

"Something I can help you with?" He seemed earnest, his blue eyes tinged with worry.

"Sure. How about conjuring up hot sand, aquamarine surf, lots of palm trees . . . and oh, yeah, don't forget it should be ninety degrees in the shade."

"Can I throw in a couple of margaritas?" he asked.

"Only if they're blended and doubles."

"Man, your fantasies are pretty damned specific."

"Why dream if you don't know what you want?" she tossed back and felt some of the tension leave her shoulders.

"Do you? Know what you want?"

"Mmm." She nodded. "Most of the time. You?"

"I thought I did . . . a long time ago." He lifted a shoulder. "Now I'm not so sure." He seemed about to say more, but thought better of it, his smile fading and the warmth in his eyes suddenly chased by something cold and secret. "I'd better shove off," he said. "Dani told me I shouldn't overstay my welcome. Something about 'letting her have her space.' Call me if she's a problem."

"She won't be."

"Or if you feel stranded out here." He looked out the window to the rolling acres edged in old-growth timber. "You're a little isolated."

"We'll be fine," she assured him, though his last words gave her pause. She'd chosen this place precisely for its remote location, but now, watching him walk to his rig, the snow slanting from the sky, the wind blowing wildly down the gorge, she wondered if she'd made a mistake. As he climbed into the cab she resisted the urge to run outside, flag him down, and beg him to stay, to admit that she wasn't as strong as she appeared, that she liked the thought of another adult, a man, around when the forces of nature were so raw and threatening.

But she didn't.

Wouldn't admit that she couldn't handle things on her own.

She felt a chill and rubbed her arms as he drove down the lane, his tires spinning in the rapidly piling snow, his headlights cutting across the white expanse of drifts.

The phone rang and she reached for the receiver.

"Hello?" she said, but no one answered. "Hello?" She heard the crackle of static, as if there were a bad cell connection, and something muted, something soft and melodic, like a song she should remember. "Hello? If you're there I can't hear you," she said strongly. "Call back."

She hung up and waited.

But no call came through.

The telephone remained silent and the house, too, seemed unnaturally quiet. The usual sounds—the hum of the refrigerator, the rumble of the furnace, the faint whisper from a television upstairs, were muted by the shriek of the wind that rattled the loose panes in an attic window. The lights quivered once more and Jenna swallowed hard as she realized what she'd heard on the phone. Not only had someone definitely been on the line, but the nearly indistinct melody she'd heard was the theme song from *White Out*, the last film she'd made, the film that had never been released. Though the theme song had become a hit, *White Out* had become a disaster of a project that had destroyed her marriage and killed her sister.

Now, she took a step backward. She caught sight of her ghost-like image in the windowpane and for a second she saw Jill. Beautiful, innocent Jill, whose physical appearance had been so much like Jenna's they'd sometimes been mistaken for twins. Now dead.

Because of you.

She felt her eyes burn with the memory of thousands of tons of snow cascading in a deadly roar down the mountainside.

You should have died, not your sister.

The recriminations reverberated through her brain, just as they had for years. "Oh, God," Jenna whispered, stumbling backward against a chair in the nook. The chair screeched against the hardwood floor, and Jenna managed to catch herself, though the strains from *White Out*'s theme song whispered through her mind. Who had called her and why had they played that music?

You're not sure they did. You really couldn't hear. It might have been some other song altogether. Or crossed wires. Look at the storm! There could be a glitch in the phone system. You're imagining things, Jenna.

Quickly she picked up the receiver and read the caller ID message—private number. "Damn." She dialed *69, hoping to hear the name of the last caller, but the recorded message repeated what caller ID had told her. Whoever had phoned remained anonymous.

Intentionally?

Or because he was hiding?

"You son of a bitch," she hissed, slamming down the receiver and trembling inside.

She tried to tell herself she was overreacting. That nothing was wrong. That her all-too-vivid imagination was running away with her.

But, of course, she knew she was lying to herself.

Again.

"Get a grip," she ordered, but knew that tonight, holding on to her frazzled emotions would prove impossible.

She was there, just on the other side of the frigid glass. Not as beautiful as Jenna Hughes, but enough like her that as he stared past the red and blue neon of a sizzling beer sign, he imagined she would do. Her body was about the same size, petite, though her breasts were smaller and her hips not quite rounded the same way. But close enough . . . for now. She was a blonde, but her hair color was unnatural, darker roots indicating that she'd been born brunette, but her hair was not as dark as Jenna's black waves. Not that it mattered, he told himself, watching as she bussed her own tables, wiped her hands nervously on her apron, and glanced often to the windows and the raging storm.

As if she knew he was there.

As if she understood that her destiny lay in the dark, frigid night.

He smiled and felt a thrill zing through his bloodstream, an impulse so cold it reminded him of other times . . . of a faraway youth and an ice-crusted lake, of freezing water washing over his skin, of a shivering girl and dark, deadly water . . . images of long ago. For the briefest of seconds he closed his eyes and thought not of the past but to the future. His imagination ran with him, called to him, painted vividly erotic images of the woman inside the diner . . . Faye . . . yes, Faye Tyler of *Bystander*—that's who she was, hiding out here under an assumed name . . .

Beautiful.

Sexy.

Perfect.

Like Jenna.

Her name rang with the clarity of church bells through his mind and he licked his lips, feeling the cold upon his skin as he imagined her. Ached for her.

Jenna.

She was the one.

Like no other.

And tonight, through this other woman, this pale replica, she would be his.

CHAPTER 12

You should never drink alone.

Isn't that what *they* say? Whoever *they* are.

Too bad. Jenna had just had one helluva day and she decided a cup of decaf coffee laced with a bit of Kahlua and Bailey's Irish Cream wouldn't kill her. She spied the aerosol whipped cream in the refrigerator and couldn't resist. "In for a penny," she told herself as she added a dollop of cream to her cup, then topped it all off with a dash of chocolate sprinkles. If her trainer Ron ever found out, he'd punish her with extra minutes on the treadmill, but so what? He was, after all, only twenty-six and certainly didn't know about the soothing effects of chocolate and alcohol when it came to times of stress. Which this definitely was.

"Right?" she said to the dog, who had settled into his favorite spot under the table. Critter, if nothing else, was optimistic when it came to the thought of scraps being surreptitiously slipped in his direction. His tail thumped loudly on the floor as Jenna sat on a chair and pawed through her bag for the mail she'd picked up earlier. With everything else that had happened in her life today, she'd forgotten about the mail until just this moment. The girls had devoured pizza, salad, and ice cream and were upstairs in their rooms while Jenna contemplated a long, hot bath in the Jacuzzi.

As she sipped her drink, she sorted through the magazines, bills, and advertisements that had collected in her post office box during the last week. Until she came to the hand-addressed envelope. Her name was written in precise block letters and there was no return address. Using a letter opener, she slit the envelope open and noted that the postmark was Portland.

Inside was a single sheet of paper.

A unique, single sheet of paper upon which was a short love poem, the words superimposed over a pale image of Jenna wearing a black sheath with a beaded neckline, a picture taken of her on the set of *Resurrection*. It had been a publicity shot taken of her in the role of the coolly seductive and psychotic killer, Anne Parks.

You are every woman.
Sensual. Strong. Erotic.
You are one woman.
Searching. Wanting. Waiting.
You are my woman.
Today. Tomorrow. Endlessly.
I will come for you.

Jenna's heart nearly stopped. Ice congealed in her veins. "Oh, God," she whispered and dropped the letter as if it burned her. Coffee from her cup sloshed onto the table, splashing over the sheet and envelope. Who had sent this to her? Why? Heart hammering, she glanced around the room, as if whoever had mailed the poem might appear.

Critter climbed to his feet and whined.

"It's—it's all right," she said, though she could barely breathe. Someone knew her mailing address, realized she lived here. When she'd moved from L.A., she'd tried to start over, had asked that all of her fan mail be sent to her agent's address . . . Her post office box here was supposed to be private.

It's a small town.
The general public does know you live here.

You know this comes with the territory.
Relax.

But she couldn't stop her pulse from racing. She'd received mail from obsessed fans before, but those incidents had been years ago. It was while she was married, when she'd lived in Southern California and was still making movies, still part of the industry, still a name that would come up time and again in the gossip columns. In the past year and a half, most of her mail had been screened and filtered by Monty Fenderson of the Fenderson Agency. She fought the absurd impulse to call him, to rant and rave, to scream that her privacy had been invaded.

Which was ludicrous.

The public knew that she lived in a small Oregon town. That was to be expected.

So a piece of mail from a sicko slipped through. So what?

Her nerves were just shot from the storm, all the talk of the murdered woman, her fights with her daughters . . . what she needed to do was calm down. Finish her drink. Take that bath. . . . Nonetheless, she walked around the house and though it was far from town, flanked by towering trees and the river, fenced off from the world, she walked from room to room and shut the blinds. A shiver slid down her spine as she read the last line again.

I will come for you.

Without a second thought, she walked to the wall where the alarm system was housed and pressed the code. A second later a tiny green light switched to red. It was a basic system, one that had been installed, the realtor had told her, long after the house was built, and was only wired to the doors. A buzzer went off when the system was engaged and a door opened; two minutes later, if the alarm hadn't been deactivated, a siren began to shriek. But she wasn't contracted with a security firm that notified the sheriff's department if the alarm went off. Yet. She'd take care of that tomorrow morning.

Meanwhile she sat near the fire and warmed her hands.

She had a crippled old dog and a shotgun with no ammunition for protection.

Don't freak out. It's just an anonymous letter . . . no big deal.

But it was mailed from Portland, less than an hour away.

From her.

From her children.

Inwardly, she turned ice cold.

I will come for you.

She took in a deep breath. *Try it,* she thought, anger overcoming fear. Tomorrow she'd not only sign up with the security company, she'd go to the outdoor store for some shotgun shells.

"Come on, Cass . . . it'll be fun," Josh insisted. "And besides, there's no school tomorrow. Meet me in an hour at the usual spot."

"If I get caught I'll be so dead." Cassie was burrowed deep in her bed, covers over her head, her cell phone against her ear. He wanted her to sneak out. Again. So soon after being caught. No . . . she couldn't risk it.

"So what? Can she ground you any more?"

"She can make my life pretty damned miserable," Cassie said and winced slightly. It was true her mom was bugging the hell out of her, always prying, always laying down rules, always treating her like a kid, but deep down, Cassie knew, Jenna was playing the part of disciplinarian because she thought it was the best thing for her daughters. Which was, of course, way wrong.

"You won't get caught. By the time you leave, it'll be after one. She'll be asleep. Guaranteed. Dead to the world."

Cassie hesitated, biting her lip before finally deciding. "I can't. Really."

"Oh, quit being a wuss. Lots of kids are going out tonight."

"Their parents let them."

"No, Cass. *They* just don't let their parents boss them around, like you do. *They're* not scared of their parents."

"I'm not scared of my mom."

"Sure you are."

"No way."

"Then why don't you ask her to let you go out?"

"She'd say 'no.' I'm supposed to be grounded. Remember?" Sometimes he could be so dense!

"So how can she stop you?"

"For one thing, she turned on the security system tonight. I saw her from the landing of the stairs. She's probably doing it just to keep me inside."

"So turn it off. You know the code, don't you?"

"Then the house would be unprotected."

"So what?" he said with a laugh.

"Look, I just don't want the hassle."

"Because, like I said, you're afraid of your mom. You've given her that power over you. This really isn't her problem. It's yours."

"Fine. But it's not yours!" She snapped her cell phone shut and turned it off so that if Josh decided to call her again, she wouldn't hear it. Sometimes he was so pushy. But his words taunted her. *You're afraid of your mom. You've given her that power over you. This isn't her problem. It's yours.* So he thought she was weak. No, she wouldn't buy into that. He was just trying to find a way to get her to do what *he* wanted. *He* was the one who was trying to exert *his* power over Cassie. Not her mother. She pushed herself from beneath the covers and clicked her remote so that her television came to life. It was too late for most shows, but there was a movie she could watch, one she'd missed because she'd been in the middle of the move from California at the time. Boy, had that been a mistake.

From the next bedroom, she heard laughter. Allie and her friend were really stoked about not going to school. They'd spent some time outdoors trying to build a snow fort. It had been too cold for that, so they'd gone to the stables, which were heated, to check on the horses, all of which were sur-

viving just fine, and then they'd come inside for hot cocoa
and popcorn and . . . Cassie let out a quiet little sob. Sometimes she felt so alone. Even Allie had a good friend. Jenna
had the people at the local theater, even though some of them
were beyond strange, but Cassie felt as if she hadn't really
connected with anyone since she'd moved up here.

Just Josh.

And he was suspect, his motives for being with her
murky.

But he's all you've got.

She considered calling her old friends in L.A. and Santa
Monica, but it was late and she'd just feel worse. Besides,
the last few times she'd talked to Paige, it had been awkward. Paige hadn't really said anything, but she'd been quick
to let Cassie know she was busy and was obviously eager to
get off the phone. And Cassie didn't really blame her. She
would have been the same way if the situation had been reversed.

Tears threatened her eyes. The movie didn't hold her attention. She flipped the channel and saw her mother. "Damn!"
There Jenna Hughes was, not even as old as Cassie was now,
playing the part of a teenaged prostitute in *Innocence Lost*.
Angrily, Cassie hit the Power button on the remote and the
image faded. There seemed no way to get away from her
mother. Even in the solace of her room. She felt a tear drizzle from the corner of her eye and she swiped it away angrily. What was wrong with her? She glanced at the clock. It
was almost one . . . and the house had become quiet. She
stole into the hallway and peered into Allie's room. Both
girls were conked out on the floor on a couple of air mat-
tresses and sleeping bags. She eased to the stairs and looked
down to the landing and Jenna's room. The door was closed,
no sliver of light at the threshold.

Everyone was asleep.

Back in her room, she reached for her cell phone and
flipped it on.

A new text message read:

I luv you.

Her tears started in earnest. Josh was the only person in this godforsaken town who even had an inkling about who she was, the only one who cared. Swallowing back more tears, she quickly typed a reply:

I'll be at the gate in 20 min. Luv U 2.

"I'm sooo outta here," Sonja announced, whipping off her apron and tossing it into the hamper in the back room as country-western music pulsed through the speakers.

Lou, the cook, grunted his approval as he scraped off the grill. The only other person in the back area of the diner was the busboy, a useless, lazy kid who was perennially petulant and usually high on some unknown substance. He was wearing earphones, listening to God-knew-what, making his usual statement against his Uncle Lou's choice in music. Now, he managed to look up and sent Sonja a "so what?" glance as he swabbed a mop inefficiently over the tile floor.

Tonight she didn't care. She just wanted to get home to her husband and three kids. The last customer had left fifteen minutes earlier, and Sonja had wanted to pry him off his bar stool and physically toss him out the door. Who in his right mind would be out on a night like this?

Only the regulars at Lou's, she decided, not for the first time, and made a mental note to find herself a better job.

She bundled into a ski jacket, wool hat, and gloves, then grabbed her beat-up backpack.

"I'll see ya tomorrow, if the roads are passable," she said, and elicited another grunt from Lou the Silent. Which was probably better than Lou the Chatterbox, or Lou the Know-It-All. Or Lou the Lech, she thought, as she fished through her purse, found her keys, then braced herself against the cold as she walked outside. "A damned Ice Age, that's what it is," she muttered.

The wind hit hard, slapped at her bare cheeks, and brought with it snow filled with hard little ice crystals.

To think she'd let Lester Hatchell convince her to move from Palm Desert to come up here. Palm-friggin'-Desert, where tonight it was probably seventy degrees—make that seventy degrees *above* zero. Unlike here on the shores of the Columbia Gorge. Beautiful? Yes. Even in winter. Livable? Hell, no! At least not in the middle of winter. *Lord, please, give me palm trees, hot sand, and a piña colada any day of the week. Make that a bucket of piña coladas! It beats the hell out of pine trees, drifting snow, and hot-damned-toddies. Winter wonderland, my ass!*

The subfreezing wind cut through her heavy coat, and even the Christmas lights glimmering on the eaves of the diner looked weak and pathetic. Why had she ever let Lester sweet-talk her into moving to this god-awful, freeze-your-butt-off spot? Why?

God, what a night!

She trudged across the parking lot to her little hatchback, a four-wheel-drive Honda encrusted in ice. Even the lock that she thought she'd covered carefully with an insulated piece of cardboard was frozen solid.

Fortunately, she had one of those battery-operated keys that heated the locks when inserted; she forced her key into the lock and smiled to herself less than a minute later when the door opened. She was glad to be going home to Lester's incessant snoring and the kids sleeping all willy-nilly in their bunk beds. She'd had a bad feeling about this night from the beginning, that something wasn't right. The intensity of this cold front seemed unnatural, and the conversations she'd overheard in the diner over the past couple of days were all laced with talk that this particular winter would be the coldest in over a hundred years.

Great! Just what we need, she thought. The local kids were already out of their minds at the prospect of no school for days. Her boy, Cliff, had been bouncing off the walls when she'd left for her shift around five.

With the cold slicing through her coat, she slid inside her little car and closed the door, then shoved the key into the ignition and flicked her wrist.

Nothing happened.

"No," she whispered, trying again. "Don't do this to me."

Nothing. Not even a click.

She pumped the gas and felt a niggle of fear. That same dark premonition she'd had earlier.

Which was just plain silly.

"Come on, come on." Again she tried, and again. She couldn't see out of the snow-covered windshield, couldn't imagine how long she'd have to wait for a tow truck. She could call Lester, but he'd have to leave the kids alone or bundle up eight-year-old Cliff to come and get her . . . maybe Lou would give her a ride. She tried one more time and finally gave up. It was no use. The car was dead.

Perfect, she thought sarcastically as she threw open the door and stepped outside.

Then she saw him.

Striding purposefully up to her.

She felt a second's fear before she recognized his build and the way he walked. A regular at the diner. As he neared, even in the dim light she noticed the blue of his eyes beneath his ski cap and caught his smile. A familiar face! One of the regulars. Someone she could trust in this isolated lot. "Hey!" she said, climbing from the interior. "Thank God you're here."

"Got a problem?"

So he wasn't Sherlock Holmes. But he'd do. He'd have to.

"Yeah. My car won't start. Deader'n a doornail."

"Why don't you let me try?"

As if she was too stupid or clumsy or feminine to know how to turn on her own car. Men! But she pasted a smile onto her face as she stepped into the crunchy, ankle-deep snow again. "Be my guest," she invited, sweeping her hand wide toward the open door as the force of the storm took her breath away. "If you can get it started, I'll see that Lou gives you the ten-percent-good-guy discount for the rest of your life."

"That won't be necessary," he said, leaning close to her and placing something hard against her jacket. Before she could say a word, a white-hot blast jolted through her body. Pain shot through her system. Panic exploded in her brain.

She tried to scream, but his gloved hand was over her mouth. She smelled something sickeningly sweet and cloying and she coughed, unable to breathe . . . What was he doing? And why? Oh God, she thought crazily, he's going to rape me . . . or worse . . . *No, oh God, no,* she silently screamed, trying to kick and fight, though her limbs wouldn't react, her legs and arms disjointed and weak. *No! No! No!*

But she couldn't fend him off. Couldn't scream. Muscles, hard as steel, wrapped around her and she sagged against him, flailing uselessly. Her body seemed to be melting and was unresponsive. Fear cut through her and she thought disjointedly of her children. This couldn't be happening. Couldn't!

"Don't fight it, Faye. There's nothing you can do," he whispered.

Faye? I'm not Faye! He's got the wrong woman . . . oh, please. She tried to tell him that he was making a horrible mistake, but the rag over her nose and mouth made her woozy, her tongue wouldn't work, the words forming in her throat came out as mewling pleas. *I'm not Faye! Don't you understand? Please look at me! I'M NOT WHO YOU THINK I AM!*

Her head lolled back. She tried to focus on him, to will him to read her mind, but it was too late. Through the pelting beads of ice and snow, the world spun eerily. Huge, looming, ice-covered eighteen-wheelers, tall street lamps, and the Christmas lights strung on the eaves of the diner blended and blurred in her vision. Her weak, impotent thrashing stopped and her legs finally gave out completely. Blackness pulled at the edges of her vision, taking her under.

As she let go of consciousness, Sonja Hatchell knew she was doomed.

CHAPTER 13

The bedside phone blasted at 4:15.

Carter, dragged from sleep, reached over and knocked the hand-held from its base. "Damn," he muttered as he grabbed the receiver and jammed it to his ear. Whoever was on the other end didn't have good news. Not at four in the morning. "Carter."

"Hey, Sheriff, it's Palmer with Dispatch."

"What's up, Dorie?" Carter said as he ran his free hand over his face and tried to wake up.

"Just got a call from Lester Hatchell, and I thought you'd want to know about it. Sonja didn't show up after her shift. He just called in. Really upset. Her car isn't at the diner; he already checked. He also drove her usual route and didn't find her anywhere. I sent Hixx out to the diner to check, but it's not like her."

"Any accidents reported on surrounding roads?" Carter was suddenly wide awake. Lester Hatchell was a friend of his.

"Yeah. One since midnight. Single-car, one driver, a male taken to a hospital. The accident was ten miles north of Falls Crossing."

"Hell." He threw off the covers, his bare feet hitting the cold wood floor.

"I thought you'd want to know."

"I do, Dorie. Thanks." He slammed the receiver down, walked to the small bathroom off his bedroom, and turned on the hot water in his shower. By the time he'd stripped out of his boxers and run a toothbrush over his teeth, the water was hot enough and he walked through the shower. Ten minutes later, he'd shaved and dressed and was hurrying down the stairs from his sleeping loft.

The woodstove had burned to nothing and he let the fire die. No telling when he'd get back, and the furnace would keep the place from freezing. The remains of last night's dinner—the crust of a frozen pizza and two empty beer cans—mocked him, but he didn't have time to clean up.

By the back door of the small cabin he clipped his Glock into his holster, threw on his jacket and hat, then let himself into the garage, where he pulled on his gloves and felt the first bite of the raw morning. He'd heard the weather report last night. More of the same. No sign of a break in the cold front. Snow, snow, and more snow had been predicted and the meteorologists were gleefully talking about ever-lowering temperatures, enough that the falls and river might freeze.

More bad news.

He slid into his Blazer and frowned as he thought again of the last time the falls had frozen solid. He'd been sixteen at the time. Sixteen and a teenaged idiot.

His jaw clenched as he backed out of the garage, his tires crunching on the fresh snow, the windshield fogging. In his mind's eye, he was looking up at Pious Falls, the cascading water having frozen in thick, icy plumes that tumbled over a hundred feet to the frozen river below.

"Let's do it," his best friend, David Landis, had said eagerly. David's face was red from the cold, his eyes bright with the challenge as he'd squinted up to the top of the cliff, the spot where the frozen creek started its free fall.

David and Shane had been friends from the first day of elementary school.

"I don't think so."

"Why not?" David had already been putting on his crampons, his ice pick was tucked into his belt—ropes, harness, and carabiners attached to his jacket. "It'll be fun." He'd cast an amused look over his shoulder. "Don't tell me you're afraid. Shane Carter, ace downhill racer, extreme rock climber, and what? Ultimate chickenshit? Pussy-to-the-max?"

"I just don't think it's a good idea." As if to add emphasis to his words, the wind had screamed down the gorge, rustling the dead leaves and rattling the brittle branches of the surrounding trees. Thick ice coated everything, glistening in a clear, cruel glaze.

David had been undaunted. Fearless. As ever. He'd adjusted his ski mask. "You never think it's a good idea," he'd taunted as his breath fogged the air. "I'm tellin' ya, man, this is a chance of a lifetime. When does it ever get cold enough to freeze the falls? By tomorrow this place and Multnomah Falls will be crawling with climbers. Today, we climb alone." With that, he'd tightened the strap on his helmet and slid goggles onto his face. Once again he'd looked up at the tumble of ice columns that rose to the cliffs high above, so high that they were lost in the low-lying clouds. David's smile had stretched wider, his enthusiasm palpable. "I'm going with or without you, Carter, so make up your mind . . ."

Now, twenty-odd years later, Carter squinted through the windshield as the wipers slapped snow from the frozen glass. The Blazer slid and whined until he reached the highway, where the road had been plowed and sanded, but new snow was already piling over the older icy mounds.

Where was Sonja Hatchell?

He feared the worst. From the diner to the Hatchell place, the road wound up the foothills, crossing three or four bridges over swift-moving creeks. He only hoped she hadn't hit a patch of ice, swerved off the road, and ended up trapped in her little car while icy water flooded the interior.

Don't even think that way.

Sonja's probably fine.

Maybe she and Les just had a fight and she decided not to go home . . .

Carter didn't believe it for a second, but he didn't want to think about the unknown. Not yet. Because it scared the hell out of him.

At 9:30 Jenna pushed open the door of the theater with her hip as she balanced two cups of steaming coffee drinks she'd picked up from the local espresso bar. She made her way to Rinda's office and announced, "One large, sugar-free caramel latte with extra foam and sprinkles for you." Placing one of the cups on the corner of Rinda's desk, she added, "And a skinny double mocha grande with whipped cream for moi."

"You're a lifesaver." Rinda picked up the solitary chocolate-covered espresso bean balanced on the lid of her cup and plopped it into her mouth. "I needed this. It's freezing in here, the furnace is threatening to give out, and the copier is on the fritz. And that's just for starters." She touched the rim of her paper cup to Jenna's. "Here's to things improving."

"Amen," Jenna said and settled into the faded, overstuffed chair in the corner that was often used in productions.

The door to the theater banged open and a few seconds later, Wes Allen ambled into the room. Despite the near-zero temperatures, he was wearing jeans and a fleece pullover with a hood. No jacket, coat, or hat. "What is this—the theater's new coffee klatch?" he asked, parking one hip on the side of Rinda's desk.

"That's the espresso klatch," Rinda said, brightening at the sight of her brother.

"Froufrou drinks." He snorted. "Give me the real stuff anytime. Black coffee—nothing added."

Rinda laughed. "A real he-man's drink."

"If you say so." He winked at Jenna and she forced a smile she didn't feel. What was it about him that bothered her so much? He was Rinda's brother, for crying out loud! But he always seemed to stand an inch or so too close, was quick to touch her shoulder, or, like now, wink at her conspiratorially, as if the two of them were in on some private joke.

Chill out, she told herself. She was still a case of nerves, that was all.

"So—what are the dire circumstances that made you insist I get out of bed at the crack this morning?"

"The furnace and copier, to begin with. Also, Scott said one bank of lights keeps shorting out—he was fussing with them last night and couldn't fix them."

"That's because he's just a kid. I, on the other hand, am a pro." He rotated his hands skyward as if expecting applause.

"Yeah, right. I seem to recall you were trying to fix that short just the other day."

"Point taken. Now, what about *your* problem?" he asked, swiveling on the corner of the desk to stare Jenna straight in the face. "Your pump?"

"All fixed. Harrison Brennan and a friend of his, Seth Whitaker, came by yesterday."

Wes pretended to be crestfallen. "You could have called me."

"Next time," she promised and took a sip from her mocha.

Footsteps sounded in the staging area. "That's probably Blanche. She wanted to go over some changes in the sheet music," Rinda said, just as the woman in question poked her head into the room.

"Am I interrupting?" Blanche asked, eyebrows lifting above narrow, black-rimmed glasses. Though, according to Rinda, Blanche was over sixty, she appeared much younger. Short, spiky hair that was more orange than red framed her round face. When she smiled, the thin lines beside her eyes and lips became more pronounced. Single now, there were rumors that she'd been married several times and possibly had children, but Jenna wasn't certain as the older woman rarely spoke of her personal life. In the theater, Blanche was already shaking off the cold and unwinding a fuzzy scarf from around her neck.

"Not at all. Come on in and join the party. I'll put on a pot of coffee."

"About time," Wes said as he pushed away from the desk. "While it's heating, I'll look at the furnace."

"About time," Rinda threw back at him, then turned her attention to Blanche and the changes she wanted to make in the sheet music. Twenty minutes later, the coffee had brewed and Blanche had downed a cup before checking her watch, gasping, and muttering that she was late for an appointment as she flew out the door. Wes was still banging on the furnace before Rinda and Jenna were alone in the office again.

"I want to show you something," Jenna said as she reached into her purse.

"What?"

"Something I got in the mail yesterday."

"A fan letter?"

"You might call it that . . . if fan means fanatic." She handed Rinda a Ziploc bag with the note and envelope inside. "Don't open it. You can read it through the plastic."

"Okay." Rinda peered at the envelope and as she did, the color drained from her face. "Jesus, Jenna, what the hell is this?"

"I don't know."

"*You are every woman? You are my woman?*" she whispered, her eyes rounding. "Who sent this to you?"

"Anonymous."

"Whoever did it took the time to print it on a picture of you."

"It's a copy of a promo photo from *Resurrection*."

"This is sick, Jenna! Demented! Psychotic! You take this letter and picture to Shane Carter pronto!" Rinda ordered, and then read the text out loud. "*I will come for you?* God, that's scary as hell." Rinda dropped the plastic bag as if it had burned her fingers, letting it fall onto a pile of unopened mail upon her desk.

"Beyond scary as hell."

"So how'd the freak get your address?"

"I don't know . . . I suppose it wouldn't be all that hard, not with computers, the Internet, public information. It seems anyone can find anybody these days. I'm not sure even people in the witness protection program are safe. Identity theft is rampant."

"This is worse than identity theft."

"I know," Jenna agreed before finishing her mocha and crumpling the paper cup. There was a series of loud clicks and banging on metal; presumably Wes was trying to fix the furnace and she was reminded of the other day when he'd overheard part of their conversation. Was he listening now?

"So don't be an idiot," Rinda was saying. "Take the letter to the authorities. Start with Carter."

Jenna groaned inwardly. She didn't want to face the taciturn sheriff again.

"Your ranch is in his jurisdiction. Either he'll help you or point you in the right direction." Rinda bit the edge of her lip and deep furrows lined her brow. Jenna could almost see the wheels turning in her friend's mind. "Don't you think it's more than a little coincidental that some of the things you donated were stolen from here? I mean *everything* that was taken from this place . . ." she jabbed a finger at the worn floorboards of the theater "—was yours. From one of your movies. Nothing is missing from the things that anyone else gave to us. We've received tons of stuff . . . *tons* . . . all donated in the last couple of years, and the only things missing were originally yours. I don't like it."

"I don't, either," Jenna agreed, her anxiety level spiking again, though she attempted to stay calm and not let the paranoia that had followed her around since discovering the note get a stranglehold on her. Everything Rinda had said, she'd already thought. "To tell you the truth, I don't like a lot of things lately."

"Did something else happen?"

There was a loud *click* and the theater became suddenly silent, the normal whisper of moving air and rumble of a motor quiet. Eerie.

Or maybe it was just Jenna's case of nerves.

Oliver, who had been hiding behind the bookcase, let out

a worried meow before hopping onto Rinda's desk and starting to groom himself.

"I did get a weird phone call," Jenna admitted. "I couldn't really hear because the connection was so bad, but I thought . . ." She hesitated. Had she really heard music in the background? Or was she getting paranoid?

"What kind of weird call?" Rinda prodded, her voice belying her worry.

"One where no one talks but you can hear music from the score of *White Out*."

"That does it! You *have* to talk to the police. Pronto." She shot to her feet and Oliver, startled, flew off the desk. He was out the door in a striped yellow blur.

"I know, I know. I will." At Rinda's insistent stare, she added, "Today."

"Have you told the girls?"

"I mentioned that I got a strange piece of fan mail and that they were to be extra careful. I also told them to let the answering machine take all the calls so we have a record of who phoned in on the main line. I didn't want the kids to freak out, and I didn't let them read the letter."

"Allie's pretty young but maybe you should have let Cassie read it."

"I just didn't want to upset her any more than I have already. She and I aren't exactly having a great mother/daughter relationship right now."

"She's a teenager. What else is new?"

"I know, but lately she and I are *always* at each other's throats. I caught her sneaking out and grounded her, but I don't think it's doing any good."

"Is she giving you the cold shoulder?"

"Make that a subzero shoulder," Jenna groused, then wished she'd said nothing. What went on between her daughter and herself wasn't anyone's business but their own. However, there were times when Jenna needed someone to confide in, another parent who had dealt with teenagers, a mother who understood the frustration and worry of raising kids.

"You just don't like her boyfriend," Rinda charged as the furnace snapped on again and the steady movement of air filled the silence.

"That's what Cassie says."

"Is it true?" Rinda dumped the dregs of her coffee into a potted fern.

"What's not to like? He smokes, drinks, does weed, I think, doesn't work, and isn't a great influence on my daughter. He's going to graduate this year, I hope, if he doesn't get kicked out for ditching class, and he can't decide whether he wants to go to the local community college, join the Army, or take a job laying carpet for his uncle. All he thinks about is sex, drugs, alcohol, and getting into trouble."

"So he's like most eighteen-year-olds."

"He's nineteen and should be getting his act together."

"Like you did?" Rinda said with a lift of one eyebrow, stretching one arm behind her head.

"At least I was working."

"For a producer nearly twice your age who was taking advantage of you."

"Robert wasn't taking advantage of me. And I ended up marrying him," Jenna said, before she heard herself and winced. "Oh God, I hope Cassie's not thinking of marrying Josh."

Rinda gave her a don't-kid-a-kidder look. "It's probably crossed her mind. Not that she's serious."

"But she's got so much potential. She's smart and pretty and . . ." Sighing, Jenna shook her head.

"Don't you just love being a single mother?"

"I do—it's being the heavy and the disciplinarian that I hate. The rest of it's a piece of cake."

"If you say so," Rinda agreed, though her eyes had darkened, as if she were thinking of her son, Scott. "I kinda think it's all a trial."

"I've heard it gets better when they turn forty."

Rinda laughed, but her smile was tenuous and didn't chase the worry from her gaze. "Lesser women have raised 'dren into adulthood. However, they weren't dealing with this—" Rinda motioned toward the Ziploc bag on the desk. "Do you want me to go down to the sheriff's office with you?"

"I don't need a keeper." Jenna grabbed the plastic bag and dropped it into her purse. At the thought of facing Sheriff Carter again, she withered inside. It was obvious he didn't like her and had considered her last complaint frivolous.

No doubt he wouldn't think much more of this one.

That was just too damned bad.

Sonja was shivering. Sluggish. Her blood felt as if it were congealing and there was a noise . . . a buzzing over the sound of some kind of music.

Where was she, and why the hell did she feel so woozy? She moved slightly but didn't have control of her body . . . wait!

Her eyes flew open and she blinked hard, but it was still dark . . . or kind of. No . . . she was situated in the light, an intense, small circle of illumination, as if she were center stage beneath a spotlight while the surrounding area was pitch black.

Were there people just outside that small arc of light? People *watching* her, unseen eyes studying her? She tried to move and realized that she was naked and strapped into some kind of leather chair with a footrest and a headrest . . . a dentist's chair—or one of those antiquated electric chairs she'd seen in the movies?

God, no, she thought, the cobwebs clearing from her mind with a fear so deep, she thought she might pass out again.

Or maybe she was still asleep. *Oh, Lord, please. Let this be a dream.* But what kind of weird dream was this? Her bare skin pressed hard against the cold leather. Her head was forced against the back of the chair, strapped tight, her mouth wrenched painfully open by clamps she couldn't see.

Get me out of here!

And the feeling that she was being observed . . . *If you're out there, please, PLEEEASE help me!* She strained to s caught only glimpses of shadowy images in the surrounding area.

"Waking up?" A disembodied male voice said from somewhere in the darkness. Her body jumped within its tight constriction, causing sharp pain where her hands and legs were restrained. "We'll have to fix that."

Where are you, you bastard? Why the hell are you doing this to me? She tried to talk, but her voice was just a squeak, her jaw immobile, and she remembered the abduction, her car not working . . . Oh God, where was the monster who had done this? Where? She glanced upward at an apparatus hanging over her head . . . the arm of an old dentist's drill shining wickedly under the intense light. Her blood turned to ice as she stared at the cruel steel instrument. *Oh, God, no!*

Her heart thudded.

Despite the chill, sweat broke out on her skin as she strained to move.

If she could only throw off these bonds and get out of here! Panic ripped through her. She flung herself against her shackles, struggling wildly to no avail. The buzzing intensified a second before the volume of the music increased . . . it was a song she should recognize . . . maybe from a movie, though she was too freaked out to think about it.

She had to get out of here. Now! Frantic, she attempted to twist in the chair, but could barely move, her muscles sluggish, the bands over her wrists and legs and chest holding her firmly, cutting into her flesh. For the first time she noticed a needle pressed into her skin and the long, snakelike plastic tube of the IV strapped to one wrist. Clear fluid slipped drop by drop into her bloodstream.

This was macabre. Surreal. A nightmare. Had to be. *Had* to be.

She tried to yell. To scream. To kick. To no avail. *Who are you, you sick bastard?*

"It's no use, Faye," the disembodied voice said, seeming

aye, she tried to tell him, her eyes moving wildly

from one side to the other. *Oh, God, he's got the wrong woman! This was all a horrid mistake! I'm Sonja! Can't you see you've got the wrong woman, you son of a bitch? Let me go!*

She caught a glimpse of movement in the darkness, someone slowly circling, moving just out of the perimeter of light.

Her skin crawled and she nearly peed herself.

This *couldn't* be happening. She was tripped out somehow, that was it. And yet he circled closer, a tall male figure, all muscles and taut skin. Her eyes moved crazily from one side of her head to the other, trying to follow him.

Suddenly, as if dawn had somehow pierced this hellhole, light began to glow, radiating from the floor, illuminating the area surrounding her, allowing her to see that she was center stage and the others she'd felt near her, the people staring . . . no, not people, mannequins, naked, bald, and expressionless, had been placed strategically around her. Holes where eyes should be stared at her.

As if she were some sacrificial lamb on an altar.

She shriveled with dread.

What in God's name was this?

"See them, Faye?" the disembodied voice said. "They're waiting for you."

I'm not Faye and these are dolls. They're not waiting for anyone!

From the corner of her eye, she saw movement. He was close, a muscular man who was completely naked. His body was scraped free of hair, like the mannequins, and a tight skullcap was pulled over his head.

She knew this monster. Had trusted him. And now, he rounded in front of her, wearing nothing but surgical gloves and an intense expression. In one hand he held scissors. In the other was a portable razor, buzzing loudly.

Her insides shredded as he lifted a lock of her hair and quickly clipped it off. The long blond lock fell to the floor. Involuntarily she started, but she couldn't get away from him, couldn't kick or claw or fight him, couldn't scr

You sick son of a bitch, she silently yelled while the sightless mannequins watched as ever so slowly, he started cutting her hair. Clip, clip. Snip, snip. In time with the music.

Again she was reminded of the scenes in prison movies, where an inmate's head is shaved before he's executed. Oh, no . . . no . . .

As the buzzing became a roar near her ear and the empty-faced dolls looked on, she felt the first cold touch of the razor's blade against her skin.

There was no escape.

CHAPTER 14

"I'm sorry, Les . . . no word yet," Shane said, and felt as if the weight of the world had been heaped upon his shoulders. "I've talked to the State Police. They've got nothing. Neither have my deputies. Nor the city guys. We checked with the nearest hospitals. Sonja wasn't brought in. I've spoken with Lou Mueller, who said you talked to him as well, and his nephew, Chris Mueller, who helped Lou close up. Looks like they were the last people to have seen her."

"What about the customers?" Lester asked, his voice edged with hope and something more, something darker.

"We're looking into it. Lou's given us names of the people he knew—the regulars—and we've got descriptions of a couple others as well as the credit card receipts. I've got deputies interviewing anyone who was at the diner last night and we've got a be-on-the-lookout-for bulletin out for Sonja's Honda." And so far they'd come up with nothing. The weather was against them, of course, the dogs unable to cover a lot of territory, the helicopters grounded, even the troopers with night-vision goggles unable to work well in the cold. "What we could use is the most recent picture of her you've got."

"Okay. Anything else I can do?"

"Stay by the phone, talk to all of Sonja's friends and relatives, and take care of yourself. I'll send someone over." It hadn't been twenty-four hours since she'd last been seen, but Shane had a bad feeling about Sonja's disappearance. It wasn't like her. At all. Lester had sworn that they hadn't had a fight, and even if they had, would she take off in the middle of the worst storm in half a century? Nah, that didn't make sense. Lou, at the diner, had told a deputy that Sonja hadn't seemed out of sorts or worried or anything out of the ordinary. He'd thought she was going straight home after work, but hadn't seen her leave, just noted that her car was gone when he'd taken off.

Not good.

Not good at all.

"Thanks, Shane." Les's voice trembled a bit and then there was a *click* as he hung up.

Shane stared at the phone. "Son of a bitch." What had happened to Sonja Hatchell? He finished his second cup of coffee, wadded the paper cup in his fist, and dispatched a deputy over to the Hatchell house. His job here in Lewis County was usually filled more with meetings, red tape, and small-time crime than anything else. There were drug busts, traffic accidents, DUIs, underage kids partying, and a fair share of vandalism. Of course, his deputies had been called out on domestic violence disputes, but usually the charges were dropped before the parties headed for court. His department had helped break up a meth lab ring two years back, and there had been a chop shop in East County that they'd helped shut down, but dead women didn't roll out of hollow logs, nor did citizens go missing.

Until now. He glanced out one of his windows. Over the tops of buildings, steely gray clouds moved slowly. Ominous and deadly. Life had changed here in Falls Crossing. And not for the better.

He glanced through the open blinds of his office. The de-
~~~~ment was a madhouse. Phones jangled and overworked
bustled inside to file reports and book prisoners,
time to stamp the snow from their boots and

warm their near-frozen fingers around cups of coffee before hitting the icy streets again. There were more accidents and reports of power outages and falling tree limbs. The hospital was crammed, the ER a zoo. And Amanda Pratt, ever the ambitious Assistant D.A., was riding his butt about the woman found on Catwalk Point. She'd e-mailed twice and called once, wanting more information. And then there was the press, already calling, and one local reporter, Roxie Olmstead, who wouldn't take "no" for an answer.

Carter was about to phone Lieutenant Sparks when he noticed a familiar figure wending her way through the cubicles. Though she wasn't very tall, it was hard to miss Jenna Hughes when she breezed into a room. She was bundled in a thick ski jacket and tight-fitting ski pants tucked into slim boots. Heads swivelled as she walked by. Carter wasn't immune himself and noticed the way her stretchy pants hugged her hips, thighs, and calves. She was just damned sexy without seeming to care.

He hung up the phone without dialing. Through the blinds, Carter observed her glance in his direction, then stop at his secretary's desk. *Jenna Hughes was getting to be a regular around here,* he thought, as he watched her try to finagle her way past Jerri.

With everything else going on in the county, he didn't need nor want the distraction of the Hollywood Princess. No matter what her problem. But like it or not, he was going to get her. He stood as Jerri tapped on the door and poked her head inside. "Jenna Hughes is here and would like to talk to you." Jerri didn't look any too pleased. But then, these days, she rarely did.

"Send her in."

Barely were the words past his lips before Jenna strode into the room. He tried not to notice that without much make-up, or the soft focus of the camera lens, or special lighting, she was still a knockout. Great. Just what he needed.

"Get those taillights fixed?" he asked, and was rewarded with a harsh glare.

"As a matter of fact, yes, I did."

"Glad to hear it." Waving her toward one of the chairs facing his desk, he said, "Have a seat."

She dropped into a side chair as she tugged off a wool cap and her gloves. A long braid of black hair fell past her shoulders. "Look, I really hate to bother you. Really. I know you're busy. It's got to be a madhouse here with the storms."

"We're holding our own."

"Good." She sighed, tugged nervously on the gloves in her hands, and beseeched him with those famous green eyes. "I've got a problem."

Haven't we all, lady? "More missing props at the theater?" he asked, half joking and not even scaring up a hint of a smile on her often-photographed lips.

"I wish."

Fishing in her oversized purse, she shook her head. There was a tension about her he hadn't noticed before, a hardness to her mouth, tiny lines of worry visible between her delicately arched eyebrows, a nervousness as she dug into the bag. "It's a little more serious than the stolen things, I think. Rinda said I should tell you about it as I live out of town and am therefore in your jurisdiction. Lucky, you, huh?" Still no smile as she looked up at him, then retrieved a plastic Ziploc bag and dropped it into the middle of his desk. "I received this in the mail, at my personal post office box."

"What is it?" he asked, picking up the bag. "Fan letter?"

"Oh, it's way beyond a fan letter." Her voice was brittle with sarcasm as he picked up the bag and studied the note written over the picture of her.

He scanned the words through the thin plastic sheath. With each obsessive line, his gut tightened. No wonder she appeared about to jump out of her skin.

You are every woman.
Sensual. Strong. Erotic.
You are one woman.
Searching. Wanting. Waiting.
You are my woman.

Today. Tomorrow. Endlessly.
I will come for you.

"Who sent this to you?" he demanded.

"I don't know."

She had his attention now. "You have no idea who would send you something like this?" He held the bag more closely to his eyes and examined the envelope. Same type as in the letter. Postmarked in Portland—on the east side, he thought.

"That's right, none."

"Ever happened before?"

She let out a small sigh and lifted a shoulder. "Well, yes. Once."

He dropped the plastic bag onto the desk, grabbed a pen from a cup on his desk, clicked it, and slid a notepad closer. "Go on."

"The other time was a while back when I was still living in L.A. There were always obsessive fans, of course. Always. But . . ." she gnawed on a corner of her lip, then caught herself and met his gaze steadily again, ". . . but I thought I was safe here."

"Anyone ever stalk you?"

"Not recently."

"In the past?"

She hesitated, then nodded. "There are some fans who step over the line, get a little too close, try to move into your space, and once there was a guy who just wouldn't take 'no' for an answer." Her clear eyes clouded with the memory. "He called and showed up at my house, followed me when I was jogging, showed up on the set, even when I was out to dinner. And yeah, he sent me a letter. It was . . . unnerving, to say the least. I was married at the time. My husband and I got a restraining order against him."

"What happened then?" he asked.

"I never heard from him again. I guess he got the message."

Her explanation didn't seem right. "Wait a second. The restraining order was the end of it?" Carter wasn't buying it.

Not for a second. "He was obsessed with you to the point that you went to the police and then he just went away?"

"Yeah." She shrugged. "I don't know what happened to him, but he left me alone."

Carter didn't like it. He clicked his pen several times. "The guy's name?"

"Vincent Paladin."

Carter scratched it out on his legal pad.

"Address?"

"I told you, I don't know what happened to him. He was kind of a vagabond type, I think. About twenty-seven at the time. Never lived in any one place more than a month or two. At the time he had an apartment in Compton, which is in L.A. County—south-southwest of USC. Claimed he was a student there, but the police found out that was a lie. Actually, he worked at a copy store—Quickie Print, I think the name of it was."

"How long ago was that?"

"Five . . . almost six years," she said.

"And you've never heard from him since?"

"Not a word."

Odd. Was it possible Paladin had relocated up here?

"Was the letter similar to this one?"

"Not at all. It was a long, rambling thing, handwritten on a yellow legal pad. There were seven pages, I think."

"Do you have a copy?"

"No." She offered him a small, self-deprecating smile. "It's not something I like to dwell on."

"But the police in L.A. have it on file, right?"

"I would assume. Detective Brown, Sarah Brown, was in charge of the investigation."

Carter wrote down the detective's name and made a note to call LAPD. "Anything else you can tell me about Paladin?"

"Not much." She shook her head, the long braid swishing between her shoulder blades. "He was an introvert with this odd obsession about me."

"Did he ever harm you?"

"No, and I really don't think that was his intent. He was never violent, never got into the house, though he did hang around outside the gates. It creeped me out to see him there, but he never stayed long."

"What about this picture?" he asked, picking up the bagged note again and studying the photo beneath the words, a beautiful photo in which Jenna Hughes was sexy, sultry, and sophisticated.

"A publicity shot for *Resurrection*, a movie I made nearly ten years ago."

"Any significance to it? Any reason this picture would be chosen over all the other publicity shots of you?"

"Not that I know of. It was just part of the promo for the film. Available anywhere. Video stores. The Internet. Collectibles. Movie paraphernalia, I suppose. Right before the movie came out, there were thousands of pictures available, but, as I said, that was a long time ago."

Carter asked more questions about Paladin, didn't find out much, and made a note to find out what the creep was up to, where he'd most recently dropped anchor. Could he have followed Jenna north? Been stealing some of her things? She mentioned the phone call and the fact that she thought she'd heard music from one of her movies playing in the background, and he felt a tightening in his gut.

"Do you have any enemies?"

"Other than my daughter's boyfriend?" she said, and then looked immediately contrite. She fiddled with the gloves in her hand. "Strike that, would you?"

"Why?"

"It's not him . . . I was just joking."

"Not a joking matter."

"No," she said soberly, her eyes suddenly a darker shade of green. "It's not."

"What about your ex-husband?"

She shook her head. "Robert's too into himself, and he and I get along."

"What about boyfriends or ex-lovers?"

She smiled and blushed as if embarrassed. "None," she

said, dropping the gloves onto her lap and looked directly at him. "Surprised?"

"Yeah."

"I'm not like the characters I play, Sheriff," she said quickly, a flash of anger coloring her cheeks.

"I assumed not."

She arched an eyebrow, silently accusing him of the lie. "A lot of people do, you know. They think I'm the person they see in the film. They tend to forget that what I do is called 'acting' for a reason. They identify with me as the character I'm portraying, and that's just not the way it is. I—"

His phone jangled and he held up a hand, took the short call, then hung up.

"Sorry," he apologized, and scanned his notes.

"You were asking me about my love life," she reminded him, an edge to her voice, the anger still simmering in her eyes.

He didn't blame her for not wanting to discuss what happened behind her closed doors, but that was just too damned bad. Today, if she wanted his department's help, she had to provide answers. To all of his questions. "So what about it?"

Her jaw slid to one side and she looked as if she wanted to spit nails. Instead she gripped the arms of the chair. "The deal is this: I really haven't dated much since the divorce. I've seen a couple of men for coffee and dinner and that's about it. It probably totals four or five dates, if you can call them that."

"Who were the men?"

"Jesus."

He waited, stared at her, gave her time.

"I don't want to drag everyone into this."

"It's important." He was firm and getting tired of her backpedaling. "Either you want me to help you or not."

"Yeah, I know. Okay, I've gone out to dinner twice with Harrison Brennan—he's my neighbor and does some odd jobs around the place. I've had coffee with Travis Settler, the father of one of my daughter's friends, a couple of times. Believe me, it's all pretty tame. Nothing X-rated."

He ignored the jab. "Why haven't you dated more?" he asked, and looked at her hard again. He had assumed that men would be all over her, but she didn't seem to be bull-shitting him.

"I guess I'm too busy, and I intimidate a lot of men, I think."

"Because of your fame?"

"Exactly."

"Okay, so tell me who *you* think would send you the letter?"

"I don't know. That's why I'm here."

He narrowed his eyes at her. "I don't have a lot of time, Ms. Hughes. Why don't you give me your best guess."

"I wish I could," she snapped, unable to come up with anyone she thought might want to torment her. Then she gave him the names of the people she'd met since moving up here, most of whom Carter knew personally, none of whom he considered a nutcase who would send an obsessive letter like the one she'd received.

But then, no one knew what a person did privately.

He glanced down at the letter she'd found in her mailbox again. So meticulous, the text painstakingly placed so that the words didn't mar her face nor detract from the sensual atmosphere of the photograph.

"*Resurrection* was the movie where you played a killer, right?"

Little lines framed her mouth. "A psychotic murderess."

"Who was into sadomasochism."

"Mainly sadism," she corrected. "Anne Parks inflicted pain on her lovers, not herself."

He remembered the film. Had seen it in the theater with Carolyn. Remembered talking during the long drive home about the level of eroticism versus violence in the thriller. "Doesn't it seem odd that of all the publicity shots of you, he chose this one?" he said, and felt a real sense of foreboding. Gone were any of his thoughts that Jenna Hughes was just a Hollywood princess who was missing a few baubles she'd donated to the local theater.

"I don't think it was random," she admitted, and licked her lips nervously. "And that's what's scary."

"But the music you heard was from another movie?"

"*White Out*. The song was a hit. The movie never came out." She cleared her throat, then explained quickly about the accident that had closed production of the film. He remembered reading about the avalanche and tragedy. Looking at her now, he saw the pain in her eyes, noticed the slight droop of her shoulders and he realized she'd never gotten over the loss of her sister who had been killed during the filming. There had been a freak accident; explosives that were to be used in a later scene had inexplicably gone off, creating a killer avalanche. Jenna's sister had been in the path of hundreds of tons of wildly rolling, roaring snow and ice. She'd never had a chance. Jenna, he guessed, somehow blamed herself for not being able to save her younger sister's life.

He asked a few more questions, and they were just wrapping up the conversation when BJ knocked on the door. "When you've got a minute," she said, poking her head into the room. Her usual smile was nonexistent.

"We're about done here."

Jenna stood. "Look, I don't want to take up any more of your time. Just let me know if there's anything else I can do."

"I'll keep this, run it down to the lab," he said, motioning to the plastic bag. "In the meantime, be vigilant. Lock your house and cars."

"Okay."

"I'll get back to you. Let me know if you hear anything else, get any more disturbing mail or calls, or if you think of anything that might help."

"I will."

"You have a security system?"

"Yes."

"Use it. You might consider a guard dog."

"I have a dog."

He remembered seeing the ancient mutt in the old truck and at the theater. For a second he considered telling her to upgrade to a younger, tougher animal that might at least be able to hear, but decided to hold his tongue. "Good."

He stood and shoved his hands in his back pockets. "Look, you take extra precautions, okay? For you and your kids. I'll make sure that the road near your house is on the nightly surveillance for the county, but I have to tell you, my men are working overtime already. It's up to you to be on guard and stay safe. You might consider hiring a bodyguard and getting a more . . . aggressive dog." He didn't so much as crack a smile as he held up the plastic bag. "I'll have the lab check this out, see if we can get prints or other trace evidence or find out what kind of paper, ink, and printer we're dealing with."

"Thanks."

She seemed sincere. Maybe he'd misjudged her by immediately tossing her into his mental bin of preconceived stereotypes that all Hollywood actresses were egomaniacs. "I'll let you know what we find out."

"Great." She nodded curtly, then hurried out of his office. As he watched her go, he knew he hadn't seen the last of her. Surprisingly, that wasn't such a bad realization.

Jenna Hughes was one hell of an intriguing woman.

CHAPTER 15

"Trouble?" BJ asked, watching Jenna walk briskly through the desks toward the front door of the sheriff's office.

"Always." Carter, too, was eyeing Falls Crossing's most famous citizen's backside. Even hidden beneath fleece-lined layers, her ass was definitely tight and oh, so female. He drew his eyes away, but figured BJ had seen his silent appraisal. "So, what's up?"

"Charley Perry. Apparently he likes being a celebrity. Station KBST has been offering up sound bites all morning about their 'exclusive interview' with him."

"Give me a break," Carter grumbled. "I thought I told him to keep his mouth shut."

"That's like telling a grizzly to be gentle when you're offering him a piece of steak."

"I suppose. Any news from missing persons about Jane Doe?"

"No matches yet."

Great, Carter thought, and found the remote to the small television that was balanced atop a filing cabinet. *Just . . . great.*

"What's this?" BJ was looking at the plastic envelope on Carter's desk.

"Looks like Jenna Hughes found herself another fan."

"*You are every woman? You are one woman?* Jesus, who does this guy think he is? Julio Iglesias?" She was studying the envelope.

"That's Enrique—you're dating yourself." He glanced at the note again and it bothered him. More than he wanted to admit. He considered her beautiful face. "Whoever sent it thinks he owns her."

"She have any idea who would do this?"

"Nope—but she did come up with the name of a stalker who chased her around a few years back. Vincent Paladin, some creep who hung out in video stores."

"Does he live around here?"

"Don't know. Yet." He tapped the desk and scowled. Was it just coincidence that Jenna Hughes received the note at the same time that a Jane Doe was discovered up at Catwalk Point and Sonja Hatchell came up missing . . . the incidents seemed unrelated . . . or were they?

Jane Doe appeared to be the victim of a homicide that had occurred a while back.

Sonja Hatchell was missing. But she could have taken off on her own, or been lost in the storm.

And now Jenna Hughes was being terrorized, if not stalked.

"Hey, what's going on?" BJ was staring at him. "I see gears grinding in that brain of yours."

"Just thinking about coincidence. You believe in it?"

"Never."

"Me neither," he said, and chewed on the edge of his moustache as he pointed the remote at his TV and clicked it on.

"Uh-oh, here we go." BJ was already staring at the small television screen and there, in all his glory, was Charley Perry, chatting up a reporter. Charley's white hair was combed, his beard trimmed, his plaid shirt clean and pressed. "Look at him, all gussied-up and dignified-looking."

"Idiot." Disgusted, Carter clicked up the volume and listened as Charley Perry shot off his mouth. "I should have his ass arrested for impeding an investigation."

"And think of all the negative publicity the sheriff's department would get then." BJ winked at him. "Remember, you're an elected official, sworn and dedicated to upholding the law and—"

"Yeah, I get it." He watched Charley expound on his theory of what had happened to the unidentified woman, then tell the story of how he and his faithful dog, Tanzy, had found the remains. The screen had switched to the dog in question, a white-and-liver-spotted mutt that seemed to have some springer spaniel in her. Tanzy whimpered and hid behind Charley's bowed, jean-clad legs, avoiding a treat offered by the reporter. The segment was soon over, and Carter clicked off the set. "That was newsworthy," he groused.

"Charley's harmless."

"And a moron." Carter's mood darkened. With no news on the Jane Doe, Sonja Hatchell's disappearance, Jenna Hughes's stalker, and Charley Perry mouthing off to the press, the day was going rapidly from bad to worse.

God, it's cold. So cold . . . and the music . . . where are the strains of music coming from?

Teeth chattering painfully, Sonja opened a bleary eye and struggled to stay awake. She'd been in and out of consciousness, she thought, though her mind was thick, her thoughts disjointed. She knew time had passed, though she wasn't certain if it was in minutes, hours, or days. Her brief seconds of wakefulness had been without clarity. Vaguely she remembered being abducted, but she couldn't recall her captor—had it really happened? And there was a fragmented image of stripping her, but again, the memory was dreamlike . . . surreal. Then she remembered that the monster had not only shaved her head but filed her teeth . . . she tried to feel her incisors with her tongue, but tasted blood and felt only sharp little nubs where once her teeth had been.

Oh, God . . . it hadn't been a dream.

So where was she now? Why was she still alive?

She seemed weightless, but freezing . . . every inch of her skin felt as if it were cloaked in ice. Shadows crawled around her, colors that blurred and had no form or meaning in the vast, dark expanse.

Where am I?

Where the hell am I?

This is wrong. So wrong. And weird as all get out!

She strained to see, but the shifting shadows were without form. Her ears were tuned to every noise, but all she heard were the plaintive notes of a ballad that seemed familiar, a song she should recognize.

Was it her imagination, or did she detect malice lurking in the surrounding murkiness, something or someone evil observing her?

Shivering, she tried to concentrate, to remember . . . to think. Beyond the cold. Beyond the fear that threatened her.

Come on, Sonja! What the hell is this?

Fragments of memory, jagged shards like serrated icicles, cut through her brain.

Jesus, it's cold!

She stirred and everything around her shifted. Traces of dim light playing eerily around her naked body—yes, naked, she thought frantically and a new, horrifying dread began to pulse through her brain. Every inch of her skin was exposed and colder than it had ever been in her life. She struggled to breathe, felt as if the liquid in which she was nearly immersed was freezing her body from the outside in.

Don't panic! Just figure your way out of this.

She had the sensation that she was standing, though she felt no pressure on her nearly numb feet . . . as if she were suspended. Without wires.

Oh God, this was one weird trip . . . like LSD gone bad. Think, Sonja, think!

She squeezed her eyes shut, trying to clear her mind, hoping that the distorted images would disappear, but when she opened her eyes again, nothing had changed.

With every bit of strength she could muster, she strained to tilt her head and look down at her feet. Her bare feet. Her bare, frozen feet that stood on nothing. Dangling, but not moving. What the hell? Her heart clutched as she tried to focus and looked straight ahead again, to the warped images, the odd play of bits of light. It was as if she were captive in some big tank . . . a huge glass vat filled with something clear and thick, like water about to freeze, and she did have some kind of straps holding her still, straps connected to a huge lifting device—a mechanical arm, stretched overhead; she just couldn't feel them, as she was so cold. *What is this? What kind of weird sci-fi crap is this?* Frantic, she tried to look around. The tub of water itself was housed within a darkened building, a vast warehouse with faint light and shadows that wavered eerily. Through the curved glass, she saw women, softly backlit and unmoving, in odd poses, juxtaposed to each other. The mannequins! They were on the stage, but the dentist's chair and drill had been moved.

How long had she been out? She remembered him adjusting the IV drip, adding something with a hypodermic needle before passing out and then . . . then she'd woken up here.

There was still music, a haunting melody from some movie, seeping through the cavernous room.

Desperately she tried to move, to propel herself to the side of the tank and try to climb up the sheer glass walls and over the rim. *Move, Sonja. NOW!*

She strained. Put every bit of strength into her efforts. Her heart pounded. Her blood pumped. But her arms and legs remained slack. Motionless. Unheeding.

No! Oh, no!

Again she tried. So hard, her filed teeth clenched and she felt as if a blood vessel might pop.

Nothing.

Oh, God.

Help! She tried to scream, but her voice came out in a squeak. As if already beginning to freeze.

Fear surged through her.

Adrenaline spurted through her near-frozen blood, and yet she didn't move. Couldn't so much as wiggle a finger.

Why the hell couldn't she move or speak?

Why couldn't she scream?

What happened to her voice?

What the hell is this?

Stay calm, she told herself, as the music reverberated through her head.

The water seemed even more dense as if it, along with her body, was slowly turning to ice. But that was crazy. Insane.

Suddenly the music halted.

There was silence, which was worse, and then footsteps, quiet but steady . . . deadly . . . approached. From behind.

Frantically, she tried to turn, to scream, to plead for help, but it was useless. Her neck wouldn't budge a fraction of an inch.

"Awake so soon?" The voice was a deep, male whisper. Yet it echoed through the room, bounced through her brain. The same voice she'd heard before. *His* voice.

Let me out of here, you bastard!

"I wondered if you'd come to, Jenna."

Jenna? I'm not Jenna! She tried to yell to tell him that he had the wrong woman, that this was all a mistake, but her voice failed her.

"Or should I call you Faye?"

Faye? No! I'm not Faye. I'm not Jenna. I'm no one you want, you idiot! Frantically she struggled, trying to move, but her brain was fast becoming as sluggish as the rest of her. She couldn't move, couldn't feel . . . she knew instinctively that if she were to let go, to allow herself to slide into the seductive blackness of unconsciousness, she would never reawaken, never breathe again, never see her boys . . . *Let me go, please, oh, please . . . don't do this . . . it's a mistake!* But even as her words came to her mind, even as she tried to scream, she felt herself slipping under, giving up her valiant struggle to maintain clarity, realizing that she was soon to embrace death.

She fought hard to stay awake, but her eyelids became heavy, her body numb, and as the man who had been only a disembodied voice stepped around the tub. She saw his face, distorted through the curved glass, the sadistic beast.

"Your time has come, Faye," he said softly, as if savoring each syllable, and as Sonja's gaze met his, she recognized the pure evil lurking in his icy, unblinking eyes.

CHAPTER 16

They were getting nowhere fast. At least, that's the way it seemed to Carter as he threw his keys onto a shelf near the front door of his cabin. Physically he was dead tired, but his mind was working overtime, fueled by caffeine and the nicotine he'd inhaled when he'd bummed a couple of cigarettes from Jerri. He'd kicked the habit ten years earlier, but at times when he was dog tired and trying to work out a problem, or when he'd had more than two beers, he tended to fall off the wagon, though never enough to buy himself a pack. That's where Carter had drawn the line—paying for smokes. Even though he knew his rationale was foolish. The only person he was kidding was himself.

He unzipped his jacket and hung it on a hook, then kicked off his boots. His house was cold enough that his breath fogged, the frigid air seeping up from the old wood floor and penetrating his wool socks. He spent the next ten minutes stoking the fire and adding a couple of mossy chunks of oak he'd carried in yesterday.

Once the fire was crackling, heat beginning to radiate from the old stove, he rocked back on his heels and stared at the flames through the glass window set into the door.

The Oregon State Police Crime Lab hadn't come up with any more evidence to help identify Jane Doe. So far, from talking to the companies who manufactured alginate, no huge amounts of the gooey stuff were missing, nor had there been any record of a large amount being sold to individuals who weren't dentists or artists, or people who used the stuff legitimately in the past couple of years. But the detectives with the State Police were still checking with other distributors, some in Canada. Jane's face was being reconstructed by both a computer and police artist, but neither was complete as yet.

All these operations took time.

Sonja Hatchell had now been missing for forty-eight hours, and the prospect of finding her was becoming more grim with each passing minute. Deputies had organized volunteers in a search party that was continuing, but hampered by the inclement weather. All the roads and bridges that were passable had been checked and double-checked. Still nothing. It was as if she and her car had fallen off the face of the earth.

Then there was still the issue of Jenna Hughes's missing things, frightening phone call, and anonymous letter, along with the ravages of a storm that hadn't yet abated. In the past couple of days the wind had died down and the snow had stopped just long enough to give the sanding crews a chance to catch up to the plows, then it had started all over again. There had been two more accidents on I-84 and the State Police had shut the Interstate down once again.

Homes without power had been evacuated, and all of the mountain streams had completely frozen over. Even the larger rivers were beginning to ice up. All in all, it was a mess, and the damned weather service kept predicting more of the same. The media, all dressed in their designer ski gear, gleefully reported the number of inches of snow, showed video images of kids sledding down city streets, cars sliding off roads, semis backed up because the truckers couldn't get across the mountains, and cross-country skiers making their way through the streets of Portland. Meanwhile, Carter and his overworked crew, along with the State Police, the department of transportation, and all the utility companies, were working around the clock to keep the roads and residents safe. Which was impossible.

God, he was tired.

Outside, the wind tore through the forest and Carter grumbled under his breath. He walked to the kitchen, opened the freezer, and ignored a man-sized dinner in favor of a tray of ice cubes and a bottle of Jack Daniels tucked away in the cupboard. With a flip of his wrist, he slapped the tray onto his counter, sent a few frozen cubes flying, then poured himself a drink. He was supposed to be off duty for the next two days but figured he'd be called in before daybreak.

But he still had time for a short one.

Sipping the whiskey, he hankered for another smoke, but ignored the craving as he sat at his desk and booted up the computer. His electricity flickered, and he had to try again, but the lights managed to stay on and he was able to access the Internet. Without hesitation, he called up a search engine and typed in Jenna Hughes's name.

The number of sites that could be accessed was astronomical. Especially for an actress who was no longer working, a once-upon-a-time star who should have fallen off the public's radar. Carter pulled up the first fan club site and found himself staring at a computer image of Jenna, the Internet's answer to an 8x10 glossy head shot. In the picture, she was half-turned toward the camera's lens, and a hint of a smile tugged at her full lips. There was a glimmer of naughtiness in her green eyes, a shadow of a sexy imp beneath her serious facade. Shiny black hair fell in tangled disarray and framed her face coquettishly. Though the image was only of her shoulders and head, you had the feeling that she was naked in front of the camera, that she was teasing whoever had the audacity to stare at her.

Carter's gut tightened.

He felt a current of lust in his blood, just a tiny bit of want, which, he knew, was exactly what the publicity shot was meant to inspire. And the kind of imagery that could cause not only sane men, but those who were unbalanced, to think of Jenna Hughes intimately, to want her, to imagine themselves with her sexually.

A scary proposition.

And now his problem.

He viewed several pages, read some facts about her, checked out some of the posts to the bulletin board, then surfed again. Without too much trouble, he found the picture of Jenna that was used for the publicity of *Resurrection,* the same sensual shot that had been copied, printed over, and sent to her by some sicko.

It was easy enough to download the picture.

A six-year-old could do it.

By the time Carter had finished his drink, he'd looked through a dozen sites, and only scratched the surface. He typed in several lines from the poem and came up with nothing significant, then gave up. Jenna Hughes had a serious problem, yes, but so did a lot of other people. He thought of Lester Hatchell and frowned.

What had happened to Sonja?

Even in an ice storm, people in cars didn't just disappear. Or did they?

He walked into the kitchen and poured himself another stiff shot. The wind was raging, rattling the windowpanes, howling in the trees, forcing brittle branches to slap against the old siding. God, he hated the cold.

How many times had he considered moving to a warmer climate?

To Tempe, Arizona, or Sonoma, California, or Taos, New Mexico. He'd gotten literature from over a dozen towns in the Southwest, weighed the pros and cons of pulling up stakes and chasing the sun, but had never followed through. It was almost as if he were fated to be here, that the invisible ties that bound him to Falls Crossing were strong as steel cable.

Back at his desk, he settled into his chair again and before he concentrated on the computer screen, he caught a glimpse of a Lucite cube that was forever beneath his desk lamp, yet never noticed. It had been a gift from Carolyn on their first wedding anniversary, and beneath the plastic surfaces were faded snapshots of him as a much younger man, a much less jaded man, a man who, at that time in his life, had known how to smile. Six photographs. All were of him, four included Carolyn, another was with David when they were gangly-looking freshmen in high school, and the last was a group shot that included Rinda Allen and her brother Wes, along with Carolyn and a few others. They'd been ringing in the New Year and were all wearing stupid little hats and blowing those ridiculous noisemakers . . .

That New Year's Eve party had been so long ago.

During another bone-cold winter.

He closed his eyes for a second. Tried to call up Carolyn's face. But all he could remember were images from photographs or home movies that had been taken over the years. Knowing he was making a mistake, he walked to the hall closet, pushed aside some loose tools, and found an ancient cardboard box. Inside were videotapes from a life he'd led long ago. He pulled out the first cartridge he came to, then walked into the living room. Hesitating only for a second, he shoved the tape into his VCR and clicked on the television.

A few seconds later, there she was.

His heart clutched.

She was laughing, her blond hair poking out of a red stocking cap, her scarf unwinding, her boots slipping as she ran through the snow and hurled hastily packed snowballs back at the cameraman.

"Don't . . . Shane, don't you dare," she ordered, laughing as the image wiggled and a snowball came from the direction of the camera to splat against her back. "Oh, you devil! That was dirty! Just you wait." She threw a few back at the camera. "When I get you home . . ."

"You'll what?" his voice demanded.

"I'll make you pay!"

"How?"

"I'll take it out of your hide."

"Can't wait," he'd said, and another snowball flew past

her head before the image stopped altogether. The last movie he'd ever taken of her. Three days later he was called to an accident. She'd been driving, hit black ice, slid off the road, down a steep canyon to Cougar Creek. Her neck had snapped. She'd been killed on impact.

Carolyn.

His wife.

The woman he'd sworn to love until death.

And he had.

Oh God, he had.

Long after he shouldn't have.

Faye just wasn't right.

Standing naked near the clear glass tank, he eyed the woman's near-dead body as it hung in the freezing chamber and wondered why he'd thought she'd do. True, she had a slight resemblance to Jenna Hughes, but her skin wasn't the correct shade; the tattoo of a ring of roses around her ankle was all wrong. The set of her jaw was sharper, her eyes smaller, her nose not quite as straight. She just wasn't perfect.

But then no one was.

Except Jenna.

Unhappy with his choice, he unstrapped this pale replica from her bonds and couldn't help but feel a thrill as her cool skin brushed over his. The sensation of cold flesh touching him caused his heart to pump, his blood to flow more freely. There were things he could do to her. Sensual acts he'd been planning for a long while. And he could do them now, while she was still alive, breathing so shallowly from her near-frozen lungs.

He drew in a short breath. Shut his mind to any erotic image with this woman—this fake. Lying with her, touching her, kissing her in this state would be sacrilegious. He had to save himself.

For Jenna.

The time was near . . . so near. He had to force himself to

be patient. With the woman draped over his shoulders, he glanced around the room again, his gaze moving to the walls where he'd trained floor lights upward to the artwork surrounding the entire room. Pictures of Jenna Hughes stared down at him. Photographs he'd downloaded anonymously from the Internet, movie posters he'd bought over the years, blown-up pictures from magazines and newspapers, even grainy shots from the scandal sheets. She was everywhere, her image carefully and lovingly fastened to the ceiling and walls.

And to think that he'd even considered fornicating with this . . . this sad, pale, bald replica.

Shame burned through him as he carried her to a dark corner of the room and gently placed her into his specialized long box. She twitched a bit as her skin touched the previously mixed alginate, but he settled her into the coffin, where the gelatin-like substance oozed over her. Slowly, her body sank lower. The trick was to make sure that the alginate would suspend her body, that her buttocks and shoulders wouldn't rest against the bottom of the tank while the alginate was at the perfect consistency, to ensure that the mold of her body was flawless. It was tricky work, as the stuff congealed quickly.

He was trying to create a full-body mask, though so far his attempts had proved unsuccessful, and he'd been forced to use mannequin bodies with head casts. His hope was to hone the process so that by the time he'd abducted Jenna, he would be able to cast her perfect body over and over, perhaps in different positions if he could find a way to keep her alive long enough, and build his shrine to her. He'd already made some mistakes.

In his first attempt, he had not shaved the woman's head properly, leaving her hair to mess up his image. A stupid, amateurish blunder. That mistake had been time-consuming. A waste. What had he been thinking? Since then, he'd worked more carefully, had honed his art to a science, planned the smallest detail, knew who he would use for his work . . . He'd spent the last two years creating a list of women who would be as near-perfect as possible for his shrine though he hadn't started actually sculpting his creations until last winter. Before Jenna Hughes had moved up here, he'd been studying specimens, looking for women with the right facial structure, acceptable frames.

Now, as Faye sank into the pink, oozing depths, he felt a sense of accomplishment. She didn't move. Couldn't, as she was immobile from the freezing. The alginate seeped upward between her legs, through the space between her arms and torso, over her closed eyes. It slithered into her most intimate recesses and molded to her. The process would only take minutes. She would die of suffocation, but not struggle, as she was comatose, already a victim of the frigid ice water and relaxants.

Soon he would have a perfect mold. With extreme precision, he would extract her from the solid alginate, then stuff her useless body into the freezer before he disposed of it permanently.

He watched as the alginate began to solidify.

Just as he'd planned.

Leaving the coffin, he walked through a separate doorway to his computer room and sat at a desk with several keyboards. Anonymously, he logged on, and, starting with e-Bay and some of his favorite vintage dress shops, he began searching. Somewhere, if he took enough time and exercised patience, he would find articles of clothing and jewelry that would suffice as a full costume for Zoey, his next project, the character Jenna played in *A Silent Snow.* Smiling to himself, he imagined showcasing Zoey as well as all the others. He already had found the costume for Faye Tyler of *Bystander,* and the black dress he'd picked up at the theater that Anne Parks of *Resurrection* would soon wear.

His grin widened as he thought about what Jenna would say when she saw his tribute to her. No doubt she would be awestruck. Speechless. Forever in his debt.

That would be a time to savor!

He hoped to keep her alive long enough for her to realize

how much he loved her, how much he cared for her, how he planned to immortalize her.

Through the glass door, he peered into the freezing chamber where the alginate was hardening over Faye Tyler.

But soon his work would be complete.

He walked to the window, where he could see his full-length reflection in the glass, a pale image of a tall, muscular man with a full head of hair, sharp features, intelligent eyes.

He prided himself upon being a near-perfect specimen.

A man any woman would want.

A man who only wanted one woman.

A man who intended to have that one, unique woman.

Soon.

CHAPTER 17

"So do you and Carter have a truce?" Rinda asked.

She and Jenna were sitting in the theater's office and sorting through the pre-sold tickets.

"We were never at war."

"But you two were sure prickly around each other."

"Prickly? Oh, give me a break." Jenna shook her head. "Forget the matchmaking, Rinda, okay? And don't try to deny it. I see what you're up to, and it won't work."

"I think you two would—"

"Yeah, yeah, I know. But forget it." The last thing Jenna needed now was the distraction of a man, *any* man, in her life.

"He's kind of a hunk."

Jenna had noticed. "So what? Who needs a hunk?"

"I wouldn't mind one."

"Then *you* date him." She counted all the tickets for section A and placed them in a stack on Rinda's desk. "The man's a pain in the ass."

"So you *do* like him."

"Give me a break." She started counting out section B and lost track. "He's stubborn, all business, seems to go by his own rules. A cowboy."

"Nothing wrong with that."

"Lots wrong with that," she argued, and hated the fact that Rinda could see right through her. "Let's forget Carter for the moment, okay?"

"Fine . . . let's see here . . ." Rinda leaned closer to the computer monitor. The seating chart was computerized, but the old desktop was straining, its capacity stretched to the limit with the new software Wes had added in the past couple of weeks. In his estimation, the new programs would make life at the theater easier; so far, just the opposite had proved true as the old hard drive struggled with even the most simple commands. Biting her lower lip in concentration, Rinda was trying to print out a chart while Jenna, in a folding chair scooted close to her friend's desk, was counting out the preprinted tickets that had not yet been sold.

The furnace roared in the background, blasting out hot air that quickly dissipated in the drafty, old theater, and notes from a piano drifted through the rooms as Blanche was tinkering with the score of the next production. "What is it you have against Carter?" Rinda pestered, still staring at the screen.

"I thought the subject was closed."

"It's a simple question."

"Well, other than the fact that he gave me a citation and then acted like I was some Hollywood prima donna the first time I went to his office, I've got nothing against the man."

Rinda looked over the tops of her computer glasses.

"Just admit it, Jenna. The man gets under your skin," Rinda said, as Oliver hopped onto the corner of her desk. Absently, she petted the cat's tawny head.

"You mean, he irritates me."

"Whatever you want to call it. But you're getting along with him now, right?"

"Okay, yes, I suppose." She lost count of section B again and swore under her breath. "Damn, where was I?"

Rinda chuckled.

"Okay, I give up! If you really want to know, Carter was fine when I went in to see him about the note. Interested. Concerned. Professional. Not like the other time, when he acted like he thought I expected some kind of special treatment. I got the feeling that he expected me to show up in a limo, that I'd be wearing sunglasses and tons of lip gloss and Gucci shoes . . . something straight out of *The Idiot's Guide to Hollywood Stereotypes*."

Rinda laughed. "You've got him all wrong. He's just busy. I know Shane. He'll be on this stalker thing like a flea on a dog."

"I hope so." She picked up the B tickets again.

"You might consider doing some of the things he suggested."

"Great—you, too. Well, just for the record, I'm *not* trading in Critter for a newer, sleeker, fiercer model," Jenna said, and the old dog, curled on a mat at the base of the stairs to the belltower, thumped his tail at the sound of his name. "I'm also not hiring a damned bodyguard."

"You've got the alarm system fixed, though. Right?"

"I'm working on it. I've called the company, but they're booked solid."

"I supposed that's a start. How are the girls taking all this?"

"With trepidation. I don't want either of them to freak out, so I've downplayed this whole stalker thing a bit, but I'm not leaving them alone much. Hans and his wife Ellie are willing to hang out at the house whenever I need them."

"The Dvoraks? They're ancient."

"You're as bad as the kids. Hans is in his early seventies, not exactly ancient, and Ellie's even younger. They're both sharp as tacks and in good physical shape. Wait a minute— why am I defending them to you?"

"Sorry I asked."

"You should be, and besides Hans and Ellie, I've got Estella coming over to clean a couple of times a week."

"Weather permitting."

"And Ron stopping by for the personal training sessions. For the record, he's twenty-six—young enough for you?"

"I said I was sorry. For God's sake, Jenna, you're touchy,"

Rinda said, then smiled. "Okay, I guess you've got a good reason."

Scott, climbing down from the rafters where he'd been adjusting the lights, had obviously been eavesdropping. "You know, I could help with the alarm system," he offered, not meeting Jenna's eyes. He was a gawky kid, with spiky red hair and eyes that seemed a little too round, ostensibly because of the fact that he never had gotten quite comfortable in his contacts. "Just give me a chance, Mama."

"*What?* Oh!" Jenna's flesh crawled as she recognized the line from her first movie, *Innocence Lost*. As Katrina, a thirteen-year-old prostitute, she had uttered the very same line when begging her reticent madam of a mother for a chance to earn her own money by giving up her virginity.

"Scott!" Rinda hadn't missed the reference, either. "Enough with the quoting of dialogue, okay? Jenna gets it. You're a fan. Geez."

Scott blinked rapidly and blushed. "Sorry."

"You should be. Cut it out." It wasn't the first time Scott had come up with a line and inserted it into the conversation, but Rinda had never said anything before, and Jenna had let them pass. But it was strange, and she was glad Rinda put the clamps on her son.

"I, uh, just thought that I could make sure that Jenna's got a security system that has all the new stuff like infrared sensors and motion detectors. State-of-the art equipment." Scott turned to Jenna. "Didn't you say you wanted a new system?"

"Yeah, I'm considering it," she said cautiously, sensing what was to come.

"I could install it for you!" he said with a smile that seemed genuine enough, yet she couldn't shake the sensation that something wasn't right with the kid. "Piece o' cake!"

"I don't know," Jenna hedged.

"Sounds like a good idea to me." Rinda was peering through her computer glasses, frowning at the screen. "Why not?"

Jenna said, "I think I should probably have a security

company install it, one with guards and connections to the police department if, God forbid, there ever was an intruder and the alarm went off."

"Isn't that what you have now?" Rinda asked.

"Well, kind of. But the system doesn't work, and the company that installed it years ago is now defunct."

"So it's pretty much useless as is. If I were you, I'd have Scott get the old one up and running as best as he can until you get the new one installed. With this weather, that could be weeks. Maybe months." Rinda pressed a key, then swore under her breath as the screen flickered and then died. "Oh, crap," she growled, slapping her desk and jostling her coffee cup.

Startled, Oliver scrambled off the desk, scattering mail and disappearing down a stairway to the dressing rooms.

"Perfect," Rinda said as she and Jenna scooped up the letters and envelopes. Rinda said to her son, "While you're so gung ho to fix electronic things, maybe you should look at this stupid computer."

"It needs a new motherboard and a bigger hard drive and about a dozen other things. It would be cheaper to replace it."

"Wonderful." Rinda stacked the mail on the corner of her desk again. "I'm a complete moron when it comes to anything technical."

"Okay, okay," Scott said, lifting his hands in mock surrender. "Let me take a look at it. Move over." He knelt beside his mother's desk, his fingers typing frantically on the keyboard. All the while, his frown increased and his mouth became razor-thin as he studied the screen. "The program's too big," he finally muttered.

"That much I do know," Rinda admitted.

"Maybe I could try something different . . ." His fingers flew over the keys again, and he stared as if transfixed at the odd assortment of symbols that scrolled across the screen.

The front doors banged open, then shut with a loud *click*. The piano music stopped abruptly. A few seconds later, Wes, in jeans and a thick jacket, sauntered into the small room.

"Problems?" he asked, eyeing Scott kneeling before the computer. "Don't tell me—the hard drive."

"That would be it, yes." Rinda folded her arms under her chest. "It's making me crazy."

"Just a second." Scott was still staring at the monitor that was blinking to life. "Okay . . . it's fixed now. But probably just temporarily. You really need some new equipment."

Wes yanked off his gloves. "Let's see."

Scott's jaw tightened a fraction. "I said, it's running now."

"Yeah, but I'd like a look." Moving in on the younger man, Wes rubbed his hands together, then motioned for Rinda to vacate her chair, which she did, albeit begrudgingly. He sat down, started to type, then swore and started again. "Damned fingers are nearly frozen solid." He slid a glance up at Jenna. "I spent the last two hours with the search party looking for Sonja Hatchell."

"Any luck?" Rinda asked as she leaned against a post, but from the expression on Wes's face it was obvious the missing woman hadn't turned up.

"Nah. It's nearly impossible in this weather, but the police are still trying."

Rinda rubbed her arms. "I wonder what happened to her?"

Nothing good, Jenna thought, but didn't state the obvious.

"I heard that she and her old man weren't getting along." Scott lifted an indifferent shoulder. "I bet she just took off."

"Why would you say anything like that?" Rinda demanded.

"Because I saw her at the diner sometimes. She was always complaining about the cold weather. Came from somewhere in Southern California and wanted to go back. I bet she had a fight with Lester and thought 'what the hell' and just started driving south."

"Leaving her children behind?"

"Some parents do," Scott said, his tone sarcastic just as Blanche Johnson, wearing a hand-knit beret, poked her head into the office. "I'm taking off now. If you need anything, just call," she said, then seemed to take note of the somber faces. "Is something wrong?"

Rinda said, "We were just talking about Sonja Hatchell."

Blanche frowned. Deeper lines etched across her forehead. "I keep thinking she'll show up. You know, call from somewhere. Or . . . something."

"That's what I think," Scott said.

"Sonja would never be so irresponsible." Rinda shook her head. "I know her. Even if she was pissed at Lester, she would have called her kids."

"Maybe." Scott wasn't convinced.

"Anyway, her taking off would be the best-case scenario," Rinda whispered and touched her throat. "You know, it's creepy. First that woman they found up at Catwalk Point, and now Sonja missing. It makes you wonder if they're related."

"I'm sure the police are checking it out," Blanche said, then scrounged in her purse for her keys. "I've really got to go." She cast a glance at Jenna as she retrieved an oversized key ring. "I've cancelled my private lessons this week because of the weather, so tell Allie to keep practicing. We'll catch up once the storm passes and the roads are clear again." She caught a glimpse of the icy window. "I hope it's soon. I hate this weather."

"Don't we all," Rinda tossed over her shoulder, though she was watching Wes work with the computer.

Jenna promised, "I'll make sure Allie spends some time at the piano."

"She'll hate you for that. Most kids love to play outside in this weather. Sled, build snowmen, ice skate." Blanche was already halfway out of the office. "Piano practice will be low on her priority list, I'm afraid."

"We'll see."

"Mmm. That we will." Blanche's footsteps faded through the old theater.

"Strange old bird," Wes said, as if to himself.

Jenna agreed, but didn't say so. These days everyone seemed to be acting oddly. Maybe it was the weather. *Or all in your mind . . .* She wasn't going there. Not today.

"That should do it." Stretching, Wes leaned back so far in the desk chair that his back cracked. "Oh, that's better."

Straightening, he added, "The program's working now, it's just slow."

Scott scowled. "Isn't that what I said?"

"Geez, Scott, did you get up on the wrong side of the bed or what?" Wes asked, and made the mistake of rumpling his nephew's hair. "A little heavy-handed with the sculpting gel, kid."

Scott cringed, stumbling backward. "Knock it off!" He blushed as red as his hair and his round eyes took on a sinister gleam. "I'm *not* a kid."

"Yeah, right. You need to quit using all those women's hair products," Wes needled. "They're sissy stuff."

"Knock it off, Wes," Rinda cut in.

"He doesn't bother me," Scott growled. "Old fart."

"Ouch!" Wes's grin stretched from one side of his face to the other. "Okay, I get it. I embarrassed you. Let's forget what I did, okay?" He offered his hand.

Scott wanted to pout, but thought better of it, though he didn't shake his uncle's outstretched palm. "Fine. No sweat." He shrugged sulkily, then inched toward the door, where he stopped. "So, Jenna," he said uncomfortably, "if you want help with the alarm system, let me know."

Jenna wanted to drop through the floor as Wes turned toward her. "You've still got problems with your security system?"

"Of course she does," Rinda said.

"Then I'll come fix it."

"You don't have to—"

"That's a great idea," Rinda cut in and motioned to her son, who was glaring at his uncle. "Take Scott with you, Wes." When Rinda noticed Jenna about to protest even further, she added, "Look, Jenna, do this for me, okay? So I worry less. Getting the alarm system up and running only makes sense."

Jenna stopped arguing. If a security system would make the place safer for her and the kids, she may as well use it. Hadn't she already decided as much? So what if both Wes and Scott made her nervous? It seemed that everyone did these days. Even the no-nonsense sheriff with his cold, judgmental eyes.

Because of her fame she was used to curious stares, interested looks, furtive glances, and even out-and-out gaping at her. But she'd rarely come across the cool, clinical detachment the cop had shown. He'd been all business to the point of being brusque the first time out of the chute, a little warmer the second, but there was still mistrust between them. Or, as Rinda had suggested, was it something worse than mistrust?

Wasn't it true that she found the lawman attractive?

How ridiculous.

She'd never been drawn to the dark, silent, cautiously brooding type of man, but this one . . .

She stopped herself short. What the hell was she thinking? About Shane Carter? *Get real, Jenna!* She hurried outside, thoughts of Carter refusing to be dislodged from her brain. Yes, he was handsome. And single. And sexy. But who needed it? He was off limits. And he obviously had no use for her. She remembered some of his advice.

Buy a pit bull . . . Hire a bodyguard . . . Yeah, right!

Hiking her collar against the wind, she crossed the snowy parking lot to her Jeep. Carter was just one more example of a burned-out lawman who had already seen too much. And what more could she expect? That he'd kiss her feet because she'd once been a movie star?

She climbed into her Jeep and told herself to take a quick reality check.

"I'll be there Wednesday morning. Early."

"Seven?" Dr. Randall asked, glancing at his watch. It was late, nearly eleven o'clock at night. He'd already turned out most of the lights in his condo and was waiting for the latest news report on the television that was glowing in his den.

"Six, if that works for you."

The psychologist wanted to argue that the appointment at that hour would be too early, but held his tongue. Let the man make his own decisions. That was part of his makeup. A take-control individual who never could quite get it together. Oh, on the outside he appeared calm and determined, a man who knew his own mind. Macho type. But inside . . . that was a different story.

And an interesting one.

Not for the first time, Randall was tempted to tape the session covertly, to keep records. There was a book in the making here, he was sure of it. Yet he'd promised. And so far, he'd never lied or broken his own personal code of ethics.

He was a man of his word.

But wouldn't the press have a heyday with this one?

Or the law enforcement agencies. Wouldn't they love to uncover what Dr. Emerson Randall knew about his client?

That was the problem with his job, the dichotomy of it. Perceived truth vs. reality. And what was reality, anyway? There were all kinds of philosophical arguments about what was real and what wasn't.

Then there was the ethics angle.

An interesting one.

He felt the chill of winter seeping through the walls of his condominium and smiled. Unlike his client, he enjoyed the cold weather, loved the change and variety of the seasons, even the snow and ice. It was cleansing somehow, and the violence of weather, the power of Mother Nature, or the strength of God, whatever you wanted to call it, made man more humble, more aware of his place on this rapidly spinning planet.

The winter cold was good.

His hand was still gripping the receiver and he forced himself to let it go. Thoughtfully, he rubbed the beard covering his chin as the grandfather clock in the hallway struck the hour.

His responsibility was to his client.

But as he stood on the thick carpet, he speculated that if his patient ended up dead—and considering the circumstances, his death could happen at any time—then what would it hurt to write that book?

He pulled out a small recorder, pressed the red button,

and as the tape began to turn, began speaking. A few notes, that's all he'd keep on this case, just to refresh his memory. Then he'd lock up the tiny cassette in his safe. He wouldn't use the information for his own gain.

At least as long as his client was alive.

CHAPTER 18

"Sheriff? It's Montinello. Looks like we've got ourselves a little party up at Catwalk Point."

"A party?" Carter repeated, slowing his rig, then making a quick one-eighty on the plowed road. The snow had stopped for the time being, another lull that was only temporary, according to the weather service.

"Teenagers."

"Great. Hold 'em. I'll be there in twenty minutes."

"Shouldn't I call the State Police? This is their crime scene."

"I'll let Sparks know." He hung up and swore roundly. Dumb-ass kids. What were they doing out in the middle of the night disturbing the scene of a murder investigation? He shifted down and took a turn into the foothills. There was always talk that the criminal returned to the scene of the crime. Maybe that was the case sometimes, but not in Carter's experience. Who would be so stupid? Teenagers. Of course.

One of them could be involved, or know someone who was. Maybe they'd overheard something.

Possibly, but he doubted it. He suspected these were kids just out screwing around. Drinking, smoking a little dope. Getting high at the scene of the biggest crime to hit Falls

Crossing in decades. Idiots. Carter decided to scare the liver out of them.

He called in his position, left a message for Sparks, and drove steadily upward, his tires slipping a bit, the four-wheel drive grinding through the steeper turns. For once it was clear, moonlight silvering the snowbanks and heavily laden branches, but the temperature was still below freezing, as it had been for over a week.

As his Blazer crossed the bridge spanning Cougar Creek, he noticed that the waterfall was frozen solid, spectacular sprays of water crystalized to ice while tumbling downhill.

Just as the surrounding falls had been frozen the winter David died. Carter's eyes narrowed but he didn't see the road winding through the snow-laden trees. Instead, he saw another time and place, a frozen hell where his best friend was a smart aleck with shit for brains.

"I'm tellin' ya, man, this is a chance of a lifetime. We can be the first to climb this mother!" David had laughed as he'd tightened the strap of one of his gloves with his teeth. He and Shane had been standing at the base of the falls, staring up at the incredible frozen plumes of water.

Shane had eyed the cliffs over three hundred feet above. "I don't know."

But David hadn't been able to wait. A few seconds later, he was inching up the ice, higher and higher.

"Goddamn it," Shane had sworn, squinting upward while fumbling with his own equipment. "David, wait!"

"Can't do it, man!"

"Shit."

Shane's heart had been beating like a drum, and even in the frigid temperature, he'd been sweating beneath his layers of fleece and down.

David had always been fearless, the daredevil, the guy who grabbed life by the tail and swung it over his head. But this—climbing Pious Falls—was a damned fool's mission. Carter had known it, even though he'd barely passed his sixteenth birthday.

"Jesus, Carter, don't be a wuss!" David had been inching up the gargantuan icicle, yelling over his shoulder to Shane standing at the base of the frozen waterfall.

Shane's head had been angled upward as he'd watched his friend's slow, steady progress up the sheer sheet of frozen spray. He hadn't wanted to climb. His boots were sliding as he tried to stand on the solid sheet of ice that had been a wide pool at the waterfall's base. As he glanced down, he noticed two dead trout frozen in the iced pool beneath his feet, staring up at him.

"What are you waiting for, ya dumb ass! Come on!" David had yelled over his shoulder, his voice echoing through the silent, snow-crusted canyon. *"This is the kind of thing you can tell your grandkids about!"*

Those words had haunted Shane Carter ever since that gut-wrenching day.

Now, his radio crackled, bringing him crashing back to the present. A transformer had blown east of Falls Crossing and more residents were suddenly without power. From the chatter back and forth on the radio, he knew that emergency crews were on their way. "Son of a bitch," Carter swore, and feared the end of this god-awful weather was nowhere in sight. If the cold front didn't let up, there would be more homes without electricity, more people who would have to be evacuated, more stranded drivers, more ERs overcrowded.

His mood dark, he eased his rig up a final rise to Catwalk Point.

Blue and red lights strobed the surrounding forest in eerie colors.

Montinello's rig was parked in the middle of what had been the logging road, headlights shining on three other vehicles—two pickups and a Bronco—parked at odd angles near the crime scene. As Shane cut his engine, Montinello waved at the vehicles and a dispirited group of teenagers climbed out of their rides. *The usual lot of underachievers,* Carter thought, eyeing Josh Sykes, Ian Swaggert, and a few others who tried to keep their faces averted.

"Okay, they all say they were up here just hanging out. No big deal. Some claim they didn't know it was a crime scene."

"Yeah, right." Shane's breath fogged in the air as he looked pointedly at the yellow tape still strung from one copse of trees to another. "I guess they can't read."

That got him a snarly glare from Sykes.

Carter bummed a cigarette and lit up, feeling warm smoke curl through his lungs. "You get statements?"

"Such as they are. On tape."

"Rights read?"

"Yep."

"Good. Anything illegal besides them being up here?" he asked, as the wind knifed upward from the river far below. Two girls were in the group, huddled close to their motley group of boys.

"Minors in Possession. Alcohol. Marijuana. Some unidentified pills."

Great, Carter thought as he took another deep drag. *Just what we need right now.* "All the kids ID'd?"

"Yep."

In the distance, another rig's engine whined up the hill.

"Probably the state guys," Carter said. "I informed Sparks. This scene is the OSP's jurisdiction."

"Officially." Montinello stomped his feet and lit a cigarette. "A couple of the kids are underage. I mean, younger than eighteen. Two girls. One's BJ's kid. I already called her. She's madder'n a wet hen and on her way."

"Holy shit," Shane growled under his breath. In his mind's eye, he could see the headlines in the *Falls Crossing Tribune* now: DAUGHTER OF DEPUTY CHARGED WITH CRIMINAL MISCHIEF. Except that since Megan was under eighteen, her name wouldn't appear in the paper. At least, he hoped. "BJ's gonna be fit to be tied."

"Already is, but wait, it gets better," Montinello assured him as another blast of wind rolled through the hills.

Carter braced himself. "How?"

"The other girl is Jenna Hughes's daughter." He motioned

with a gloved finger to the taller girl. "The one in the purple stocking cap."

"Hell." Of course the daughter of Falls Crossing's most celebrated citizen would be involved. He looked over the group of kids huddled together, still copping attitudes, even though their teeth were chattering, and they were hopped up on fear as much as anything else. His gaze landed on the Hughes girl. Daughter number one, who had been in the truck when he'd pulled Miss Hollywood over.

The kid's resemblance to her famous mother was remarkable. Same high cheekbones and dark, arched eyebrows. A larger nose but intense eyes. Unruly strands of streaked hair escaped from her knitted hat, blowing across a face that was already beautiful. Her jacket collar was turned up against the wind, and she was standing next to the Sykes kid, a big, gangly boy with a tough-guy attitude and not much else going for him.

Carter had been a cop around here long enough to know Josh Sykes's family. On a professional level. The way he figured it, Josh was a poster child for what happens when a kid's neglected and left to his own devices. Josh wasn't a bad seed, just bored and in need of direction. Otherwise, he'd land himself into big trouble. And soon.

While Carter finished his cigarette, Lieutenant Sparks parked his rig. A big man with dark, curly hair and intense brown eyes, he took a look around, his state-issued uniform and bearing causing all the kids to watch him cautiously. He let out a long whistle of disappointment as he approached the shivering bunch of teenagers. "What in the hell did you guys think you were doing?" he asked rhetorically and didn't wait for an answer. Shaking his head, he ordered the older kids hauled into town and allowed the two sixteen-year-olds to be cited and released to their parents.

Another big engine roared loudly through the woods. Bright headlight beams splashed against the trunks of the trees.

"Uh-oh," Montinello muttered.

A pickup belonging to BJ Stevens slid to a stop. She left

the truck running, headlights drilling light through the darkness, and flew out of the cab. The proverbial wet hen.

In jeans, a sweatshirt, and an oversized ski jacket, she stomped through the snow. "What the hell is going on up here?" she demanded, as she didn't so much as look at the men, but walked up to the small group of teenagers. Without makeup, devoid of sleep, fury radiating from her, she read her daughter the riot act.

"Jesus H. Christ, Megan, don't you have a brain in your head? This is a *crime scene,* for crying out loud!"

Megan stared at the ground.

"I'm a cop!"

Still no response.

"Come on, get in the truck. *Now!*"

As she herded her recalcitrant kid toward her idling vehicle, she paused at the group of men. "I don't know what to say," she admitted, her lips razor-thin, her skin as white as the snow covering the underbrush. "I'm sorry. I had no idea she'd snuck out."

"It happens," Sparks said.

"Yeah, well, I didn't think it happened to me, and believe me, it won't again! Throw the book at her. She deserves it. God, will she ever learn?" BJ said, and rolled her eyes toward the starless heavens.

"They all do," Carter said.

"Not all of them." BJ wasn't about to be patronized. "This is just what I need right now. Just what I friggin' need." She cast a weary glace at Carter. "You don't know how lucky you are that you don't have a teenager."

She took off toward the truck and said, "I mean it, Megan, this crap has got to end. Right now!" With that, she opened the passenger door and waited as her silent, simmering daughter climbed inside.

"I don't believe this!" BJ said before rounding to the driver's side and stopping to glare over the hood at one of the boys. "Listen to me, Ian. No more. Got it?" BJ jabbed an angry finger in the frigid air, pointing at the group. "If this ever happens again, I'll take it up with your mom and that

preacher dad of yours and you won't like what I have to say."
With that, she turned, climbed into her idling truck, threw
the big rig into reverse, then shoved it into first and roared
away, snow spewing from beneath the tires as she hauled her
wayward daughter with her.

"I'd hate to be Megan about now," Montinello thought
aloud.

Or her mother, Carter silently agreed as BJ's vehicle's
taillights winked out of view.

Sparks motioned to Cassie Kramer. "Can you see that she
gets a ride home?" he asked Carter. "I was going to ask BJ,
but she's got her hands full."

"And already out of here." Carter nodded. He wasn't keen
on the idea, but everyone else was busy with the other kids
and trying to preserve what was left of the crime scene.
Fortunately, most of the evidence had been collected.

He motioned toward Cassie. "Hop in," he ordered, then
asked for her home phone number. Before they took off, he
dialed and his call was immediately switched to voice mail,
where a computer-generated woman's voice instructed the
caller to leave a message. He did.

"What about a cell?" he asked, and again Cassie rattled
off a number that he quickly dialed. That connection, too,
went directly to Jenna Hughes's voice mail. He didn't bother
with a second message.

He'd hoped to soften the blow and not blindside Cassie's
mother. If Jenna had already figured out the kid was AWOL,
Carter wanted to relieve her worries quickly. If not, he wanted
to prepare her before they showed up on her doorstep.

No such luck.

But, so far, this wasn't a night for luck.

As he started his Blazer, he glanced in the rearview mirror. The kid was okay. Huddled in a corner of the SUV and
looking miserable, but okay.

He wondered how her mother would react, then remembered Jenna Hughes wearing tight ski pants and sitting in a
chair at his desk while explaining about a stalker.

The stalker's poem came to mind again. *You are every*

woman. Sensual. Strong. Erotic. Whoever had written it had gotten the sensual part right. But tonight, Carter suspected, Jenna Hughes was going to be just another distraught, worried-out-of-her-mind mother. Unless she didn't give a damn about her kids. Unless she was the kind of parent who only considered children as accessories, who were so self-involved that their children were neglected, only brought out and worn like jewelry to be shown off.

Carter didn't think so. That wasn't the impression he'd gotten from the few times he'd met Jenna Hughes. Rumor was that she'd moved up here to get away from all the glitter and spotlights of Tinseltown. For her kids. He looked into the rearview mirror again and noticed that daughter number one kept her eyes pointedly averted, rebellion fairly seething from her.

Swearing silently, he rammed the Blazer into gear.

CHAPTER 19

The night felt strange.

Disturbed, somehow.

Jenna opened an eye and strained to listen.

Beside the bed, Critter gave off a soft, disgruntled growl. He lifted his graying head as if he, too, sensed a change in the atmosphere, a shift in the noises of the night.

Then she heard it. The sound of a truck idling nearby. Close to the house.

She glanced at the clock: 3:53.

What the devil?

Quickly she slipped from the covers, threw on the robe she'd tossed over the end of her bed; then, stuffing her arms through the sleeves, she made her way to the window. She peered through the blinds and saw a vehicle from the sheriff's department parked near the garage.

Her heart froze.

"Oh, God," she whispered.

What was wrong? Why was the sheriff here?

The stalker? Had he found who had written the note . . . or was the guy here? Panic tore through her.

Critter growled. The hairs on his back sprang to agitated attention.

Jenna was out of the bedroom in an instant, her bare feet

slapping against hardwood floors. She ran up the half-flight of stairs to Allie's room, the dog on her heels. Her youngest was asleep in the bed, covers thrown off, arms akimbo, mouth open, and snoring softly. Jenna darted to the next room. Her heart was beating a terrified tattoo. She pushed open the door and nearly died from fright as she spied the empty bed.

"Oh God, no," she whispered, just as a heavy knock resonated through the house. Something horrible had happened to Cassie! That's why someone from the sheriff's department was pounding on the door. Fear propelled her down the stairs, dread took a stranglehold of her heart. *Dear God, please don't let anything be wrong,* she silently prayed just as she heard the kitchen door creak open. She hurried to the stairs.

"Mom?"

Cassie's voice!

Thank God!

Relief flooded through her.

Jenna nearly stumbled on the last steps. Critter was growling and barking, his claws scrambling on the hardwood.

Jenna flew into the kitchen as Cassie snapped on a light. "What's going on? Why aren't you in bed?" Then her gaze landed on the man with Cassie, Sheriff Carter. Stern, chiseljawed, dark, suspicious-eyed Sheriff Carter, whom she'd seen so recently.

The dog was barking his fool head off, baring his teeth at the lawman and circling.

"Critter. Hush! Now!" Jenna ordered.

With a final suspicious growl, Critter slunk under the kitchen table, where he studied Carter with wary, dark eyes.

"I'm sorry," Jenna said, cinching the ties to her robe, her gaze landing on Cassie. "What's going on? Where the hell have you been?"

Carter said, "Your daughter and some other kids were up at Catwalk Point tonight."

She was caught short. *Catwalk Point?* "Isn't that where they found the body of that woman?"

"That's right." Carter nodded. Serious as death. Cassie shifted from one foot to the other and studied the floor.

"Why?" Jenna asked her daughter. "Why did you sneak out in the middle of the night and go up there?" She pushed her hair from her eyes as her heartbeat started to slow. What the devil was going on here?

Cassie lifted a shoulder. Her chin stuck out stubbornly.

"You were supposed to be in bed. What were you thinking, sneaking out?"

Defiance sparked Cassie's eyes and her jaw tightened, but she didn't say a word.

Carter said, "I tried to call, but an answering system picked up."

"What? But I was home and not on the other line . . ." Jenna said, then realized what had happened. "Wait a second. Did you leave the phone off the hook?" she asked her daughter, and a dark shadow of belligerence passed through Cassie's eyes.

"Oh, Cass," Jenna sighed, feeling suddenly so much older than her years.

"We tried your cell as well, but you didn't pick up."

"I always recharge it at night. It's turned off," she said, sensing his disapproval.

"I thought you had an alarm system."

"I do . . . I armed it before I went to bed . . . Oh, geez, Cassie, did you turn it off?"

Cassie's lips flattened, but again she was silent.

"Cass . . ." she said. "How could you? I told you about the letter and the phone call and . . ."

"It wasn't working anyway. You know how it is," Cassie cut in churlishly. "The red light wasn't on or anything."

"Enough about the alarm system, okay? I've asked Wes Allen to see what he can do to make it operational until a new security company can come in and install one."

Was it her imagination, or did Carter tense a bit at the mention of Wes Allen, Rinda's brother?

"Look," she added, "because of the storm, we're forced to

deal with the one we've got and it does work sometimes. So, Cassie, for God's sake, let's use it." She sighed and stared at her oldest daughter. "For the love of God, Cassie, what were you thinking?"

"That I just wanted to have a little fun. Do you know how boring it is around here?" Cassie blurted, then her gaze skated to the sheriff and she clammed up again.

"We had to cite her for Minor in Possession."

Jenna's heart sank.

"They were drinking up there, doing some drugs."

"Oh, God." Jenna sagged a little and braced herself on the kitchen island. "The other kids. Are they okay? Was anyone hurt?"

"No. It was just a party."

"At a crime scene." Jenna's gaze slid to the clock again. "At 3:30 in the morning?" The severity of the situation hammered at her. Stupid kids. Both her hands clenched and she stuffed them into the pockets of her housecoat and stared at her daughter.

Despite all her bravado and tough-girl attitude, Cassie looked scared. Good. That was a start.

"You were with Josh, weren't you?" Jenna accused, but once again, her eldest daughter didn't respond. As if she were protecting that big lummox of a boyfriend. Jenna's problems with Cassie ran far deeper than she'd imagined. "Do you have anything to say to the sheriff?"

Cassie studied the hardwood floor as if it were suddenly fascinating and mumbled a quick, barely audible, "Thanks for the ride."

It was the best Jenna was going to get, and at that moment she heard the floorboards overhead creak. Critter perked up his ears and wagged his tail. Allie was awake. "Uh-oh."

"She doesn't need to know about this," Cassie said quickly as footsteps scurried overhead and tumbled down the staircase.

"Fine." For once Jenna agreed with her eldest. She was in no mood to create more of a scene, especially in front of Sheriff Carter. "We'll discuss it in the morning."

More footsteps, moving quickly down the stairs.

Allie, red-blond hair sticking out at odd angles, face knotted in confusion, eyes half-open, stumbled into the room. "I heard yelling," she grumped, then stopped short when she spied Carter.

"This is Sheriff Carter," Jenna explained reluctantly.

"I know. He gave you a ticket."

That he did, Jenna thought. "He brought Cassie home."

"Home? But wasn't she already here?" All the sleep in her youngest daughter's eyes scurried away. Allie gave the officer a wide berth, regarding him with distrustful eyes as she sidled closer to her mother.

Jenna said, "Cassie had decided to go out."

"Out?" Allie repeated, glancing through the window to the cold night beyond. "Where? Isn't she still grounded?"

"It's none of your business," Cassie said sharply.

"What time is it?" Allie focused on the clock for a second, then turned her gaze back to her sister. "I don't get it," she said, but as the words spilled out of her mouth, her expression changed from confusion to understanding. She blinked. Rolled her lips over her teeth. Held her tongue. She got it. Her questions stopped abruptly and, to her surprise, Jenna witnessed a silent look passing between her daughters, an unspoken pact Jenna hadn't suspected existed between them until this moment in time.

"We'll talk this out in the morning, when we've all had some sleep and we can think a little more clearly. All that matters is that everyone's fine tonight, so, both of you"—she motioned to her daughters—"go on up to bed." Jenna hitched her chin toward the stairs.

Cassie, as if she expected to be called back at any instant, made haste to the staircase. She pounded up the steps, unlike the noiseless way she'd tiptoed down earlier on her way out. She'd had practice. Jenna hated to think how many times the girl had padded silently down the hallway and eased down the stairs. How many times had Cassie lied to her? How often had she disengaged the alarm and locks to slip into the darkness and meet Josh?

Jenna's stomach curdled. What did they do? Drink? Of course. Have sex? Most likely. Smoke pot or crack? Oh God, she hoped not. What were the drugs that were so available here? Methamphetamine? Ecstasy? For sure. Oh, Lord.

Jenna sighed audibly. There was a chance that Cassie was already pregnant.

Have a little faith, would you? Trust her.

After she's been caught twice in the last week sneaking out? I don't think so.

As much as she wanted to trust her kids, Jenna had a hard time believing that Cassie and Josh weren't having sex. And Cassie was only sixteen. What a mess!

If she could, she'd wring Josh Sykes's scrawny neck and then castrate him!

"Great," she muttered angrily before realizing that Sheriff Carter was still standing in the kitchen, hands in the pockets of his jacket, and staring at her with his damning brown eyes. "I'm sorry about this," she said quickly, "and I really appreciate you bringing Cassie home."

He nodded. "No problem," he said, but his expression belied his words. "Unfortunately, this isn't over. She'll still have to report to the juvenile court."

"Which might be a good thing, considering. Cassie needs to be scared or shocked or shaken into some sense of reality and responsibility." Jenna scraped her hair away from her face and shook her head. "My daughter doesn't take much advice from me anymore."

"What about her father?"

"Robert?" Jenna let out a short, humorless laugh. "Yeah. Well. I'll call him in the morning . . . no, first I'll have Cassie call him, have her cop to what she's been doing." She dreaded the confrontation. No doubt Robert would blame Jenna for not having control of their daughters. He was a great one to point out blame rather than handle the situation. Dealing with Robert on tough issues was tantamount to walking through quicksand. Impossible, pointless, and mired in all kinds of emotional muck that just kept dragging

Jenna down. Robert's knowledge of the situation wouldn't improve things one iota.

Again, she found Carter watching her and she was suddenly aware of what she must look like—her hair mussed, not even a trace of lipstick, her face lined with worry, her checkered flannel pajamas peeking out of her favorite, slightly worn, chenille robe. *So much for the glamorous Hollywood babe look,* she thought wryly. "Gee, where are my manners?" she mocked, feeling her lips twist in self-deprecation. "I guess I'm not used to guests at four in the morning."

"I didn't stop by as a guest." His voice was deep, and not as harsh as usual. As if he understood the trauma she'd been through tonight. Gee, maybe the guy actually had a heart hidden somewhere deep in that big chest of his. Nah. Jenna wasn't betting on it.

"Well, you're here now. So . . . would you like a cup of coffee or something?" she asked, then spied her coffeemaker sitting on the edge of the counter. Day-old sludge was congealing in the glass pot.

Carter's gaze followed hers.

"I'll make fresh," she offered.

"Don't bother. I've got to get going." He stepped toward the door, but she was suddenly on a mission. And sick to death that every time he saw her, she was some kind of victim.

"It's the least I can do." She knew that she was too hyped-up now to sleep, so over his protests she washed the glass pot, dumped yesterday's grounds down the sink, and poured fresh beans into a grinder. Over the screech of the whirring blades, she said, "I've got a thermal cup you can take with you."

"Really, this isn't necessary."

"No, and it's not a bribe to get both me and my daughter out of trouble, either," she tossed over her shoulder. "You know, it's funny, but every time I see you, and it's been a lot lately, I've been in some kind of trouble."

"Comes with me being a cop."

"I know. But it seems like, in the last few days, every time I turn around, I'm facing you."

"A nightmare, huh?"

"Well, yeah. It has been." She looked over her shoulder and actually caught a glimpse of his smile, a flash of white teeth beneath his dark moustache, a crack in his serious facade. When he smiled he was handsome in that rugged, outdoors-man way that had never much impressed her before. But now, spying the crow's-feet near his eyes and the shadow of his beard adding to his all-male image, she noticed his good looks. Which was ridiculous. It was four in the morning, for God's sake. He'd spent the last few hours dealing with her juvenile delinquent of a daughter when he had so much more to do. Yet, tonight, she noticed just how well he filled out his jeans and parka.

"Sleep deprivation," she muttered under her breath as she poured water into the coffeemaker and turned on the switch.

"Pardon me?"

"Nothing."

The kitchen seemed to warm with the aroma of coffee brewing.

"Do you have any kids?" she asked, though, from the rumors she'd heard in town, she guessed not.

"No." He was leaning against a bank of cupboards, his gaze moving from her to the window over the sink where snow had collected in the corners of the panes.

"They're a blessing . . . and sometimes . . ."

"A curse?"

"Well, let's just say . . . a trial," she admitted, swiping at the counter with a towel.

"But worth it?"

"Absolutely. Ya gotta take the bad with the good." She opened a cupboard and saw the travel mug she was looking for about two shelves out of her reach. Leaning against the counter, she stood on tiptoe and stretched, but her fingers barely brushed the bottom of the shelf. Jumping was out of the question, but she hoisted herself agilely onto the counter and was twisting around when he stepped closer.

"Here. Let me get it." He was in front of her before she had time to scoot away. Suddenly she was pinned by the sheer presence of the man, her legs dangling close to his hips. He smelled of the outdoors and faintly of tobacco and some kind of aftershave, but she only got a whiff as his fingers wrapped around the mug in question. "This what you want?" His face was close to hers, near enough that she saw the striations of gold in his brown irises, noticed that a few rebellious gray hairs dared appear in his dark moustache.

"Uh-huh," she managed to say.

"Anything else?" He handed the mug to her.

"That'll do."

He backed away then, and she felt as if she could finally draw a breath. More flustered than she wanted to admit, she hopped off the smooth tiles, poured the coffee, and screwed on the cap, before saying, "Oh . . . what about sugar or cream?"

"Black's fine." His cell phone beeped and he snagged it from his pocket. "Carter," he said, his gaze grazing hers for a second. "What?" The skin over his face tightened, lips folding over his teeth. "Where?" he asked, and listened hard as coffee continued to drizzle into the pot. "Okay. I'll be there in half an hour . . . meanwhile, hold the kids that were up at Catwalk Point at the station until I get there to talk to them . . . I don't care where. Isn't there a free cell? If not, the drunk tank . . . yeah, let them get to know the regulars. See if that scares some sense into them." He snapped off his cell and offered her a quick, humorless smile. "I've got to go, but I'll be in touch. I haven't heard back from the lab about the note you received, but I'll call today. Put some pressure on them. I assume you haven't had any more trouble?"

"Other than Cassie? No."

His smile was a flash. "Double-check your alarm system. Make sure it's working. And the gate. Why's it open?" he asked, pointing his chin at the kitchen window from which Jenna saw the entrance to her premises.

"Broken," she admitted. Beneath the security lamps the double iron gates, mounted on pillars wrapped in rock, were flung open and packed with snow and ice, immobile. "It's the electronic lock. Broken. Again. I've had it fixed twice." She lifted one shoulder. "I don't know what it is with me— bad karma, I guess. Everything mechanical or electrical around here is on the fritz."

"Need help? I know some people around town who might be able to fix the alarm and the gate and even install cameras or whatever you want." The small lines etching his forehead deepened as he added, "Of course, with the storm and power outages, most of the electricians are working around the clock. You'd be lucky to get someone before the spring thaw."

"I know. But I think I've got a couple of people who've offered to help."

"Good." He glanced down at Critter and the old dog finally wagged his tail as he crept from beneath a cane-seated chair. "Yeah, a fine lotta guard dog you are," Carter said, patting Critter's head.

"I'm not replacing him." She handed Carter the travel mug. One side of the sheriff's mouth lifted.

"I guess I wouldn't, either," he said, then lifted the cup toward Jenna. "I'll get this back to you."

"Don't worry about it." Motioning to the high cupboard where she kept a few odds and ends she never used, she added, "You can see how much I was using it."

"Okay. Good night, or maybe I should say, good morning, then." He took a sip, then headed out the back door. "Make sure you lock up behind me."

Jenna did just that, bolting the door and watching through the kitchen window as Shane Carter walked briskly through the breezeway, then followed his own trail of broken snow to his Blazer. A few seconds later he drove off, lifting a hand as he passed the house.

She waved back automatically and didn't move until the red glow of his taillights had passed through the main gate and disappeared into the gloom.

Jenna shivered and felt more alone than she had since moving to Falls Crossing. It was still pitch-dark outside, no glow of dawn illuminating the eastern sky.

Just the cold, dark morning.

CHAPTER 20

"So you know what they say about the plumber's faucet always leaking," BJ grumbled the next morning. She looked tired. Bags appeared beneath her eyes, her hair was unruly, and her shoulders slumped. An aura of allover weariness accompanied her. "I guess it works for cops, too. Their kids don't obey the law. Or at least mine doesn't." Disgustedly, she flung herself into the side chair at Shane's desk.

"Maybe it's a good thing Megan got caught while she's still underage."

"Oh yeah? Why is that? You don't think this is just the beginning?" BJ's usually animated expression was flat and exasperated, the corners of her mouth pinched with worry. "You know, if I could send her off to military school, I would."

"Don't you think you're jumping off the deep end?"

"Diving in it. Wallowing in it. Drowning in it." BJ leaned back in the chair and closed her eyes. "Lord give me strength."

"Megan will be fine."

"When? When she's twenty-five? Thirty? I'll be dead by then. I'm tellin' you, she's killin' me. *Killin'* me."

Carter laughed. "I don't think she has a chance against you."

"Goddamn, I hope you're right." BJ opened her eyes and straightened. "So did you interview the boys?"

"Yeah. Along with Sparks and another officer from the OSP." He remembered the sullen faces of Josh Sykes, Ian Swaggert, Anthony Perez, and Cal Waters, all of whom had kept up the bravado for hours before being released to their parents this morning. Only when faced with their disappointed mothers or furious fathers did the kids show any signs of cracking. If they'd been scared by being locked up, they'd managed to hide it. "I'd be surprised if any of them had any connection to the dead woman. I think it was just a case of showing off—driving up to the scene where a murder victim had been found, kind of a truth-or-dare kind of thing." He rotated a pencil between his fingers.

"I'd like to break their necks. Especially that little prick Swaggert's."

"Better not. Might be considered police brutality."

"He deserves it. They *all* deserve it." A muscle worked in her jaw and she blinked rapidly. "Little jerks. Sex, drugs, and alcohol . . . that's all they care about."

"There are laws protecting underage girls."

"I know, I know. But anything that was done was consensual."

"She's only sixteen."

"Yeah, and they're what? Seventeen, eighteen? Not a brain between all of 'em."

"Is Megan okay?"

"If you ask her, she's fine. Her only problem is her . . . let's see . . . let me get the lingo straight . . . her only problem is her 'stupid, overbearing, nosy, old-fashioned, out-of-it cop of a mother'—that would be me—who won't let her do what she wants." BJ closed her eyes again and touched her fingertips to her forehead. "I haven't told Jim yet. He'd tear the boys limb from limb, which, let me tell you, is a fantasy of mine right now."

"How is it that he doesn't know?"

"Slept right through everything. Can you believe it? He's on one of those breathing machines because of his apnea and he's been sleeping in the spare room where there isn't a phone. Didn't hear it ring, me yell, or Megan slam her door.

He took off for work around six this morning just like normal, and I figured I'd spare him the bad news until tonight. Maybe by then I will have cooled off and possibly have a few more answers about what those kids were doing." She let out a long breath that shifted her bangs and stared straight at Carter. "Then the you-know-what is gonna hit the fan. In a major way. Jim has this antiquated attitude that his precious little daughter would never drink or do any drugs and that she'll be a virgin until she gets married, which will probably be sometime in her thirties if Daddy gets his way." BJ straightened in the chair. "I think it's time for a reality check. For all of us." She stretched her arms in front of her until her knuckles cracked. "Okay, so enough about my perfect fairy-tale family. What else is new?"

"Nothing good," Carter admitted and brought her up to speed. "I was called over to the Tanner place about a break-in *after* taking Cassie Kramer back to her mother. Someone had ripped off some tools in his back shed. There were tracks leading down the hill to the road. Then I dealt with the boys, and I've spent the rest of the morning talking to OSP. The Jane Doe remains unidentified, and so far there's not a trace of anything on Sonja Hatchell. I've talked to Lester twice today already and a search party has been scouring the woods around his place as well as near the diner again. They've come up with nothing. I've double-checked with the hospitals and clinics. No one's seen Sonja Hatchell."

"What about her car?"

Shane shook his head. "Haven't found it. No citations issued against it. No record of it showing up in any repair or body shop. When the weather clears, the State Police will send up helicopters to see if she somehow drove off the road and her car is stuck somewhere." He met her worried gaze. "But if that's the case, there's not much chance she's still alive."

"It's a bitch," BJ said, her troubles with her daughter temporarily forgotten. "People just don't vanish off the face of the earth—there are no aliens in UFOs plucking citizens out of Falls Crossing, no matter what Charley Perry says."

"She could have been kidnapped, not by aliens, but there's always the chance someone was waiting for her with a weapon and forced her to drive somewhere."

"Then where was his vehicle?" BJ asked, her face puckering as she thought hard about the crime scene. "How did he get to the diner? Was he on foot? Or did he come back for a car he'd hidden nearby that no one saw?" BJ was thinking aloud, her eyes focused on a corner of his desk, though Carter knew she was someplace else, envisioning what had happened to Sonja Hatchell.

"If she was kidnapped, and we don't know if that's the case, it might not have happened at the diner," Carter pointed out. "He could have forced her off the road somewhere—flagged her down or something—and forced his way into her car. Maybe she even let him in—it was late and that wasn't smart, but she might have thought she was helping someone stranded in the storm."

"Somewhere *he's* got a car or van or truck."

"Somewhere close to where she was taken. But it's been several days—he could have come back for it."

"How, by walking? In this cold? Or hitchhiking?"

"Or with an accomplice."

"Jesus, more than one guy?"

"It's possible," Carter said. "Sparks is working on that theory, too. He's even suggested that the State Police might talk to the press, see if they can help us. I agree with him." It was a thought that had been with Carter for a while. Reporters were usually a pain in the ass, always hanging around, looking for a scoop, speculating on what had happened. But at other times they helped rather than hindered an investigation, either warning the citizens of danger or asking the populace for help.

Left to his own devices, Carter would rather keep the Fourth Estate out of any investigation, but maybe it was time to ask for help from the local television, radio, and newspapers in order to find Sonja Hatchell. The State Police had already asked the public to come forward with any information they might have concerning her disappearance, only to learn that the last people to have seen her were Lou and his nephew, who worked at the diner. She seemed to have disappeared the moment she stepped outside after her shift.

"So if Sonja was forced back into her car and taken at gunpoint, she would have had to drive somewhere. How far could she get in a storm like that?"

"Her car had four-wheel drive."

"Doesn't mean it can get far on icy roads, a lot of which had been closed."

"You think this guy is a local?"

"Could be," BJ said, "and I have this feeling—call it gut instinct or feminine intuition, that Sonja's disappearance could be connected to the Jane Doe case."

Carter stopped wiggling the pencil and looked BJ straight in the eye. "Let's not call it feminine intuition, because I had the same hit. It's far-fetched, there's no link to the two women or cases."

"Except that both incidences are odd. Out of place for around here." BJ's nostrils flared slightly, as if she'd picked up a bad smell. "It's all too coincidental for me."

"The OSP isn't buying it. But I did talk to Sparks about a possible link. He's a good guy, won't just ignore it. He'll chew on the idea awhile. In the meantime, all the law enforcement agencies have been alerted and a be-on-the-lookout-for bulletin has been issued for Sonja and her car in Oregon, Washington, Idaho, and California. Sonja's picture's already been on the news." He drummed his fingers, was well aware of the time passing, the promise of even more bad weather, and the ever-slimming chances of finding Sonja alive.

"How's Lester?" BJ asked as she stretched out of the chair.

"Holding together. Barely. But he has to. For the kids."

"What a mess." BJ walked to the window, looked out in the direction of Danby's Furniture. "It's the damned weather. It's making everyone crazy."

"Is that what it is? And here I was blaming the water."

"Funny, Carter," she mocked, but managed to scare up a grin as she left his office. "Real funny."

"I thought so." But he was lying. The truth of the matter was that he didn't find anything funny these days. Nothing at all.

". . . I'll be sure to tell Robert you called," his secretary promised.

"Do that." Jenna hung up the phone. "Perfect." Once again, during a crisis, the kids' father was nowhere to be found. Once again, she'd handle things her way. Which would probably make things easier in the long run.

It was ten in the morning, and neither one of her girls was yet awake, but that was about to change. Jenna climbed the stairs quietly and passed Allie's room before rapping lightly on Cassie's door and pushing it open. The room was a mess. Even with the blinds drawn and the lights out, Jenna noticed that Cassie had peeled off last night's clothes and left them in a heap at the end of the bed. CDs and books were scattered over the floor, jars of makeup, fingernail polish, creams, and perfume cluttering up the desk and bookcases. Plates and glasses, soda bottles and empty cartons took up floor, desk, night-table, and window-ledge space. The wastebasket was overflowing.

Either Cassie was an inveterate slob, or she was depressed.

Probably a little of both. Which Jenna understood.

Cassie had suffered through her parents' separation and divorce. Moving to Oregon had been difficult for her. Nonetheless, there was no excuse for open rebellion and living like a pig.

"Cass, wake up," she said softly and sat on a corner of the rumpled bed.

She was rewarded by a confused growl coming from under the comforter.

"We need to talk."

"Now?" Cassie raised her head, opened a bleary eye, focused on the bedside table where her clock radio glowed red. Groaning, she grumbled, "Mom, I'm sooo tired."

"I imagine. But you know what I say about 'soaring with the eagles.'"

"Yeah, yeah . . . 'If you want to soar with the eagles at night, you have to rise with the sparrows the next morning.' It's a dumb saying."

"Yeah, but words we're going to live by. So come on downstairs before your sister wakes up."

"But it's sooo early."

"I don't think so. I'll make breakfast."

"Ugh." She sighed loudly, as if she were the most persecuted teenager on earth.

Oh, save me, Jenna thought, but stood and said, "You've got five minutes." She slid quickly out of the room and hurried down the stairs before her daughter could utter another syllable of protest. She wasn't as angry as she'd been last night, but still wanted to shake some sense into Cassie. What had the kid been thinking? *She wasn't, Jenna. That's the problem. Cassie's just a kid. She was just out joyriding and raising a little hell with her friends. Something you did more than once.*

Still, Cassie was on a course set straight for big trouble—life-altering, if not life-threatening, trouble—and it scared Jenna to death.

She was wiping up spilled coffee grounds when she heard her daughter's muffled footsteps on the stairs.

"Okay, so I'm awake," Cassie groused as she stepped barefoot onto the hardwood floor of the kitchen. She was wearing pajama bottoms that exposed her navel, a cropped-off flannel top, and a major pout. "Couldn't this wait?"

"It's waited too long already."

"Great." Yawning, she padded to the coffeepot, poured herself a cup, and plopped down at the table. "So talk."

"Can the attitude, Cass. I'm sick to the back teeth of it. Today I want you to clean your room, and I mean top to bottom, then I want you to call your dad and tell him everything about last night. I already tried to reach him, but he was 'out.' Maybe you'll have better luck. Besides, I think you should be the one to tell him what you've been doing. Then, once all that's accomplished, we'll discuss your social life."

"Meaning Josh."

"Right now, I'm not too crazy about him."

"You've never liked him," Cassie charged, sipping from her cup.

"It's not him—I've told you that—I don't like what's happening with *you*. What in the world were you doing sneaking out and going up to the Point?"

"It was no big deal."

"Tell that to Sheriff Carter."

Cassie leaned back in her chair. "He likes you, too, doesn't he?"

"What do you mean?"

"Come on, Mom, you're not stupid. The guy is turned on by you. Isn't it weird? All the male attention you get? Mr. Brennan. Mr. Settler. Now the cop. Geez, do you know how many of these local yokels are cruising the Internet, checking out your Web site and all the other ones dedicated to you? I bet even Hans rents your movies and . . . oh, shit . . ." She blinked quickly and swiped at her eyes, then sniffed loudly. "It was just so much easier in L.A."

"Maybe it was," Jenna allowed, "but you don't need to use foul language, and we're not talking about me or my Web site or the move. We're talking about you, your attitude, and your lies to me. You're going down the wrong path, Cassie, and I'm scared for you. Really scared. You could be making choices that will change your life forever."

"I'm okay," Cassie said, her eyes dry again, her chin jutted, lips folded over her teeth.

"Are you?" Jenna demanded, angry and worried and knowing she wasn't getting through to her daughter.

"You know, Mom, maybe this isn't all about me. You've been really uptight lately. But then you always are around Christmas."

That much was true. Ever since the tragedy surrounding

White Out, filmed during the holidays, Jenna had developed an aversion to anything remotely connected with Christmas.

Cassie leaned low in her chair, cradling her cup on her bare midriff. "Most families have fun around the holidays, you know? They have parties and Christmas trees, and go caroling and shopping and sledding."

"Is that what you want to do? Carol and shop and sled?" Jenna asked, pouring herself a cup of coffee and noticing that her hands were trembling slightly. *Get a grip. You can't bring Jill back. It was just an accident, remember?* But the niggling thought that what had happened in Colorado was more than a freak accident had always stayed with her, lingering at the edges of her mind, tinged with guilt that she'd survived while her baby sister had been killed.

"Maybe," Cassie said indifferently.

Jenna couldn't imagine her eldest daughter wearing a wool coat, a scarf wrapped around her neck as she walked down the frozen streets of Falls Crossing and happily caroled the neighborhood with *Silent Night* or *The First Noel*. No—it just didn't fit.

Cassie set her cup on the table. "Geez, I just want to have some fun. Is that so bad?"

Jenna stirred cream into her cup. "And sneaking out and going up to the site of a murder to get high is fun."

"Yeah!" Cassie leaned back in her chair and folded her arms under her breasts, stretching the skin of her abdomen. Her belly-button ring winked in the kitchen lights. "It beats hanging out here and doing nothing." She glanced longingly at the windows. "I'm so sick of this weather. I *am* gonna call Dad. He'll let me come home for Christmas."

Come home. Jenna's heart twisted as she took a chair across the table from her daughter. Cassie had never thought of this house as her home, still considered Southern California as where she belonged. "Maybe that would be a good idea," she said, hating the words. "In the meantime you can help me put up decorations around here. Now . . . let's talk about sex and drugs and alcohol."

Cassie groaned. "Do we have to?"

"Oh, yeah," Jenna said, taking a warming sip of her coffee. "We have to."

Carefully, he painted her face. Dipping his brush in the pallet, gently blending the flesh tones, he worked tirelessly. Music was playing, the score from *Bystander* reverberating from nearly twenty speakers that he'd wired throughout his own personal soundstage and workroom. He loved this music; it was his favorite, and as he looked up to the stage where mannequins were posed, he felt a sense of pride.

Most of the figures were dressed in perfect replicas of originals from his favorite Jenna Hughes movies. Some were still naked, waiting for the right costume, and all, so far, were faceless, no features distinguishable on their blank, bald heads. That part was changing.

He studied the stage where the women of his dreams stood motionless. Though not finished, he imagined them as perfect as they had been in Jenna's films.

Marnie Sylvane, the lonely schoolteacher of *Summer's End,* stood next to Katrina Petrova of *Innocence Lost.* Katrina had been Jenna's first movie; she was a teenager when she'd played the young prostitute. Facing away from Katrina was Anne Parks, the psychotic murderess of *Resurrection.* A little farther upstage was Paris Knowlton, the young, frightened mother from *Beneath the Shadows,* who shared the spotlight with Rebecca Lange, the downhill racer of the never-finished *White Out.* In the far corner, Zoey Trammel, an autistic woman of *A Silent Snow,* sat in the rocking chair that had been used in the movie and now, in his hands, Faye Tyler, a sexually adventurous woman of the seventies, was nearly finished. How much he'd accomplished in so little time!

And there was still so much to do. Soon, he would have to get rid of the corpse and the car. He had a plan, but had to wait for a while before he drove Faye . . . no . . . not Faye, just the cadaver which was the shell for his art. He had to drive the husk of Faye in the hatchback to the cliffs over-looking the Columbia River, then let it roll over the edge. The car wouldn't be found for a long, long while . . . if ever. The body, trapped inside, would stay in the river and slowly decompose.

Getting rid of her would be easy. All evidence destroyed. No muss. No fuss.

But sculpting and painting the faces, that was the difficult part of his mission. He just couldn't get the features right, no matter how hard he tried. It seemed impossible to capture Jenna Hughes's beauty. The faces he cast, from women who had a resemblance to her, never turned out quite to his lik-ing. They somehow cheapened her image and seemed ama-teurish.

Frowning at the mask in his hands, he worked even harder, feeling the sweat bead upon his brow despite the cool temperature. With a steady hand, he outlined the eye hole, making a thin black line around the lid where he would in-sert the lashes, imagining what his work would look like when the false eye, a perfect shade of green, would be in-serted. He already had the wig, shaped in the style Jenna wore as Faye Tyler, a chin-length bob with feathered bangs cut just beneath the eyebrow ridge.

He paused for a minute, set down his brush, and picked up his remote control. As he'd done a hundred times before, he clicked on the big-screen television he'd mounted into a far wall, then fast-forwarded the DVD of *Bystander* already inserted into the player. He knew exactly where the scene he wanted was—a close-up of Jenna Hughes's beautiful face. He found it easily and there she was, staring directly into the camera, her eyes taking on an erotic, catch-me-if-you-can spark, the hint of a smile pulling at the corners of lips tinted a soft rose . . .

His heartbeat accelerated as he imagined she was looking directly at him. Flirting with him. Teasing him. Enticing him. She wanted him. His gaze never leaving the screen, he hit the Play button. Watched as she carelessly tossed her hair away from her face, turned, and began walking . . . slowly away. The camera focused on her buttocks, covered by a swingy, light skirt and bare legs lifted by four-inch heels.

He trembled inside.

Licked his lips.

Waited.

Then it came. The second in time he lived for.

Slowly, Faye Tyler turned her head and looked over her shoulder.

He hit the Pause button. Studied that come-hither glance and felt his groin tighten, blood pumping furiously through his veins.

She was so perfect.

Tears filled his eyes as he stared at her unadorned beauty.

Softly he vowed, "You are my woman. Today. Tomorrow. Endlessly. I will come for you."

CHAPTER 21

The good news was that the storm had abated. Near-zero temperatures had warmed, and the digital display on his Blazer hovered in the low thirties.

The bad news was that another cold front, worse than the first, was on its way, and nothing was going to melt soon. Add to that the fact that, after nearly a week, there was no sign of Sonja Hatchell. He doubted she was alive, though he'd never admit it to Lester. At least not yet.

Carter drove along a winding stretch of road leading to Falls Crossing and listened to the police radio as the defroster in his Blazer worked overtime. He'd checked twice daily with the Oregon State Police and Sparks had kept him updated, but there was just nothing to report. They still had no idea who Jane Doe really was, even with the widened missing persons sweep; nor did they yet have a composite picture of the woman, either from the computers or by having an artist sculpt a face onto the bones. The alginate lead hadn't come up with anything, either, but the lab technicians had found traces of another substance in Jane Doe's hair, a fine little piece of plaster that made no sense whatsoever.

But it was something.

Not much, but something.

It was morning, the first light of dawn filtering through

the ice-crusted trees that lined this stretch of the highway, heavy snow piled high on the roadsides. He passed a few abandoned cars on his way into town, met a snowplow headed the opposite direction, and noticed a sanding crew not far behind. He was dog tired, a knot of tension twisting between his shoulder blades, and all the coffee in the world couldn't chase away the fatigue that had settled upon him.

He just couldn't sleep.

Maybe it was the weather.

Maybe it was Jane Doe and Sonja Hatchell.

And maybe it was Jenna Hughes, who had, though she didn't know it, invaded his life. He'd studied the note sent to her, made inquiries about her missing things, checked e-Bay and talked to the pawn shops in Portland, even looked up her fan sites online and come up with nothing. He'd checked with video rental and sales companies, asked for lists of customers who had asked for Jenna Hughes movies, but so far hadn't come up with anyone suspicious. Worse yet, though he wouldn't admit it to a soul, he'd started dreaming about her. Scenes from her movies had invaded his nights and he'd woken up sweating, hard as granite, and feeling every bit the fool he was.

He'd called her twice, and though she'd received no more threatening notes and no more of her personal items were missing, she had managed to get her security system and electronic gates working.

He drove into town where the street lamps were just winking off; colored holiday lights blazed in all the storefronts, and as he passed by the local theater, he automatically checked for Jenna's Jeep. There were no vehicles in the snow-covered lot, just a back-lit sign announcing tickets were on sale for the next play, *It's a Wonderful Life*, which would be performed near the end of December.

At the courthouse, he pulled into his reserved spot, braced himself, and headed inside. He grabbed a cup of coffee before settling into his office and sorting through reports, mail, phone messages, and e-mail.

BJ showed up around ten and seemed relieved. Her

daughter and friends had been cited with misdemeanors for their part in the party up at Catwalk Point. As it turned out, nothing was disturbed, none of the kids had any link to the crime, or so it seemed, and there was no harm done to the crime scene or the case. Sparks had decided to go easy on the group, citing the young ones with breaking the curfew and the older ones with contributing to the delinquency of a minor, then having the D.A. drop the charges in exchange for some community service. It seemed fair enough, though Carter feared it would do nothing to change any of the delinquents' behavior.

BJ, however, thought it was for the best. "No one was hurt, so the parents should deal with their own kids. Megan knows where Jim and I stand." Carter wasn't certain this was the right tack. He remembered interrogating Josh Sykes while the insolent kid had sat leaning back in the metal chair, his scraggly bearded chin belligerently thrust forward, eyes at half-mast, almost daring Carter to make a move that would result in a lawsuit. "I ain't sayin' nothin'," Josh had repeated over and over again, and Carter had wondered what Cassie Kramer saw in the young punk.

Now, BJ settled into the chair facing his desk, suddenly got to her feet, left the room, and returned with a cup of water which she poured around the near-dead plant on a corner of his desk. "This Christmas cactus should be blooming," she reprimanded. "Just give it a little TLC."

"Fresh out," Carter grumbled. "I just received the word on Vincent Paladin, the guy who stalked Jenna Hughes in the past."

"Yeah?"

"He's in Florida. On parole. Being a good boy and visiting his parole officer every week. He was in Tampa on the day the letter was mailed from Portland."

"He could have an accomplice."

Carter finished his coffee in a final gulp, then crushed the paper cup in his fingers. "Don't think so . . . these guys, stalkers, they're usually loners."

"So you're ruling him out?"

"I'm not ruling anyone out," he said quickly.

One of BJ's eyebrows arched. "Get up on the wrong side of bed this morning?"

"Don't I every morning?"

"Yeah, but lately it's been more obvious."

He snorted. "Maybe it's just that I don't like the cold."

"Then your mood isn't going to improve much, is it? The weather service claims we're in for a whole lot more of this. Guess we'd better get used to it."

Never, he thought, but kept his mouth shut.

The evening rehearsal had turned into a complete disaster. Two actors hadn't shown up—one woman claiming her car wouldn't start, another staying home because he was recovering from a sprained ankle after slipping and falling on the ice. The other cast members were alternately cold or hot, depending upon the whims of the furnace, and only a few remembered their lines. The piano seemed out of tune, and there were the continuous problems with the lighting and sound systems.

By the time the two-hour rehearsal was over and the last of the would-be performers had left the theater, Jenna was ready to tear out her hair. She'd volunteered as the acting coach and after tonight, regretted the decision. Why had she agreed to help Rinda put on this production? What kind of masochist was she? Was she so desperate to fit into this community that she'd put herself through this torture for the next few weeks? *Never again*, she silently vowed as she and the rest of the staff were gathering their things and discussing the performance.

Blanche, at the piano near the stage, was picking up her things while Lynnetta, who was hemming a costume, sat in a back pew. Wes and Scott were presumably overhead, working on the faulty lights, while Jenna, Rinda, and Yolanda Fisher sat on the edge of the stage where once there had been a pulpit.

"That wasn't so bad, was it?" Blanche said, picking up her sheet music from the piano and pressing it into a folder.

"No," Rinda said glumly. "'Bad' would be an improvement."

Blanche zipped the sheet music into a leather briefcase. "Oh, that's what you always say about this time in each production."

"For what it's worth, I agree." Yolanda Fisher was wrapping a magenta-colored scarf around her short-cropped curls. Yolanda, a lithe Afro-American woman, gave dance lessons in the theater on Tuesday and Thursday nights, and sold insurance during the day. Tonight, she'd volunteered to help with the blocking. "It was worse than bad." She swathed the ends of her scarf around her neck. "'Pathetic' would best describe it. Not that I'm criticizing."

"Humph!" Blanche pursed lips tinged a washed-out red, as her lipstick had faded sometime during the first act. "What do you think, Jenna?"

"That we need divine intervention?"

Rinda and Yolanda laughed, and even Wes, hidden somewhere in the rafters as he worked on the lights, chuckled, but Lynnetta frowned as she broke the thread she'd been using with her teeth, and Scott, Rinda's son, if he was still helping with the sound system, remained silent. Jenna felt her skin crawl a little, which was ridiculous, but she couldn't stop herself from looking toward the high ceiling with its darkened beams and hidden niches. Once there had been a choir balcony, crying room for young mothers with babies, and a couple of small closets in the converted attic space. Above the balcony, accessed by stairs, rose the belltower, a tall spire that, in Jenna's estimation, should have been condemned twenty years earlier.

Blanche let out a puff of disgust. "I would think you all know this kind of thing just takes time and practice, practice, practice." She pulled on her beret and a pair of leather gloves.

"You're right," Jenna agreed. "Practice will help." Inwardly she thought they also needed a little more talent and a lot more dedication. However, this was a local production, the actors were unpaid, and the proceeds of the ticket sales were to be added to the fund to improve the theater and pay some of the staff, so no one could really complain.

Yolanda said, "I'm outta here. See y'all later," as she made a quick exit out a side door to the parking lot.

Lynnetta jabbed her needle into a pincushion and folded the dress over her arm. "I think we should give the actors a break and chill out. Blanche is right. We all get nervous around this time."

"Too true," Rinda admitted as the furnace kicked into overdrive, rumbling loudly as it forced hot air through the ancient pipes. "Okay, let's put this behind us. One step at a time. We rehearse again in two days. Let's hope *all* the actors show up."

"Oh, I'm sure they will." Blanche took off her pink Keds and stepped into fur-lined suede boots that just covered her ankles. "Have faith!" She smiled then at her own little joke, though her lips didn't seem to have any mirth as they stretched across her teeth. "Oh, I guess that line's been said a time or two in here." She slid her briefcase from the piano bench. "I'll see you all in a couple of days. Seven o'clock, right?"

Rinda nodded. "Weather permitting."

"Oh, honey, I don't think the weather is going to permit anything this winter." Blanche offered another flat smile and, heels of her boots clicking on the hardwood floor, left the theater.

"What's her problem?" Wes called from overhead before he clomped down the stairs at the base of the belltower and appeared at a rear exit of the stage.

"She always tries to be upbeat," Rinda said.

Jenna wasn't sure. There was more to the piano teacher than met the eye. Blanche lived alone with five cats, three pianos, a house full of Depression glass, and stacks of paperback books. She'd been married, but no one knew if she was divorced, widowed, or just separated. Or if there ever really had been a husband or the son she'd alluded to occasionally. A talented musician, she was a little on the eccentric side. And, in Jenna's estimation, not necessarily "upbeat."

"I think we should all try to be more positive." Lynnetta smoothed the dress she'd folded and placed it into a small athletic bag.

"Okay, okay." Nodding, Rinda shoved her hair from her eyes. "You're right. This is just the first real rehearsal— everyone will improve." She glanced at her watch and her eyes widened. "Damn. It's late. The dog's been shut in the house all day. I've got to run." Her gaze swept the theater. "Scott!" she yelled toward the rafters. "Let's go." There was no immediate response, and Rinda turned to her brother. "Wasn't he with you?"

Wes nodded. "Earlier. But I haven't seen him since the second act."

"Scott!" Rinda yelled.

Jenna looked upward to all the darkened areas. "Hey, bud. Get a move on!"

Still no response.

"He didn't leave, did he?" Rinda pushed herself off the stage and walked to one of the tall, arched windows. She found a clear spot in the stained glass and peered out to the darkened parking lot. "My car's still outside."

"He wouldn't have left," Lynnetta said, but she didn't seem certain.

"Scott?" A note of worry sounded in Rinda's voice. "Scott!"

"He was in the audio booth half an hour ago. I'll go check." Wes was already flying up the stairs and Jenna told herself there was no reason to get worked up. Scott was always out of step, just a little out of sync with the rest of the world. But Rinda was working her way up to an emotional point somewhere between irritation and panic.

"Not up here!" Wes called down over the speaker system, his voice reverberating through the vast room. "Scott . . . you're M.I.A. and your mom wants to leave!"

"He's got to be here," Rinda said, heading for the stairs leading behind the stage to the basement dressing area when he appeared in the doorway. "Oh! God, you scared me," Rinda cried, a hand flying up to cover her heart.

"I thought you were looking for me." Scott's pimply face was the picture of innocence. Around his neck dangled a set of headphones from which rap music was audible several feet away.

"I was, but . . . where the devil were you?"

"Downstairs, cleaning . . . isn't that what you wanted me to do?"

"Oh . . . Well . . . Yes . . . I guess," she said, slightly confused. "Look, it doesn't matter, and it's late—let's get a move on . . ." Rinda's anger dissipated as she threw on her coat and hat, then shepherded her son out the door.

Jenna grabbed her things and followed, leaving Wes and Lynnetta to lock up.

Outside, the night was calm, nerve-stretchingly so, only a few snowflakes falling from a dark, starless sky. Hands in her pockets, Jenna glanced back at the theater with its tall spire and narrow stained-glass windows and felt a chill as deep as the night. Her eyes were drawn upward, to the top of the tower and the sharp roof where once church bells had tolled. She saw a movement, a fleeting shadow, and had the strange feeling that something or someone was standing in the tower, hiding in the frigid darkness, staring down at her.

But that was nuts.

Paranoid.

No one was in the theater but Wes and Lynnetta . . . unless Wes had quickly climbed the rickety stairs to the top of the spire.

She was about to say something to Rinda and Scott, but they had already climbed into their car. Scott was behind the wheel and Rinda gave a quick wave as they eased out of the parking lot. Once at the street, Scott gunned it and the car fishtailed before settling into the right lane. Twenty-four years old and acting as if he were sixteen, the kind of kid whose emotional growth had been stunted somehow and had never really matured. Still living at home with an overprotective mother.

Who are you to criticize—think about your own daughter. Cassie's not exactly an angel.

Jenna unlocked her Jeep and slid inside.

She'd just pulled out of the parking lot when her cell phone jangled. She picked it up and eased down the street. "Hello?"

"Mom, can you pick up a pizza?" Allie asked.

She smiled at the sound of her younger daughter's voice. "You know, that would be a good idea. If the pizza parlor's open."

"And can I go to Dani's?"

"Now?" She glanced at the clock. Nine-thirty. "Isn't there school tomorrow?"

"I mean after school. Tomorrow."

"You have piano lessons I think, depending on the weather."

"I *hate* piano lessons."

A picture of Blanche in her beret and boots galloped through Jenna's mind. The woman was a couple of steps beyond odd. "How about on Friday, if it's okay with Mr. Settler?"

"Oh, you're supposed to call him."

"Am I?"

"Yeah—he called."

"When?"

"Uhhhhh . . . after you left."

"Tonight?"

"Yeah."

"I'll call him back and we'll get things straight about the weekend," she said as she pulled up to a stop sign, then looked down the street. "Hey, you're in luck. Martino's is open. What would you like?"

"Pepperoni."

"And—?"

"Just pepperoni."

"Okay, put Cassie on the phone and I'll see if she wants anything else."

"She's in the shower."

"Pepperoni it is," Jenna said. "I'll be home soon."

Jenna clicked off her cell and pulled into the snow-plowed lot, where she parked between a black van and a red pickup with tires so big it could have entered in one of those monster-truck competitions. Music was blaring from the speakers, a bass thrumming so loudly that even though the windows were only barely cracked, the hip-hop song vibrated through the air. Three boys wearing backward-facing baseball caps sat inside the king cab, laughing, talking, and smoking.

One of the kids was Josh Sykes.

Jenna's good mood evaporated. She considered confronting him right then and there, but decided against it. Humiliating him in front of his friends would serve no purpose. Biting her tongue, she hiked the collar of her ski jacket tighter, hurried inside, and ordered her pizza and a Diet Coke.

While waiting for the pizza, she took a seat in one of the empty booths and sipped her soda. Two other booths were occupied, but no one so much as glanced in her direction. *Anonymity*, she thought, savoring the feeling of freedom it brought.

Within minutes, Josh and his friends, carbon copies of each other, sauntered in. Jenna's peace of mind dissipated immediately.

One of the boys, dressed in baggy jeans, serious gold chains, and a jacket three sizes too big, leaned an elbow on the counter and tried to flirt with the girl taking orders; another propped himself against the windows and stared outside as if he were waiting for someone, and Josh, spotting Jenna, had the good sense to quit joking around. Their gazes clashed and she thought she saw his Adam's apple bobble a bit before he donned his usual I-don't-give-a-crap-about-anything demeanor.

She supposed she should leave well enough alone, but she couldn't. Not when an opportunity like this dropped into her lap. Leaving her soft drink sweating on the table, she sauntered up to Cassie's punk of a boyfriend. "Hi, Josh."

He didn't respond until she was standing directly in front of him. "Hullo."

"How are you doing?"

A wariness flashed in his eyes. He didn't trust her friendliness one bit. So maybe he wasn't as stupid as she'd thought. "Fine. Just gettin' a pizza."

"Me, too." She glanced at his two friends, who had turned to face the confrontation. "Why don't you come over to my booth where we can talk. I'll buy you a soda."

"I'm, uh, not thirsty."

"Then just come over for a few minutes, okay? Since we're both here waiting. It's a little like fate, wouldn't you say?"

He didn't. Just followed her to the table while his friends tried to swallow their smirks. Jenna didn't care. She was trying to keep her cool, knew that flying off the handle would only make him defensive and angry, and those emotions, running rampant in a kid his age, would only serve to make him want to prove her wrong and go against whatever law or threat she laid down. So, despite the fact that her blood was boiling and she wanted to wring his scruffy neck, she motioned him into a seat and sat opposite him. "You're sure you don't want anything?"

"Nah." He looked down at his clasped hands. Set them on the table. Almost like he was praying.

"Okay, so here's the deal. I know you care about Cassie and she cares about you."

He looked up to see if she was joking. She wasn't.

"So it seems to me that you'd want to take care of her, kind of protect her." She had to force the words out; they clogged her throat because the last thing she believed in was a man protecting a woman. And Josh was the least likely white knight she'd ever come across.

"Yeah . . ." he said tenuously, as if he didn't believe what he was hearing.

"So, I'd think that you'd want what's best for her and, you know, asking her to sneak out and go to the scene of a crime

and then drink and use drugs . . . it's just not the best thing."
She tried hard to keep the sarcasm out of her words, but a little slipped through.

"We weren't doing anything wrong," he said, then caught
the warning look in her eye and changed his tack. "We
wanted to have some fun, that's all."

"I know." She said it as if she believed it. Josh's problem
was his lack of imagination, of coming from a family that
didn't give a damn about him, and boredom at the prospect
of what was the rest of his life, though he couldn't seem to
see beyond the signposts of this small town. "But the kind of
fun where you're doing dangerous things, or chancing being
arrested—that's not what's best for Cassie. Or for you. Look,
I'm going to be honest here, okay? I was really angry at
Cassie and at you, but I'm trying not to go off the deep end
and do anything that all of us would regret."

He glanced up again and she held his gaze steadily, made
sure he understood her intent, that beneath her empathetic
words, there was a veiled threat. Josh needed to know that
legally she had the upper hand and that she knew it. "So let's
all try to work this out. Come over to the house. Visit Cass.
Take her out, but no more sneaking out, okay? It's just not
safe and I'm sure the last thing you would want to do is compromise Cassie's safety and well-being."

"Yeah . . . but . . ."

"Pizza for Hughes," the girl behind the counter said, and
Jenna rose quickly.

"Thanks, Josh," she said, leaving her barely touched soda
and an astounded Josh in the booth. She forced a smile that
would have won her an Academy Award on Josh's two
friends, then scooped up the cardboard box and left
Martino's.

So she'd had a run-in with Josh; she was certain it wouldn't
be her last.

CHAPTER 22

Snow was falling again, blowing in windy swirls.

Jenna managed to climb into her rig and start the Jeep's engine. Once she'd reversed out of Martino's parking lot, she chanced another glance at the window of the pizza parlor. All three boys were now staring at her through the cold, frosty glass. No wonder she'd felt their gazes drilling into her back.

With a wave, and a smile as fake as fool's gold, she drove away. "Horny, self-involved idiots," she muttered through her plastered-on grin, then silently chastised herself for being a fraud. Yet she'd always lived by the credo of catching more flies with sugar than vinegar, so she didn't beat herself up about being two-faced. "A means to an end," she reminded herself, and the end was Cassie's safety and well-being.

As she passed the courthouse, a three-storied, yellow-and-brown brick building constructed nearly a hundred years earlier, she glanced at the glowing windows, picked out the one that belonged to Carter, and noticed the lamps were burning. Of the few cars parked in the lot, she picked out his Chevy Blazer. So he was still on the job. She'd heard that about him, that he worked around the clock, that ever since his wife had died he'd thrown himself into his job.

Local gossip had it that his wife was the victim of a one-car accident that had occurred during another harsh winter, but Jenna tried to temper every rumor she heard as being embellished over the years.

She flipped on her wipers, as the snow was coming down steadily now. Fiddling with the radio, she was hoping to find a weather report and instead landed upon a static-riddled Jimmy Buffett tune that conjured up hot sand, tropical water, and frothy drinks.

It sounded like heaven.

She hummed along. Her cell phone rang and she expected that Allie, whose patience was sometimes close to nil, was calling and checking on the pizza. She flipped open her phone and saw an L.A. phone number.

Robert.

Her stomach dropped as she answered. "Hello?"

"Hi, Jen." Robert's smooth baritone was interrupted by static. "I hear . . . we . . . trouble . . . Cassie called . . . and . . ."

"Robert, I can't hear you. You're breaking up."

". . . damned cell . . . call . . ." His words were spotty and crackled.

"Can you hear me?"

". . . breaking . . ."

"Yeah, you're breaking up, too. I'll call you back . . . when I get home to a land line. Got it?"

". . . Cass . . ."

"I can't hear you!" she shouted as she reached a sharp corner and slowed down without hitting the brakes. The tires slid and she swung wide, into the oncoming lane. "Damn!" She dropped the phone and it slid onto the floor. The pizza carton, too, careened onto the passenger-side floor mats.

Adrenaline shot through her system as she tightened her grip over the wheel and rode out the slide, swerving as she eased back into her lane, where the tires slid again. "Oh, God," she whispered as she shifted down, slowing the engine, feeling the tires try to grip. The cell phone crackled. She let it die and concentrated on the road, an icy ribbon of asphalt.

Snow was falling harder now, and she carefully flipped on the wipers. The cell phone rang again. She ignored it. Robert could call back or not. She didn't really care. She just needed to get home in one piece. Besides, she was used to being a single parent. It had been nearly a week since Cassie had been caught sneaking out and her father had finally deigned to return her call. What a guy!

She had the Jeep under control finally, but her blood was still pounding, her nerves stretched tight as the road dipped and curved, edging ever closer to the Columbia River, a fierce, dark snake of frigid water tumbling madly through the gorge.

She couldn't wait to get home, to stoke the fire, to bite into a piece of tangy pizza topped with stringy cheese and spicy pepperoni.

Maybe she'd take a bath and read the paperback she had at her bedside.

Headlights flashed in her rearview mirror.

Thank God. At least she was no longer alone. Some other idiot was driving along this isolated stretch of road winding by the river. It was comforting somehow.

She glanced back, squinting as the vehicle behind her accelerated fast, its headlights on high beam, blinding as they drew near.

Jenna took the next corner. The vehicle—a truck?—lagged behind as she took a corner, then straightened out.

On the straightaway, things changed. Quickly. The vehicle behind bore down on her. Fast. Too fast for the icy conditions. "What in the world?" Jenna lightly touched her brakes. A warning for the driver to back off. No such luck. Bright headlights dimmed off and on, flashing back. As if it were some kind of game.

The driver was messing with her? When the roads were freezing? But that was crazy.

Heart pounding with fear, she thought of Josh Sykes. Had she embarrassed him in front of his friends and now he was getting his jollies by scaring her half to death? This was nuts. The car behind was so close, its headlights blinding. Jenna slowed down, hoping the guy would take a hint. No. He just hung on her bumper, begging for an accident.

"Cretin," Jenna muttered, beginning to sweat. She thought of all the warnings about predators who intentionally rear-ended a woman alone in a car to force her to pull over. When the potential victim took the bait and stopped, hopping out of her car, intent on reaming the guy out and offering to exchange insurance information, she was abducted at gun- or knife-point, to disappear or be found later, raped or dead.

Don't panic!

Jenna's jaw tightened.

She thought of the note she'd received, of the feeling she couldn't shake that she was being watched, of the horrible fact that one woman's body had been found in the mountains and another local woman had gone missing.

Stop it. This is just some idiot kid—probably Josh and those jerks he calls friends.

She licked her lips and glanced again in the mirror. Fear pounded through her bloodstream. *Hang in there. Be smart.*

But the guy just kept coming.

She accelerated.

He kept up with her.

Trees and mile signs flashed by.

She slowed down.

Felt a bump.

Her bones jarred.

"No!" She gripped the wheel but the Jeep's tires slid.

Oh, Christ!

Another car, driving the opposite direction. Jenna flashed her lights madly, but it flew by. Where could she go? Anywhere she pulled in, he might follow. No, she couldn't stop.

Bam!

He hit her again. Harder this time.

"Son of a bitch," she growled as the Jeep started to spin. She started to put on the brakes, then eased into the turn, feeling the wheels grip as her heart beat crazily.

Think, Jenna, think. Are you going to lead whoever it is back to your house?

The sheriff's department was in the opposite direction and she didn't have enough gas to make it into Troutdale . . . oh, God . . . She wasn't far from the turnoff to her home, and the cell phone was in the car, though out of reach on the floor of the passenger seat beneath the pizza box. She couldn't risk reaching down for it.

But the moron behind you doesn't know you dropped it.

She could fake him out. Maybe.

Thinking she was out of her mind but praying her ruse would work, she took her right hand off the wheel and fished through her purse. With one eye on the road, she retrieved her small black garage door opener and held it in front of her, pretended to punch out buttons on her "phone," then held the palm-sized gadget to her ear. Hopefully the guy with his intense headlights would see what she was doing, yet not realize she was faking it. As she drove, she nodded, moving her mouth, making up a fake conversation, and sweating bullets.

Maybe the driver of the vehicle behind her was just a bad driver.

And maybe pigs really do fly.

She glanced in her rearview mirror again.

Was it her imagination or had the truck slowed down?

Dear God, please.

She swallowed hard. The turnoff to the county road that wandered past her house was less than a mile away. She was still pretending to talk on the phone as the road wound down a hillside. Still the vehicle behind her lagged. "Good, you bastard. Back off," she said into her garage door opener. Around a final curve in the road, and the Jeep slid only slightly before straightening.

She glanced in the mirror.

Nothing.

No headlights.

Yet.

She punched the accelerator, expected to see the glare of the vehicle at any second.

But the darkness of the night surrounded her.

She reached the turnoff to the county road alone.

No headlights followed, and though she turned off the radio, she heard no sound of another vehicle's engine over the rumble of her Jeep.

Had whoever was following her turned off?

Or was he following her without headlights?

That's ridiculous.

Yet her skin crawled at the thought, and she squinted hard into the rearview mirror.

Hadn't she thought someone had been watching her from the belltower of the theater? Could that hidden someone have left the building, watched her drive to the pizza parlor, and followed her? But why?

To terrorize you. Just like he did with the note.

"But he's gone," she said, then realized she was talking to herself. Not a good sign. One more quick glance in all the mirrors told her she was alone on the road.

Whoever had been following her had turned off.

And there was a chance that he'd just been a bad driver, one who tailgated, one who inadvertently hit his bright lights . . .

And your bumper? Yeah, right!

Her attention split between the road ahead and the dark night behind her, she turned on the county road leading to her home, taking the corner faster than she would have if her nerves hadn't been stretched tight, and fishtailed around the corner. Once the Jeep had straightened and the tires grabbed the road again, she punched the accelerator up a final rise and over a hill until she spied the open gates at the end of her driveway.

Gates that should have been closed, now that they were working again, Hans having melted the ice and reconnected the faulty wires.

Again her heart clutched. What if someone had gotten inside? Someone with bad intentions? *Don't be nuts. They've been open for eighteen months without incident. You're just borrowing trouble!*

She drove past the rock pillars and on the far side, hit the

button on her electronic remote. With a whir, the gates
started to close behind her. Another poke of the garage door
opener and the heavy door lifted. As she pulled in, she
caught a glimpse of Allie standing in the kitchen, backlit by
the overhead lights. She was waving frantically, and before
Jenna could get out of the car, she was racing outside, across
the breezeway, wearing only her pajamas and slippers.
Critter was bounding beside her, his entire body wiggling at
the sight of Jenna.

"Are you crazy?" Jenna demanded of her daughter as
Allie opened the side door to the garage. "Go into the house
and get your jacket and boots!" She was hauling her purse
and the pizza out of the car while sidestepping the exuberant
dog.

"But I'm hungry," Allie protested, launching herself at
the pizza carton and nearly flattening Jenna in the process.

"I'm getting it to you as quickly as I can. Come on, back
into the house. Both of you!" She shepherded her daughter
and dog into the kitchen, where warm air hit her in a welcome blast. "What're you thinking, Allie?"

Cassie, seated in a chair with her feet propped up on the
hearth in the den, was flipping through a magazine. "Sometimes she doesn't think, Mom," she said.

"At least I don't sneak out." Allie was already pulling the
pizza box from Jenna's arms.

"You're too dorky to even think about it."

"Enough!" Jenna said, in no mood for the girls' petty
bickering. "What went on tonight?"

"Nothing," Cassie said. "As usual."

"That's a lie." Allie lifted the lid to the pizza box and
flipped it open to display a gooey mess. All the cheese and
pepperoni had run off the crust to pool along one side of the
box, and the pizza itself was a bare crust with streaks of red
marinara sauce running off it. "Yuk, what happened?"

"I had to brake hard and the box slid off the seat."

Allie wrinkled her nose. "It looks gross."

"Yeah, it does, but it tastes the same." Jenna didn't need
this argument. Not tonight.

Cassie dropped her magazine and walked to the table where the pizza was congealing. "Mom's right," she said, and Jenna nearly fell through the floor. She couldn't remember the last time her older daughter agreed with her on anything. Cassie pulled a gooey slice from the box, plopped the cheese and a couple of slices of meat onto it, and took a bite. "It's great."

Allie was still guarded, but emulated her older sister and grabbed a naked slice.

"Okay, so tell me what's happened since I left. Hans is gone?"

"Yeah, he fed and watered the horses, then took off. He let me help." Allie was winding strings of mozzarella around the bare crust of her piece of the pizza.

"Good. Anything else? Anyone phone?"

"Travis Settler called and he said he'd call back," Cassie said. "And there were a couple of hangups. No caller ID— private calls. I tried dialing star sixty-nine, but that didn't help. I figure it was probably a bad cell phone connection."

"Probably," Jenna said, though it worried her. She was still jittery from the drive home. "Let me answer the phone if we get any more calls."

Cassie sighed loudly and, carrying her slice of pizza on a napkin, returned to her chair and magazine.

Allie had already zoned out of the conversation and between bites was decorating the remaining pizza with bits of pepperoni.

"What about your dad?"

"What about him?" Cassie asked.

"He didn't call?"

She shook her head, took her seat in the chair, and began thumbing through the magazine again. "Wait a minute. There was one call that Allie took."

"Allie?" Jenna said.

"What?" Her daughter looked up from her masterpiece of food art.

"Did Dad call?"

"Tonight? No."

"Another night?"

"Yeah."

"You didn't say anything."

"I guess I forgot."

"When was it?"

A lift of a small shoulder. "I don't know . . . yesterday, I think. Maybe the other day."

"Did he want to talk to me?"

Allie bit her lip and winced. "Yeah."

So Robert wasn't the flake she'd thought. She felt slightly better about her ex. "You need to tell me about all calls you take for me, okay? Or write them down."

"Okay," Allie mumbled.

"But another call came through tonight. Who was it?"

"Some guy."

The hairs on the back of Jenna's neck raised. "What guy?"

"I don't know. He said he'd call back."

"Did he say what he wanted?" Jenna asked, trying to keep the fear from her voice.

"No. Just wanted to talk to you and asked where you were and I said I didn't know."

Full-blown panic erupted. "Wait a minute, you gave a stranger information that you were here alone?"

"Uh-uh." Allie shook her head. "I wasn't alone. Hans and Ellie and Cassie were here, too. So when he asked if I was here by myself I told him 'no.'" She stuck out her chin, but her lower lip wobbled a bit. "I'm not an idiot, Mom."

"Of course not."

Cassie snorted. "Don't ever give out *any* information. Didn't you learn that before when that Paladin creep in L.A. was stalking Mom?"

"This was different!" Allie insisted, but Jenna was suddenly worried sick. The note. The feeling someone was following her . . . watching her. The missing things at the theater.

"Why weren't the gates closed?" she asked, trying to keep her cool.

"The electronic mechanism messed up again. Hans tried

to fix it," Cassie said, tossing her magazine aside and looking up at Jenna as if she'd finally sensed the undercurrent of worry in Jenna's tone. "What is it, Mom?"

"I think we should try to be a little more secure."

Cassie's eyes narrowed. "This is so I can't sneak out, isn't it?" she charged.

"Hey, Cass! It's *never* okay for you to sneak out. We don't have to discuss it again. But remember, I got a weird fan letter the other day."

"Just how weird was it?" Cassie demanded.

"Weird enough."

Allie was suddenly disinterested in the pizza, her little-girl's fear antennae activated. "The guy that wrote it, you think he was the one who called here?" she asked, furrows etching her brow. She bit her lip anxiously.

"I don't know," Jenna admitted, as she walked through the house and locked every door and window. "I just don't know."

Allie puppy-dogged her. "Are we safe here?"

"Of course," Jenna said, but in her heart, she didn't believe it. Not for a second.

CHAPTER 23

"Do I have to?" Cassie complained as Jenna handed her the phone. The last thing she wanted to do was have it out with her father.

"Absolutely!"

Cassie wanted to squirm out of it, but she dialed her dad's phone and walked into the den, turning her back on her mother as Robert answered gruffly. She bolstered herself. "Hi, Daddy."

"Cass."

His voice had a hint of emotion in it and Cassie suddenly missed him terribly. She knew he'd been a jerk of a husband, and sometimes a crummy dad, but he was all she had.

"What's going on?"

Her throat thickened. God, she didn't want to disappoint him. Sighing and wiping back tears, she said, "I guess I screwed up." And then she told him the story. All of it . . . well, she kept out the fact that they'd been smoking weed and making out . . . no reason to send him into orbit . . . but she told him the rest, including the part about sneaking out with Josh, visiting the crime scene, and being hauled home by the sheriff.

All the time he didn't say a word.

"That's it?" he asked when she was finished.

"Yeah."

"Learn anything?"

"Not to get caught?" she tried to joke, though tears ran down her cheeks.

"Well, I think you know better. Try to give your mom a break, would you?"

"Yeah." She sniffed loudly. "Do you . . . do you think I could come home?"

A pause.

Cassie's heart crumbled.

"For Christmas?"

"I meant for—"

"I'd love it!" he cut in before she could admit that she wanted to move back to L.A. for good. "The deal is, we're planning to go to Tammy's folks' vacation house for a few days. They've got a place in Tahoe, and I haven't been skiing for years." *Not since the accident during the filming of* White Out , she thought. "But I could check, see if there's room . . ." He let his voice fade away and Cassie swallowed back more tears. He was trying to nicely get out of having her come. He didn't say it, but having his daughter visit was inconvenient.

"Mom wants me and Allie here anyway—it probably wouldn't work."

"Maybe spring break . . . oh, hell, that won't work. I've got a new project and we'll start filming in March. Maybe I could find a couple of days to visit you. We're shooting in Vancouver, B.C. Or you girls could fly up!" He said it with such enthusiasm. As if he meant it. He probably did. Right now. "I'll work it out with your mom. Promise. So . . . you don't give her any more trouble."

"Sure," she said, and managed not to sniff, not to let him know how much she hurt.

"So, is everything okay?"

Okay? Was he crazy? "Yeah," she lied. But it wasn't okay. It never would be.

"That's my girl. Should I talk to your mom?"

"Nah." She shook her head as if he could see through the phone lines.

"Okay. I'll call soon. Love you . . . Oh, is Allie up? I should say something to her."

That burned Cassie. Of course he should! "I'll get her." She walked into the kitchen and mumbled, "Dad wants to talk to you," as she handed Allie the receiver; then, before anyone said another word, before she broke down completely, she flew up the stairs to her room and threw herself onto the bed. She wouldn't cry. *Wouldn't.* Not when her mother or sister could hear. Still the tears kept flowing, hot and wet, from her eyes.

She hurried into her bathroom, locked the door, and turned on the radio as loud as it would blare. She ran the shower and faucet, then held a wet towel over her face and let out little, tiny sobs, just enough to release some of the anguish, but not enough that anyone could hear her pain.

"Bastard," she whispered as she thought of her father. The trouble was, she loved him. Somehow, she'd have to find a way to stop that ridiculous emotion. He didn't care about her, not really. Hadn't even fought for custody during the divorce. What a wuss! Sniffing, she dabbed at her eyes. Robert Kramer wasn't worth all this torture.

What about Josh?

Good question. And a tough one.

If you still lived in L.A., would you even look twice at a boy like Josh Sykes? Or would you consider him someone to avoid, a person swimming in the shallow end of the gene pool?

"Oh God, I don't know."

Sure you do. Think about Mike Cavaletti and Noel Fedderson and Brent Elders . . .

The boys she'd secretly thought were cool in Southern California. Tanned, smart, privileged, going places . . .

"Snobs," she said under her breath.

Like you. Deep down, aren't you one of them? How would you like your friends in L.A. to see you with Josh, up in the snow at a crime scene . . . thrown in the back of a sheriff's car and dragged back to face your mother like a criminal . . .

"Crap, crap, crap!" she said, suddenly angry with her situation, her family, and the whole damned world. Stripping off her clothes, she stepped into the shower and let the hot spray tumble over her face and down her body. She was tired of her mother telling her what to do, her sister being such a dork, her father avoiding them altogether, and Josh pressuring her into doing things she wasn't sure she wanted to.

"So do something about it," she growled. What was that corny expression—*Today is the first day of the rest of your life*—or something like that? Close enough. Tonight, she planned to adopt it. It was time she took care of herself. The hell with everyone else. Because when it came right down to it, no one knew her, understood her, or really cared. Even Josh. *Especially Josh!*

From now on, it was time to look after *Numero Uno.*

Carefully he trained his binoculars on the compound. From his blind hidden high in the ice-encrusted branches, he focused. The gates were closed, the lights of the house blazing. Jenna and her children had been huddled in the kitchen area. She was worried. She'd stolen glances outside, snapping the shutters closed and cutting off his view.

Don't, he thought, but could do nothing from here.

Open them, he silently commanded, moving his gaze frantically from room to darkened room, but she didn't pass by a clear window, wasn't visible to him.

Anger surged through his blood.

Don't close me out. Please . . .

His mind wound backward, tripping over memories of cold winters and slammed doors. Even after "the incident," as it was later called, the doors had been locked to him.

"Mama, no!" he said out loud, startling himself.

He was shivering, remembering the slow, ugly sound of ice cracking. He and Nina had been walking across the frozen lake that shimmered silver in the moonlight, oblivi-

ous to anything but each other as a canopy of stars winked
high in the heavens. He felt the warmth of her bare hand
through his glove, noticed the flounce of her nightgown as it
floated around her small, white ankles. Her black hair was
mussed and tangled and her eyes promised delights he could
only imagine. They'd kissed. A lot. He glimpsed her breast
through the placket of her nightgown, small . . . round . . .
with a beguiling, dark tip that was hard with the cold.

"Come with me," he'd said earlier, after tapping on her
bedroom window. She'd opened the latch quickly and
slipped through the window, leaving her baby sister snoring
softly in the top bunk. Silently hushing him, she'd placed a
finger to his lips, and he'd grinned, waited for her to pull on
her fur-lined slippers, then took hold of her hand and led her
swiftly into the woods.

Together they'd run through the snow . . . free from the
fierce glares, angry words, and bone-crushing hands that
slapped fast and quick, without provocation.

The night air was fresh and cold, unmarred by the smells
of stale breath, cigarette smoke, and not-quite-empty whiskey
bottles. Stars and moonlight were their guides.

They were free.

If only until dawn.

He didn't care how little time they had, as long as they
were together. Young. Strong. "Come on, Nina," he urged,
tugging on her arm. They ran to the lake and she laughed. It
was the purest sound he'd ever heard, tinkling through the
midnight forest as they reached the shore and stepped onto
the steady ice. She nearly slipped right then and he caught
her, tangled with her, felt his heart beat a primal tattoo that
was as exhilarating as it was frightening.

Aside from the soft hush of a breeze, the night was silent,
a few lights shining from cabins tucked into the woods,
docks jutting out into the ice, a forgotten canoe now frozen
solid at the nearest pier. He touched her hair, stared into the
wonder of her face.

Tossing her head back, she teased, "Bet you can't catch
me."

He gave her a squeeze. "I've already got you."

"Not for long." As slippery as an eel, she wiggled away from him and began running, feet slipping wildly, black hair caught in the wind.

"Wait!" he cried, but she ignored him and he had to give chase, farther and farther from the snow-drifted banks, across the frozen water. He knew it could be dangerous. How often had his mother warned him to avoid the lake as she'd closed the door? But tonight the lake was magic. Black magic.

Of course, he caught her and she, laughing, chilled to the bone, twirled in his arms. His heart was pounding frantically, his breath cold and shallow as he held her close and stared down into eyes that mirrored the night. "Kiss me," she ordered, her hands in his hair, pulling his head down insistently. Cold lips touched his and his blood stirred. Her tongue pushed against his teeth, slipping between them, touching his.

He groaned. Lost. His hands bunched up her nightgown, the hardness between his legs sudden and demanding.

At first he thought the unfamiliar sound was the rush of blood in his veins, the thunder of his heartbeat, but he was wrong. His muscles tightened instinctively as he listened and heard an eerie groan. An ominous, near-silent creak that slithered a warning through his brain.

He lifted his head. The shore was five hundred feet away. How had they gotten so far from land? "Don't move," he whispered, shivering. Maybe it would go away.

But he knew better.

Another deep groan that echoed through the valley as well as the chambers of his heart. The hairs on the back of his arms lifted.

"Oh, God."

"What?"

They were too far from shore. Too far. "Come on!" he ordered as another splintering sound reverberated through his brain. He felt it then, the subtle shift beneath his boots. He grabbed her hand. "Run!" he'd cried over the louder, sharper crack, the sound of a fissure etching frantically through the ice.

"Why? Oh, God!"

"*Run!*"

"I can't!" Her feet, in slippers, found no purchase on the glazed surface and she slid wildly. He grabbed her wrist and ran, dragging her toward the shore. She was a dead weight, pulling against him, but he didn't care. Faster and faster he ran, his own feet sliding wildly. He aimed for his house, where, through the leafless trees he saw patches of warm light in the windows, smelled the scent of burning wood drifting from the chimney, heard the soft sound of tinkling laughter and music, noticed the unfamiliar car parked in the snowy drive.

Nina was crying now, her fear manifesting in tears. "Come on," he urged, yanking hard on her wrist, forcing her forward; then he turned toward the house. "Ma!" he yelled so loudly his voice seemed to reverberate over the ice. "Ma! Help!"

The earth shifted beneath him.

Nina's hand slipped from his gloved fingers.

He spun as she screamed, a terrified shriek that sliced through the night.

Craaaack!

The ice beneath them split.

His legs slid from beneath him and he saw the crack, a great, yawning crevice that moved and slivered as if it were alive.

No!

The cleft aimed right for Nina.

She gasped. Tried to get her feet under her and run.

"Hurry, Nina!" He scrambled toward her. The crack widened into a gaping crevice and Nina—beautiful, trusting Nina—screamed horribly as she fell through the ice in a sickening, heart-stopping splash.

"No! Oh, God, no!" He threw himself to the spot from

which she'd vanished, searching the murky, frigid depths, hearing ice crack and split all around him, but she submerged quickly, disappearing into the black depths.

He didn't think. Jumped into the dark, gaping hole. Frigid water engulfed him, strangling him, dragging him down with cold, cruel fingers. He thrashed beneath the surface, searching the murky waters of the lake. *Please, oh, God, please* . . . His lungs burned from lack of oxygen. His eyes saw nothing and he was shaking from the inside out.

Where are you? Nina . . . WHERE?

Swimming in wild circles, feeling as if he was going to explode, hoping for a glimpse of her, of the nightgown, of *anything*, he searched. Frantic. Knowing he might die.

Bubbles of air came out of his nose. He let in a little breath. Frigid water rushed into his nose and throat. Desperately he kicked upward, propelling himself to the break in the ice. He gasped as his head broke free. Coughing. Sputtering. Spitting water. "Nina!" he cried wildly, his voice a croak in the cold darkness. "Nina!"

Nothing.

No sound of her sweet voice.

His gaze scraped the surface of the lake, but he saw no sign of life. Oh, God, she was still down there. Freezing. Drowning. *Dying*.

He dived downward again, deep into the inky depths. *Nina, where the hell are you? Oh, baby. Come on, come on!* The seconds ticked by and he saw nothing through the murky water. What were the chances that she would survive? How long could someone stay under water, under *near-freezing* water? Were there air pockets locked near the surface? Could she even now be pressing her sweet lips upward to the ice, hoping to find a small pocket of air trapped beneath the surface? His mind was spinning crazily, a kaleidoscope of sharp images of Nina cutting through his brain as he swam in a panic, his lungs once again on fire.

Something slippery brushed against his leg; he kicked it away before thinking it might be Nina.

Forcing himself to sink deeper, he searched the blackness. Thought he heard voices far away. His lungs were stretched tight, screaming in pain, but he couldn't leave her down here. Wouldn't. *Where are you? WHERE?*

He let out a bubble of air, his gaze trying to pierce the impenetrable black. He saw white fingers . . . a hand . . . he reached for it, then realized it was his own numb fingers waving in front of him. The weight of the lake was crushing him, his lungs bursting, when he felt another light brush against his leg. What was it? What the hell was it? Nina? Or . . . or what . . . he couldn't think, unconsciousness tugging on him, his lungs about to burst.

He let out his breath and kicked hard, shooting to the surface.

Bam!

His head cracked hard against the ice.

Air escaped his lungs.

Oh, God, he was trapped!

They both were.

Air bubbles pouring from his mouth, he slid beneath the surface, feeling with his hands, trying to find a rift in the layer of frozen water. Blackness swirled around him. He gasped and water filled his lungs. Flailing wildly, he heard the groaning crack again and then the ice above him split.

Coughing and gasping, snorting, he rose, throwing up water, holding onto the sharp edge of the clear, frozen crust splintered across the lake.

He heard voices . . . distant voices . . . angels . . . or demons? His mind was spinning, the voices muted and far away.

And then the scream. A wild screech that ripped up his spine and bored through his brain.

He spewed up more water, and then, just as he saw pinpoints of light bobbling toward him, the blackness that had tugged at his mind gave a final, angry yank.

He was certain he was going to die and gave himself up to death willingly.

But God had let him survive. Somehow he'd been spared.

Now, standing in the swirling sleet, a glaze of rime upon the branches of the gigantic fir and the floor of his blind, he felt the same darkness, the rage, that had been with him for the ensuing years.

Why had he survived?

Why had Nina died?

He'd woken up in a hospital bed and soon realized that he'd been blamed for Nina's death. He'd seen it in his mother's unhappy gaze, watched the play of emotions on the officers and counselors who had talked to him.

Though not convicted of nor charged for the crime, he was forever silently accused by all who knew.

As he was by himself.

Had he not lured her out there?

Had he not wanted her for himself?

Had he not felt a thrill, just a little tingle of excitement, at the thought that because of him, because of her *love* for him, she'd lost her life?

Could he have saved her?

Probably not.

But when those small fingers had brushed against his ankle, and now he was convinced that it was her touch that he'd felt, why had he surfaced rather than reached down? What would two more seconds have cost him?

His life?

He knew better.

She had died because of him.

His lips twisted into a smile with the knowledge. With the power. He refocused his binoculars. With calming crystals of ice pressing against his face, he observed Jenna Hughes's house from his hiding spot.

Nina had been the first to die. He'd tried to tamp down his feelings of triumphant exhilaration when he realized that he had the power of death over life. He'd attempted sadness. He'd tried guilt. But, both emotions had worn thin quickly.

He'd told himself he would never love again.

And then he'd seen Jenna Hughes.

In that split second when he'd first gazed upon her, he'd known.

She was the one.

From that moment forward, every other woman in his life seemed insignificant. Including Nina. Poor, trusting little Nina.

Beautiful.

Like the others.

He reached into his pocket and fingered the glove he'd stolen . . . a small, black leather glove, one of the two that Jenna, as Anne Parks, had worn in *Resurrection*. He closed his eyes and remembered the scene where Anne, dressed in a slick black bra, high-cut panties, this very glove, and a choker around her neck, had advanced upon her lover. Lying spread-eagle upon his bed, the lover was expecting a coy sex game and had ended up experiencing erotic death.

Perfect.

He let his binoculars dangle and closed his eyes as the cold kiss of the wind touched the back of his neck. Slowly he opened his fly. He thought of Jenna. He thought of the icy, grasping waters of the lake. He let the first needles of sleet run down his upturned face.

Slowly he slipped the glove over his cock.

Then he pretended Jenna Hughes was kneeling before him.

CHAPTER 24

It had been a long day. Hell, it'd been a long week. Carter's wipers slapped at the snow falling from the night sky and his headlights cut through the darkness to reflect on the sheet of snow and ice covering the road.

On one side of the road, hundred-year-old fir trees loomed upward into the starless night, tall, foreboding, catching snowflakes in their immense branches; on the other side, the Columbia, churning with floes of ice, moved steadily westward. Snow and ice gathered on the corners of his windshield and the defroster lagged behind the condensation that fogged the glass.

His cell phone rang as he crossed a narrow bridge that spanned Pious Creek. He noticed that the creek appeared frozen solid.

"Carter," he barked.

"It's Sparks."

"I hope you have good news."

"It looks that way. Not only do we have a composite sketch of the woman found up at Catwalk Point, but we might have an ID."

Shane's hands tightened over the wheel.

"We think the missing woman might be Mavis Gette."

The name rang no bells with Carter, but it was something.

Mavis Gette.

No longer Jane Doe.

Maybe.

"Twenty-eight years old. Last known residence was Yorba Linda, California," Sparks said, his voice distinct. "She's a loner. Estranged from her family, no friends . . . we're double-checking with a cousin who lives in Portland, if you can believe that. She's already scanned and e-mailed the two photos of Gette she has. They're not top quality, but they're damned close to the computer-enhanced sketch we've got. We should have dental records faxed by the morning, though a positive ID will be tough because her teeth were filed down . . . We'll be looking at jawbone structure, missing teeth, any hint of dental work remaining. The last time anyone remembers seeing her was last winter. She talked to the cousin around the end of January."

"And no one's missed her since?"

"The phone call wasn't pleasant, which wasn't unusual. Gette was unemployed and was asking for money again. The cousin—Georgina Sharpe—said 'no.' They argued, Gette spat out some expletive and hung up. Sharpe gave us the name of a few of Gette's acquaintances and other family members, but so far, we've only talked to an aunt. Hasn't seen or heard from Gette in nearly a year."

Carter felt a little rush, the kind that kept him on the job. Whenever there was a chance that a case was breaking open, his senses came alive. "Where was Mavis Gette at the time of the call to her cousin?"

"The cousin isn't sure, but she thinks Gette was hitch-hiking up I-5 from California."

"Hitching?"

"Yeah, well, we're not talking brain surgeon material here. Dropped out of school in her sophomore year of high school, never done much since. Anyway, Sharpe thinks Gette said she'd gotten as far north as Medford. We're already checking Sharpe's phone records to see where the call actually originated, and with her last employer, a motel where she was a maid in Yorba Linda, and with anyone who knew her. She wasn't married but had two losers for ex-husbands and a string of boyfriends, a couple of whom had criminal pasts, or at least the cousin says so . . . Not much more information now, but I'll keep you posted."

"Can you e-mail me the sketch?"

"Already done. Along with the report."

Carter slowed for a corner, his eyes narrowing on the road as he listened. "I assume you're checking out the Sharpe woman."

"And her husband. She was a bookkeeper for an independent trucking firm. Her husband owns the company."

"And the woman was hitching."

"Yeah, we're checking out all his drivers, but that's a long shot, considering the fact that the wife called in."

"Unless she's suspicious."

"We'll see. I've already talked to the FBI, and the California State Police are going through her things, the stuff she didn't clean out of her apartment when she skipped, but it's been so long, the landlady could have sold or dumped whatever was left. Not much hope there, but who knows? As soon as the ID is confirmed, we'll have a press conference. Maybe someone will come forward with more information."

"Let's hope," Carter said. "I know it's a long shot, but I'm going to talk to Lester Hatchell, see if Sonja knew the woman."

"You still think the cases are linked?"

"Maybe, maybe not."

"Won't hurt," Sparks agreed. They talked a few more minutes, then Carter hung up, his mind working overtime with the possibilities.

He didn't learn anything more, but, for the first time since the body had been found at Catwalk Point, he felt as if they were getting somewhere, as if he'd found a tiny toehold in the quicksand he'd been wading through, a toehold that could give out at any moment, he reminded himself.

A few minutes later he was home, had peeled off his gloves, jacket, and boots, stoked the fire, and settled in at the computer. He logged on, checked his e-mail, found several from Sparks, and opened all the attachments, a report, and a computer-enhanced picture of what Mavis had looked like.

She'd been a beautiful woman.

Even features, high cheekbones, strong chin . . .

Reduced to bones stuffed into a hollowed-out log.

Why?

Who had done this to her? A psychotic who happened upon her when she was hitching? Or someone she knew. He clicked on the photos sent from the cousin and saw the resemblance to the computer-generated image. Pretty damned close. The pictures weren't very clear, Sparks had been right, but in the images was a woman in her early twenties, with a sullen expression, big eyes, and untamed brown hair.

"What happened to you?" Carter murmured, staring at the image for a few seconds before walking to the refrigerator and pulling a can of beer from its plastic noose. Cracking it open, he took a long swallow, then settled into his desk chair again. The woodstove was finally putting out some decent BTUs, and he was warm as he clicked on to the Sonja Hatchell information and pulled up a shot of Sonja. Just as he'd remembered her.

He wasn't exactly a techno-wizard, but he knew enough about computers to cut, paste, enlarge, reduce, and put the images of the two women side by side. He couldn't superimpose one over the other, but he didn't need to. The resemblance was evident in their facial structure and as he glanced over their stats, they seemed more alike. Sonja was five feet, three and a half inches, Mavis at five feet four—same as the analysts had estimated Jane Doe to be. Sonja had a slim build. A hundred and twelve pounds. Mavis Gette's last driver's license, issued by the State of California, stated one hundred and fifteen. Close enough.

And similar to the height and weight of Jenna Hughes.

Not that the cases were related. There was no evidence to connect Jenna Hughes with Jane Doe or Sonja Hatchell.

Yet.

*   *   *

"I can't find the cool bracelet," Allie grumbled the next day as she picked at her breakfast.

"What cool bracelet?" Jenna was seated at her desk in the den, searching the Internet for security services. She'd called three, none of which could come and replace her alarm system for nearly a month. They were all backed up. Jenna had even inquired about a bodyguard, taking Sheriff Carter's suggestion to heart after her scare last night. Today, she was convinced the idiot riding her tail was Josh Sykes but she couldn't prove it. Nor could she shake the feeling that she was being watched, that the things that kept breaking down on the ranch were more than just time and wear and tear. *You're being paranoid*, she told herself, but decided paranoid sure beat the hell out of unsafe.

"You know the one," Allie wheedled.

Jenna rolled her chair backward, so she could see beyond the last few steps of the staircase and into the kitchen where Allie was spreading peanut butter on an English muffin.

"It's got black and white beads and kinda stretches."

"Faux pearls," Cassie clarified. She'd been in her room, ostensibly still cleaning up her continual mess, and, to her credit, was carrying down a full plastic bag of trash in one hand while balancing three plates and several stacked glasses in the other.

"I think it's in my jewelry box, the one in the closet." Jenna flipped to another Web site for a security "team."

"No, it isn't. I looked."

"You're sure?"

"Yes!" Allie snapped, obviously angry that her mother didn't believe her. They were all a little tense, trapped in the house for the most part, waiting for the storm to abate. Jenna's nerves were strung taut, and Cassie was in a bad mood because she was still grounded. Her phone call to her father hadn't helped, the only result being that Robert was quick to blame Jenna, and from what she could tell, his blood pressure was probably skyrocketing with the pressures in L.A. "I don't need this right now," he'd told Jenna when Cassie, near tears, had handed Allie the phone last night. Later, when she'd gotten on the line, Jenna had pointed out that Cassie's behavior wasn't about Robert, but he'd managed, as always, to turn the conversation around. She'd hung up feeling more frustrated than ever. Even Allie, usually all smiles and enthusiasm, seemed bored and at loose ends. "I wanted to wear it over to Dani's."

As if Dani Settler would care. The kid was a tomboy's tomboy.

"Let me see if I can find it." Jenna walked up the stairs to her room and searched through her jewelry box. The bracelet was M.I.A., so she checked another, older box that housed costume jewelry she rarely wore. Not there. Where was the danged thing? The last time she'd seen it, she'd used it like a rubber band to pull her hair off her face, but she'd remembered putting it away. Of course, either of the girls could have "borrowed" it, but she'd thought the piece was in the box. Hadn't she seen it there just last week?

Frowning, she searched through the bedrooms, even taking a quick look through the kids' rooms as well as the guest room on the upper floor. She headed upstairs to a loft where Allie sometimes played. Still nothing.

So what? Things were misplaced every day, but she couldn't help the niggle of worry that ate at her. Once again, the missing item was something she'd worn in one of her movies—in this case, as Marnie Sylvane in *Summer's End.* Maybe that was significant, maybe not. She walked into her bedroom again and did a 360-degree turn, eyeing shelves and window ledges, her bedside tables, anywhere she'd sometimes left her things, but everything was where it should be and there was no bracelet.

She thought about calling her cleaning lady, Estella, but didn't. It wasn't a big deal. So another thing was missing . . . no—misplaced, *not* missing. Jenna would find it. Eventually. She sat on the edge of her bed and told herself to relax. She was just too uptight and a headache was building behind her eyes.

She walked into the bathroom, downed three ibuprofen with a glass of water, and returned to the bedroom. Out of habit, she opened her nightstand drawer and found the usual things she always kept there—change, a flashlight, a small package of Kleenex, and a paperback she'd been reading. Then she looked across her bed to the other bedside table, one she never used, a perfect match to the one on the side of the bed where she slept.

Of course there would be nothing in it, she told herself, but rolled across the bed and slid the drawer open. She peered inside.

Her heart dropped to her feet.

"Jesus," she whispered, her skin crawling.

Inside the drawer was a single envelope.

Addressed to her.

In the same block letters she'd seen before.

Identical to the envelope she'd received in the mail a few days earlier.

She swallowed hard. Fought panic. How long had it been there? How had it been delivered? Had the person who had written it been here? In her house? In her *bedroom*?

A cold sweat broke out between her shoulder blades and it was all she could do not to scream. Fear prickled her skin.

"You son of a bitch," she muttered under her breath. "You can't do this to me . . . I won't let you." But inside she was terrified. Quivering.

Carefully, using a tissue, she lifted the white envelope from the drawer and, using her fingernail, slit it open. A single letter fell out. Another poem. Superimposed over another photo, a promo shot for *Bystander*.

I am every man.
Hungry. Strong. Ready.
I am one man.
Knowing. Watching. Waiting.
I am your man.
Today. Tomorrow. Endlessly.
I will come for you.

CHAPTER 25

Jenna didn't wait for clearance from the secretary, just barged into Sheriff Shane Carter's office and plopped into his chair. "I need your help," Jenna said, adrenaline pumping through her blood. She had to do something. Now. "And if you can't help me," she added, "then you need to tell me who can and point me in their direction. I received another note."

"What?" he said, dead serious.

"That's right. My personal Wordsworth has struck again." She tried to keep her voice light, but she couldn't hide the fear that had nearly congealed her blood. To think that he'd actually been in her house. Her bedroom. Her flesh crawled as she pulled a plastic bag holding the horrible poem from her purse. She dropped it without ceremony onto Carter's desk. "And last night someone tried to run me off the road, and there are more things missing, movie paraphernalia, from my house. Things keep breaking down and I don't know whether someone's trying to totally freak me out or I'm paranoid or—or . . ." She stopped suddenly, realizing that she was notching herself up, that she was sounding as scared as she felt. "Oh, God." She pushed her hair from her eyes and forced herself to take a deep breath.

"You want to slow down and start over?" He was leaning back in his chair, staring at her over tented fingers. His expression was grim, his lips compressed, but for the first time since she'd been introduced to him, she thought she detected a bit of tenderness in his eyes. A tad of compassion. "Wait a sec." Reaching toward the phone, he pressed an intercom button on the desk and said, "Jerri, if you don't mind, would you bring Ms. Hughes a cup of coffee or a soda or . . . ?" He lifted bushy eyebrows in her direction, hoping for her to choose, she supposed.

"I don't care. Anything . . ."

Carter nodded as she wrapped her arms around her middle and tried to make sense of the note. Who would stalk her here—in lazy, little Falls Crossing, though it hadn't been all that lazy in the past few weeks. Had someone followed her from L.A., or had she met her personal nutcase somewhere in this little town and hadn't realized it?

"Decaf, Jerri," Carter said and visibly winced at the reply. "I'll remember it when you're up for review. Oh—and hold all my calls . . . well, I know, but aren't they *all* emergencies? Okay, fine, if they call, put through Sparks, Messenger, or anyone from the state crime lab—especially Merline Jacobosky. Anyone else I'll call back . . . yeah, thanks." Clicking off the intercom, he focused all of his attention on Jenna. Coffee-brown eyes scrutinized her. "Now, Ms. Hughes, let's go through this again. Slowly."

"Okay." She did. Cognizant of the whirlwind of activity going on outside his office, knowing that he was responsible for a county that the governor was hoping the federal government would declare a disaster area, she told him everything she claimed she could remember. He read the note through the plastic and scowled, the lines near the corners of his eyes becoming deep creases.

". . . I'd already decided to take your advice," she said as her story wound down. "I've called several security companies, looking for a bodyguard and someone to replace my alarm system. Unfortunately, with the weather and red tape, it'll take some time. But Wes Allen—you know him, I think—" Carter nodded, his jaw shifting to one side, his muscles bunching reflexively. "I work with Wes at the theater and he's agreed to help with the existing system to try and make it functional until I can replace it."

"Good idea."

"You mentioned me getting a bodyguard earlier."

He nodded.

"Do you have anyone who would be interested?" she asked. "You know a lot of people in the area. People who have been in law enforcement and might be looking for a job like this. Otherwise I'm stuck with the Yellow Pages and the Internet." She managed a thin smile. "That's a little like jumping from the frying pan into the fire."

His eyebrows rose and he grinned. "Well, we don't want that. You've got enough trouble with this." He tapped the bag on his desk. "I'll ask around. I've got some friends that might consider the job."

"Good." Though she wasn't certain having a stranger on the premises "protecting" her would make her feel any better.

"There's a studio apartment off the garage or an old bunkhouse that I use for storage right now."

He made a note and said, "In the meantime, I'd like to check out your house and anyone who has access to it." He thumbed through a stack of files on his desk, pulled out one with her name written on it, then flipped it open. Spying the page he was looking for, he twirled the file on his desk so she could read it. "This is a list of the people who have had access to your house in the last sixty days, or so you claimed the last time you were in. Any changes? Additions?"

She picked up the file and mentally ticked off each of the names. Friends, family, workmen, delivery people, even a couple who had come door-to-door, selling religion. "This looks pretty complete," she said.

"When do you think this note was delivered?"

"I don't know. I never look in that drawer. It could have been yesterday, or three months ago . . . maybe longer."

"Your house cleaner, does she . . . look in the drawer?"

"I doubt it—just dusts on top."

"What about the kids? Sometimes they nose around where they shouldn't."

"I asked the girls before I left. Neither one of them had opened it."

"Are they alone now?"

"No. I won't do that anymore, even though my oldest is sixteen . . ." Her voice trailed off and her gaze clashed with Carter's. He knew about Cassie already; he'd dragged her home the last time she'd snuck out. "Well, you've met Cassie. She thinks I'm treating her like a baby, but that's too bad."

"Isn't that the mantra of most sixteen-year-olds?"

"Unfortunately."

He read the note again. "Our poet repeats himself."

"Limited vocabulary," she cracked, but the joke fell flat.

"I'll have the lab check this out," he said. "I'll send a deputy right now with a fingerprint kit, and I'll be out later. We'll talk to your neighbors and anyone who's been at your place recently, see if anyone saw anything suspicious."

"Wouldn't they have said something already?"

"It could be they didn't recognize it as suspicious. I'll try to jog some memories." His smile was hard, barely twitching the lips beneath his moustache. "As I said, I'll stop by and hopefully have a couple of names of potential bodyguards." He leaned back in the chair.

"Thanks," she said, and feeling only slightly better, left the sheriff's office and headed for the sporting goods store. She didn't believe in guns, hated the thought of having a loaded one in the house, but now that her family was threatened, she decided she needed protection. She'd considered getting shotgun shells earlier and had been too busy. Now was the time.

You've never shot anything other than paper targets in your life.

"Yeah, well, there's a first time for everything," she muttered as she walked down the steps of the courthouse and tightened her wool scarf around her neck.

* * *

Carter watched her leave. She was scared and he didn't blame her. She disappeared down the stairs and he stood and stretched, walking to the window and staring outside through the frosty panes to the parking lot below. Blazers, an Explorer, a truck, and two Crown Victorias were in the lot along with a few pedestrians, heads bent against the wind as they walked past. Across the street, at Danby's, there was yet another sale, the advertising for this one including Santa painted on the storefront windows.

Small Town, U.S.A., he thought.

Small Town, U.S.A., with one missing woman and another woman found dead. Carter didn't like it. He didn't like it at all.

Lieutenant Sparks had called earlier. The dental records for Mavis Gette were hard to match because of the filed teeth, so now they were waiting for DNA. That would take some time, but Gette's cousin had confirmed that Mavis had once broken her collarbone—the clavicle that they'd found near the body had, according to the Medical Examiner, once been fractured. In Carter's estimation, Jane Doe was Mavis Gette. The FBI agreed, according to Sparks, as he was dealing with the local field agents. So why had her teeth been filed down? Why the alginate in her hair? Was this guy some kind of weird, psychotic dentist? How did a woman who was last heard from in Medford end up at Catwalk Point?

He moved his head around, releasing the tension in the back of his neck and, from his vantage point, saw Jenna Hughes hurry across the parking lot. Her boots slid a bit and she had to catch herself on the fender of one of the Crown Vics.

It was funny how he felt about her. He'd assumed she was a Hollywood princess, pampered, used to the good life. But he'd been wrong. At least here, in Falls Crossing, she wasn't a star—no, far from it. Here she was a single mother who was scared out of her wits. Mentally he considered all the ex-cops he knew who might be willing to come to her aid and hire on as a bodyguard. He rejected them all, and then gave himself a swift mental kick as he realized the reason. An unlikely spurt of envy that sped through his blood.

He didn't like the idea of one of the people he knew looking after her.

However, the thought of her being unprotected was worse.

He couldn't accept the job.

He had more than he could handle as it was.

His gaze followed her as she slid behind the wheel of her Jeep and eased out of the lot. The pathetic dog was sitting in the passenger seat.

"Don't tell me." BJ's voice brought him up cold.

He turned to find her in the doorway, one shoulder braced against the jamb. "What?"

"You know what," she chided. "You and every red-blooded male in this county—no, make that this country—have a hard-on for Jenna Hughes."

He snorted.

"How about that? You don't even deny it." Her smile stretched wide. "I never thought I'd see the day."

He sighed. "I think we have work to do."

"You're in love, Carter. Admit it. Or at least you're in lust."

"You've got an overactive imagination."

"You son of a bitch," she said, but she was smiling. "I thought you were above this sort of thing."

None of us is immune, he thought, and walked back to his desk. "The lady's got a problem," he said, showing BJ the second note. "Someone's definitely stalking her, and I thought you could work some of your computer/Internet magic and help me find the son of a bitch."

"Gladly," BJ agreed. "I'm still working on a list of people who rent her movies, but I can check the Web as well."

"Good," he said, before realizing she'd dropped by his office unsummoned. "Was there something you wanted?"

"Not me. It's the press. They're clamoring for a statement."

"They can take it up with the OSP."

"Yeah, that's what they've been told, but a few aren't taking 'no' for an answer. The most stubborn one is Roxie Olmstead, the local reporter for the *Banner*. She wants an interview with you. Caught up with me on the street, knows I work with you, and blah, blah, blah, could she have an exclusive interview."

He remembered her from an earlier case. Pretty. Petite. Persistent. Pain in the butt. "You told her to get in line, right?"

"I told her I had absolutely no influence over you. She'd have to try and reach you herself."

"Thanks a lot."

"Just wanted to give you a heads-up."

"Thanks." He reached for his phone.

"It's hell to be popular," BJ said, and started to leave.

You got that right, he thought, but held his tongue as he called Montinello and sent him over to Jenna Hughes's ranch. He doubted they'd find any fingerprints, but then again, who knew? Maybe they'd get lucky. Nonetheless, BJ's observations hit too close to home. What the devil was he doing fantasizing about Jenna Hughes? Christ Jesus, he was more of a fool than he'd ever admit.

"A bodyguard? Are you serious?" Cassie stopped opening the boxes labeled *Christmas Decorations* and stared at her mother in horror. "You're going to have some stranger come live with us? No way. No friggin' way."

"He'll stay in the studio behind the garage." Jenna was adamant. Ever since finding the second note, she'd been on edge. Jumpy. Out of her mind with fear. The usual noises of the house bothered her, and she was forever double-checking the locks. She'd picked up shotgun shells from the sporting goods store, but hadn't yet loaded the old gun.

Allie unwrapped a crystal ornament in the shape of a snowman. "You could hire Mr. Settler."

"Save me," Cassie whispered.

"No, really. He sometimes does detective work."

"Is that right?" Jenna asked.

"Mm-hmm." Allie set the ornament on the table, where it reflected the reddish glow from the fire burning on the other side of the room.

"Did he tell you that?" Cassie demanded.

"Dani did."

"Dani tells stories to anyone gullible enough to listen."

"It's true. I saw his gun."

"What?" Jenna was slitting open the plastic tape on another box, but she looked up sharply. "What were you doing snooping through Mr. Settler's things?"

"I wasn't. He was wearing it. In a shoulder holster. I saw it under his jacket."

"Weird." Cassie wadded up a layer of newspaper before pulling out a string of lights. "Did you know he was a P.I.?" she asked her mother.

"No. He never mentioned it."

"Even weirder."

"I don't think we'll hire Mr. Settler."

"Thank God," Cassie muttered under her breath.

"But it would be cool."

"You just want Dani to come live with us," Cassie accused, and Allie's face darkened.

"He could do it. He was in the Army. In the Special Forces, or something like that."

"Another tall tale. God, Allie, grow up, would you?"

"It's true!"

"Yeah, right." Cassie plugged in the string of lights and they winked on, shining bright and reflecting in little spots of color on the floor.

"Enough. We don't know anything about Mr. Settler."

"Except that he has the hots for you."

"Cassie!" The box cutter slipped and she nicked the thumb of her other hand. "Damn!"

"It's true."

Allie turned on her sister. "He was in the Army. Dani

showed me some stuff, okay? Medals and pictures and awards. Mr. Settler was—like a sergeant—in some kind of elite unit."

Jenna's shoulders tightened as she pressed her bleeding thumb to her mouth. She reached into a cupboard by the sink for a box of Band-Aids and tore one of the smaller plastic strips open. Why hadn't Travis mentioned his past? She wrapped her thumb with the Band-Aid, covering the cut. It showed red through the plastic, but the blood didn't seep out. She was back in business again. "So," she said, leveling her gaze on her youngest daughter. "Did Mr. Settler know you looked at his things?"

Allie shrugged.

"Allie?" Jenna reprimanded gently as she sliced open a box of clear lights.

"Dunno. Dani said it didn't matter."

"Geez. What's with that girl?" Cassie asked, uncoiling a final strand of lights. "Doesn't she take tai-kwon-do and shoot guns at the rifle range and ride horses bareback?"

"So what?" Allie said, bristling even more.

"Does she think she's a guy, or what?"

"Hey! Maybe we should all do some of the things Dani does," Jenna said as she untangled the string of lights. She thought of the holiday ahead and wondered how she'd ever find a shard of Christmas spirit. Not only was she still dealing with Jill's death, but now she had this . . . this stalker . . . watching her—entering her house.

Happy Holidays, she thought morbidly.

CHAPTER 26

The neighbors were a bust. One of the ranches bordering the Hughes estate was boarded up, no sign of life; another was owned by an elderly couple who'd noticed nothing out of the ordinary. Aside from Harrison Brennan being overly concerned and bristling at the prospect of someone "bothering" Jenna Hughes, no one had seen or heard anything they thought was worth mentioning.

By the time Carter parked his Blazer in Jenna Hughes's driveway, it was early afternoon and Montinello was just leaving. He'd finished taking prints, remarking, as he met Carter, about the chances of finding a needle in a haystack. "There were so many prints in the house. She's got two kids, friends, a housekeeper, a ranch foreman, a personal trainer, and then the kids have friends and she's had repair guys in." Montinello was standing next to one of the department's SUVs, the rig he'd parked in front of Jenna Hughes's garage. "Unless whoever left the note is a class-A moron, I doubt if we'll get lucky," he said, shaking his head. A few snowflakes swirled from the sky, and though it wasn't yet twilight, the day was dark, the gloom of winter settling into the surrounding trees and buildings.

"You never know. How many prints in her bedroom?" Carter asked, looking up at the behemoth that was her house.

Smoke curled from a tall rock chimney, and steam rose from a side deck, where, he supposed, a hot tub was uncovered. Nestled in the trees, complete with icicles dripping from the roof, the rustic house looked like something out of a Christmas card. But beneath the quaint facade lurked something treacherous, something evil.

"There were a few prints around the room . . . some larger than hers."

Carter nodded, his jaw suddenly tight at the thought of a man in Jenna Hughes's bedroom.

Montinello lifted the small case he was carrying. "I took everyone in the household's prints to compare them to. If I need to, I'll check with the other people who've been there—her personal trainer, the guy who keeps the ranch up. His wife. But for now, I'll start with these. Meanwhile, I told her to beef up security, and while I was here two guys, Wes Allen and his nephew, were fixing the alarm system and the electronic gates. Both work now. I double-checked, but she says the security system needs to be either completely updated or torn out and a new one installed. She's called someone, so she's on it, I think."

"Good." Carter should have felt better about Jenna's safety, but didn't. There was something about this place—picture-postcard perfect and yet so isolated—that worried him. He glanced at the surrounding forest and isolated, snow-covered acres and too many outbuildings. Stable, barn, garage, windmill, pump house, sheds . . . a lot of places for a criminal to hide. Too many.

Montinello opened the door of his Blazer and tossed the kit inside.

"Let me know what you find out."

"You got it."

As Montinello drove away, Carter walked along the breezeway and knocked sharply on the back door. The dog began to bark and as Jenna inched open the door, threatened to rush out.

"Shh! Critter," she ordered as she pushed the door open. The dog was going out of his head, turning in circles wildly.

"And you didn't think he was a guard dog," she said with a laugh. Her hair was pinned to the back of her head and she smelled faintly of the same perfume he'd noticed before.

"He seems to have risen to the occasion."

"It was the threat of being replaced by a pit bull, I think." She grinned as she caught hold of the dog's collar. "Come in if you dare." Her eyes seemed to sparkle a bit at the sight of him, and he told himself that he was being an idiot. She was glad to see him because she was scared and he was the law, or she was faking it—she'd had a lot of practice. All those years of acting. "Welcome to my nightmare," she invited.

He took off his boots as she let go of the dog, who immediately nuzzled his legs and whacked him hard with his tail.

"Oh, Critter, you're blowing your cover," Jenna admonished as she led Carter into the kitchen.

Along with Christmas decorations, boxes, tissue paper, and lights strewn all over the floor, there was also black or silver dust in a few places, residue from the prints Montinello had taken. The younger girl was fiddling with a string of lights, changing bulbs and barely looking up.

"Allie, this is Sheriff Carter, remember?"

"Yeah." She barely glanced up.

"You can call me Shane," he said. To Jenna, he added, "It's less intimidating. Right, Allie?"

The girl shrugged and kept at her task.

"Kids love me," he joked, and Jenna laughed, her gaze touching his for the briefest of instants, just long enough to captivate him.

"I can tell."

"Whatever you say." Her eyes took in the mess on the floor. "Kinda makes you feel like you're in a winter wonderland, huh?" she quipped, calmer than she had been earlier in the day.

"Right." He eased around an open box of tree ornaments and pulled a piece of paper from the inside pocket of his jacket. On the page were the names and phone numbers of three men he trusted. "I haven't called these guys, but they might be available to help with security."

"Bodyguards?"

"Potentially. Yeah." He nodded. "I can personally vouch for them."

Something seemed to soften in her and she bit her lip, then looked up at him, her eyes shinier than they had been. "Thanks, Sheriff. This was above and beyond."

"Part of the job."

She arched a dark brow. "If you say so."

"I do," he said, but the silence stretched between them and he noticed how her eyelashes swept her cheek when she blinked. He heard the clock ticking and a television in another part of the house. "Want to show me where the note was discovered?"

"Oh . . . sure . . . this way . . ." She cleared her throat and stepped over a long string of bubble lights, then led him up the stairs. Carter tried not to notice her hips moving beneath her jeans or the way a few strands of black hair escaped from the knot clipped to her head as he followed her, but it seemed impossible. He barely noticed the dog streaking ahead as she opened double doors on a floor midway up the staircase. Her bedroom was on a floor all its own, and as he stepped into the room, he knew he was in trouble. The smells of cedar, soap, and lilacs assailed him. A queen-size bed was pushed against one wall and a white silk robe was tossed casually over one of the iron bedposts. Candles and potpourri were scattered around the room, and thick rugs covered the smooth, hardwood floors. A television peeked from behind doors slightly ajar in a large armoire, and a bank of paned windows looked out to the forested hills.

Black or silver fingerprint dust was pretty much everywhere, especially around one of the nightstands, the bureau, armoire, window latches, and doors.

"Mind if I look around?"

"Be my guest," she said, and he stepped into an attached bathroom with sunken tub, shower, and sauna. Next to it was a walk-in closet the size of his living room. It was cut up by different shelves and rods, even drawers. Long gowns, slacks, blouses, dresses, sweaters, all hung above cubbyholes filled with shoes and shelves lined with handbags. More clothes than any one woman had the right to own. One of the drawers was open slightly, revealing a red lace bra. His throat tightened a second and he visualized her in the garment, then brought himself up short and walked out of the closet to the bedroom again.

She was standing near a bedside table, waiting for him.

"This is where I found the note," she said, opening a drawer gingerly. It was empty now. "As I said, no one uses it. I don't think it's been opened since I moved in."

"Except by whoever left the note."

"Yeah." Shivering, she wrapped her arms around her middle and walked to the windows. "You know, when I first came here, I felt so free. As if this was a haven. But lately . . ." She turned, faced him, and stared at a rug for a half a second. "I know this sounds paranoid, but I've had this feeling . . . a sense that someone's watching me." She bit at the edge of her lip. "And I had it before I got this note, even before I got the first one. It's . . . just . . . this strange sensation. I get cold inside just thinking about it." She blushed a little. "I know— paranoid, huh?"

"Maybe not."

"Yeah." She stole a glance at the nightstand. "To think that he was *here. Inside* my house. *My bedroom.*" Her voice quivered a bit. "He could have been inside when I was sleeping. God, he could have been in the girls' rooms. Do you know how creepy that is?"

He nodded and heard the sound of a truck's engine rumbling closer. "You might consider moving into a hotel for a while."

"I'm not letting some . . . weirdo push me out of my own home. No way. I'll hire people. I called a locksmith this morning. He's already changed all the locks. Wes Allen worked on the security system earlier today, and I bought shells for the shotgun."

"You did what?" He was shocked. This little woman with a weapon? "Do you know how to use one?"

"I'm hoping I won't have to."

"But you have kids in the house and—"

"And I'm going to protect them. I did learn how to shoot years ago, for my part in *Resurrection*. Anne Parks was a killer. She usually used other weapons, but there were two scenes with guns. My director wanted me to look like I knew how to handle a handgun, so I took lessons. Have I ever shot a living thing? No. Would I? Yeah. If it meant protecting my kids."

"That was a handgun, right?"

"Yes."

"You might want to practice with the shotgun. Shot scatters and . . . it wouldn't be my weapon of choice."

"It's what I had and better than nothing."

He thought of all the statistics about gun owners killing themselves or their loved ones with their own weapons. "Just be safe."

"That's what I'm trying to do," she said as the dog lifted his head, then growled loudly. Nails clicking as he scrambled over the hardwood floors, Critter began barking his fool head off and took off down the stairs.

"He takes his job seriously," Jenna quipped as she followed Critter downstairs.

He'd better, Carter thought, *he'd damned well better.*

Harrison Brennan was on the back porch, peering through the window mounted into the door.

He was also looking angry as all get-out.

Great, Jenna thought as she opened the door and the dog let out a disgruntled woof. Critter had never been a fan of Harrison Brennan, but then neither had either of her girls. With all his good intentions, he was still irritating.

"The sheriff here?" he asked. "He stopped by my place earlier." Brennan looked over her shoulder and his jaw tightened slightly, his lips becoming a flat, unhappy line.

"Harrison," Carter said, close enough behind her that she felt his breath against the back of her neck. A little tingle danced down her spine, but she ignored it.

"Guess that answers your question." Jenna tried not to be irritated with her neighbor. After all, Harrison always seemed to have her best interests in mind. Critter didn't seem to be of the same mind and growled at Harrison.

"Shh," she warned the dog, "or you'll be out in the snow."

"Damned mutt never has warmed to me," Harrison said, but tried to reach down and pat the dog's head. The growling ceased, though the hairs on the back of Critter's neck never quite laid flat and his tail remained motionless. He accepted the touch, but kept his head down, his eyes watching Harrison's every move. "Hell, he'd like to bite my hand off."

"Ignore him. Come on in," she invited, then shot the dog a warning glare. "You. Be on your best behavior. Go to your bed."

Critter shuffled off to his favorite spot under the table, and Carter, as if to give her some privacy, said, "Mind if I look through the house . . . I'd like to check out the layout."

"Anything you need to do," she said, waving him off and grateful that he was taking her threats as seriously as she was. It felt safe to have him in the house and she relaxed a little, even though Harrison was fit to be tied. As Carter moved from one room to the next and eventually up the stairs again, Jenna shepherded Harrison into the den, fending off his questions out of Allie's earshot, then explained what had been happening over the past few days.

With each turn in her story, Harrison grew more grim, his jaw tightening, his thumbs rubbing restlessly against his forefingers. But he didn't say a word, just stood in the den, staring at her with intense blue eyes, his lips compressed tightly.

When she was finished, he rubbed his chin and glared at her. "You mean you're telling me you had someone leave a threatening note in your house and you didn't call me?"

"I thought the police could handle it," she said, hearing the creak of footsteps on the stairs.

"Or me. I'm next door," he pointed out, his eyebrows knotted together. "And I've got connections. The FBI should be in on this!" He shoved one hand through his short, bristly hair, making the silvery strands stand straight on end. "Just what the hell is going on here?"

"That's what we're trying to find out," Carter said.

Brennan was agitated. Face flushed, he turned his anger on Carter. "So do you think she's safe here?"

"I'm fine, Harrison," she cut in.

"But the security system. It's been a mess. I'll call Seth. If he can't fix it, I'll find someone who can."

"Already done," she said. "Wes Allen was over earlier."

Beside her, Carter tensed. Brennan snorted through his nose. "What does *he* know? He tinkers around with sound systems and the like. This is serious."

Jenna snapped, "Believe me, I realize that."

"I'll double-check the system. Get someone who knows wiring. If not Seth Whitaker, then Jim Klondike—he's a helluva handyman." She started to argue, but Harrison wasn't about to be put off as he turned his attention to the sheriff. "What are you and your department doing about this?" he said, pointing a finger at Carter's chest.

"Everything we can." The sheriff folded his arms over his chest and didn't give an inch.

"Humph." Harrison lifted disbelieving silver eyebrows, then faced Jenna again. "You need protection. A woman all alone with kids out here. I don't like it."

"This is my home."

"And it's not very secure." He rubbed the back of his neck. "I guess I could stay over."

Carter's nonchalance dissipated in a heartbeat, and Jenna said, "That won't be necessary, Harrison. I'm hiring a bodyguard."

"A bodyguard? Who?" he demanded.

"I'm not sure yet. I'm hoping to start interviewing today. Sheriff Carter came up with some names—"

"Jake Turnquist," Brennan said quickly, his blue eyes narrowing. "I'd feel better if it was me staying here, but if not, then contact Jake. He's a friend of mine and an ex-Navy Seal. Has done P.I. work after a stint with the Portland

Police. He lives in Hood River now, and single—no wife or kids to tie him down, so he could probably move in."

Jenna felt every muscle in her back tighten as she tried to keep her temper in check. She was dead tired and scared, hadn't eaten for nearly a day, and she wanted to jump down Harrison's throat. What was it about her that made Harrison Brennan think he could run her life? Was she such a wimp? "Look, Harrison, I'll see what *I* want to do," she said, her jaw locked, quiet fury shooting through her bloodstream. "But first I'll talk to the people the sheriff knows." Slowly she unclenched fists she didn't even realize had curled.

"Turnquist's on the list," Carter said, staring Harrison Brennan down. "Harrison's right. Turnquist is a good man. I worked several cases with him before he retired."

Brennan's expression lost a little of its rigidity. "Then it's decided."

"Not yet," Jenna said, wanting to strangle the man. "But I'll give him a call."

"Good." Carter glanced around the house one more time. "I'll stay in touch. Call me if you have any hint of trouble or need anything."

"I will," she promised, and felt more than a little trepidation as she walked him to the back door. Then she was waiting, staring through the panes on the back door and watching as the sheriff drove through the open gates. That warm feeling of safety she'd felt in his presence dissipated in his wake. She was left with Harrison and the bald fact that he was becoming a nuisance. A concerned nuisance, but a nuisance nonetheless. She didn't push the button to close the electronic gates that, Wes had promised her, were working again. She'd lock them once Harrison left.

He was waiting for her in the kitchen, one hip pressed against the counter, her portable phone in his hand.

"I called Jake," he said with a smile that told her he was proud of himself. "Mission accomplished."

"Meaning?"

"He'll take the job."

She was floored. "Sight unseen? Without meeting me or

even looking around?" She motioned to the interior of the house. The setup didn't seem right. "Did you discuss pay? Hours? Jesus, Harrison, you've got to stop doing this, right now. You cannot run my life." She was advancing upon him, her face turned up to his, anger radiating from her in hot, furious waves.

"I'm just trying to help."

"You're suffocating me."

"You'll like Jake." The man was impossible, staring at her as if he didn't understand a word she said.

She squared her shoulders and set her jaw. "That's not the point, okay? I don't need you to protect me."

"Because you're doing such a bang-up job on your own?" he asked, a nasty gleam surfacing in his eyes.

"Because I don't want you to! It's as simple as that. Maybe you should just leave, okay? Whatever you think we've got going here, is a mistake."

He stared at her as if she'd gone insane. "Wait a minute. You're not making any sense. You need help."

"But I don't need to be smothered! I'm a grown woman, for crying out loud. So back off. And, please, just leave me the hell alone."

For a second he just stood in the kitchen, his boots unmoving, his mouth slack, and then, as if he finally got it, he sucked his breath in through his teeth. "If that's what you want." Zipping his jacket, he made his way to the back door. "I'm sorry I was so pushy, Jenna," he said, one hand resting on the doorknob as he looked at her over his shoulder. "It's just my way. Years of taking command, you know."

She didn't back down. Just glared at him.

"Listen, I'll look over the security system just for my own peace of mind, and then I'll leave you alone. If you change your mind, give me a call."

She wouldn't. She knew it.

Most likely, he did, too.

His blood was pumping. Thrumming through his veins. Snowflakes melted against his flesh, drizzling cold trails of water down his face and along his bare skin. He wore only gloves, no other article of clothing. His muscles quivered as he pulled himself up on the bar he used for chin-ups, a cold metal rod lodged deep into the rough bark of giant firs.

Pull up . . . slowly . . . let down even more slowly. Body rigid. Feet together. Up. Down. Up. Down. One hundred times.

Exercise was part of his daily regimen. Day in, day out. Regardless of the weather.

"Neither snow nor rain nor heat nor gloom of night . . . yeah, that was it, just as regular as the U.S. Postal Service.

Dependable

But deadly.

Invincible in winter.

Made strong by the very cold he abhorred. Mentally clicking off the reps, feeling the ache in his muscles as he strained, he felt the need to kill again, the pulsing need begin to throb through him. Gritting his teeth, he finished his regimen, then dropped lithely to the ground, his bare feet sinking into the drifting snow.

The sheen of sweat on his skin mingled with the icy drops of snow. Hot and cold. Freezing air rushing over his nakedness. Steam rising from his flesh.

The wickedness of the night crept under his skin.

He closed his eyes for a second.

Imagined the hunt.

It was the killing time.

And he knew where to find her . . .

CHAPTER 27

If Mohammed wouldn't come to the mountain, then the damned mountain was going to haul ass to him.

Roxie Olmstead was tired of getting the "no comment" routine from the Lewis County Sheriff's Department, and she was pissed that she couldn't get through to Carter. The guy was stonewalling her, no doubt about it.

She'd left voice messages and e-mail messages and even hung out around the courthouse, hoping to flag Carter down and get some kind of information about Mavis Gette, the woman found in pieces up on Catwalk Point. Even after the corpse had been identified, Carter had refused her calls—well, actually, that bitch of a receptionist, Jerri Morales, had coolly informed Roxie that Carter was "out" or "in a meeting" or "unavailable." She'd only found out about Mavis Gette from a statement issued by the Oregon State Police.

"Hell," she muttered, walking out of the offices of the Lewis County *Banner*. The wind blasted her, pushing her hood off her head and running icy fingers through her hair. Clutching her laptop, thermos, and purse, she hurried through the blowing snow to her car and unlocked the little four-door. Her stomach was acting up again and she popped a couple of antacids after she scraped a vision hole in the ice covering the windshield, then flicked on the ignition and the Toyota's

defroster started warming the glass in front of her. Her
Corolla had over two hundred thousand miles on it and was
beat to hell, the interior shot, but with an engine that wouldn't
quit. With a standard "three-on-the-tree" transmission and
studded snow tires, the old car could get Roxie just about
anywhere. Including Sheriff Carter's house.

She smiled to herself as she considered the lawman. Tall
and good-looking, Carter appeared more like Hollywood's
vision of a cowboy than a real sheriff. It bugged the hell out
of Roxie that he wouldn't give her the time of day. Well,
tonight things were going to change.

She turned on the wipers to help scrape off the ice, and
switched on her favorite radio station, one of the few that
came in here, and listened to '80s pop as the ice slowly
melted and the car's interior warmed. Before she could really see much, she swiped a spot clear on the inside of the
windshield and picked her way through the few cars in the
lot, then gunned it onto the street. Her car slid a bit and she
grinned. God, she loved the snow, watched as it swirled and
danced in front of her headlights. At a stoplight, she braked,
found a tube of lip gloss in her purse, and swiped a little
pinkish stain over her lips. She was admiring her work in the
rearview mirror when the light changed; she stepped on it
before the guy on her bumper got impatient and laid on the
horn.

Driving out of town, she mentally sketched out what she
would say to Carter when he answered his door.

If he wasn't home, she'd wait. She had a thermos of coffee, a blanket, and a book that was interesting enough to
hold her attention, but not so consuming that she'd lose track
of time or her quarry. If he didn't show up in an hour, she'd
bag it and try again tomorrow. As much as she wanted to
corner him, there was only so much time she could spend in
this cold, and she wasn't going to use up all the power in her
little battery.

But, by God, he was going to talk to her.

Face-to-face.

She had questions to ask him, and, in her mind, was plotting what she intended to say to him, how to approach him, how to avoid getting his door slammed in her face. She even thought of using a ploy—"Sorry, Sheriff, I ran out of gas, right up the road"—but knew he'd see right through it. What to do? How could she get past his formidable facade and into the real man beneath his tough veneer? Just what was it that made Carter tick? She knew all the standard facts about him: age, education, that he'd lived in Falls Crossing most of his life; he'd been married, and his wife had died in a deadly cold snap not unlike this one, but she'd like to pierce through that invisible armor of his. What was the man behind the badge like?

She'd hate to think how many times she'd fantasized about him. There was something about a brooding, quiet, secretive man in a uniform that turned her on. Oh God, she'd hate to think what some shrink would make of that, especially since her father had been a cop.

So intent was she on her inner thoughts that she braked and signaled by rote, driving into the snowstorm and heading toward his home. Humming along to an old Billy Idol tune, she barely noticed the thin traffic, the few cars she met on the snowy roads, nor anyone following her.

Engine humming, her Toyota skimmed along the road, snow tires holding onto the icy pavement, headlights sending thin beams that cut through the night and glistened against the dirty, sandy, packed snow. The song ended and she glanced in the rearview mirror, noticing for the first time how close a car was behind her. Right on her ass. "Jesus," she growled, as if he could hear her. "Hey, buddy, this isn't L.A." She sped up, her tires sliding a bit, and he was right with her. An idiot. One of oh, so many. Man, if she could get his license plate. That was it. She slowed, but he didn't pass, just hugged her bumper, probably afraid to try and make it around her on these twisting, icy roads.

Fortunately, the turn-off to the road leading past Carter's house was just a mile ahead. No doubt she'd lose this bastard then.

She shifted down for the corner, put in the clutch and felt

it give. Oh, hell, it had been temperamental lately. The car behind her didn't slow. "Watch out," she said, managing to ram her Corolla into second gear, then tried for first just as she reached the turn-off. The prick was still on her butt! Not backing off an inch. What the hell was he thinking? Carefully, she eased her foot onto the brake and started into her turn.

Bam!

Her head snapped.

What the hell? The idiot behind her had clipped her bumper!

Her Toyota began to spin crazily.

Instinctively she stood on the brakes.

Wrong! The car slid out of control, still cutting 360s and reeling wildly toward the trees. "Shit!"

She tried to remember to turn into the spin, not to lock her brakes, but the side of the road and the trees were whirling ever closer. Too close. "Damn it, damn it, damn it!" she yelled, trying not to freak out, praying the car would slow. She was at the edge of the road now. A huge Douglas fir with thick, twisted bark loomed into view.

Closer. "No!"

Closer, the NO TRESPASSING sign right in front of her. "Jesus, no!"

Thud!

Metal groaned.

She covered her face.

The car jolted to a stop.

She started to fly forward, her head hit the steering wheel, but the seat belt snapped her body against the seat.

Glass shattered, raining down on her as ice and snow spewed into the Toyota.

She tasted blood where her teeth had cut into her lip.

Dazed, she reached for the seat belt clasp and in the cracked side-view mirror saw someone approach. The idiot who had hit her! Woozy, she undid the seat belt and fumbled for the door. She felt like she was going to puke.

"Are you all right?" a male voice asked.

No, you fucking moron, she thought groggily. *I'm not, thanks to you.*

"Let me help you."

Good. Fine. Before I give you a piece of my mind and then sue the hell out of you.

The car door opened and she retched, throwing up all over the snow and door frame. Her mouth tasted sour and she managed to swipe at it with the back of her gloved hand. God, she was shaky, and she couldn't afford to be. "Why the hell were you driving up my ass?" she demanded as a big hand clasped around her arm. She looked up through her hair and the glass that had sprayed her. Didn't she recognize this guy? Hadn't she seen him around town?

"I just wanted to get your attention, Marnie."

"What?" She tried to think. "Marnie? I'm not Marnie! What kind of idiot are you?"

"One who's here to help." He smiled then, and she saw something sinister in his grin, something that touched on cruel.

"Then get your hands off me. I'll be fine," she said, her head clearing. She had mace in her purse, an ice scraper in the side pocket of the Toyota's door.

"I don't think so." He was pulling her out of the car and she started resisting when she saw his weapon, a gun of some sort, and her heart stood still.

"What is this?" she whispered, staring into eyes as cold as ice.

"Salvation."

"But you've got the wrong woman." She was fighting, trying to reach for the ice scraper, for her purse, for anything.

"I know," he said, and then he aimed the gun at her and a jolt of electricity shot through her system. She jerked and he shot her again with the stun gun before she went limp. "Of course you're the wrong woman, Marnie. But you'll just have to do."

* * *

Randall checked his watch. He hated to end the session, as they were becoming less frequent. His client had cancelled the last one that was to have been so early in the morning, then called back a day later and set up this appointment. Unfortunately, it was time to end their talk for the evening. Another client, his last of this god-awful night, would be arriving by the front staircase within fifteen minutes. He was surprised she hadn't cancelled, considering the weather, but she was a die-hard, a lifer. She'd been in counseling fifteen years and probably would be for the rest of her life. As this one should be. He tapped his pen, the one he swore not to use, on the edge of the desk, then caught himself and stopped.

The action didn't go unnoticed. "So you're telling me I have to face my fears."

"Essentially." Randall nodded, set his pen in a cup on the desk.

"I do that every day."

"Do you?" Randall nodded his agreement, though his client remained suspicious and tense. Sitting on a corner of the couch, he clenched both hands into fists, thumbs rubbing anxiously along the top of his index finger.

Steely eyes stared him down. "You know, I'm beginning to suspect this is all bullshit."

"You came to me."

"It was 'suggested' by one of the people I work for."

"And you took the suggestion."

A beard-stubbled jaw slid to one side. "I thought it might help."

"Has it?"

"You tell me—you're the professional."

"I can't read your mind."

A hint of a smile. "No? Then why the hell am I wasting my money?"

"Because you wanted to get over your feelings of guilt."

The fists opened and closed again. "I don't think that's possible." Thick eyebrows slammed together.

"I think we're making progress."

"Do you?"

"Mmm. But these sessions are not only confidential, they're optional. No one is forcing you to come here." He stared over the tops of his glasses and waited for a confirmation of his statement.

"That's right."

"You do know that you weren't responsible for David's death."

A muscle worked in that hard jaw.

"Nor Carolyn's."

His client looked out the window and plucked at a seam in the smooth leather of the couch.

Randall stared at the sheriff's disbelieving profile as Carter attempted to wrest his demons from the cold winter night. "You don't believe me," Randall said.

"You weren't there. You only heard my side of it. If either David or Carolyn were here now, they might tell a different tale." He faced the psychologist and his face was set. "They each depended on me. I let them down."

"As they let you down."

Carter snorted. "I didn't die because my best friend was a fool and my wife cheated on me."

"You didn't kill them. You couldn't climb the ice fast enough to catch David, and Carolyn was off to meet her lover and hit black ice—her car slid off the road and down a ravine. You couldn't have stopped that."

"We'd had a fight."

"Nonetheless."

"I should have stopped her from getting into her car."

"Could you have?" he asked, and the seconds ticked loudly from the clock on the fireplace.

"I don't know." He shook his head. "Probably not." Carter shifted on the couch, reached into his pocket, pulled out his wallet with his badge. "Protect and Serve—isn't that what it says?" His eyes were dark and thunderous. "And I couldn't save my best friend or my wife."

"You weren't an officer when David died."

"But I was when I demanded a divorce and Carolyn left the house crying."

"Didn't you try to follow her?"

"Only until the edge of town," Carter said, and his eyes narrowed. Randall knew the lawman's gaze had turned inward and he wasn't seeing the night outside the window, but was revisiting the scene of the accident that had taken his wife's life.

"And why was that?"

"Because she was going to his house," Carter said, turning to look at the psychologist again. "Look, I don't think we're getting anywhere." He grabbed his coat and jacket from the hall tree, then reached for the door. "If I think I need another session, I'll call."

Randall just smiled. "Whatever you want. But I think there are issues you need to explore."

"You know what, Doc? There always will be." With that he exited, taking the back stairs to the first level. Randall waited, then walked to the very window Carter had stared out of just moments before. The sheriff brushed snow from the windshield, then climbed into his Blazer. As he pulled out of his parking spot in the alley, another client was driving into the small lot.

Randall walked back to his desk and reached into the drawer. With only a quick pang of guilt, he clicked off the small recorder that had taped the entire session.

Sheriff Carter probably didn't know it, but he had a death wish, one that came with the snowfall. Not only had the lawman lost those dear to him in winter, Carter had experienced more than his share of life-threatening incidents, all in the deep winter months. His own vehicle had slid off the road more than once, and when rescuing a child from a cabin where her parents were having a violent argument, the father, despondent, drunk, out of work and mad at the world, had accidently shot Carter in the leg. Carter had evacuated an elderly shut-in during a winter storm like this one, and as he arrived, the gas heater, set ridiculously high, had exploded. Both he and the woman had survived, surprisingly. Then there was the fishing incident, when his boat had hit a snag and capsized in the turbulent, frigid waters of the Columbia. Another boat had seen the accident and, miraculously, had gotten to him in time.

Sooner or later, though, Carter's luck would run out and his recklessness would catch up with him.

It always did.

Finally the cameras were working again . . . He stared at his screen and watched through the hidden lens, seeing Jenna Hughes walk through her bedroom, stripping off her sweater, bending as she wiggled out of her jeans, her perfectly round buttocks covered only by lacy bikini panties . . . black panties cut high on the sides that barely covered her most private of places.

His cock jerked a bit, starting to harden as she stepped into the bathroom, reached in and turned on the shower, then unhooked her bra and tossed the flimsy black scrap of cloth onto a hook near the glass door.

"That's it," he whispered, staring at the screen, his mouth suddenly devoid of spit. He heard a moan from the outer room and was irritated. Marnie was waking up. The slut! A schoolteacher who chased after the wrong men in bars . . . risking everything to get laid. He refused to listen to her while he was watching Jenna. Perfect Jenna. She pulled off her panties, exposing all of her beautiful body, kicking the tiny briefs out of the way, then stopped in front of the mirror to quickly pin her hair up on her head. In the mirror he saw her breasts—large, firm, with pointed little nipples.

Steam was rising from the shower as she stepped inside and closed the glass door.

He was suddenly rock-hard and he let his hand wander down to his own nakedness, to stroke the smooth, cool skin of his erection. Light fingers. He imagined Jenna's hands upon him, the sensual wonder of her fingers . . . and then her tongue. Touching. Stroking.

"Ooooh."
Jenna?
No, Marnie.
From the other room. Waking up.
His erection withered.
It was time to deal with her.

CHAPTER 28

Carter hadn't been kidding when he'd called the last session with Dr. Randall "bullshit." They were getting nowhere, slogging through the same old emotional territory time and time again. He'd initially contacted the psychologist because of his grief, upon the advice of the District Attorney, but his sessions had been spotty at best—and uncomfortable.

He'd stopped the sessions altogether a few years back, but had started them up again this winter because the nightmares had returned with the cold weather. Horrible nightmares where he saw David's face beneath the ice, staring up at him and moving silent lips as the air left his lungs, and even darker images of Carolyn, her bloodied face and body trapped in her crushed car. While David remained silent in the dream, Carolyn's voice droned over and over, "Why, Shane, why? Why can't you forgive me . . . ?"

A good question.

Had it been Carolyn's fault that Shane had spent more time as a deputy than as a husband to his wife? Had it been her fault that he hadn't been ready for a child she wanted so desperately? Had it been her fault that Shane had encouraged her to go out with friends without him, when he'd been working? Had it been her fault that Wes Allen, an artist at heart, had known just how to make a lonely woman feel wanted?

"Son of a bitch," Carter muttered, closing his mind to the image that had haunted him for years: the thought of Carolyn and Wes in Carter's bed on the nights when he was on duty. His hands gripped the wheel as his cell phone blasted.

He picked it up before it chirped a second time. "Carter," he barked.

"It's Hixx. We've got ourselves a single-car accident on Southeast Rivercrest—1973 Toyota registered to Roxie Olmstead."

The reporter. Close to his place.

"Is she all right?"

"Don't know. She's not in the vehicle, and there's snow piling up on it."

"Where is she?"

"That's the problem. No one knows. She left her office around seven, logged out at six-fifty, and, according to her landlady, hasn't been home, not even to let her dog out. She's single, lives alone. We called the local hospitals and she hasn't been admitted—she also didn't call for a tow, nor in to the police to report the accident. We haven't started in on her friends or family yet."

"Maybe she took off. Had one too many drinks and didn't want to face the consequences, went somewhere until she sobered up."

"It looks like someone did pick her up. Another vehicle's tire tracks and boot or shoe prints. But what's odd is that her purse and laptop are still in the car. She didn't take them with her, nor did whoever showed up on the scene."

Carter felt a frisson of fear skate down his spine.

"Then there's something else. She printed herself a route map, off of the Internet. Directions to your house, Sheriff."

"My house?" What the hell was that all about? A razor of guilt sliced into his brain. Hadn't the Olmstead woman been dogging him for the last week or so, hoping to get an interview or at least a quote? He'd ignored her. "Secure the scene," Carter said, punching it. His Blazer shot forward, sliding just a little. "I'll be right there."

Carter didn't like the sound of it, thought about how Sonja Hatchell had disappeared. How Mavis Gette had been discovered up at Catwalk Point. Two cases that weren't necessarily linked, both entirely different situations, a hitchhiker who took a ride with the wrong guy and a waitress who, along with her vehicle, had vanished into a frozen night. But they all had connections to this area. *Don't go jumping to conclusions*, he warned himself, but he had a bad feeling about this, a real bad feeling. It didn't go away as he drove through the snow to the turn-off where not only a patrol car from the OSP had arrived, but several reporters, not just from the *Banner*, but a local news van as well. Probably because of the call to the newspaper by the police to try and locate Olmstead. Someone had tipped the TV guys.

A small woman in a blue parka was quick to accost him, shoving a microphone in his face. "Sheriff Carter? I'm Brenda Ward, KBST." A cameraman was tagging after her. "Do you think Roxie Olmstead's disappearance is linked to Sonja Hatchell's?"

Carter turned and faced the reporter, noticed the camera's lens focused on him. "We don't know that she has disappeared. What we have so far is a single-car accident, probably because of the storm, and other than that I really can't speculate or comment at this time."

She started to step closer, waved her cameraman in, but Carter ignored her and walked to the scene of the accident. Luckily, she didn't follow past the tape.

The situation was just as Hixx had explained over the phone, but as Carter stood with his back to the wind, snowflakes swirling all around him as he observed the smashed front-end of the Toyota, he had doubts. Something was wrong here.

Very wrong.

Lying on a cold, hard slab she awoke. Every muscle in Roxie's body ached. Her head pounded. Her mouth tasted like crap. And above all, she was freezing. So damned cold she could barely draw a breath. She opened an eye as memories collided in her brain. She'd been driving to see the sheriff, some nutcase had forced her off the road, there had been a horrid crash, and then she'd been zapped with a stun gun.

Worse yet, she was naked.

Wearing only her goose bumps.

Jesus, what had that creep done to her?

She was tied, unable to move much, and scared to death, but she tried to tamp down her fear. Wherever she was, she had to get out. ASAP. And she had to be quiet, so as not to alert the pervert that she was awake. Slowly she twisted her head against cold, smooth concrete, craning her neck, straining to see, hoping to determine where the hell she was and how to escape.

The lights were dim but she focused and saw that she was in a warehouse or big, yawning building with high ceilings covered with posters and pictures. Of one woman. Jenna Hughes. Holy crap, what kind of sicko was he? She saw no windows, no doors, but knew there had to be an exit somewhere. In the middle of the big room was a stage filled with half a dozen people or so. Half-dressed women. Some bald. Some completely naked. A couple with waxy painted faces, some without any features at all.

Roxie's heart nearly stopped as she gazed at this group of women, none of whom moved so much as an inch . . . no, she realized, not women, but statues. Surreal statues. She blinked twice and realized they were actually mannequins, the kind she'd seen in Saks and Neiman-Marcus.

What the hell was this? Some crazy *Stepford Wives* scenario? And why was it so damned cold? Didn't the creep believe in heat? Or was this part of his torture? At that thought, her insides turned to water. Torture. Oh, God, no. She studied the mannequins clustered around a recliner—no, not a La-Z-Boy but a dentist's chair, complete with drill.

She heard a noise and froze.

Music filled the room. Music from *Summer's End,* one of Jenna Hughes's movies. Roxie had seen it half a dozen times on cable TV, had identified with Marnie Sylvane, the central character, a lonely schoolteacher who could never find love. *Marnie* Sylvane. Hadn't the creep called her "Marnie" when he'd attacked her?

What kind of weird shit was going on here?

From the corner of her eye, she caught a glimpse of him. Stark naked, standing in a glassed-in room, staring at a computer monitor. She shivered with a new fear, and as if he sensed it, he turned suddenly, eyes focusing on her.

"Ah, Marnie. Awake, are you?" He smiled chillingly and walked through a glass door to the large room.

"I'm *not* Marnie," she said, and his smile slipped a little.

"Of course you are."

"I'm Roxie Olmstead, a reporter with the Lewis County *Banner.*" She was struggling to get to her feet, but her ankles were tied with thick ropes and she couldn't push herself upright. Damn it all. "My husband is going to miss me and he'll call the police, but that's not the worst of it. He'll come looking for you and he'll break your neck when he does!"

"You're not married, Marnie."

"I told you, dick-wad, I'm *not* Marnie." *And I'm not married, either*, Roxie thought desperately, hoping he'd buy into her bluff.

"You're just embarrassed."

"*What?*"

"Because you've let yourself go . . . but I'll fix that. You'll see."

"What the hell are you talking about? I don't need any fixing—hey!" She had pushed herself into a sitting position when she saw the stun gun at his side and stopped moving. Her blood turned to ice water.

"That's better," he said, his voice just audible over the music. Her eyes were fixed on the ugly little weapon. "Now . . . relax."

Like hell, she thought, and threw herself at him, clawing

with her nails, determined to get a piece of him. He yelped as she scratched his cheek. The stun gun sizzled and she felt a jolt of pure electricity slam her to the floor.

Bam!

Her chin bounced on the cold concrete.

Pain exploded in her head. She nearly passed out.

"Stupid bitch," he growled, touching his face, smearing the blood running from beneath his left eye. "That's the problem with you, Marnie. I guess it's time you learned a very valuable lesson."

No, Roxie thought frantically, helpless for the first time in her life. *Whatever it is, no!* She couldn't speak, couldn't move, but watched as he withdrew a gleaming hypodermic needle from his pocket. Holding the syringe aloft, he squirted clear liquid into the cold air. Her terrified gaze locked with his and he smiled again . . . the cold, calculating grin of a killer.

For the first time in fifteen years, Roxie Olmstead began to pray.

CHAPTER 29

Jake Turnquist was all Harrison Brennan had promised, and more. With the build of an athlete and blue eyes that seemed to miss nothing, he met with Jenna, struck a deal, and, after doing a perimeter check of the property, chose to live in the studio apartment over the garage. He claimed it had a bird's-eye view of the house. He had agreed to spend his nights in the studio and drive the girls to and from school. Jenna was more concerned about their welfare than her own, and she agreed to carry her cell phone with a Global Positioning System chip, a walkie-talkie, and have a GPS system added to her Jeep. Each girl would have a cell phone that would be fitted with a chip as well and they, too, would carry walkie-talkies.

"This is gonna be weird," Cassie predicted as she, through the kitchen window, watched Jake unload equipment from a camper attached to the bed of his pickup. A duffel bag slung over one shoulder, he carried two equipment cases up the exterior stairs. "It's like Big Brother's watching."

"But it makes your mother feel so much safer." Jenna slammed the dishwasher shut and her gaze followed Cassie's.

"How long will he stay?"

"As long as it takes."

His breath fogging in the cold air, Turnquist was hurrying

down the exterior steps of the apartment. He jogged to the back of the truck and pulled out a sleeping bag, a laptop computer case as well as a rifle with a scope.

"Scary," Cassie whispered.

Jenna placed her fingers around her daughter's hand and squeezed. "Safer."

"I don't know how much safer I feel about a stranger living here with guns and night goggles and spy stuff," Cassie muttered as Jenna released her hand. "It's like he thinks he's Rambo or something."

Rambo would be good, Jenna thought, but said, "Let's give the guy a chance, okay?" He'd personally handed her a three-page list of references the day before. Jenna had called nine of the names on the list, all of whom had lauded Turnquist with glowing recommendations.

"I'd trust him with my daughters. Or my granddaughters, for that matter," one man had proclaimed.

"He helped us figure out who was terrorizing us," another woman said. "Jake Turnquist found the hooligans who had burned a cross in our yard and slit the tires of our truck. Rounded 'em up and called the authorities. We could finally sleep easy again."

No one had said so much as one word against the man.

Jenna had hired him on the spot.

Now, as she watched him duck into the garret over the garage, she felt a little sense of relief. Even though Jake Turnquist wasn't the first man she would have chosen for the job. There was a part of her that silently wished she could have hired the sheriff to protect her and the girls. Ever since considering a bodyguard, she'd silently imagined Shane Carter filling the studio apartment with his things, watching the property, sitting with her at night, ensuring that all the doors and windows were locked, that the fence surrounding her ranch wasn't breached.

As much as Carter put her on edge emotionally, Jenna had come to trust his instincts and respect him as an officer of the law. From Rinda, Jenna knew enough about him personally to believe that he would do whatever was necessary to keep her and her daughters safe.

Except that he had an entire county to protect, not just her little family.

Still . . . she imagined him carrying his suitcase up the garage stairs.

Oh, come on, Jenna, you know better. It's not in the studio where you really want the man, is it? There's a part of you that would like to know what it was like for him to hold you, to kiss you, to make love to you.

Wow! She slammed the door to her mind shut at that thought.

Where had it come from?

She would be a fool to deny that Shane Carter was a rugged, sexy lawman, but so what? She had only to look at the latest batch of mail lying on the kitchen table, and the envelope containing her receipt for her traffic ticket, to remember what a jerk Carter could be. He was off limits. Way off limits. What in the world was she doing, fantasizing about the man? Hadn't she overheard what he thought of her when he'd caught her complaining to Rinda at the church? Hadn't he insinuated she thought herself to be some kind of Hollywood royalty?

Yes, but that was before you knew him, before he showed some concern for you and your daughters, before you noticed the wink of laughter in his eyes, the hint of kindness. Face it, you're falling for the man.

"Oh, no way!" she said out loud.

"'No way' what?" Cassie asked.

"Nothing. I . . . I got lost in my own thoughts." She glanced out the window again and saw that Jake had finished taking his things up the stairs and was walking to the gates. He'd mentioned that he was going to double-check the gates and security system, then walk the fence line and get a feel for her property.

After that, he might have more suggestions.

She was willing to listen to them all.

She hadn't gotten over the feeling of uneasiness every time she stepped into her bedroom. How had an intruder slipped in and out to leave his terrifying note? How many times had he been in her house? In her bedroom? Had he sat on the bed when she was gone? Stretched out on it? Imagined her with him? Touched himself while looking at the picture of her and her daughters on her bureau?

"Mom? Are you okay?" Cassie asked, bringing Jenna crashing back to the present. Cassie was staring at her as if there was something wrong and Jenna suddenly realized she was leaning against the counter, scratching her arms with her opposite hands. She hadn't even known it. "You're not freaking out or anything, are you?"

"Nah!" Jenna forced a smile and lied through her teeth. "Just thinking about the production. We're going to have another rehearsal tomorrow night and the last one was a bust. We scheduled another and had to cancel because of the weather, but . . ." she looked outside again to the gray clouds, "the weather's supposed to clear. That means school tomorrow for you—"

Cassie let out a melodramatic groan.

"—and yet another gripping rehearsal of *It's a Wonderful Life* for me! Now, let's go find your sister and see what she wants for lunch."

"Let me guess. Mac and cheese, chicken nuggets, or pizza."

"Or nachos," Jenna added, glad to have changed the subject. "Later, you can help me put up the outdoor lights." She surveyed the mess still pushed into one corner of the den. Christmas lights, garlands, bows, and ornaments peeked out of boxes.

"Can't Hans do it? Or the new guy—Turnquist?"

Jenna chuckled. "I don't think that's what he signed on for. You're the one that brought up families doing Christmas stuff together, remember? Baking cookies? Singing carols? Well, we're going to start with the lights. It'll be the beginning of a new tradition."

"Great," Cassie said with a sigh. "Why did I open my big mouth?"

"Because you're filled with the spirit of Christmas."

"Oh, save me," she whispered, but laughed—and Jenna felt better than she had since discovering the note in her bedroom, if only slightly.

Two days after the accident, Carter drove into town and passed the fir tree that Roxie's little car had smashed into. Since her crumpled, abandoned car had been discovered, no one had heard a word from her. Nor had search parties found any indication of what had happened to her. The tree bore a nasty scar, bark splintered, bare wood now covered with rime.

The Oregon State Police were working with the FBI, but Lieutenant Sparks kept Carter in the loop. Because of the suspected abduction, the state crime lab had processed the site where the car had been wrecked and the Corolla, towed to a police garage, had been gone over by technicians. They'd found little evidence except to note that apparently Roxie had been on her way to Carter's house when she'd lost control of the car. A fresh dent on the rear bumper and fender indicated that she might have been hit, though there were several other dents on the car, all of which appeared older that this new scrape. The lab was working with the scratches on the bumper, but no paint had been left behind.

Roxie had left her purse, gym bag, laptop computer, spilled thermos of coffee, and a map she'd printed off the Internet which included driving directions to Carter's front door. According to her editor, she'd been working on several stories at the time, one of which had been Sonja Hatchell's disappearance, and now she, too, was missing.

Ironic.

Fated?

Or just plain bad luck?

Carter had talked to the detectives from the OSP and had

admitted he'd been avoiding Roxie Olmstead as well as anyone else from the press prior to her disappearance. Now, of course, he was second-guessing himself and was fighting his own personal battle with guilt demons about the accident. If he'd granted her an interview, would she be alive today?

There's no evidence that she's dead. Remember that. You're looking for a missing woman, not a dead one.

But deep down, he felt a dread so vile, he couldn't face it. Didn't want to be the first to say the words "serial killer" when there were no bodies to suggest the horrid thought.

Nonetheless, he couldn't help wondering, had he granted her an interview earlier, would she have traveled that stretch of road? Been hit from behind? Been abducted?

"Son of a bitch," he muttered to himself as the police band radio crackled and he passed the theater. Christmas lights burned around the windows and a backlit sign reminded everyone that tickets were currently on sale for the troupe's next production, a local version of *It's a Wonderful Life.*

Since when? Carter thought, his mood as gray as the clouds overhead. At least it wasn't snowing. Crews had finally managed to scrape and sand the roads and electricity had been restored to all but a handful of citizens of Lewis County, but the temperature was still below freezing and now the ice floes in the river were beginning to cause concern. Sleet mixed with snow in the higher elevations and wasn't supposed to improve.

He noticed Jenna Hughes's Jeep was parked in the theater's lot and he wondered if she'd hired Turnquist or if she was still looking for a bodyguard. He didn't like to think of her and her girls alone and isolated at their ranch. Since he had a few minutes before he was officially on duty, he pulled into the lot. Before he second-guessed his reasons, he headed up the steps to the front doors and walked into the theater.

Music was playing from the speakers and he heard the sound of voices coming from the lower level. His boots ringing along the hardwood, he made his way to the sound and found Rinda and Jenna bending over a computer screen.

"Hey, handsome," Rinda said, standing and hugging Carter before holding him at arm's length and studying him. "Bad morning?"

"Aren't they all?"

Rinda rolled her eyes, but Jenna, leaning against the desk, actually cracked a smile. And what a smile it was. Damned near radiant. Probably practiced.

"I saw your Jeep out front and I wondered how things were going. You hired Turnquist, right?"

She nodded.

"But he's not here."

"He took the kids to school and is going back home. We have a deal. He stays overnight in the studio over the garage so that he's got a bird's-eye view of the place, and we've got cell phones and walkie-talkies on all the time." As if she read the questions in Carter's eyes, she added, "Look, I'm freaked out, of course I am, but I can't have someone breathing down my neck every second of the day. I have to have a little privacy. Some independence."

"The security system's working?"

"So far, so good. Jake's double-checked everything and he walks the perimeter every night . . . I feel a whole lot safer. Thanks."

"Just do what he says."

Rinda let out an exasperated breath, "The polite response is 'You're welcome.' Jesus, Carter, when will you quit being such a hard-ass?"

"When I think things are safe."

"Things are never safe," Rinda pointed out, her good mood dissolving. "But yeah, right now it's not a great time around here. First Sonja and then Roxie." She clucked her tongue and rubbed her arms. "I don't suppose you have any news on either one of them."

"Not yet."

"Jesus. I hate this. Roxie was a good kid. Headstrong, but, well, she was young."

"You knew her?"

"Not all that well, but when Scott and I moved back here

from California, I met Lila, Roxie's mom. We were both newly divorced and so we connected. Scott hung out with Roxie even though she was a couple of years older."

The door to the theater opened and footsteps heralded Wes Allen's arrival. "Hey, what's going on . . . ?" His gaze clashed with Carter's. "Shane," he said and nodded, though his smile was forced. Had been for years. To think they'd all been friends once.

"Wes."

"In here fighting crime?" Wes asked, winking a steely blue eye.

Rinda let out a nervous little laugh.

"Wherever I can find it," Carter said, refusing to be baited. No more. There had been a time when he'd wanted to bash in Wes Allen's face and he'd given it a good shot one night, jeopardizing his job for a chance to pummel the man who had seduced his wife. But that had been years ago, before Carter accepted the fact that Carolyn had probably done the seducing and that he, Carter, had been instrumental in pushing her away. Maybe those years of therapy hadn't been wasted after all. He nodded toward Jenna Hughes. "I'll stop by later."

Was it his imagination, or did her green eyes brighten just a fraction? "Do that."

"I will," he promised, and for the first time in over two weeks, Carter felt as if there was light at the end of the tunnel. "See ya around," he said to Rinda and clapped a stunned Wes Allen on his shoulder.

Why is it so dark?
And cold . . . so damned cold.
Pain screamed up her arms.
Groggily, she opened one eye.
Where am I?
Roxie's head was thick, her thoughts unconnected, her memory fragmented. Her mouth ached. Her teeth felt weird.

Shivering violently, her painful teeth chattering so hard they rattled in her skull, she tried to think.

Frigid air swirled around her, whispering over her bare skin.

Was she naked?

She forced her other eye open and saw that she was in some kind of chamber . . . or laboratory, a dark, cylindrical room that was so cold that her breath fogged in shallow wisps. Suspended over a large tank.

What! Suspended?

Jesus, Roxie, think! Where the hell are you?

Little bits of memory emerged. The accident. The stun gun. The needle. Oh, God, some pervert had her!

She tried to scream but couldn't force a sound. Her arms were stretched over her head, her wrists bound to a crossbar, her legs, too, strapped against a long, steel beam that pressed against her spine.

Looking down, she saw that the vat was glass and filled with a clear liquid.

Oh, God, it's acid, she thought wildly, trying to struggle, as she remembered the horror movies she'd watched so avidly. Panic squeezed through her insides. Ice-cold air swirled around her. She had to escape. Now! Frantically, she searched the large, frigid chamber. The ceiling was twenty feet above her, the rounded walls far away and darkened, but there were people in one corner. No, not people, but the faceless mannequins she'd seen earlier, all dressed in weird clothes . . . or costumes . . . clothes she was certain she'd seen somewhere, but that couldn't be . . . She swallowed back her fear as she spied posters plastered upon the walls surrounding the macabre stage, posters from movies she'd seen:

Resurrection.

Beneath the Shadows.

Innocence Lost.

Summer's End.

Movies starring Jenna Hughes . . . and her pictures were everywhere, tacked to the ceiling and walls. This was some kind of, what—macabre shrine to her? What the hell kind of madness was this?

This is a dream. A nightmare. That's all. Calm down.

But her heart was racing, thundering in her ears. Though she was frigidly cold, she began to sweat, the thin, wet drops of pure fear.

Was she alone?

"Help!" she yelled. "Oh, God, please, *someone* help me!" But her voice was garbled and muted, even to her own ears. Fear and desperation clawed through her.

Then she saw him. Again.

The dirt-wad who had done this to her.

Stark naked, standing in the eerie blue glow of a computer monitor.

"You fucking bastard!" she tried to yell. "Get me down from here, you prick!" Her words were useless . . . unintelligible.

He stared up at her. Even smiled.

Oh, God, he was enjoying this.

Her bravado crumbled.

"Help me!" she tried to plead. "Please!"

He moved slightly and she noticed his erection . . . thick and hard. He was really getting off on this. Oh, God . . . she thought she might be sick.

He pushed a button on the computer. Music filled the chamber. A song she recognized. The theme from some movie. *White Out*, that was it—the movie was never finished but the song had been released.

The beam jolted.

Terror scraped down Roxie's spine and she screamed.

With a whirring sound, the steel cable began to unwind.

Slowly the beam began to descend. By inches she was being lowered, closer to the tank of clear, deadly liquid.

"No! Oh, God, no!" She began to whimper and shake, struggled vainly against her bonds, watched in terror as she was lowered ever downward. "Please, for the love of God, let me go!"

The volume of the music increased until it was echoing in

the chamber, ricocheting through her brain as the beam touched the clear liquid. She sucked in her breath, the cold burning her lungs as her toes hit the icy liquid.

Not acid.

But water.

Cold enough to freeze solid.

"Stop! Please! Why are you doing this to me?"

Her feet were submerged, muscles cramping against the cold as it crawled upward, ever upward. Past her calves to her thighs and higher still. She screamed wildly, trying to thrash, her legs and arms unresponsive, the bonds too tight, her blood congealing in her body. As the water reached her breasts, she knew that she was doomed. Through her tears and the curved glass of the vat, she saw the son of a bitch again, now so much closer. She spat at him, hitting the glass above the surface of the water. He didn't so much as flinch. Just stood naked and hard.

Watching.

Waiting.

Killing her by frigid, deadly inches.

CHAPTER 30

Fifteen minutes after deciding to quit holding an old grudge against Wes Allen, Carter was seated at his desk in the courthouse. He spent most of the morning answering e-mail, filling out reports, taking phone calls, and handling the regular business of the department, but all the while he thought about the missing women, Mavis Gette, and the notes Jenna Hughes had received. Were they connected? Not that he could prove anything.

But he wasn't done trying.

It didn't help that the D.A.'s office was on his ass. Amanda Pratt had stopped by his office earlier, sweet as pie, inquiring about the Mavis Gette case. The broken collarbone, a bit of an overbite, and finally, DNA, had proved that Jane Doe was Mavis Gette, whose killer was, presumably, still on the loose. As an Assistant D.A., Amanda was getting pressure from the District Attorney, who, in turn, was being pressured by the media and community to find Mavis Gette's killer.

"We need to come up with some answers," Amanda had said when she'd swung into his office earlier.

Get in line, Carter had thought, but had said, "We're working on it. If anything breaks, you'll be the first to know."

"Thanks, Carter." She'd laid a hand on his, as if they'd somehow bonded. Then she'd wrinkled her nose and offered him a smile that was supposed to be cute and unthreatening. It wasn't. The woman was a shark in a tight skirt and three-inch heels, out to promote number one and eventually become D.A. She didn't care whom she skewered with her stiletto heels on the way up. Carter knew it. Everyone in the department knew it.

Fortunately, she'd finished with him and, shoes clicking down the hallway, had left him to his work. He spent the next few hours fielding calls, finishing reports, and studying pictures of the two missing women and Mavis Gette. Physically, they were similar in build, though not coloring. They were all pretty and petite, around five feet, three inches, all around thirty, all Caucasian. But Mavis had been a transient. Roxie a career woman. Sonja a wife and mother trying to make ends meet. Mavis and Sonja had lived in California, Roxie hadn't.

But there was something that tied them together. He just couldn't see it yet. Absently, he wrote the names of the women on a legal pad, thinking about each.

Mavis Gette's dead.

Sonja Hatchell and Roxie Olmstead are missing.

You can't tie them all together by the evidence.

And yet . . . as he stared at the computer images of the three women, he felt that they were connected. He just hadn't figured out how yet.

"Hey!" BJ said, poking her head into his office. He'd been so engrossed in his own thoughts that he hadn't heard her approach. "How about I buy you lunch?"

"What's the special occasion?"

"We both need a break."

"Don't we always?" he asked, but was already reaching for his jacket. "Don't we always."

"Listen, Carter, don't you know the old adage about looking a gift horse in the mouth? So shut up and keep up, unless you want to buy your own damned burger."

"And I thought you were springing for steak."

"In your dreams," she said as they headed down the stairs and outside. Despite the cold weather, they walked the few blocks to the Canyon Café and grabbed a booth. Though it was late, the little restaurant was crowded, filled with patrons who had driven into town after over a week of cabin fever. The kids were back in school, all the businesses open, the Interstate no longer closed. Yeah, life was back to normal, except that he had one dead body, two missing women, and a stalker to deal with along with the regular crimes.

The strains of country music could barely be heard over the buzz of conversation, rattle of silverware, and crackle of the fryer. Two waitresses were hopping, pouring coffee and water, while a short-order cook placed orders on the counter and the smells of frying onions and sizzling hamburgers competed with the aroma of freshly baked pies.

BJ had snagged a recently vacated booth and they waited while a single busboy cleared the table and pocketed the two-dollar tip left among straw wrappers, napkins, and dirty dishes. Once the Formica had been swabbed clean, a waitress who'd worked at the café for as long as Carter could remember poured coffee and took their orders.

"Anything new with the bust of the kids up at Catwalk Point?" BJ asked.

"So that's what this is all about—you want the inside scoop. From the OSP."

Her eyes narrowed at him over the rim of her coffee cup. "Right—consider the fish and chips a bribe. I'm a high roller. But yeah, since you and Sparks are tight, I thought you might know more."

Carter laughed. "The girls are safe. No charges, but because of Megan, you know that much already."

"What about the others?"

"The boys will probably have to do some community service for providing alcohol, even though they aren't twenty-one themselves. Actually, they're getting off pretty easy."

"Too easy," she said. "But the good news is that Megan finally saw the light and broke up with Ian Swaggert."

"Will it last?"

"Too early to call. But I'm hoping." She lifted crossed fingers for Carter to see. "Ever since the 'incident,' and that's what we call it, mind you, 'the incident,' Megan's been toe-ing the line around the house. Jim doesn't go ballistic like I do, just kind of mopes and looks at Megan with big, sad, dis-appointed eyes. You know the routine—his expression says all too clearly, 'How could you do this to me?' Like it's all about him. Hey, I'm not complaining. It seems to be effec-tive, at least for now. We'll see, though, if that little worm Swaggert leaves Megan alone. He'd better, or he'll have to answer to me." She took a long swallow of her coffee. "See how you're missing out, not having kids?"

The waitress deposited their lunch, a burger and fries for BJ, halibut and chips for Carter. BJ dug in as if she hadn't eaten in a week. "I'm blowing my diet today," she admitted. "It's hell to try and lose weight during this weather. I mean, who wants a spinach salad with no dressing when it's ten below?" She bit into her burger with gusto.

They talked about nothing important for a while, waved to a few local patrons they knew, and were nearly finished eating when BJ said, "I've finally got a report for you about who's been renting or buying Jenna Hughes's movies. Believe me, the list is long and infamous." She pushed her basket aside. "Your name came up a few times." He didn't comment. "But then, you're in bad company." She pulled her wallet out of her purse and slapped some bills onto the table. "I checked with the video stores in town, in the surrounding areas, on-line, and even the library's records. A lot of people have been watching Jenna Hughes movies around here, let me tell you. At least since she moved up here, and I'm not even talking about those people who have personal collections that they taped from their televisions."

They walked outside and BJ huddled deeper into her coat. "So, aside from mine, any names pop out at you?"

"Mmm. Her biggest fan seems to be Scott Dalinsky."

"Rinda's kid?"

BJ nodded. "He's got every movie she ever made—or-dered them all online and even bought some movie para-phernalia through e-Bay."

"You checked his credit card records?"

Her grin was wicked. "I've got my sources."

"Who else?"

"Just about everybody in town," she admitted, stopping on the curb and waiting for a truck to pass before she stepped into the crosswalk. The snow on the road was patchy, scraped by plows and melted by the warmth of vehicle engines as they passed. "And out of town as well. There's a guy in Hood River and a woman in Gresham who are uber-fans, it seems. Around here, Wes Allen has a collection, as does Blanche Johnson and Asa McReedy, the guy she bought her place from. Then there's a lot of kids in the high school including Josh Sykes . . . well, you'll see the entire printout, but believe me, it only expands our suspect list rather than shrinks it." They were walking up the courthouse steps to the warmth inside. They passed the security checkpoint and the records room before taking the stairs to the second floor. "Give me a minute," BJ said, and showed up in Carter's office five minutes later with not one stack of printouts, but three. The first list, of people who had rented or bought videos, was over thirty pages.

"This many?"

"That's right," she said. "And we're just getting started. These are the people who've rented or bought a Jenna Hughes movie in the last two years and live within a hundred miles of Falls Crossing." She sent Carter a sly look. "I was afraid the department might run out of paper if I expanded the search, but we can always change the perimeters, go back more years, or increase the physical area. I went a hundred miles because that will include the Portland metro area and the zip code for the postal station where the letter was postmarked. It allows an extra twenty-five miles around that zip code, so if our creep decided to be clever and drove across town, or from the suburbs, we've covered his ass. If he drove farther, then we need to expand the perimeters, but this seemed right to me, assuming that the guy lives within driving distance of Jenna Hughes's place. We know that either he or an accomplice left the note in her bedroom." She dropped the second list onto the first. Again, the printout was a thick sheaf of typewritten papers.

"Popular lady," he said, reaching for his pencil and wiggling it between his fingers as he skimmed the list of people who had rented or bought movies.

"Too popular, it seems."

"Mmm." The names were arranged in descending order. Those who'd purchased/rented the most copies of her movies at the top of the first page, the least on the last page. "Too popular. And too sexy. Though you probably haven't noticed."

He shot her a look, then skimmed the list of names. Scott Dalinsky was at the top of the list. "Have you cross-referenced this with the people she knows?"

"Mmm. Last page."

He flipped through the pages, and there, big as life on the final sheet, were at least thirty names, including his own. Scott Dalinsky, Harrison Brennan, Wes Allen, Travis Settler, Asa McReedy, Yolanda Fisher, Lou Mueller, Hans Dvorak, Rinda Dalinsky, Estella Trevino, Seth Whitaker, Blanche Johnson, Jim Stevens. "Your husband?"

"Hey, Jim's a red-blooded American male. Not immune. How about this one? Derwin Swaggert, the preacher. Ian's dad. You think he rented *Resurrection* because of its Christian overtones, maybe used it for reference in his Sunday sermon?"

Carter snorted.

"Or *Beneath the Shadows*—probably has something to do with the Twenty-third Psalm. You know, there's that passage about walking through the *shadow* of death."

"You really have a thing against the Swaggerts," Carter observed.

"Just their kid. And only when he messes with mine." She motioned to the list. "I'll leave this with you, and oh . . . check this out, uh, page seven, I think . . ." Quickly, she flipped the pages over and ran a finger down the list. "Here ya go. Roxie Olmstead rented *Innocence Lost* less than a week before she disappeared. Chew on that awhile."

"I will," he said, then eyed the other computer printouts she hadn't yet handed him. "More information, I presume."

"Ah, Sherlock, there's a reason you've been elected sheriff. It must be your keen detective skills."

"Oh, hell. All the while I was sure it was good-ol'-boy charm."

"Oh, yeah, that's it," she said, sarcasm dripping from every word. She slapped the second set of sheets onto his desk. "I checked with the Webmaster for Jenna Hughes's official site, found out who sends her the most e-mail, who logs in the most frequently. I've got a huge computer file, but only printed out the names of fans, again, who live within a fifty-mile radius. I can expand that as well."

He eyed the reports. "Efficient, aren't you?"

"I like to think so." She leaned a hip on the edge of his desk. "The next step I took was to look over the fan Web sites dedicated to Jenna Hughes—not only the official fan site, but all those other nonsanctioned 'unofficial' fan Web sites. What a trip. She garners more than her fair share of obsessive types, let me tell you."

Carter's jaw hardened and he didn't like the turn of his thoughts—that any sicko with a computer could have a little piece of Jenna Hughes.

Like you do? his mind taunted, and he shushed the guilty questions, didn't want to go there.

BJ was still explaining. "Some of those sites are filled with all kinds of crap, including nude photos that could be fake, sexual references, and all sorts of discussions about how sexy she is.

"If this is the kind of thing that happens when you're gorgeous, rich, and famous, count me out. Browsing through some of those Web sites, I thought I should be wearing hospital gloves because my keyboard was probably contaminated. And all the while that I searched, I was getting pop-up after pop-up screen, in continual loops. Damned irritating. I think I should be getting not only overtime, but hazardous-duty pay as well."

"Put in for it. See what the powers that be say," Carter suggested without much humor.

"I'll tell them it was your idea," BJ teased as she turned back to the printouts.

Carter had realized, of course, about the dark side of celebrity, the lack of privacy, the photo-hungry paparazzi, the obsessed fans, the tabloid exploitation, but he'd always figured it just came with the territory, the quintessential price of fame. But now, as he considered the fear that had become a part of Jenna Hughes's life, the ugliness seemed more real, the danger more certain. He felt an inner rage, a quiet determination to find the creep who was terrorizing her and put him away.

BJ was still talking about what she'd uncovered on the Internet. "It was more difficult to find someone who took responsibility for the more bizarre sites, of course, but I was able to go through to the chat room logs and the bulletin boards and figure out those who seemed most obsessed with Jenna Hughes and her movies. The problem is, those people aren't required to use their real names—they use all sorts of strange aliases, so I'm still trying to find out who some of them are."

"But you can?"

BJ winked. "I think so."

"Legally?"

She stared him straight in the eye. "Absolutely."

"So that if we find this son of a bitch, we can nail his ass. He won't be able to pay for some high-priced, sleazy defense attorney to whine about his client's rights being abused by the police and beat the rap."

She hesitated just a beat. "No."

"You're sure?"

"Don't worry, Carter. Everything I find will hold up in court."

"It had better." He ruffled the edge of the computer printouts with his thumb. "Tell me you did some kind of sort/merge thing and came up with a list of names you know who visited her Web site and rented or bought the most movies."

"And who lives in the area." Smiling smugly, she slid a slimmer printout across his desk. "Here ya go, boss," she said. "All the unusual suspects."

CHAPTER 31

"It's like a prison at home," Cassie complained as Josh picked her up after global studies. She was taking a chance ditching study hall, but didn't care. She was already hopelessly behind in some of her classes. He opened the door to his truck and waited as she climbed into the elevated cab. Once he was inside, she lit a cigarette and said, "We've got this bodyguard who's like a drill sergeant or a spy or something. He wants to know *every*thing I do."

"*Every*thing?" Josh asked, his eyebrows rising.

"And more." She didn't take the bait and exhaled a stream of white smoke. "It bugs me."

"How long is he going to be there?"

"Beats me. Probably until they find out who's sending Mom some weird letters."

"Who do you think it is?" he asked as he pulled out of the high school's parking lot, hit the gas, and sent the back of his truck sliding crazily on the ice.

"Hey!" she cried, just as his big tires grabbed the asphalt. "Knock it off, okay? I'm not in the mood."

But Josh only gave her a smug glance as he slowed for the cross street.

He acts like he just won the Indy 500, she thought in a

blinding flash of understanding. *What's wrong with him? With me? Why the hell am I with this big bohunk?*

"So who's sending the letters?" he repeated, sounding like a broken record.

"Geez, I don't know." She let out a disgusted puff of air. "Maybe that same kook who did last time. When we were still in L.A. Or maybe a new creep. I just wish he'd go away." She glanced across the seat to Josh, watching his reaction. "The police are involved, too. The sheriff's trying to figure out who sent the letters."

"That dirtbag couldn't find his own ass with a magnifying glass."

"Jesus, do you always have to be so gross?" she asked.

"It's true," he said, pouting. "He's always lookin' to bust my balls."

"Well, now he's after whoever is sending Mom those notes. My guess is he's going to try and find out who it is that's got such a weird fascination with her."

"That could be half the men in the county."

"Yeah, I know." *Including the sheriff himself,* Cassie thought. Sheriff Carter, now there was an interesting guy. Quiet. Smart. Good-looking . . . the same with the new body-guard, even though he was really old—in his thirties or something. She liked his short blond hair, intense blue eyes, and straight nose that matched perfect teeth. He was fit, muscular, and, even though he didn't smile a lot, when he did, he looked like a poster boy for one of those "Have-it-all-with-the-Marines" type of ads on TV. On top of it all, he was whip-smart. She recognized that straight up. It was true that Jake Turnquist made life a prison, but Cassie could think of worse jailors. She cracked the window, letting in a little cold air so that the smoke was sucked out of the cab as Josh, one eye on the road, slipped in a CD and pumped the bass up to the max. His sub-woofer was pounding, his fingers tapping out rhythm on the wheel, his head bobbing to the loud music.

"So is your mom still pissed at me?"

"Majorly pissed."

His face knotted up. "Shit."

"You care?"

"Sure. If she's mad at me, it'll be tough to get to see you." He slid her a lecherous smile that, she supposed, was meant to be sexy.

Instead it irritated her. Sometimes she wondered what she saw in Josh. Ever since the fiasco up at Catwalk Point, she'd thought about breaking up with him. *And then you'd be alone.* So what? Being alone might be better than being embarrassed by Josh, who sometimes seemed to act fourteen rather than his age. Maybe that was why she found the bodyguard so attractive. He was a grown-up. "You know, you could come over. Hang out. When Mom's there. We could study or watch TV."

"With the bodyguard dude, too? Sounds like a blast," he mocked, and shook out a cigarette from his pack on the dash. With a flick of his lighter, he lit up, then continued driving and rocking-out. Cassie flicked the butt of her cigarette out the window. Being with Josh was making her nervous. He stopped at a minimart, bought them each a soda, and then cruised through the frozen streets, waving at friends who passed, showing off in his tricked-out truck, doing not much of anything.

Cassie was bored out of her mind.

"If you came over, at least you could see my mom," she said, and it was her turn to lift an eyebrow.

"What's that supposed to mean?"

"Whatever you think it means."

"Oh, geez, Cass, not that again. I'm tellin' ya, I don't have a hard-on for your mom."

"Nice to know," she muttered under her breath.

"My folks aren't home." He offered her a kinder smile. "We could go there and have the place to ourselves."

Like sex would fix everything. Suddenly she felt tired. She glanced at her watch. "I really can't. Jake's picking me up right after the last bell."

"Jake?" he repeated.

"The bodyguard."

"I thought he was guarding your mom."

"And me and my sister. He and Mom have this whole program worked out where he drives us around during the day and watches the place at night. I'd better be at the school when he shows up." She took a long sip of her drink and watched shadows play across Josh's face, as if he was just beginning to understand that she had other things to do—that, perhaps, she had other things she *wanted* to do other than just hang out with him.

"Come on, Cass—"

"Really, Josh. I can't mess up anymore. Mom was really, really ticked off about the last time I snuck out up to the mountain and the cops came."

"Shit." He didn't argue any further, just put on his best I'm-really-pissed face, and drove recklessly back to the school. He dropped her off and didn't bother kissing her, just peeled out of the lot, music blaring, foul mood following after him like the smell of burnt rubber.

Oh, grow up! she thought, and wondered about her change in attitude. It's as if ever since being caught at the crime scene, she'd seen Josh with new eyes. He claimed to love her, but she still didn't believe him. He was just a good-time, damn-the-consequences country boy who would rather be racing cars or hunting, or watching near-porn movies and drinking beer, than anything in the world. Josh Sykes was going nowhere fast in a cherried-out, old pickup with a cranked-up cab and extra-wide tires with mag wheels.

Big whoop.

Cassie had better things to do.

Lots better.

Carter skimmed BJ's lists for the twentieth time. Throughout the day, whenever he was in the office, between his other duties, he'd looked over the names of the people he'd known most of his life, but the one person on the report that kept running through his head was Scott Dalinsky. Rinda's kid. An oddball, but certainly harmless. Right? Or was he coloring his judgment because he was Scott's godfather? What about Harrison Brennan? The neighbor who seemed all-too-possessive of Jenna.

Shane drummed his fingers on the desk and perused the list, his gaze landing, not for the first time, upon Wes Allen. Carter's one-time friend. Carter knew from personal experience that Wes couldn't be trusted, but he tried not to let what happened with Carolyn color his judgment.

He forced his eyes to examine other possibilities. What about Ron Falletti, Jenna's personal trainer, or Lester Hatchell. Les had purchased two of Jenna's flicks long before his own wife had gone missing. And he wasn't the only one, by far. Nearly everyone in the department, including Lanny Montinello and Amanda Pratt, had rented several of the movies and hell, even good old Dr. Dean Randall, Ph.D., had bought *Innocence Lost* and *Resurrection* within the last two months.

It seemed as if the whole damned town had a little piece of Jenna Hughes in their homes.

Which wasn't such a surprise, considering what a splash it had made when she'd moved up here from Hollywood. Everyone for miles had taken a sudden interest in her and her work. A lot of the rentals and sales had occurred within the first six months of her move.

Even he had a few of her DVDs. Which was a joke. His entire collection consisted of *Rocky*, *The Terminator*, *The Godfather* series, and three of Jenna Hughes's movies. He'd had more CDs and tapes at one time, but he'd donated them to the library when he'd cleaned out Carolyn's things after the accident.

Aside from a few pictures and the home movies, he'd pitched everything after her death, as if in so doing he could erase her from his life, wipe away the pain, pretend her betrayal hadn't existed. Hell . . .

His phone jangled and he picked up the receiver, but he kept one eye on the list. The stalker was on those pages, he was certain of it. Carter just had to figure out how to flush him out.

* * *

The rehearsal had been abysmal, Jenna thought, as she hiked the strap of her purse over her shoulder and walked toward the front doors of the theater. Tiffany, one of the girls in the cast, had come down with a case of laryngitis. Madge Quintanna, as Mary Bailey, had shown a range of emotion that vied with the animation of statues on Easter Island. The man playing Mary's husband, George, had hobbled across the stage on crutches and forgotten thirty percent of his lines. The lights had flickered eerily throughout the first act, and Rinda had snapped at Wes, who had blamed Scott.

Jenna was dead tired and already thinking about a long, hot bath and a paperback that was boring enough to put her to sleep as Blanche, carrying her satchel of sheet music, walked with Rinda and Jenna to the front door. As if reading the exasperated expression on Rinda's face, Blanche said, "What Tiffany's mother should do for that laryngitis is give her hot water with lemon and honey. It beats any of that over-the-counter stuff they sell at the pharmacy."

"Hot water?" Rinda said.

"With honey. And lemon. I've heard that you can add whiskey to it, but I never did with my kids, didn't believe in that. And they didn't need it. Would you like me to call Jane? I wouldn't mind. I know her pretty well, as Tiffany's been taking piano lessons from me for two . . . or is it three years?" she asked, seeming confused for a second. "Two, I think it is—anyway, it doesn't matter. I'd be glad to place the call."

"If you think it'll help, go for it." Rinda looked at Jenna as Blanche, beaming, bustled off. Once the front doors slammed behind her, Rinda said, "I doubt if anything other than divine intervention will help now."

"Things will get better," Jenna said, and wrapped a scarf around her neck.

"When hell freezes over." Rinda glanced to the windows and snapped her fingers. "Well, maybe you're right. It's cold enough—I think hell is freezing over as we speak."

"I didn't know Blanche had any kids," Jenna said, realizing how little she knew about her coworkers and friends.

"Scary thought, huh?" Rinda joked.

"Extremely," Jenna said with a chuckle as she and Rinda moved along the aisle between the row of pews to the front door.

At the front door Rinda paused. "We're the last to leave, right?"

"No—I think Lynnetta was still working on costumes in the dressing room."

"Geez, that's right. Lynnetta!" Rinda called, her voice echoing through the apse. "Lynnetta?"

"Yeah?" a soft voice called back.

"We're leaving now."

Which was a blessing, Jenna thought, after that god-awful, miserable, nerve-grating rehearsal.

"Okay." Lynnetta's soft voice floated up from downstairs.

"You coming?" Rinda called.

"In a minute. You go on ahead. I'll lock up."

Rinda shrugged and rolled her eyes. "Okay," she yelled back. "I'll lock the door behind us. You lock it again when you leave. And turn off the lights."

"Fine, fine," Lynnetta said loudly, her voice echoing against the high rafters.

"The acoustics in here leave a lot to be desired," Rinda muttered under her breath. "One more thing to fix."

"Let's wait." Jenna knotted her scarf around her throat. "I don't like leaving her here alone."

"She's not alone. Oliver's here."

"Oh, and a fine lotta protection he is."

Rinda wasn't listening to any of Jenna's arguments. "Lynnetta will be okay. I'll lock the dead bolt so no bogey-man can get in."

"It's serious—you know that two women are missing, another one found dead." Jenna didn't like it. "I think we should stay."

"Knowing Lynnetta, she could take another half-hour or so. Don't worry about her. She only lives a couple of blocks away, and she always calls her husband to come over and walk her home after dark. The reverend is quick to oblige and I think it's damned romantic."

"But this town isn't safe anymore."

"I'll *lock* the door, okay?" Rinda put a hand on Jenna's arm. "Really, it'll be all right. Relax."

"If only I could."

"Look, she'll call her hubby and Romeo will come escort her home."

Jenna had trouble thinking of Lynnetta's husband doing anything the least bit romantic. "Just let me double-check." She yelled toward the staircase near the stage. "Are you sure you're okay, Lynnetta?"

"Yes! Please. I'll be fine."

Rinda tossed Jenna an I-told-you-so look. She arched a knowing eyebrow and whispered, "Maybe she wants us to vamoose because her husband comes over here and they do it center-stage."

"You're awful," Jenna said, thinking of Reverend Derwin Swaggert, barely forty yet a serious, long-faced preacher with a full black beard, bushy eyebrows, and a voice that boomed as he delivered fire-and-brimstone sermons.

"This was a church not all that long ago, remember? Sex where the altar once stood would definitely have appeal."

"Come on. Let's get out of here before the conversation sinks to an even lower level."

"Is that possible?" Rinda's laugh was low and totally irreverent.

"Probably not." Jenna yanked open one of the twin double doors. A rush of brittle winter wind swept through the vestibule. Outside, she gazed up at the starless night and shivered. "God, when is it gonna warm up?"

"Never," Rinda predicted as she locked the dead bolt behind her and pulled on the door handles, double-checking that they were secure. "No end in sight, according to the weatherman at KBST." They headed down the exterior steps. "Time to think of moving south *before* the play opens and we get panned by the local press."

"Has anyone ever told you that the cup is half full some of the time?"

"Never," Rinda said as they followed a cement path to the

nearly empty parking lot where their two vehicles waited beneath a solitary lamppost. It shed a weak blue haze over the
cars, making them shimmer under a thin glaze of ice. The
wind swept through a back alley and rushed over the lot, cutting through Jenna's heavy down jacket as if it were made of
gossamer lace.

"Got time for a beer?" Rinda was fumbling with her key
ring. "I'll buy. The least I can do for your donation today,"
she said, mentioning the clothes, shoes, and purses that
Jenna had brought to the theater.

"Don't worry about it. A tax deduction, you know. My
C.P.A. will be thrilled."

"Then *you* buy."

Jenna giggled. "Better not tonight. I've got to report in,"
she said, and with a gloved hand, pulled her walkie-talkie out
of the pocket of her jacket. "Besides, I'm beat. Haven't slept
that well since I got that fun little missive from my 'friend.'"
Not sleeping well was an understatement. Ever since discovering that her bedroom had been violated, Jenna had been
unable to relax. She'd been hearing things—strange noises,
or footsteps, and she'd felt all the while that someone was
watching her every move, that someone not being Jake
Turnquist. Just knowing that someone had been in her home,
sneaking through the corridors, pawing through her things,
had made her jumpy and anxious.

"Hey, you've got the bodyguard now. Things should be
better, right?"

"I know, that should help, but . . ." Jenna glanced up at
the steeple rising high, piercing the low-hanging clouds. ". . .
I'm still a little uptight."

"All the more reason for a beer or glass of wine. Besides,
I think we need to discuss the play. I'm sure you noticed that
Madge hasn't really grasped the role of Mary Bailey," Rinda
said. Her car door unlocked with a loud click.

Jenna agreed, but said, "She's getting there."

"And when is she going to arrive? In the *next* millen-
nium?"

"It's not *that* bad."

"Oooh, I think it is. Face it, Jenna, Madge is hopeless! Terribly, horribly, indecently miscast." She frowned in the eerie blue light. "My fault. I should have gone with someone else."

"You're exaggerating," Jenna argued, though watching Madge try to emote as Mary Bailey had been painful.

"No, I'm not. I've got some ideas about the part."

"If it involves me stepping in, forget it. Madge will get it right." Jenna checked her watch. A glass of wine sounded like heaven. Coffee laced with Kahlua, even better. She needed to unwind, to forget about all the stresses in her life, but it was already late. "I'd really better take a rain check. We could discuss this over coffee in the morning, though."

"Fine, spoilsport," Rinda acquiesced. "Coffee it is . . . say, ten at the Canyon Café?"

"I'll be there."

"And you're buying."

"Right." Jenna unlocked her Jeep and slid inside. Shivering, she started the engine; then with the doors locked, fired up the defrost, turned the fan on to its highest setting, and waited for the ice on her windshield to melt. Within five minutes there was a patch of visibility in the window. She drove out of the lot a few seconds after Rinda did, following the red taillights of her friend's car, bothered slightly that the lights in the theater still blazed and Lynnetta was alone in the basement.

"Don't worry about it," she told herself, but worry had been her steady companion over the last few weeks. Everything in her life was eating at her, keeping sleep at bay. Driving through the snowy streets, she noticed that the town seemed inordinately quiet; few cars were traveling the narrow streets lined by storefronts proudly displaying holiday decor.

None of the lights, garlands, or wreaths brought Jenna any joy, nor any comfort. As was the case ever since Jill had died, Jenna dreaded the holidays, a time of year that felt empty and cold and riddled with guilt.

You should have died instead of Jill.

How many times had those words echoed through her skull?

A hundred?

A thousand?

Ten thousand?

"Stop it!" she said out loud. She was overreacting to the coming of Christmas. The disturbing letters she'd received and the missing women only added to the tension she felt as the holidays approached. She turned on the radio and, as if the DJ had sensed her mood, the strains of *Blue Christmas* wafted through the speakers. Elvis Presley was warbling about a sad holiday. Just what she needed.

"Great," she said to herself, clicked off the radio, and reached for her cell phone. She dialed home and Allie answered before the second ring.

"Mom?"

"Yeah."

"You've got my backpack, right? I mean, I left it in the car and forgot it and I didn't have it all day and I need it for my homework and—"

"Hey, whoa! Slow down, honey." While trying to keep the SUV on the road, Jenna turned on the dome light and hazarded a quick look into the backseat. "I don't think it's here."

"It was in the way back. Remember? Critter jumped into the backseat with me yesterday and I threw my backpack into the cargo space, you know, with all that other junk you were taking to the theater."

Jenna's heart sank. "You mean with the bags of clothes and purses I was donating?" Jenna flashed back to her arrival in the parking lot. Wes Allen had just been getting out of his truck and had offered to help her unload the back. She'd been grateful for the help at the time. "It's probably at the theater, then."

"I have to have it," Allie whined.

"Tonight?" Jenna asked, trying to think of some way to avoid a return trip into town. "You want me to go get it?"

"Pleeeeaaaase, Mom. If I don't do my algebra assignment, Mrs. Hopfinger will *kill* me."

"I doubt that the situation's that dire."

"It's dire-er!" From the sound of it, Allie was on her way to a mega-meltdown, the last thing Jenna needed to deal with tonight.

"Life and death?" Jenna teased.

"Yes!" Allie wasn't in the mood for any jokes.

"Okay, okay," Jenna said, resigned to her fate, her eyes already narrowing as she searched through the misty windshield for a place to turn around. "Relax, honey. I'll go get it."

"Thank you, thank you, thank you!"

"You're welcome," she said, a few flakes of new snow swirling and dancing in the path of her headlights. "Is Jake there?"

"Um-hmm."

"Why don't you put him on?"

"'Kay."

There was a second of dead air. Jenna spied a wide spot in the road and slowed as a deep male voice said, "Turnquist."

Jenna launched into what was happening. "Look, here's the deal with Allie's backpack." She explained what she thought had happened and said, "I'm going back for it now."

"Wait a minute." Concern edged his voice. "I don't like you going back there. No one's at the theater. Let me handle this."

"It'll take too much time, Jake, and it's safe. The theater's locked up tighter than a drum, and I've got one of the few keys. I probably won't even be alone. Lynnetta Swaggert was there when I left ten minutes ago. Rinda locked her in, and her husband comes over to walk her home, so I think I'll be okay. Besides, I don't want you leaving the girls alone out at the house. I'm only ten minutes out of town. I'll turn around and pick up the backpack and have my walkie-talkie, mace, and cell phone with me. If I'm not home in forty minutes, send in the cavalry."

She could tell that he wanted to argue, but thankfully he

didn't and she hung up, promising to call him if she sensed that anything was wrong.

What a joke. The problem was that everything was wrong right now. Nothing was right.

"Damn it all to hell," she whispered, then, despite her own trepidations, she pulled a quick one-eighty and headed back to Falls Crossing.

If she was lucky, Lynnetta would still be in the theater.

If not, she'd make this a very short trip.

CHAPTER 32

It was probably her case of nerves, but the town seemed more deserted than when Jenna had driven through it a few minutes earlier. The parking lot of the theater was empty and ice-glazed. The old church-cum-theater stood like a lonely sentinel, dark, cold, and foreboding, its spire knifing upward through the falling snow.

As she stared through the rapidly fogging windshield, Jenna felt a cold tickle on the back of her neck, a warning not to go any farther.

It's just your imagination. You were inside less than half an hour ago! Get this over with, for God's sake!

Briefly, she considered calling Jake again and keeping him on the phone as she searched for the backpack, then discarded the idea. It seemed foolish, would make her appear a helpless female.

What kind of a baby are you? Just get the damned pack and go home.

Before she could change her mind, she climbed out of her Jeep, locked it behind her, and felt icy pellets of snow rain down her neck. She dashed across the slippery parking lot, then hurried up the stairs. A block away she heard traffic, told herself she wasn't really alone, and rammed her key into the lock. She twisted, but the bolt didn't slide. "Come on, come on," she urged, wondering if this was some kind of omen when suddenly the lock sprang open. "Thank God."

Inside, the theater was cold and still. Weird plays of light seeped through the stained-glass windows in strange, shifting patterns. She felt a tremor of fear. Even the few remaining religious images tacked to the walls took on a demonic rather than heavenly guise in the shadows.

"Get a grip," she mumbled under her breath and snapped on the lights. Immediately the old nave was awash with light and her trip-hammering heart slowed a bit. She hastened down the main aisle, her footsteps clicking loudly. "Lynnetta?" she called, more for the sound of her own voice than anything else. "Are you still here? It's Jenna." She paused, listening, but, as she expected, there was no response, just the creaking of old rafters and the rush of wind against the steeple. No doubt Lynnetta had already gone home, probably on her husband's arm.

Jenna hurried down the few stairs past Rinda's office, then took the rest of the flight downward to the basement and costuming area where the hint of Lynnetta's perfume still lingered. She reached for the light switch but her hand paused in midair.

Again she sensed a tickle of cold breath against her skin, a hint that something was wrong. Out of place. She braced herself against the wall. "Lynnetta?" she called, certain she felt someone in the building, sensed someone breathing. She held her breath, straining to listen.

Nothing.

"Jesus," she whispered, her nerves strung tight as piano wire. Once again, her heart was beating a wild tattoo as she flipped on the lights and the warren of dressing rooms, makeup stations, and closets was suddenly awash with bright, near-blinding fluorescence.

The sacks of clothes were where they'd been dropped near the closets. Jenna wasted no time pawing through the bags. No backpack. A small pile of purses and shoes had been left on an ancient, battle-scarred bureau, but Allie's pink-and-purple camouflage pack was again missing in action. "Terrific," Jenna whispered sarcastically, searching again and trying not to hear the moaning of the wind in the rafters or the creak of old timbers as they continued to settle.

She flung up her hands in surrender, figuring Allie had been mistaken about leaving the backpack in her car, when she heard it.

The soft scrape of a boot against hardwood . . . or was it? The hairs on her nape raised. Her skin prickled. "Is anyone there?" she shouted, reaching into her purse for her can of mace. "Hello?"

Quiet.

Unearthly silence.

And yet . . . she felt as if she wasn't alone . . . *knew* there was another presence nearby.

Her diaphragm slammed hard against her lungs.

She shouldn't have said a word. Now, if someone evil was lurking in the shadows, he'd know exactly where she was and she'd be trapped in the basement. Unless she took the stairs to the exterior exit near the kitchens. But that was too far, down a long, winding, dark hallway. She was better off using the main stairs.

Nervous sweat broke out on her skin and a chilling fear took hold of her throat.

To hell with the damned backpack. Clutching her can of mace as if it were a silver cross and she was about to face a vampire, she slowly eased up the stairs. She reached into her pocket for her cell phone and flipped it open. It beeped. *Oh, God, how did she mute the damned thing so whoever was in the theater with her couldn't hear it?* Her heartbeat pounded in her ears. Her breathing was nonexistent, the spit in her mouth dried. She swallowed hard. Hit the cell's autodial key for her house and heard the phone try to connect. *Please answer. Please.* Carefully, she turned at the landing, her ears straining.

Crash!

"Oh, God!" Jenna whirled, her finger on the mace can's button. She dropped her cell and it clattered noisily to the floor.

Something brushed against the back of her legs.

She jumped, nearly squealing in fright before spying Oliver. The cat was staring up at her with big green eyes, an old umbrella stand tipped over and rolling against the floor. "For the love of God, Oliver, you scared the hell out of me!"

He meowed plaintively up at her and she instantly forgave him, relief rushing through her bloodstream as she petted his soft head and righted the umbrella stand. "I'm sorry," she cooed as he purred as loudly as the rumble of a single-plane's engine. "And am I glad to see you. If you only knew."

She found her cell phone and pocketed it. "It's pretty obvious that I'm a little on edge these days, isn't it?"

The truth of the matter was that her nerves were stretched so thin they were about to shatter, and she'd forgotten all about the cat.

As if proud of himself for scaring her witless, Oliver rubbed up against her legs as she, calmer, put away her mace. "You stay here and guard the place," she ordered, before he trotted off to Rinda's office, hopped onto her desk, and began washing himself. "Good. That's real good. No bad guy will get past that defense," she told him.

Bam! Bam! Bam!

A loud knocking rattled the windows and echoed through the theater.

Jenna nearly jumped out of her skin.

"Jenna? It's Shane Carter," the sheriff's voice boomed through the door.

Her knees turned to water. Carter? Here? Relieved, she raced along the main aisle and unlocked the dead bolt.

His expression as dark as the night, he was standing beneath the overhang of the roof.

Tears of relief sprang to her eyes as he stepped inside the theater.

"Are you all right?"

No! Are you crazy? I haven't been all right since I got that first note! She swallowed hard and lied through her teeth. "Yeah—I guess."

"Sure?"

"Oh. I'm . . . I will be fine." She felt like a fool and forced the tears away before he could see how near she was to falling into a million pieces. "But I am relieved. And glad you're here."

He wrapped an arm around her and she wanted to burrow deeply against him, to let the tears rain from her eyes, to let go and fall apart right there in the vestibule. "Everything's all right," he said softly, and her heart nearly broke as his lips brushed against her forehead. "You're fine."

She laughed. "How can you say that?" She was anything but fine, and things were definitely *not* all right.

He stared past her, his gaze searching the interior. "Anyone else inside?"

"Just Oliver."

"Who? Oh. Rinda's cat."

"Yeah, he nearly gave me a heart attack. Considering my state of mind, I'm afraid that's not very hard to do these days."

Carter gave her shoulders a squeeze before letting go. "Let's lock up and get you home. Safe."

"Sounds good." In truth, it sounded like heaven. In her mind's eye she saw herself with a glass of wine as she soaked in the hot tub, her fears and tension dissipating in the warm water and mist that would rise into the cold air. The trouble was, she saw Carter in the Jacuzzi with her . . . ridiculous. Before her fantasy got out of hand, she shut off the lights and the theater was suddenly dark as death.

She stepped over the threshold and into the frigid night. Again she had trouble with her key; then, finally, the tricky dead bolt slid into place.

Carter tested the doors and they held. "Let's go."

"How did you know I was inside?" They walked, bodies close, breaths misting and mingling in the air, to the parking lot where Carter's Blazer was parked next to her Jeep.

"Turnquist called," Carter said. "He explained what was happening and that he wasn't comfortable with you being out alone at night, so he called and asked if someone could check on you." Carter's eyes found hers. "I volunteered."

Her heart fluttered stupidly. "Sense of duty?"

He lifted a dark eyebrow. "I was on my way home anyway."

She felt a little jab of disappointment, and she told herself she was the worst kind of fool. What had she hoped? That Carter had eagerly come to her rescue out of some need to see her? Because he cared about her? *Get real, Jenna.*

Carter was saying, "Turnquist was right to phone. You shouldn't be out alone. I'd feel a lot better if you had someone with you all the time, preferably Turnquist. But anyone is better than no one. I don't like the idea of you being by yourself, not until we nail this guy."

"I think I was pretty safe tonight. Oliver didn't really attack me."

"This time. I don't know how much you can trust that cat," he deadpanned, and she chuckled, relieved. They reached her SUV and he touched her on the arm. "Seriously. Be careful. I wouldn't want anything to happen to you. Especially on my watch." Again, he squeezed her and it felt good to have his strength surround her. "You know, it wouldn't be too good for my reelection campaign if I lost the county's most famous citizen."

So he did have a sense of humor, she thought, and for a split second the ice and frost covering the ground seemed less threatening. "I wouldn't want to tarnish your stellar reputation," she teased, and felt herself blush. Like a schoolgirl! What was wrong with her?

"Now, that's the attitude I like."

She turned toward him and, for just a second, in the cool blue glow of the street lamp, thought he might kiss her. The intensity in his gaze said he wanted to fold her into his arms and kiss the breath from her lungs. She sensed that spark of electricity in the air, the sizzle of seduction, and trembled inside. He stuffed his hands into his pockets as if he suddenly couldn't trust them. He cleared his throat. "Seriously," he said, his voice a little deeper, "take care of yourself."

Tears sprang unbidden to the back of her eyes. "I try to."

"Try as hard as you can." The barest of smiles from the tall man. "And I will, too."

She felt as if she was breaking inside. Tenderness from this taciturn lawman? "Thanks," she said, a trifle breathlessly. "I will." Then, impulsively, before she could second-guess herself, she stood on her tiptoes and brushed her lips across the beard shadow on his cheek. "Thanks, Sheriff. I don't think I've ever been more glad to see anyone in my life as I was tonight to find you on the other side of that door." She hitched her chin toward the theater's covered porch. "You take care, too." Pausing, before climbing inside her Jeep, she cocked her head to one side as if evaluating him and felt the cold of winter brush her face. "I'm sure you don't want to hear this, but beneath that tough-as-old-leather facade lurks a damned nice guy."

"Not so nice." Again, his eyes darkened with desire.

"Oh, I think so." She caught a glint of white teeth beneath his thick moustache.

"Well, don't let it get around. It would ruin my reputation."

Pressing a gloved finger to her lips, she assured him, "Your secret's safe with me."

"Good. Now, go home before we both freeze. I'll follow you."

"You don't have to—"

"Of course I do." The speck of lightheartedness of the past few minutes fled into the frozen night, but there was still that sensation of want in the air, the ache of newfound desire existing between them, as flakes of snow whirled and fell to the ground. Her throat dry, Jenna climbed into her truck and tried to ignore the wayward beating of her heart. *This is crazy, Jenna. Nuts! You don't have time for any kind of fantasies or infatuation. And with Carter? Oh, my God, get real.* Scrabbling in her purse, she found her key ring and jabbed the Jeep's key into the ignition. Her hands were quaking in her gloves. *Get hold of yourself,* she admonished, then jumped when he tapped against the driver's window, his face pressed to the chilled glass.

She pressed a button, the window descended, and his face was only inches from hers, warm in the cold night.

"For the record," he said, "the name's Shane."

"But everyone calls you Carter, right?" Dear God, what was this tiny rush she felt, the sense of intimacy tonight? She caught a hint of aftershave. "Or Sheriff?"

"Oh, they probably call me a lot of things behind my back, none of them worth repeating. But you can call me Shane."

"Fair enough, Carter," she teased.

An eyebrow quirked. "That'll work, too." His gaze held hers for a second as snowflakes collected on his dark hair and broad shoulders and again she thought he might kiss her. Again she was disappointed. "Later." He slapped the Jeep's fender twice and turned toward his rig.

"Take a deep breath," she whispered to herself as she rolled up her window to watch him fold his big frame into the driver's side of his Blazer. What had she been thinking, flirting and bussing him on the cheek?

"Nerves," she told herself as she threw the Jeep into gear. "It's just that I've got a real bad case of nerves." He represented safety, that was all. It wasn't that he was sexy as all get-out, or that his smile, beneath warm, dark eyes, could melt the ice around her heart.

Stupid woman! With all the worry that's going on around here, the last thing, the very last thing, you need is an entanglement with a man—especially Carter. Don't even think about him like that!

Letting out her breath, angry with herself and her silly fantasies, she glanced in the rearview mirror. As promised, Carter was following her, but beyond the reassuring glow of the Blazer's headlights, her gaze skated to the theater disappearing rapidly from view.

She felt another chill. Cold as midnight. Something in the ancient church wasn't right. The lonely building, with its opaque stained-glass windows and sharp-peaked, desolate belltower, stood stark against the frigid night and seemed sinister in the snowfall. *That's ludicrous. It's all your perception, your imagination. The building has nothing to hide, no heinous secrets. It was a church, for God's sake, a joyous place for worshippers to gather and give praise.*

So why did she feel like Satan himself resided there tonight?

"Because you're a drama queen, maybe, or an over-the-top paranoid," she muttered. There was nothing wrong with the building housing the theater. *Nothing!* "You've seen one too many horror flicks." She was just letting her own fears get the better of her, that was it. Right? Even if there was some horror hidden within the old clapboard walls, it had stayed secreted away for the night and Sheriff *Shane* Carter, an extraordinary hunk of a lawman, had come to her supposed rescue. Even now he was driving behind her through the snow. Things could be worse. Lots worse.

With one eye on the road ahead, she snapped open her cell phone and tried to call the house. It took several attempts, as the phone seemed to have suffered some damage when it had dropped to the floor in Rinda's office. Finally, it connected.

Allie answered quickly. "Hello?" Her voice was barely audible over the static.

No reason to beat around the bush. "Hi, hon. Hey, look, I'm sorry, honey, the backpack's not in the car and it's not at the theater. I checked."

"But it has to be!"

"Maybe you left it at school," Jenna suggested, straining to listen.

"Uh-uh."

"Or it's in Jake's truck or your room or—"

"Mom!" Allie cut in angrily, her voice wavering. "I *know* where it was. In the back of the Jeep!" She sounded near the verge of tears, but it was hard to tell with the blips in the conversation.

"Listen, don't worry about it. Call someone in the class, see if they can give you the questions over the phone, or . . . if they have a fax machine, they can send a copy over."

"Not if they've already done their homework! And I need the book!"

"We'll talk about this when I get home. If I have to, I'll call Mrs. Hopfinger in the morning."

"I can't hear you."

Jenna repeated herself, nearly shouting, and Allie tried to argue.

Jenna's frayed nerves snapped. "Hey, slow down, Allie. I've done the best I can do. You can pout and get mad and whatever else you want to do, but it won't help, now, will it?"

There was a long, brutal silence. Jenna waited it out. Wondered if she'd lost her connection. Finally, just as she was about to hang up, Allie muttered almost inaudibly, "Jake wants to talk to you."

"Good." Jenna forced enthusiasm into her voice as she stopped for a streetlight. "Put him on."

A second later, the bodyguard was on the line.

"Everything okay?" he asked.

"Aside from the backpack being AWOL, and my cell phone trying to give up the ghost, yeah, things are fine," she said, glancing in the mirror again. Carter's rig was still following her. "Can you hear me?"

"Barely."

"Well, the cavalry came to the rescue. Thanks."

"Just doing my job," he said, his voice breaking up.

"And I appreciate it. Really. I'll be home in twenty minutes."

The connection failed before he could respond. "And a fine piece of crap you are," she said to the phone as she flung it into the seat next to her and drove, with Carter on her tail, out of town.

He watched her go.

Closeted in the darkened spire, hiding in the shadows, he trained his night-vision glasses on her and silently observed Jenna Hughes as she drove off in her Jeep.

With the damned sheriff on her bumper.

He hadn't counted on the police showing up.

Nor had he expected Jenna, *his Jenna*, to press her face into the cop's, and kiss the bastard on his goddamned cheek.

Rage surged through his blood and a tic developed under his eye. She shouldn't be kissing anyone, or talking to anyone, or laughing with anyone.

No one but him!

The police should never have come. Never!

Next time, think things through more carefully.

Still, despite the lawman, he could have taken Jenna tonight. If he'd wanted to. If it had been her time.

It would have been so easy.

But rushed.

Not part of the plan.

Precision. That was the key. Precision.

Tonight he'd nearly been discovered.

Because he'd been too eager.

Again he berated himself and he closed his eyes for a second, let the cold breeze blow across his face, chill the anger in his blood. Tiny crystals of ice caressed his face and he imagined Jenna's chilled lips kissing him. Oh, such sweet, sweet surrender.

But she'd not kissed him. Not tonight. No, she'd stood on her tiptoes and swept her chilled lips over the bastard's face.

His muscles tensed in fury.

The sheriff's arrival had caught him off guard. He'd barely finished his mission and had lingered to look through the bags of clothes Jenna had donated, searching for a perfect scarf for Zoey Trammel . . . a green scarf, with threads of gold woven through the coarse fabric—just like the one she always wore and fingered in *A Silent Snow*, a fitting title, one with ironic overtones.

He'd hoped, when he'd heard that she was giving the theater troupe more things, that he would find a few little gems for his collection. Including the scarf. He'd been sadly mistaken. Most of what he'd pawed through was trash. Old clothes her children had outgrown, or things she'd given that weren't associated with her films. He'd pressed those articles of clothing to his face, hoping to smell her scent, a lingering aroma of her perfume, but had been disappointed. He'd also thought she might have included some panties or bras, but there had been no underclothes, not even a slip or teddy.

Frustration boiled through his blood.

The search had nearly proved fruitless. Until he'd seen the backpack and recognized it for what it was. Bait. An ugly little piece of bait. That thought brought a smile to his face and he opened his eyes. From his high perch, he gazed down at the lights of the little town spread upon the shores of the murky Columbia River, its waters thick and burgeoning with ice floes that were stalling river traffic, panicking the populace. Even the streams that fed the mighty river had frozen solid, the falls tumbling over the surrounding cliffs, becoming plumes of ice.

A perfect time for killing.

A thrill curled down his spine. He recognized this new, fresh snowfall as an omen, a sign that things were nearly in place.

He waited a few more minutes, surveying the parking lot and icy streets, assuring himself that the sheriff hadn't assigned another patrol to the theater. Finally, assured that he wouldn't be disturbed, he returned to his work.

Shouldering the kid's backpack, he started his descent, his steps quick and stealthy as he hurried ever downward. The musty, skeletal interior of the belltower sheltered him from the weather, its rickety, circular stairs groaning softly against his weight.

He didn't stop until he reached the basement. It was an area he knew well.

He crept past old scenery stacked against a wall, down an aisle where makeup mirrors and lights were now darkened, and around a corner to a nearly forgotten storage area, hidden deep beneath the stage of the floor above.

His pulse pounded in anticipation as he reached the closet he considered his, a small, compact, dark space where he'd hidden behind a rack of folding chairs as a child. From this secret spot he'd heard the minister giving his loud sermons, felt the shuffle of feet overhead, listened to piano music, beautiful, tinkling notes of each hymn's introduction before the choir or congregation began to sing so loudly he covered his ears.

This was his own private sanctuary, a cold, dim place where he could sequester himself, unknown to anyone. *His* closet. Rarely disturbed.

Now, with his key, he opened the closet door, the musty air filtering out as he shined his penlight over the few boxes, crates, and trunks that had been stored and long forgotten. He flipped through his keys again, and finding the smallest on his ring, he unlocked one of the large trunks, a dusty crate no one seemed to notice.

He pushed.

The rounded top creaked open.

Electricity sang through his blood as his gaze landed on the barely breathing body stuffed inside. Unconscious. Unaware of her fate.

Just as he'd left her.

One small hand was visible, and he stared at her fingers. Not unlike Zoey's, if he found the right rings to decorate them . . . He fixated on her ring finger and frowned when he noticed the wedding band and gaudy engagement ring. They would never do. Zoey was a single woman. He'd remove the band immediately, but as he stared at the finger, he imagined what he could do with it. A shiver of adrenaline swept through him, caused a tightening in his crotch.

Oh, yes. The finger was perfect.

"Come on, Zoey," he whispered gently, dragging the small woman from her cramped confines. "It's curtain time."

CHAPTER 33

". . . I was hoping that we could have dinner sometime," Travis was saying as Jenna held the phone between her ear and shoulder. Forcing the corkscrew into a bottle of wine, she tried not to think about Shane Carter. From her rearview mirror, she'd watched Carter follow her home and hoped he'd turn into her driveway, but as the gates to her house had swung open, he'd driven past, his Blazer disappearing into the ever-worsening snowstorm. Disappointed, she'd come into the house, talked a few minutes to Turnquist and the kids, then finally, reluctantly, returned Travis Settler's phone call. He hadn't answered, but had called her back within ten minutes.

Dinner with him had suddenly lost a lot of its appeal.

Because of a country sheriff who doesn't care about you when this man does? This smart, good-looking, single father who has a great sense of humor? And you're pining for the lonesome lawman? Come on, Jenna, wake up!

She suggested, "Maybe you and Dani could come over once the roads are cleared. I could even cook, though my repertoire is pretty limited."

"When the roads are cleared?" He laughed and again, because of the connection, she had the sensation that he was driving somewhere in this hideous storm. He hadn't called her back from his house, but his cell phone. "When will that be? In May?"

"I was thinking more like a barbecue in July," she joked back, relaxing a little as she stared out the window and worked on extracting the cork. Long icicles hung from the eaves and gusts of wind blew against the house, rattling the windows and sending the barely visible windmill slats spinning crazily. The wine cork popped and she poured herself a long-stemmed glass. "How about the Fourth?"

"I'll check my calendar." He paused, then added, "Looks good. You're on. Remember, we already discussed hot beaches and drinks."

She'd forgotten about the conversation. "That's right."

"So what about sometime sooner? Seriously, Jenna, I'd really like to see you. Without the girls. I was hoping that Cassie would babysit and you and I could go in to Portland. There's a restaurant in the Hotel Danvers that's supposed to be excellent."

He sounded closer now, but that was probably a trick of the weather. She tasted her wine, then asked, "Where are you?"

Was there just a beat of hesitation?

"In my truck, trying to get home."

"Is Dani with you?"

"With a sitter," he said.

"At home?"

"I'm picking her up on the way home. Why?"

So that explained why no one had answered when she called his house. He must've picked up his messages from the road. Nothing sinister about that. Dear God, was she suspicious of everyone now, even Travis? "I just wondered how the roads are," she lied, as she'd been driving home from the theater less than an hour earlier.

"Miserable."

Sipping her chardonnay, she squinted through the swirling snow and saw taillights barely visible on the road. The hairs on the back of her arms lifted. Was it possible that he was passing by and not mentioning it?

"Are you anywhere near my place?"

"No. Why? Is anything wrong?"

Everything, she thought, as she watched the taillights disappear. *Everything's wrong.* "Nothing but the weather," she lied again.

"Let's make a date when the storm lets up," he suggested. "I'll call."

"Do that. You know, there's something I've been wanting to ask you."

"Shoot."

Jenna steeled herself. "Allie has it in her mind that you were in some kind of elite military group, some kind of special forces."

"Does she?"

"Is it true?"

"Yeah, but not something I like to talk about," he said.

"She also mentioned that you're a private investigator."

"Hell." He let out a long breath. "Dani talks too much. Brags. It's true. I do some insurance fraud or help attorneys find deadbeat dads or people who skip on their bills. That kind of thing. It's not nearly as glamorous as television would like you to think."

"And here I thought you were a rancher."

"I am. But I supplement."

"Do you carry a gun?" she asked.

"Only when I think I'll need one, but yeah, I have a permit. Jenna, what's with all the questions?"

"I was just curious," she said, wondering why she couldn't confide in him, why she suddenly didn't trust him, why avoiding the truth seemed so important.

"Listen, I'll tell you all about myself over dinner, but I'm afraid I'm not nearly as exciting or mysterious as my daughter would like people to think. Hey, I'm at the sitter's, so I'd better go."

"Tell Dani 'hi,' and don't be too hard on her for bragging you up, okay?"

"Never," he promised, his voice softening slightly at the mention of his daughter. "She's the president of my fan club. Probably the only member. I'll call later."

He hung up and Jenna was left feeling ambivalent. Was he the caring father she'd thought he was, or someone she didn't really know, a man with a fiercely guarded secret life?

Oh, get over yourself, Jenna. You're jumping at every shadow that crosses your path. Travis Settler is a good guy. You know that. Trust your feminine instincts, for God's sake, and quit longing for Shane Carter. Now there's a man with problems!

She walked closer to the window. Through the blizzard, she saw a movement near the stable, a dark figure moving silently. Her heart jolted before she realized the man was Turnquist, walking the perimeter of the grounds. Just as he did each night. He varied the times he checked the fence line, sometimes taking Critter with him, sometimes wearing night goggles. He secured the stable, sheds, and barn, double-checking locks, doors, and windows, and rarely seemed to sleep. Yet Jenna didn't feel completely safe and wondered if she ever would. She corked the wine bottle and put it in the refrigerator before carrying her near-finished glass upstairs. She heard water running and a radio blaring over the rush of water in the bathroom as Cassie showered. Allie, the dog at her feet, was curled on her bed and watching television. Critter heard Jenna in the doorway and lifted his head, his tail bouncing off the quilt in soft thuds.

"Everything okay?" Jenna asked, walking into the room.

Allie shrugged. "I guess."

"I'm sorry I didn't find your backpack, but it just wasn't there." Allie didn't respond. "Look, the bad news is that the storm is getting worse."

"I hate good news/bad news jokes," Allie grumbled.

Jenna pressed on. "The good news is that school will probably be cancelled and you won't have to turn in your homework anyway. Maybe you'll get lucky." She winked at her daughter. "How 'bout that?"

Allie managed a little grin and held up crossed fingers. "That would be waaay good."

"I thought so. Good night, honey."

"'Night, Mom."

Jenna paused again at the bathroom door, where the shower and radio were still audible, then decided not to interrupt Cassie and slipped down the half-flight of stairs to her bedroom. *The room where he'd been.* She felt the same sick, crawly sensation she always did when she considered the creep walking through her house, touching her things, opening her drawer. Her eyes were drawn to the bedside table and she wondered . . . no, it wouldn't be possible . . . but her heart thudded in dread at an inner vision of her stalker having left another missive in her room.

That's crazy. You know better.

Swallowing back her fear, she finished her wine in one gulp, walked to the nightstand, and slowly opened the drawer. Her breath was tight in her lungs as she peered inside.

Empty.

Thank God! She let out a breath and the lights blinked. Once. Twice. Three times.

"Damn."

From the upper floor, Cassie squawked and the sound of music and running water stopped simultaneously.

Quick little footsteps pounded down the half-flight. Paws clicked against the hardwood floors. "Mom?" Allie asked, her voice tremulous, opening the door. "My television blinked."

"I know. Come on in."

The invitation was too late. Allie was already through the door. Not to be left out, Critter scrambled into the room and flew onto the bed.

Another set of flat, wet footsteps slapped against the floor. "What the hell's going on?" Cassie, wearing a hastily donned nightgown, her wet hair wrapped turbanlike in a towel, appeared on the landing just outside Jenna's open bedroom door. Her eyes were smudged with mascara and bits of shampoo clung to her forehead and cheeks.

"I'm afraid we might lose our electricity."

"Oh, great. You've *got* to be kidding!" Cassie was angry, her arms crossed over her chest, the towel starting to list to one side. "Living up here is a nightmare, Mom. *Beyond* a nightmare."

"So you've said." The lights flickered again, Cassie swore under her breath, and Jenna's tight nerves began to unravel. She forced a smile. "Everyone calm down." For once she didn't take Cassie to task on her foul language. They had bigger problems. "Okay, we've got the fire going and we all have warm pajamas, down quilts, flashlights, and candles. Jake is outside, so we're fine."

"You call this fine?" Cassie asked, righting her turban.

"Think of it as an adventure."

"Yeah, right," Cassie mocked, but left the room. "Oh, Mom, you are sooo pathetic. An *adventure!*"

"Watch it, Cass," Jenna warned her retreating daughter's backside. "I'm in no mood for this."

Cassie closed the door to her room.

Give me strength, Jenna thought.

"She's a pain!" Allie observed.

Amen. "Sometimes."

"*Most* of the time." Allie threw herself onto her mother's bed and the dog curled into a ball beside her. "I'm gonna stay here for a while."

"Good idea." Jenna decided not to run after Cassie. Let her cool off. They were all upset. She sat on the corner of the bed. "Why don't we watch a movie together?"

"'Cause there's no school tomorrow?"

"We think."

Again, Allie flashed both hands, showing that all her fingers were crossed for good luck, her thumbs crossed as well, her fears about the blinking lights allayed for the time being.

"Not a scary one, okay?"

"I think we can find a comedy." Using the remote, Jenna turned on the television, lit a couple of candles, and found extra pillows for their backs. She couldn't admit it to the kids, but she, too, was jittery as all get-out about the potential loss of power. The last thing they needed was to be trapped in a house without any lights or heat.

And someone out there . . .

Knowing. Watching. Waiting.

She walked to the windows and snapped all of the blinds shut. As she did, she caught a glimpse of Jake Turnquist trudging past the stable, his boots breaking a new path in the piling snow, white powder visible on his dark jacket and hat.

A lonely sentry on a cold winter night.

Jenna shivered and crossed her own fingers, silently praying that the bodyguard was enough protection from whatever evil was watching her.

I will come for you.

Like hell, she thought, and remembered the shotgun lying ready beneath the bed.

Carter mentally kicked himself all the way home.

What the hell had he been thinking at the parking lot of the theater?

When women were being abducted in his county and a murder was yet unsolved, he was hitting on Jenna Hughes? Thinking horny high-school-kid thoughts of a Hollywood princess? Jesus H. Christ! What kind of idiot was he?

Well, actually, she had been hitting on him, he reminded himself. He'd caught a glint of desire in her eyes, felt more than a hint of arousal as she'd swept her cool lips against his face. But had she really been interested? Or had her little display been just a performance by a convincing actress?

"Damn," he muttered, craving a cigarette.

Squinting as his wipers tried to keep up with a fresh onslaught of snow, he nosed his rig along the winding road that passed his property. "Put it out of your mind," he told himself. He'd done his duty. She was safe. Nothing had happened. So she'd kissed him out of gratitude. So what?

He passed Roxie Olmstead's accident site and wondered about the missing woman. From the notes on her laptop computer and information gleaned from her co-workers, the police had decided that she'd been on her way to Carter's house to try and pry information out of him, information regarding the mystery of Sonja Hatchell's disappearance. Had someone found out about her quest and tried to thwart Roxie's attempts at a story, or had she been the next victim? Was she stalked purposely. Or selected at random?

How organized was this guy?

Did he plan his abductions in advance, search out his victims, or just run across a woman who appealed to him and then get lucky? He couldn't wait to see what the FBI's profiler thought.

Cranking on the steering wheel, he felt the tires spin a little before finding purchase. The Blazer whined as it plowed through the drifts covering his drive.

Though the OSP and FBI weren't completely convinced that the two missing women were connected, Carter trusted his gut. Both he and BJ considered those cases, Mavis Gette and Jenna Hughes, somehow linked. Carter just hadn't figured out how they were associated yet, though that elusive link teased at the edges of his brain. He felt that same frustration he always did on a hard case, that teasing niggle that he was missing something—something important enough that it could break the case wide open.

So what was it?

Through the curtain of snow his headlights flashed on the rustic siding of his cabin, a home that was comparable in size to Jenna Hughes's garage. The Blazer rolled to a stop and he cut the engine. The differences between Jenna Hughes and himself were so vast, it was ridiculous that he even entertained fantasies about her. He was, he'd always told himself, a realist.

So why did she continue to haunt him, not only at night when his dreams would take him into her bedroom and into her bed, but during the day?

The images were vivid and visceral.

Ice glazed the windows. Snow fell steadily outside. A fire crackled near the bed where he made love to her in every position, his muscles straining, her body soft but compliant, her lips warm, her eyes gazing up at him with innocent eroticism. Their coupling was feverish, nearly brutal, filled with

wanting and a desire that didn't stop until both their bodies
were soaked with a sheen of sweat.

Afterward, Carter would awaken.

Feel like a fool.

His body sated.

What the hell was he thinking?

Realist, my ass.

*Wasn't Carolyn also above your station, the daughter of
an ex-governor? A woman who had once modeled for print
ads in* The Oregonian? *Why can't you settle for a nice, local
woman, someone who owns a bakeshop, or works for an insurance agent, or runs an ad agency, someone who would
look up to you rather than the other way around?*

Teeth clenched so hard his jaw ached, he snapped his keys
out of the ignition. He was hungry, dead tired, and whether
he liked to admit it or not, horny as hell. "Shit," he growled
as he slid out of the truck, and walked the few steps to his
front door, where he kicked off his boots and hung his jacket.

Unbuckling his shoulder holster, he reminded himself
that he had a job to do—he couldn't be distracted by a
woman. *Any* woman. He draped his holster over the back of
a chair, dropped his briefcase onto the couch, stoked the fire
in the woodstove, and tossed a frozen "man-sized" dinner
into the microwave and set the timer.

Pouring himself a stiff shot, he tried to keep his mind off
of Jenna Hughes. He had too much to do to be thinking
about a woman, especially *that* woman. She was the intended victim of a stalker and he had to keep his perspective.
Which, of course, was proving impossible. She'd somehow
gotten under his skin and burrowed deep into his thoughts.

An idiot, that's what he was.

As the microwave hummed and he sipped his drink, he
clicked on the television and found the news. Old footage of
Charley Perry up at Catwalk Point came into view, then a
discussion of Sonja Hatchell and Roxie Olmstead's disap-
pearances. A police source "close to the investigation" had
said there was no link to the crimes, but the newscasters

speculated upon the possibility of a serial kidnapper, or perhaps a serial rapist or serial killer.

"Great," Carter said sarcastically.

The two anchors, a woman and man in matching suit jackets, chatted about the public taking precautions and promised a statement from the Oregon State Police. *Fine.* Carter rattled the ice cubes in his drink. *Let Lieutenant Larry Sparks handle that one.*

The microwave dinged and he refreshed his drink, carried the hot little plastic plate on a towel into the living room, and using his ottoman as a table, watched the weather report.

More bad news. Yet another cold front was blasting in via Canada and temperatures were expected to drop to the lowest level in more than fifty years. A reporter standing in front of Multnomah Falls was dwarfed by six hundred feet of frozen, cascading water. The ice climbers were already arriving to try and scale the second largest waterfall in the contiguous United States.

"Damned fools," he muttered, swallowing a forkful of lasagna. *Like David.* Inside he cringed, refused to think of the day that David Landis had slipped, fallen, and plunged to his death. He muted the television, left part of his dinner uneaten on the ottoman, and carried his drink to his desk. Typing rapidly, he logged onto the Internet, checked his e-mail, then clicked onto Jenna Hughes's official home page before surfing through her fan sites.

Who, he wondered, was doing the same? How many people across the country, or throughout the world, were, at this moment in time, trying to learn more about the sultry actress? Who was nearby, the sicko close enough that he could gain access to her home?

Pulling BJ's list from his briefcase, he cross-referenced the people who had rented or bought videos of her with the list of people she'd said had been in her home within the last few months.

He came up with Wes Allen, Harrison Brennan, Scott Dalinsky, Rinda Dalinsky, Travis Settler, Yolanda Fisher, Ron Falletti, Hans Dvorak, Estelle Thriven, Joshua Sykes, Seth

Whitaker, Lanny Montinello, Blanche Johnson, and Shane Carter. He cut the women's and his own name from the merged list and realized the resulting "suspects" were really just a start. There were probably people she couldn't remember, workers who had been at the place, friends of friends, and the truth of the matter was that the guy might not be anyone she knew. It could be someone who either had a key from a previous owner or access from another source, perhaps someone she'd never known had set foot upon her land. Carter drummed his fingers on the desk and studied the picture of Jenna Hughes still radiating from his screen, a publicity shot where her long hair fell over one shoulder and she looked at the camera as if it were a lover. Her shoulders were bare, suggesting that she was naked, though that was just an illusion, as was much of the public's perception of her persona. He flipped through a series of screens showing Jenna in her various roles. Katrina Petrova, her first starring role, a teenaged prostitute in *Innocence Lost,* Marnie Sylvane, the schoolteacher living a double life in *Summer's End,* Paris Knowlton, a scared young mother in *Beneath the Shadows.* There were other images as well, from films where she'd played bit parts, and finally, there were several shots of her in her last, doomed movie, *White Out,* produced by her husband, never released, where her sister, Jill, had been killed on the set. Jenna played Rebecca Lange, a downhill racer, and for the part her looks had been altered slightly.

In the pictures from the set, Jenna's eyes were a clear blue, the result of contact lenses, Carter guessed. Her hair was blond for the role, and in one of the photographs, there was a picture of her battered and bruised, when Rebecca was in the hospital recuperating from a near-fatal skiing accident. Her face was swollen, her skin discolored, her teeth broken, and she was barely recognizable as beautiful Jenna Hughes.

It was as if she was a different woman.

Because of the art of makeup and prosthetics.

Carter stared at the image and a slow recognition stole over him. *Makeup!* That was the key.

His brain spinning ahead, he clicked onto a Web site he'd bookmarked on his computer. It was dedicated to alginate. He scrolled down quickly, skimming the article about alginate's use for taking dental impressions, and flashed to Mavis Gette's filed-down teeth. He'd thought it might be to disguise her identity, but maybe not.

Remembering Jenna's broken teeth in her role as Rebecca Lange, he imagined the process used to achieve that look. Someone, either a dentist or a makeup artist, had taken an impression of Jenna Hughes's bite, then fitted a set of fake, broken teeth over her own to make it appear as if she'd lost and cracked teeth in the skiing accident. Kind of like the vampire teeth a kid would buy for a Halloween costume.

"Hell," he whispered, as he considered the possibilities and kept reading. He noticed a mention of alginate as used in making prosthetics and masks, and he felt as if the wind had been knocked out of him. Was it possible? Had he missed something so obvious?

Eagerly he spent the next hour researching the making of masks and molds, learning that masks could be made by covering a subject's body part in liquid alginate to create a reverse image or mold. Once the alginate had solidified, the body part was carefully removed, leaving a space, or the reverse-image mold. If plaster was cast into the mold, the artist would have a perfect copy of the original body part, be it face, hand, foot, or whatever.

"Hell," he whispered, realizing the copy would be the mask that would look like the subject's original body part. From this point, the mask could be painted, added to, or cut. Other pieces of alginate or latex could be glued to the original mask to change or distort the image.

There were artists in the movie industry who created monsters or comic book characters or aged characters in just this fashion.

Carter stared at the screen and watched a short, fast-forwarded video of a normal-looking Hollywood actor transform into a werewolf by the use of an alginate mask, prosthetics, contacts, false canine teeth, and a shaggy wig.

Not only his face, but his hand, too, morphed slowly from a human hand to a furry paw with razor-sharp talons.

"An artist or a makeup person," Carter said to himself as he thought of the traces of alginate found on Mavis Gette. "Not a dentist."

They'd been looking in the wrong direction.

He watched the video again. When casting the actor's face in alginate, straws were inserted up the subject's nose so he was able to breathe.

And live.

But what if the subject, such as Mavis Gette, had been dead already? Then her face and other body parts could be used for a mold without the need of straws to keep her breathing.

Except that the crime lab had found traces of alginate internally. As if she'd ingested it.

His thoughts turned dark. Was the liquid alginate applied while Mavis had still been alive, the ultimate death mask? Why hadn't she struggled and ruined the mask? Perhaps she had. Or else she'd been drugged or somehow comatose . . . Jesus.

This was something out of an old B sci-fi flick.

Leaning back in his chair, he stared at the computer monitor. He felt the urge for a smoke—he could always think better when he relaxed with a cigarette. Rummaging in his desk, he found an old stick of Nicorette gum and popped it into his mouth. It was weak, far from a real hit, but he chewed the stuff and began surfing again, this time to Web sites dedicated to the making of movie monsters.

He watched another short video and witnessed an actor transform into an alien, another morph into a frightening image of Satan, while a third was aged by decades.

Was it possible?

Had the guy cast a mask of Mavis Gette's face?

Why else would there be traces of alginate attached to her skull?

Was this the same creep who had kidnaped Sonja Hatchell?

Carter chewed thoughtfully and took notes, doodling as

he tried to make sense of what he'd just learned. What kind of psycho would kill a woman for a mold of her face or body?

Could Mavis Gette's killer be a studio artist, someone connected to Jenna Hughes? Someone who had been in the business?

His mind went to Vincent Paladin, who had worked in a video store, but Paladin had no history of being involved in maskmaking or filmmaking as far as Carter knew. And he wasn't around. Carter had double-checked with his parole officer. Vincent was minding his Ps and Qs in Florida.

So who else? Someone local? A transient? What kind of guy was he?

Carter looked at the list of people who had rented Jenna's films. Wes Allen led the pack. Wes Allen was an artist, though never with makeup, to Carter's knowledge and Wes Allen had never lived in California. *But he had visited his sister and nephew when they resided near L.A.*

Leaning back in his chair, Carter listened to the fire hiss in the woodstove. He had to be careful and not let his personal feelings about Wes get in the way of his perspective. Associating Wes Allen to the crime had to be real, not a personal vendetta.

Examine the evidence!

Sitting up, he tapped the eraser end of his pencil on the desktop. His mind ran in circles and he thought of Jenna Hughes. Beautiful. Smart. Sexy. And now a target.

Of adoration?

Or murder?

Pulling the keyboard from its tray, he clicked onto his list of favorite bookmarked Web sites, then scrolled down to her name. Again. With a touch of his finger, her image appeared on his monitor. He couldn't help the tightening in his groin as he slowly flipped from one picture to the next. Each image was gorgeous, the kind of photos meant to be sexy and innocent and intriguing.

Even so, the computer screen was a flat, poor replica of the vital, real woman.

Chewing his tasteless gum, he thought about Jenna longer than he should have and figured BJ was right—he was in lust.

With a Hollywood star.

Just like a hundred million other men.

One of whom was stalking her.

Possibly Wes Allen.

Who could easily be eliminated from the suspect list? He spat his gum into the trash and pulled open the top desk drawer, searching in the back until he found a small cardboard box. Inside, lying upon a bed of cotton, were three rings. His wedding band and Carolyn's engagement set, complete with a one-carat diamond.

Ignoring the jewelry, he lifted the cotton. Tucked into the box was a single, worn key from an ancient lock. One he'd never used, though he'd been tempted over and over again.

Without a second thought, Carter slipped the key into his wallet. Just in case.

At that moment, his cell phone beeped.

He hit the Answer key and stared at the images playing upon his computer screen. Pictures of Jenna Hughes.

"Shane Carter."

"Sheriff, it's Dorie." The dispatcher sounded breathless and unnerved.

Carter braced himself.

"Yeah?"

"We just took a 9-1-1 call," she said. "Derwin Swaggert's wife is missing."

"Lynnetta?" Time seemed to stand still.

"That's right."

"Hell." Carter knew in an instant that another woman had been abducted. "How long has she been missing?"

"Only a couple of hours, but he's out of his mind with worry. He's already called the city police, but wants you involved, so I'm giving you a heads-up. I know it hasn't been the full twenty-four hours, but I figured you'd want to know."

"You figured that right," Carter said, imagining the preacher's petite wife, a sweet woman with an overly pious and stern husband and a rebel for a kid. "Where was the last place she was seen?"

"The Columbia Theater."

Where he had been.

Where Jenna had been.

"I've already dispatched the nearest unit. They haven't reported back yet."

"Thanks, Dorie." He was pushing his chair back and reaching for his holster. "I'm on my way."

CHAPTER 34

Not Lynnetta . . . Oh God, please, not *Lynnetta.*

Jenna might have collapsed if Carter hadn't grabbed hold of her arm. "I'm sorry," he said, standing in her kitchen at six in the morning. The refrigerator hummed, a fire in the grate hissed and crackled as it burned, lacing the air with the scent of wood smoke. But the world had changed drastically overnight, and all those reassuring sounds and smells faded into the background.

Carter had phoned her to say he was stopping by and had shown up less than five minutes later with the horrible news that Lynnetta Swaggert was missing.

He looked like hell. Bags were visible beneath eyes red from lack of sleep. Deep creases ran in worried lines across his forehead. A day's worth of stubble darkened his jaw, and the scent of tobacco clung to him. Physically, he appeared bone-weary, but there was something else beneath the tired facade, a fired-up Carter running on adrenaline, caffeine, and nicotine. "I wanted to tell you in person," he said, "and ask you about last night, before I came to the theater looking for you. You and Rinda might have been the last people to see Lynnetta Swaggert."

Alive.

He hadn't said it, but that one word hung in the kitchen

between them, unspoken but palpable. Jenna looked away and fought tears. *Lynnetta. Why Lynnetta?* There was a distinct chance Lynnetta Swaggert was dead. Just as there was an ever-increasing probability that Sonja Hatchell and Roxie Olmstead were no longer living.

"Lynnetta never phoned her husband?"

"No. He figured she was working late and started calling her around nine-thirty."

"Just after we left," she said, a little stronger now, her backbone once again rigid.

After Carter's phone call had jolted her awake earlier this morning, she'd thrown on a pair of jeans and a sweater and clipped her hair onto the top of her head, hurrying down the stairs with the dog tagging after her just as Jake was letting the sheriff's Blazer through the gates.

"There's always the chance she left," he said thoughtfully, though they both knew it was a platitude.

"Without a car in temperatures below freezing?"

"Someone could have picked her up. Someone she knew." Along with a determination in his dark eyes, there was sadness.

"You don't believe that."

"Not for a minute," he admitted, and finally, as if he just realized he was holding onto her arm, released it. "So let's go over what happened last night. Who was at the theater, if Lynnetta took any calls, who stopped by, who phoned, if she used e-mail, if something seemed to be troubling her, that sort of thing. My guess is you'll be called by the State Police, too, probably by Lieutenant Sparks. He's a little intimidating at first, but is one of the good guys. I don't know who will contact you from the FBI, but the field agent who works this territory knows her stuff. We'll get this guy."

"Before he abducts someone else?"

Carter's lips tightened and she wished she could have recalled the sharp words. "That's the plan."

"You'll have to work fast," she said, and walked to the coffeemaker and ground some beans. "Whoever he is, he seems insatiable." She poured water into the pot and hit the On switch.

Carter nodded. "It looks like he's upping the stakes. Escalating."

Critter gave a soft woof as the back door opened. "It's me," Turnquist called, and she peered down the short hallway to spy the bodyguard stopping near the laundry room to unlace his boots. "What's up?"

Carter set his hat on the table and draped his jacket over the back of a kitchen chair. His shoulder holster and pistol were strapped on, reminding Jenna how dangerous her life, and the lives of the other citizens of Falls Crossing, had become.

As water dripped through the pot and the scent of Kenyan roast filled the room, Carter sat at the table and explained that Lynnetta Swaggert had never phoned her husband, wasn't in the theater, and never went home. The reverend had called everyone he knew last night, searching for his wife, and Carter, along with the OSP, was checking everyone who had been in the theater or seen Lynnetta in the last few days.

"So he took her between the time I left and returned for Allie's backpack," Jenna said, knotting up inside. *If only you and Rinda had stayed until Lynnetta had finished with whatever she was doing!*

"Or he was there when you went back, inside the theater with her."

Jenna cringed inside, remembering the feeling that she wasn't alone while searching for the backpack, the sense that someone was nearby, breathing softly, moving noiselessly. To think that he might have been as near to her as Carter was now. And she'd blamed it on the cat. Her hands shook as she poured coffee and carried cups to the table, then sat across from the sheriff. As Carter took notes and sipped from his cup, Jenna told Carter everything she remembered from the night before, including the eerie sensation that someone had been in the theater. She also explained the few facts she knew about Lynnetta Swaggert—that she was devout, married to a preacher Jenna had met a few times but didn't know, that Lynnetta had one son, who was a friend of Josh Sykes, and that she was an excellent seamstress who created or altered costumes for the troupe. Jenna thought Lynnetta was about thirty-eight, looked younger, had the energy of five women, and worked part time as a bookkeeper for a local accountant.

"What about her personal life?" Carter asked.

"I don't think it was unhappy. Or if it was, she didn't complain." Jenna had never heard Lynnetta say that she was dissatisfied with her life, her husband, her job, or even her son, Ian. Jenna knew pitifully little about the woman, but Lynnetta had mentioned a brother in the Cincinnati area.

". . . and that's about it," she said, rubbing her arms as if from a sudden chill. She felt terrible. Responsible. Even though she knew better.

Her coffee sat untouched in front of her.

"Do you have any clues?" she asked, when Carter had finished taking notes.

He hesitated and she expected him to give her some line about not being able to talk about the case. Instead, he frowned darkly into his cup before taking a long gulp. "Nothing yet. But there's something else I wanted to ask you about."

"Shoot."

"Did you know any makeup people in Hollywood?"

"Of course. A lot."

"I'm talking about the kind of individual who makes the masks that fit perfectly to an actor's head, something that would make him change dramatically but retain his own facial features, the kind where they make a mold of the subject."

"Yes . . . the monster makers. There are companies that do that kind of work. Robert, my ex-husband, worked with several when he was into his horror-flick phase," she said, her thoughts still on Lynnetta. "Why?"

"A long shot, just a theory," and one Carter obviously wasn't going to share. "Could you give me a list of the companies who worked with the films you made or anyone you know in that business?"

"Sure."

"You think some Hollywood makeup man is stalking Jenna?" Turnquist asked.

"I don't know who is, but I want to check out every possibility." He drained his cup as his phone rang. "Carter." If possible, his face became more grim as he listened to whoever was on the other end of the line. "I'll be right there," he said, then hung up. "Gotta run. A would-be ice climber just fell off of Pious Falls. Looks like he shattered his pelvis." He plowed tense fingers through his thick hair. "I'd appreciate it if you could jot down the names of the makeup companies."

"We'll fax it later," Jake said, and watched as Hans Dvorak's rig rolled up to the gate and stopped. Hans rolled down the window and punched in the code. The gate swung open.

Carter noticed the foreman's truck drive through. "How many people have the security code?" he asked.

"Six . . . maybe seven. People who work here," Jenna said.

Turnquist nodded and finished his coffee. "I've got their names."

"Fax that, too, and change the code every day."

"Every day?" she repeated, stunned.

"That's right."

"I'll call Wes Allen to reset it," Turnquist said.

Carter rubbed his jaw, scratching his whiskers. "Why don't you try someone else?" he suggested, his frown deepening.

Turnquist's eyes narrowed. "Something wrong with Allen?"

"He's real busy, what with his own business and the theater." Carter pulled his jacket off the chair and stuffed his arms through the sleeves.

"Wes would make time," Jenna said, sensing an undercurrent she didn't really understand, then remembered Rinda saying there was some bad blood between her brother and the sheriff. Something about Carter's wife.

Turnquist said, "Then I'll call the guy Harrison knows, Seth Whitaker."

"I don't really know him." Carter glanced at Jenna.

"I've met him—he seems okay," she said.

Turnquist nodded. "I'll vouch for him."

"He did work for you before?" Carter was eyeing Jenna.

"Yes, when the pump froze."

"Then have him show you how to program it and you change it every day. The only people who will know what it is are you, the kids, and Turnquist here." Carter nodded at Jake as he zipped his jacket.

"And Hans and Estella," she corrected.

"No. You buzz 'em in. Have the electrician, Whitaker, work it so that you have control from the house."

"That might take a while." She wondered how the girls would keep up with the ever-changing access code.

"Then find someone else. A company who will install the buzzer today or tomorrow." He eyed Jenna as he squared his hat upon his head. "You won't have to do this forever," he assured her as he headed for the door. "Just until we get the son of a bitch."

Rinda called less than an hour later. She was a wreck, her voice trembling as she cancelled all activities at the theater—dance classes, voice lessons, even the rehearsals for the coming play. "It's just too weird, too disrespectful," Rinda whispered, her throat sounding clogged as if she were fighting tears. "You were right—we should have stayed later last night until Lynnetta's husband showed up. We should never have left her alone."

"You don't know that we could have made a difference. If the creep who took her wanted her, he would have found a way to get to her."

"God, who is he?" She cleared her throat. "He waited until after we left to pounce, didn't he? He was watching. He might even have a key." She was working herself up, her voice rising. "This wasn't random, Jenna. It was planned. I know it. Oh God, why would anyone want to hurt Lynnetta?"

"I don't know." Jenna rested a hip against the counter and stared at the fire. She couldn't think of a single soul who would want to harm the preacher's wife.

Rinda sniffed, then asked, "Has Carter been by to see you?"

"Yeah, this morning."

"He was here, too, asking all sorts of questions. Just left. He or some officer from the State Police is going to talk to everyone in the theater troupe, all of the actors, stagehands, the janitor, you name it. Even Scott, if you can believe that."

Jenna could, but didn't say as much. As it was, Rinda sounded slightly miffed, her grief spilling into anger.

"I can't believe this mess," Rinda admitted. "I hope—I mean, I pray—that Lynnetta's okay. Maybe her disappearance is all just a big mistake . . ." But the desperation and pain in her voice said she believed otherwise. As did Jenna.

"Let's not give up hope yet."

"I haven't. But it's hard. And you'd better brace yourself. That reporter for KBST, Brenda Ward, she's already called me. Twice. And someone from the *Banner,* where Roxie Olmstead worked. They've left a couple of messages. I'm tellin' ya, these people are cannibals. One of their own is missing and they're trying to make a story out of it." She blew her nose and added vehemently, "But just try to get them to write a human-interest piece on the renovations to the theater and see what happens. Nothing, that's what! It's all murder, scandal, blood, and sex these days!"

"I think the theater's going to get a lot of press now."

"Exactly. *Bad* press. Just what we need . . . and Lynnetta. I can't quit thinking about her, about last night . . . Oh God, Jenna, what's happening around here?"

Nothing good. "I don't know."

"Look, I've got to go," Rinda said. "And warn Scott."

"Warn him?"

"Yeah. He doesn't even know about Lynnetta, and they were pretty tight. He drove into Portland last night for a concert that should have been cancelled because of the weather, but wasn't. Anyway, he has no idea Shane's on the warpath. Jesus Christ, that makes me mad! To even suggest that Scott might know something. Shane Carter is Scott's godfather and still he doesn't trust him."

"It's his job. He can't trust anyone right now," Jenna said, bristling slightly as she defended the man that, for months, Rinda had lauded and now was cursing.

"Oh, no!" Rinda gasped.

"What?"

"Turn on your television. Check out KBST."

With the phone to one ear, Jenna picked up the remote with her free hand and clicked to the station Rinda had suggested. There, on the screen, a reporter was planted in the snow in the foreground. Behind her was the theater. Police cars and a few uniformed men were visible, as was the sign announcing tickets on sale for *It's a Wonderful Life*.

Rinda groaned.

"You wanted publicity."

"No one will come to the play now."

"You don't know that—the first performance is still a few weeks away," Jenna said, wondering why she was trying to cheer her friend up. Rinda was right, the situation was dire. Poor Lynnetta.

"This isn't the right kind of publicity."

"According to my agent, there is no wrong kind," Jenna said, hoping to lighten the conversation, but Rinda wasn't to be consoled.

"Uh-oh."

"What?"

"A city cop car in my drive. Probably Officer Twinkle."

"Who?"

"Old joke. Bad one. Never mind." She sighed as if the weight of the world was on her shoulders. "I suppose this is going to be unending."

"Maybe they'll find Lynnetta."

"Let's hope," Rinda said, and hung up.

Jenna continued to watch the television. She felt empty

inside as the reporter, Brenda Ward, a pert little redhead in a blue parka and gloves, squinted against the falling snow-flakes and explained about Lynnetta Swaggert being abducted. From Lynnetta's disappearance, the newscast segued into stories about the other missing women, and Jenna felt as if she had a huge stone in the middle of her stomach. The weather report was next, along with a reminder that the schools were closed. Jenna, thoughts on Lynnetta, barely noticed. Finally she snapped off the TV.

They spent the day inside. Both girls, though they didn't say it, were bored to tears and neither one was interested in a) baking an early batch of Christmas cookies; b) helping string interior lights and putting up all the decorations except for the tree; or c) playing cards or any kind of board game. They both preferred their own company.

Cassie talked on the phone, instant-messaged on the computer, or watched some soap opera on television. Allie, with Jake at her side, broke a fresh trail through the snow to help Hans with the horses. Two hours later, she returned, her cheeks red, her nose running; Jenna made her hot cocoa and a peanut butter sandwich and urged her to practice the piano. Begrudgingly, she agreed, and now, as Jenna sat at the table going over her checkbook, the clear notes of several Christmas carols wafted into the den.

Jenna was able, through Harrison Brennan, to get through to the electrician, but of course, Seth Whitaker had barely arrived when Harrison, hell-bent on helping out, drove through the open gates. He parked next to Turnquist's truck. Over Jenna's protests, Brennan helped his friend, and though Jenna sensed that Whitaker would rather have done the job himself and made tracks to his next project, he didn't complain, even when Harrison handed out orders.

"If he's bothering you, I'll ask him to leave," Jenna said to Whitaker as she, dressed in ski gear, carried out a thermos of coffee. Brennan was a few feet off, standing near Whitaker's white truck and out of earshot as he rewound a roll of wire. He wore a tight-fitting jumpsuit made out of some thin, insulated material and a thick jacket and ski mask.

"I'm okay." Whitaker, bundled in a heavy jacket and pants, a hunter's cap with flaps covering his ears, was intent on his work at the gate post and barely looked up. His toolbox was at his feet, getting buried by the blowing snow.

"All right, but I know he can be bossy."

"Comes with being in the military, I guess," Whitaker said, as he screwed the faceplate on the keypad at a gate post. "Here. Time for a quick lesson." He took the thermos from her gloved hands. "Now, depress the key that says PID—that's Personal Identity. Put in three numbers that mean something to you and hit the PID key again." She punched in two, two, six. "My birthday," she explained.

Whitaker snorted. "Well, that's okay for now, but in the future, use something that's a little more obscure. Now that you've entered your PID, you need to punch in a code of four numbers—these are the ones that will change daily. Go ahead, use any numbers. We'll change the code again, once you understand how it works."

Jenna keyed in one, two, three, four.

He grinned, his brown eyes crinkling at the corners. "Fair enough. Now hit reset." He pointed to a button with the tip of his Phillips screwdriver. She did as requested. "Okay, now try your new code." Once again, she keyed in the numbers. After the last digit, the gate swung open. She used the same process to close the gate and return it to its locked position.

Whitaker kicked open his toolbox and dropped his screwdriver onto the tray holding wrenches, pliers, and screwdrivers. Then, as he kicked the lid closed again, he began twisting off the thermos lid. He seemed satisfied with his work, even grinned. "You can do the same thing up at the house. I'll wire it in."

"What's to prevent anyone from taking off the faceplate and resetting it themselves?"

"Nothing. As long as they have your PID. So that's why I suggested you come up with something more creative than your birthday. Got it?" He poured a stream of coffee into the thermos cap.

"Yeah, I think so. I just hope I can remember the codes if I change them every day."

"You might want to work out some kind of system that only you and your kids know. Like adding thirty-three to the total numbers. You just punched in one, two, three, four, or one thousand two hundred and thirty-four. Tomorrow you'd add thirty-three and your code would be one thousand two hundred and sixty-seven, or one, two, six, seven. The next day you'd add another thirty-three and the code would be one thousand three hundred, or one, three, zero, zero."

The numbers spun in Jenna's head. "I think we'll come up with something simpler."

Whitaker shrugged and sipped the coffee. "Whatever's easiest for you to remember."

"Got it figured?" Harrison asked as he carried the coil of wire to the gate and joined them.

Turning her back to the wind, Jenna reached into her pocket. "Never." She pulled out a small cup. "I thought you might need something to warm you up."

Harrison's blue eyes met hers and a small smile tugged at the corner of his lips, barely visible through the ski mask. As if he were touched by her act of kindness. Lately, the words they'd shared had been sharp. "Thanks," he said, accepting the cup. "It is a mite cold out here."

"Like ten below," Whitaker agreed. "If you add in the wind chill, it's even worse."

Smiling as the snow swirled around them, Whitaker handed Brennan the thermos. "What about you?" he asked Jenna.

"I've got a cup inside. I'll let you two freeze out here and drink mine by the fire," she teased.

"Nice," Whitaker mocked.

"Come in when you're finished and you can warm up."

"Soon," Whitaker muttered. "We're about done out here."

"Thank God—it's colder than a well-digger's butt." Brennan looked at Jenna, his blue eyes assessing. "Not that I'm complaining, mind you. I've never really minded the cold. Winter's usually my favorite time of year."

CHAPTER 35

The sheriff's department was a madhouse. Even though the FBI and Oregon State Police were involved in the kidnapping and murder cases, the department was stretched thin, plagued with new problems. With damage from the storm, icy roads, shut-ins, power outages, and idiots like the kid who broke his pelvis in eight places while trying to scale Pious Falls, his men and women had more than they could handle. The press had convened in Falls Crossing en masse despite the bad roads.

A search party had been started for Lynnetta Swaggert. The group was largely made up of volunteers—neighbors, friends, and members of the church—who were already tired from tromping through the snow-covered woods and fields looking for Sonja Hatchell and Roxie Olmstead. Even the Explorer Scouts, young people who aspired to be cops and were often used in searches, were weary, cranky, and cold to the bone. A usually eager group, they were dispirited with the prospect of yet another search.

Carter sat at his desk behind an ever-growing pile of paperwork, a couple of empty coffee cups, and a stack of phone messages he hadn't returned yet. Most of the paperwork would have to wait. The missing women were the highest priority, and Lynnetta's husband was making the most of the grim situation.

The Reverend Derwin Swaggert had been on the television, dry-eyed but shaken, spouting about God's will and asking for prayers for his wife. A candlelight vigil was planned for this evening, and The reverend was encouraging everyone to pray not only for Lynnetta but for the other missing women as well.

Morale was low.

Deputies and office workers alike needed a break.

Even BJ wasn't herself.

She stopped by his office and shut the door. "You know, I have a problem with Ian Swaggert, a big problem. He's still hanging around Megan, and the kid is trouble, but this . . ." She lifted a hand and let it fall to her side. "This is real bad."

"We could still find her."

"Alive!" BJ snapped. "We need to find her alive."

Jerri tapped on the door and dropped two sheets of paper on his desk. "Fax for you," she said. "From Jenna Hughes."

BJ said, "What kind of fax?" as Jerri left and closed the door behind her again.

"A list of makeup studios who specialize in monster-making." He quickly scanned the list. "Companies that might use alginate for molds."

"What are you talking about?" She was interested, leaning a hip against his desk, reading the list upside down as he explained what he'd found out and how he thought the alginate might be the link between Mavis Gette's murder and Jenna Hughes's stalker.

"You're serious about this?"

"Absolutely."

BJ studied the list and scratched her arm. "I don't know, it's pretty far-fetched," she said. "Did you tell the feds or OSP?"

"I called Larry Sparks. He said he'd check it out. Run it by the FBI. They've got a profiler working on the serial kidnapping case now, but they're still not convinced the cases are linked, so maybe this'll help."

"Or maybe they'll laugh you out of the office."

He snorted. "It wouldn't be the first time." Running a finger down the typed names of the companies, he said, "Now, what we need is a roster of their employees and anyone with roots up here, maybe someone who was working for them in California and moved north." His eyes narrowed and he tented his fingers under his chin as he leaned back in his chair, making the old metal groan. "And we need to find out if any of them are or have been missing alginate. Did you have any luck finding out if any suppliers shipped to anyone around here?"

"Other than the dentists?" She shook her head. "No."

"What about Portland? Or Vancouver? Even Seattle. Somewhere within driving distance."

"Still working on it."

"Good."

Another tap on the door and Jerri stuck her head in. "KBST is camping out in front," she said, "and one of the reporters, a"—she glanced at her note—"Brenda Ward, wants to interview you."

"Not now."

"She asked for a statement."

Carter leaned forward. "Tell her to call Lieutenant Sparks of the Oregon State Police."

Jerri ducked out of the office and BJ picked up the list. "Mind if I make a copy?" she asked.

"Go for it. Once you get a printout of any employees who have moved recently, or quit, or taken a leave of absence, we'll cross-reference it with our list of people who have rented or bought the movies, not just around here, but in the greater metropolitan area of Portland, maybe all of northern Oregon and southern Washington. If that doesn't work, we'll expand the search." He crushed an empty cup and tossed the crumpled remains into his trash. "But I have a feeling this guy's close." His eyes narrowed as he thought. "And efficient. Maybe knows his victims. There wasn't any sign of a struggle in the church, nor at the scene of the Olmstead accident, nor at the parking lot of Lou's Diner. Either this guy somehow disables his victim without a struggle or blood loss or he cons them into helping him out. Remember Ted Bundy? Sometimes he wore a cast, I think, or bandages to disarm his victims, make them less wary."

"Roxie Olmstead wrecked her car. No conning there."

"He could be smart enough to adjust to each situation. If one way doesn't work, he uses another."

"Let's hope he's not smart," BJ said, "but just lucky and that his luck is about to run out." She grabbed the two sheets of Jenna Hughes's fax and started to walk out of the room. "Oh, wait," she said. "I thought you might want to know that there are a couple of lines from the poems that I came across on the Internet. *Today. Tomorrow. Endlessly.* It's from a poem written by Leo Ruskin—have you heard of him?"

Carter shook his head.

"Similar to a New-Age Timothy Leary. Writes poetry that means nothing to me, but get this—the line was going to be used as a promo line for *White Out*, the Jenna Hughes movie that never was finished."

Carter's head snapped up. He drilled BJ with his eyes. "Wouldn't she remember that?" he asked. "Her husband was the producer of that movie and it lost millions."

"You'd think, but maybe she wasn't in on that end of things, and then her sister was killed and her marriage fell apart. She could've blanked the whole business out, if she ever knew it at all."

Carter felt a rush in his blood, a surge of adrenaline, the same excitement that he always felt when he was about to solve a case. This could be it. "Where is Ruskin now?"

"Still searching."

"Find him. Find out all of his previous addresses. And when you start with the makeup studios and firms in L.A., start with the one hired for *White Out*."

"Will do," she said as she left the office and Carter's phone rang. As he picked up the receiver, he hoped he'd just gotten lucky.

* * *

What was this?

Dear Lord in heaven, what was going on?

Lynnetta opened a bleary eye and shivered.

It was so cold . . . freezing . . . Her skin was probably turning a dozen shades of blue. Yet there was a dullness to her, as if her brain was filled with mud. Blinking, she slowly looked around the vast room . . . or was it a warehouse? . . . She couldn't tell from her position in a chair, a recliner of sorts. Somewhere music was playing, but it sounded far away and when she blinked, she saw women standing on a stage. Half of them faceless, naked, bald, but three dressed, their hair combed, their faces . . . Lynnetta swallowed hard. They were all Jenna Hughes! No, that couldn't be. They were likenesses of Jenna, strange mannequins.

What was this?

She rolled her eyes upward. Above her head was the long, stainless-steel arm of a dentist's drill . . . shining bright in the dim lights. Glinting like pure evil.

No . . . this couldn't be right. Something was wrong here. Very, very wrong. She had to get a grip or wake up or . . . She heard a sound, a soft rasp that set her teeth on edge.

She was groggy and certain that she, like Alice, had fallen down a rabbit hole. Everything was surreal. Bizarre. Topsy-turvy. She blinked again to clear her vision and her mind.

But it didn't hone the dullness.

In her peripheral vision she saw him. The man who had startled her in the theater. But now he was naked.

Oh, no.

She remembered being in the theater under the stage. She'd heard a noise as she was putting away the dress she'd hemmed. Thinking the sound was just the cat nosing around where he shouldn't, she'd called to him. As she'd rounded the corner to Rinda's office, she'd come upon a man who had been waiting for her in the darkness. She'd thought he'd held a gun and had tried to run. But he'd grabbed her, placed the cold metal against her neck, then zapped her. Electricity had shot through her body. She'd crumpled, but he hadn't been finished and slammed a needle into her arm.

Fear slithered down her spine as she tried to see him more clearly, attempted to recoil. But she couldn't escape; she was bound to this damned chair and realized with a sickening feeling that she, too, wore nothing. Her skin was pressed against cold leather. Oh, Lord, was he going to rape her? Why? What had she done to deserve such a wretched fate?

Tears filled her eyes, but still, through the blur, she saw him, his genitals exposed, a tattoo she couldn't make out upon his chest. He was holding something in his hand, something she couldn't quite see.

Help me, she silently pled. *Please, God, help me.*

Who was this man? She thought she'd known him, had seen him in town, but he'd changed. He was slimmer than she'd remembered, his hair thinner and dyed a different color. As if he was wearing a disguise . . . or had worn one for all the time that she'd known him.

Even his eyes were different. Cruel. Like glittering blue rocks set deep into his skull. The purest form of evil she'd ever witnessed.

She swallowed hard as she stared at the contraption in his hand. It was a dental appliance, a rubber dam with stainless-steel frame, equipment that would force a mouth open.

No! She began to panic, though her mind was mush. She had to get out of here! Now! Oh, God, there was no escape. She was bound to this chair. Over the music and the sound of her own frantic heartbeat, she heard a voice.

Stay calm, Lynnetta, I am with you.

Was it God's voice she heard . . . yes? Or a hallucination from some weird psychedelic drug that was being piped into her bloodstream via the IV pierced into her wrist. She glanced down at her hand and for the first time noticed the bandage . . . a thick strip of gauze wound tight over her fingers, binding them together. What was that all about? There was a dark red stain . . . no doubt blood . . . on the gauze, seeping through from her ring finger . . . Yet she felt no pain and something about her hand seemed weird. Frantically attempting to wiggle her fingers, she failed. Probably because of whatever drug was flowing through the darned IV. There had to be something in the clear liquid that was keeping her mind fuzzy, dulling the pain.

So why was her hand bandaged? Had she struggled? Fought? She couldn't remember. Didn't have time to think.

He was coming closer.

Fear screamed through her bloodstream.

Trust in me. The Father's voice again, trying to calm her, hoping that her faith would sustain her.

Please, Father, have mercy, she prayed, closing her eyes as she felt Lucifer's hot breath upon her cold face. She thought of the martyrs who had gone before her, the fearless souls who had accepted God's fate. For some reason, The Father was testing her, but she would fear not . . . He would deliver her. She was certain of it.

She thought of springtime and her dear, departed parents, then of Derwin, a hard-driven man, but a man who had loved her . . . and she thought of her son, Ian, not yet an adult, tempted by all that was available to youth these days. *Be with them, dear Lord,* she prayed, and despite whatever torture this evil incarnation of Satan had planned for her, she would never lose her faith. Never! Soon, she would be home. Soon, she would be with Him. She, like those before her, like Jesus who had suffered on the cross, would endure the agony on earth to accept her eternal reward.

I'll be with you soon. Sweet Jesus, I'll be with you soon.

Her eyes still shut, she complied as the monster roughly forced the rubber dam into her mouth, didn't so much as squeak as he tightened it so that her jaw was opened painfully wide, her lips pulled harshly back, her tongue and teeth at his mercy. She flinched only slightly when she heard the hum of the drill, but closed her mind to everything other than her prayer.

Our Father, who art in heaven . . .

The drill squealed against her teeth, shrieking wildly as the scent of burning enamel filled her nostrils, and she knew it was only a matter of seconds before the ungodly drill bit hit a nerve.

CHAPTER 36

Technically, it wasn't breaking and entering.

He had a key.

The key Wes Allen had given Carolyn years before, and it was now in the front pocket of Shane Carter's jeans.

But you don't have a search warrant. Anything you find will be thrown out of court. You'll lose your job.

Carter had wrestled with that decision for nearly four days, ever since the night Lynnetta Swaggert had been abducted. He had hoped to gather enough evidence against Wes, to get the damned search warrant, but then Amanda Pratt and her boss, the D.A., hadn't been impressed with the fact that Wes Allen dabbled in art, knew Jenna, had bought or rented all of her films on DVD or tape. And Wes had no link to Leo Ruskin, the Leary-esque poet from L.A. who seemed to have disappeared off the face of the earth.

Even Shane had known the evidence was thin at best, and his gut instinct didn't count for much. Besides, there was that little matter of a personal vendetta Amanda Pratt had brought up.

"Isn't this guy a friend of yours . . . oh!" Sitting on the edge of her desk, legs swinging, she'd snapped her fingers as if struck by a sudden bolt of insight. "Wait a minute . . . this was the guy that had an affair with your wife, right? The one you, in a fit of rage, swore to kill? Isn't this the reason they suggested you go to counseling, to deal with your grief and rage? I think this little incident nearly cost you your job."

"That was a long time ago," Carter had said.

"And they always say something to the effect that revenge tastes best when served up cold."

She hadn't budged, so here he was, hours later, parked on an old logging road a quarter of a mile from Wes's farmhouse, hankering for a cigarette and contemplating breaking the law and losing everything he'd worked for all his life.

Because of a gut instinct.

And because he was losing his perspective when it came to Jenna Hughes. What had Dr. Randall observed about him, that he was the kind of person who basically shot himself in the foot, who always found a way to thwart himself? Hence, Carolyn. Now . . . his job.

Tough, he thought, climbing out of his truck and making his way through the woods. He was wearing a pair of boots that were a size too big, a pair that had been left by Wes himself at Carter's cabin years ago. Fitting, Carter thought with a trace of irony. The boots were a common brand, the favorite of hunters and hikers in the Northwest. Hard to trace. Carefully, he walked through the woods, using a flashlight, grateful for the lull in the blizzard that had been ripping through the gorge. He knew the deer trails well, had followed them while hunting as a kid, he and Wes and David together.

It had been years ago. Carter hadn't been through this part of the forest since the day David Landis had fallen to his death while trying to climb Pious Falls. But the terrain hadn't changed much—the forest still remained, and Carter skirted the falls, now solidly frozen pillars that stretched from the ridge overhead to the pool of ice at his feet.

The night was quiet. Eerily so. Without the cascading rush of water tumbling over the cliffs or the wind howling through the canyon cut by the Columbia River, the forest held a silence all its own. A bit of moon peeked through the thick clouds, but the stars were obscured, as if they didn't want to witness his crime.

Sometimes a man had no choice but to take the law into his own hands. That's just the way it was.

Angling down the hillside, he recognized Wes's home, visible through the trees, one tall security lamp lighting the small farm with its ancient farmhouse and cavernous barn. Wes's truck was missing, which wasn't a surprise as Carter had spied it parked in front of the Lucky Seven Saloon, a favorite watering hole just outside of town. Wes usually spent a couple of hours there each night that the Trail Blazers played; Carter was gambling that his pattern wouldn't change tonight. The game had started an hour earlier, which should leave plenty of time. Unless Wes didn't stay through the fourth quarter.

Carter had considered enlisting BJ, telling her to stay at the bar and sip beer, making sure that Wes stayed firmly seated upon his bar stool. But BJ would have started asking questions, and then he would have involved her in something if not strictly illegal, then certainly borderline. No, he was better going it alone.

Pausing to double-check that no one was lingering on the farm, he leaned against the trunk of a Douglas fir that had somehow escaped the logger's axe and watched his breath fog in the still night. Headlights flashed along the highway in the distance, few and far between. Somewhere a train rumbled on distant tracks, but no dog was barking. The two-storied farmhouse with its wide porches, steep roof, and peeling paint was dark and appeared deserted.

"It's now or never," he told himself and circled through the woods to the barn, where he stopped and listened for the sound of a dog or other animal, but no noises erupted, no startled neigh, no sharp, warning bark. Through a sagging gate and up the back porch he crept, as he had often years ago.

Before Wes and Carolyn had become lovers.

Jaw set, he climbed up two steps to the porch and reached

the back door. He pulled off one glove with his teeth, then using his exposed hand, extracted his wallet from his pocket and removed the key.

In a second it slipped easily into the old lock and turned. Carter winced, bracing himself for the sound of an alarm that Wes could have installed in the past few years. The lock clicked and no other noises erupted.

So far, so good.

He left the boots on the porch; then, in stocking feet, he slipped through hallways that had been, years before, familiar.

The smell of the house hadn't changed, and he noticed a row of empty, sixteen-ounce bottles of Coors on the counter. The furniture—a hodgepodge that suited Wes and no woman would claim—was the same, a little dusty, but no clutter in the living room with its dueling recliners, long couch, big-screen and surround-sound TV.

Floorboards creaked beneath his feet as he searched each room, sweeping the beam of his flashlight across a dining room table with a dried centerpiece that had to be ten years old, dust collecting on the once-glossy wood, then into the small room by the stairs, a parlor Wes used as an office. Along the wide top of the desk, next to a state-of-the-art computer, were neat stacks of mail. Bills in one pile, newspapers in another, magazines in a third. Nothing looked out of the ordinary; the bills were for utilities and such, offers of credit cards at great rates, the magazines ranging from *Popular Science* and *Hunter's World* to *Playboy* and *Penthouse*.

The computer was on standby . . . and with a touch of one key, glowed to life. Carter checked the time. He'd been inside ten minutes—he'd only allow himself another ten just in case Wes got bored with the game.

Since he was using Wes Allen's computer, access was a snap, all preprogrammed. Carter glanced at Wes's most recent visits: e-Bay and Jenna Hughes's Web site were at the top of the list, and a check through Wes's list of favorite or bookmarked sites, again had not only e-Bay and Jenna Hughes, but her fan sites and porn sites sprinkled in with pages dedicated to basketball, electronics, home repair, and art. Carter copied the list, sent it to himself, then deleted the sent mail. If Wes were clever, and dug deeper, he'd figure it out, but Carter was betting that Wes Allen would never know he'd had a visitor.

The digital time readout on the monitor warned him that his allotted time was nearly exhausted. After wiping the keyboard clean, Carter quickly made his way up the stairs and walked through two small, cold bedrooms filled with extra furniture and clothes, unused for any purpose, including guests, from the looks of it. Stacked boxes on extra tables, chairs and a bed without a mattress, empty closets. A quick check revealed that the boxes were filled with old papers, tax information and the like, not what Carter was looking for.

He left the extra bedrooms undisturbed, then swept through a single, utilitarian bathroom and, finally, Wes Allen's bedroom. It was as stark and uncluttered as the rest of the house, a braided rug supporting a cast-iron bed, a solitary bureau that also served as a TV stand, and a night table where a lamp, reading glasses, box of tissues, and remote control had been placed. Neat. Tidy. Everything in order. Almost as if Wes had expected company.

Carter checked his watch. The fourth quarter would be about over unless there was overtime involved. He had to move fast.

He quickly searched the closet, found nothing, opened the bedside drawer, and his breath caught in his throat as he shined his flashlight into the interior. The drawer was empty, aside from a few pieces of jewelry and a stack of snapshots.

Of Carolyn.

Bile rose in the back of his throat as he quickly sorted through the Polaroids.

Pictures of Carolyn laughing, clowning, pointing, or biting her lip. Photographs of her in jeans and sweaters, in a bikini, in a lacy teddy. Snapshots of her wading in the river, seated behind the wheel of Wes's truck, on a bed with rumpled sheets.

Carter closed his eyes and let out his breath. "Son of a

bitch." His back teeth ground so hard his chin ached. "Son of a goddamned bitch!"

The old, hot pain of betrayal cut through his brain.

What did you expect when you went snooping?

Had this been a fool's mission? A personal vendetta, as Amanda Pratt had suggested? Is this what he'd really been searching for?

He thought about burning the pictures, then set them in the drawer and closed it.

This search wasn't about him. It wasn't about Carolyn. It was about Jenna Hughes and protecting her. And he'd come up empty-handed.

So far.

Yet he couldn't leave the pictures of Carolyn lying there. Silently telling himself he was a damned fool, he pocketed the full set of shots. Let Wes discover them missing. What could he do? Come down to the station and accuse Carter of the theft of snapshots of his wife?

Without second-guessing himself, he made his way downstairs and nearly jumped out of his skin as a grandfather clock near the front door began to chime the hour. He looked in every closet and cupboard and bookcase as he made his way to the back door and locked it behind him. *Get a move on. There isn't much time. Don't push your luck.*

On the porch, he pulled on boots and walked outside. He spied the cellar entrance, an exterior door that led to the basement. Locked. With a path of broken snow leading toward it.

He'd noticed a set of keys in a drawer by the back door.

Though time was ticking off quickly, he couldn't come this far, take this much of a risk, and not follow through. As swiftly as possible, Carter retraced his steps, grabbed the key ring, and made his way to the cellar door. In all the years he'd known Wes Allen, he'd never once crossed this threshold.

Carter tried six keys before the seventh slid into the lock and it sprang open. Using the beam of his flashlight as his guide, he stepped carefully inside, pulled the doors shut, and started down the ancient wooden steps to a dank, brick-lined basement just deep enough for him to stand. The thin beam of his flashlight exposed old jars, tools, unused hunting and fishing gear, rubber waders, a canoe that had seen better days.

Nothing.

He stepped farther inside, breathing slowly, trying not to consider the seconds ticking by. He swept the flashlight slowly into every cranny, the yellow beam washing over cobweb-laden beams, crumbling mortar, and around a corner to another door, this one padlocked.

What the hell?

Carter checked his watch. His time was up. More than up. But he couldn't stop now. It took several tries, but he found the right key, the lock gave way, and he pushed open the door and flipped on a light switch near the door.

He felt as if he'd been punched in the gut.

Got ya, he thought, with a needle-sharp sense of satisfaction. This small room was a shrine, a goddamned altar to Jenna Hughes.

As dirty as the rest of the cellar was, this room was pristine, the walls recently Sheetrocked and painted a soft gold, the floor carpeted, a television mounted in one wall, a VCR and DVD set up with surround sound, video camera, tripod, digital camera, a space heater set on the floor near a bookcase filled with videos, DVDs, and pictures of Jenna Hughes. Everywhere. In frames, or pinned to the wall, between candles, and among bracelets and necklaces, hair clips and garters. A short black wig was mounted on a Styrofoam head. Earrings glittered on the arm of the only piece of furniture in the room, a red leather recliner, facing the screen.

Using his handkerchief, he picked up a tiara. It looked familiar. Had Jenna worn something like this in *Innocence Lost,* when she'd played the teenaged prostitute? Were the earrings like those that had sparkled in the ears of Paris Knowlton, the role Jenna had played in *Beneath the Shadows?*

Carter had seen enough of her movies recently. He should remember. He checked his watch and frowned. He'd stayed too late.

He started to leave, the beam of his flashlight illuminating the videos and DVDs, titles he equated with porn or Jenna Hughes. Wes Allen's very private theater. Carter hated to think what Wes did while he watched.

He was about to leave when the beam of his flashlight slid over a black video case that didn't have a printed spine. His gut slammed hard against his diaphragm. A labeler had been used to identify the homemade film: CAROLYN.

"Shit!" Carter reached for the video, intent on putting it into his pocket or smashing it into a million pieces. But he couldn't. Not if he wanted to nail Wes, and damn it, he wanted to nail Wes Allen in the worst possible way. If for nothing else, then the pornography. Curiosity about what was on the damn tape burned through his brain and his guts ground.

He couldn't compromise the collar. Couldn't.

But he slipped the video into his pocket.

It was time to get the hell out of here.

A sound pierced the silence. The deep, rumbling sound of a truck's engine. Getting closer.

Hell!

He quickly slipped out of the room, slapped the light switch off with a gloved hand, closed the door behind him, and managed to click the lock closed. He was halfway across the basement when he stopped short. The truck was close, the engine growling ever louder. Through the crack in the cellar door, he saw lights flashing. Headlights sweeping across the exterior of the farmhouse. From Wes Allen's truck.

Carter froze.

Pressed himself back against the wall.

He heard the engine die, the pickup's door creak open, and the sound of Wes trudging through the snow toward the house.

Carter held his breath as the footsteps clomped up the steps to the back porch, paused for a second, then walked inside, the floorboards groaning directly above Carter's head.

Go on in, Wes, turn on the news . . . check your e-mail . . . or go on up to bed . . . sleep it off.

But the footsteps overhead stopped in the kitchen.

No sound at all came from the house.

As if Wes had felt something in the air. Had sensed someone had been in his house.

Carter heard another soft scrape. The sound of a drawer opening? Oh, crap, was Wes intending to visit his private viewing room?

Carter still had the key ring on him. If Wes was looking for his keys . . . oh, shit. He couldn't panic. Had to figure a way out of his. Wes shuffled a bit, swore. Searching for keys that were missing?

If you don't do something, he's going to come down here and you'll be trapped.

Slowly, Carter extracted his cell phone from his pocket. Sweating despite the freezing temperature, he turned the phone on and muted it. He pressed BJ's number.

She answered on the second ring. "Hello?"

"Call Wes Allen," Carter whispered.

"What?"

"It's Carter. Call Wes Allen at home. Tell him you saw someone lurking around his shop in town. He needs to get down there. Pronto. You've called me, and I'm going to meet him there. You have another emergency you have to cover."

"Carter? What the hell are you talking about?" she asked. "What's going on?"

The floorboards were creaking overhead. "What the fuck?" Wes growled.

"Just do it. Now!" Carter whispered harshly into his cell, then rattled off Wes Allen's number.

"Can't you?" she demanded, then said, "Fine . . . but you owe me." BJ sounded miffed.

Carter snapped off his phone. Hardly dared breathe in the damp, frigid basement. He could have put in the call to Wes himself, but it wouldn't have allowed him enough time to beat Wes to the shop. Someone else had to have made the call—that someone was BJ. This way, if Wes took the bait, everyone's ass was covered.

Overhead, Wes walked out the door again, his boots ringing on the floorboards of the porch.

Come on . . . come on . . . call, damn it . . .

Wes was getting closer.

For God's sake, BJ, call!

The footsteps were near the cellar door; any minute, Wes would notice the lock was open.

Rrrriiinnnnggg!

Carter waited, listening hard. Nothing.

Again the phone rang. The footsteps stopped dead in their tracks.

Answer the phone, Wes. Answer the damned phone.

"Jesus." Wes began running, over the snow, up the steps. The back door opened as the phone jangled again. Carter, standing just below the floorboards, heard it all.

"Hello!" Wes's voice was irritated as the door slammed shut behind him. "What? . . . Who is this? My shop? . . . The alarm didn't go off . . . isn't that *your* job? Oh, hell. Yeah . . . thanks. I'll check it out." Wes hung up, swore, and flew out the door. Carter heard him running to his rig, the door of his truck opening and closing, and the engine finally firing.

Carter sagged against the wall and reminded himself to send BJ flowers or take her to a ball game or something.

Tires spun. The truck roared down the drive. Carter gave himself two minutes, just in case Wes had second thoughts; then he hurried out of the basement, locked up, deposited Wes's key ring in the drawer behind some bottle openers, and let himself out. After locking the door securely behind him with Carolyn's key, he took off, running up the hill and through the woods in the oversized boots. It had started snowing again, hard, which was damned lucky. His tracks would be covered before daylight.

CHAPTER 37

"I can't, not tonight," Cassie whispered from her bed. It was late. What was Josh thinking, calling after midnight. "And don't argue with me, okay? I'm not going to let you tell me what to do."

"So you can let your mom control you."

"I said, 'Don't go there.'"

"Okay, but what about tomorrow? There's a party."

"I *can't*. Look, Josh, don't do this, okay?"

"But I love you, Cass, you know it."

Do I? "I can't risk it."

"Tomorrow. We can go earlier. There's another candle-light vigil for Ian's mom—you could say that you wanted to go. I just want to see you again."

"I don't know . . ." But there was a part of her that needed to get out, away from these four walls with a tense mom, dorky sister, and watchful bodyguard.

"Think about it," Josh said, and hung up.

Cassie bit her lower lip and looked out the window. Would the damned snow never quit? It was true she was bored to tears and her mom and her were getting on each other's nerves. Big time.

She'd nearly broken up with Josh . . . and had had second thoughts.

But to sneak out using the excuse of going to a candle-light vigil for Lynnetta Swaggert? How lame was that? How slimy?

She flung herself back against the covers and fought tears.

Her life was shit.

"I will come for you . . ." a disembodied voice whispered over the frozen terrain. Snowflakes, tiny beads of ice, rained from a moonless sky.

The voice seemed to resonate from everywhere—the mountains, the river rushing by, the dark forest.

"Who are you?" Jenna cried, scared out of her wits. She was running as fast as she could, gulping terrified breaths of cold air and looking over her shoulder, trying to catch a glimpse of whoever it was that was following her. She saw nothing, but he was there, chasing her, following her every move. She sensed him. Felt him. Knew he was chasing her.

There was no escape and yet she ran, her bare feet slipping on the hoar-frosted ground, her tight black dress, binding, restraining her from running faster.

"Jenna . . . Jennnnnnnaaaaa."

She died a thousand deaths at the sound of his voice. It seemed to come from everywhere. "Who are you?" she demanded, as the wind whipped through her hair and clawed at her face.

"You know."

"I don't!" Her legs were like dead weights, dragging her deeper into the snow, her dress ripping and peeling away as, frantic, she scrambled among the headstones, forcing herself through the snowflakes that stung as they pelted her skin.

The voice whispered against her ear, "I am everyman." Deep, male, and guttural, it echoed through the cemetery.

"Leave me alone." She tripped over a short stone wall that had been hidden in the snow.

"Wait for me . . ."

"Leave me the hell alone!" she screamed, turning to face

nothing. No ogre. No wraith. No horrid creature stalking her. The snowflakes continued to fall and spin and dance in the night.

"You are my woman . . ."

"I'm no one's woman, you fiend." She turned to run again, but something grabbed her from below, holding her fast, strong fingers curling around her ankle. Glancing down, Jenna found herself staring into the upturned face of Lynnetta Swaggert.

Lynnetta, her hair combed, an angelic halo seeming to glow around her as she lay upon the snow, smiled blissfully upward, and said, "You'll tear your dress, Jenna." Blue eyes clouded with worry. "Be careful. I can't mend it for you any longer."

"Lynnetta! Thank God you're all right."

But Lynnetta's beatific smile turned evil. "Sensual . . . strong . . . erotic . . ." Lynnetta repeated, as if she'd memorized the words.

"What are you doing here? Who brought you?" Jenna demanded.

"You are everywoman."

"Like hell!"

"Tsk, tsk. This is your destiny."

"Destiny? No . . ." In a full-blown panic, Jenna looked around at the crumbling headstones, the thick night closing in. "I've got no destiny."

"Of course, you do. I'm talking about God, Jenna," Lynnetta said. "He's the only door to salvation."

"God is no part of this."

"He works in mysterious ways."

"That's bull, Lynnetta."

"Where are your clothes?"

"What?" Jenna looked down and discovered that she was naked. The black sheath was no longer wrapped around her body and she was cold . . . so damned cold . . . shivering. Sharp bits of sleet bit at her skin, leaving tiny red welts upon her flesh. "I don't know."

"You'd best find them, naughty, sinful girl. Tsk, tsk, Jenna.

Shame on you. Making those filthy films . . ." Lynnetta's *peaceful smile faltered and she was gone; in her place was dirty snow, piled high around a tombstone.*

With horrified eyes, Jenna read the inscription:

Cassandra Lynn Kramer, beloved daughter.

What! Her heart hammered painfully. Cassie? No!

"No, no, no!" she cried, hyperventilating, tears streaming down her face . . .

Jenna's eyes flew open.

Darkness surrounded her as the nightmare slithered into the darkest corners of her subconscious. "My God," she whispered, swiping the tears from her eyes.

She was home.

In her own bed.

Safe.

Her heartbeat slowed as she caught her breath. And then sensed it. A presence. Dark and evil . . . as if someone had been standing over her, watching her writhe painfully through the nightmare. But that was impossible; probably her own mind playing tricks upon her, the remnants of the chilling, grotesque dream. Her skin prickled in fear, and she strained to listen for the sound of shallow breathing, or the scrape of a shoe against the floor. She heard nothing out of place, just the howl of the wind shrilling over the eaves and the creak of old timbers settling onto the frozen foundation.

Yet there was a shift in the air, something amiss, the cool breath of some living creature's wake.

Don't do this to yourself, she reprimanded, as she rolled quietly from beneath the covers and grabbed the robe she'd tossed over the footboard. Heart thudding wildly, she made her way to the hallway, and by the feeble glow of the nightlight, she climbed the few stairs to the next floor where the hardwood was cold against her feet and the air seemed to stir without reason.

Cassie's bedroom door was ajar and bluish light flickered from within. Quietly, Jenna pushed the door open and saw her daughter fast asleep on the bed. Cassie's face appeared innocently soft and unlined, cast in the shimmering

pale blue from the muted television. The worries and
stresses of her teenaged life had been erased by the peace
that comes with sleep.

So far, so good, Jenna thought, as she slowly let out her
breath and walked noiselessly to her younger daughter's
bedroom. Carefully, Jenna opened the door and Critter, at
the foot of the bed, lifted his furry head. His tail thumped
while Allie, disturbed, smacked her lips as she rolled over
before burrowing deeper under the covers.

Everyone was safe.

No evil presence was skulking through the halls.

"Jenna?"

She nearly lost control of her bladder.

Gasping, she whirled to find Jake Turnquist, only his head
and shoulders visible as he stood on the stairs. "Everything
okay?"

Of course not. Does it look like everything's okay? "Yes . . .
no . . . I think." She pushed her hair from her eyes and tried
to calm her galloping heart as she walked quickly toward
him. Whispering, she said, "I had a bad dream. About Lynnetta.
And when I woke up, instead of being relieved, I had the
feeling that someone had been in my room, had been standing at the edge of the bed and was staring at me."

"Maybe you heard me come in."

"To my room?" She was suddenly wary.

"No. I was downstairs. My flashlight batteries went dead
tonight and I didn't have any replacements. I knew you kept
extras in the pantry, so I came in to get some. Maybe you
heard the back door open."

"Maybe," she said, then shook her head as they walked
down the stairs together. "But I don't think so. I think . . .
Oh, God, am I going insane?" she said, and realized that she
couldn't remember her last, uninterrupted good night's
sleep. Her nerves were frayed and she was close to the
breaking point. "That's it, I'm going crazy."

"I don't think so. They say that if you think you're crazy,

then you aren't. Come on downstairs," he said tiredly. "If it makes you feel any better, I'll do another perimeter check."

"Thanks," she said, and though she sensed his reluctance, he took off for his rounds.

In the den, Jenna turned on the television, yet stared out the windows to the dark, howling night beyond. There was no moonlight. No stars visible. Just the certain, steady fall of snow.

She caught her own pale reflection in the window and watched Jake for as long as he was visible, then waited nearly an hour for him to return. She stoked the fire, heated hot chocolate, scanned yesterday's newspaper, and half-listened to a late, late talk show, all the while watching the seconds tick off the clock.

Finally the back door opened and Turnquist walked into the house. Brushing snow from his jacket and pants, his face ruddy with the chill from the wind and snow, he looked as tired as she felt.

"Nothing?" Jenna offered him a cup of hot chocolate.

He pulled off his gloves and took the cup gratefully. "Not a damned thing."

He'd seen no one outside.

Found no evidence of anyone having been on the ranch.

Was certain nothing had been disturbed.

"I guess I'm just paranoid," she said, feeling like a fool. She'd sent the man out in the bitter cold because of a "feeling" that someone had stood over her bed and watched her as she'd slept so fitfully. And Jake was more than a little ticked, though he tried to hide it. Snow was melting on his stocking cap, and his hands, despite the fact that he'd worn insulated gloves during his rounds, appeared chapped and half-frozen.

"Look, I don't think you're crazy, you know that. But your nerves *are* shot." He didn't say the words kindly as he warmed his hands by the fire, stretching his fingers as if to assure himself that they still worked. "Maybe you should take something to help you sleep."

"Sleeping pills?"

He looked over his shoulder at her, appraising her with cool blue eyes. "Or Valium, or Prozac, just enough to take the edge off."

"I think I need 'the edge' on."

He didn't reply, just picked up his cup and finished the hot chocolate. Outside, the wind tore down the gorge, keening and whistling around the eaves.

"Jake?"

"Yeah?"

"Thanks."

"Just doin' my job," he said, his voice softening slightly as he carried his cup to the sink. "Go on upstairs and I'll lock up."

"Okay. Good night."

"Is it?" he teased, shaking his head. "Hell, I don't think so."

"Me neither." Smiling at his bad joke, she headed up the stairs to her bedroom, once her sanctuary, now violated. She wondered if she could ever relax in here again. Tossing her robe over the foot of the bed, she yawned. Everyone was here. Safe. She could sleep now.

She glanced over at her dresser and noticed the jewelry box. Had it moved? *Get over yourself, Jenna. Go to sleep.*

But as she stared at the box, she noticed one of its small drawers wasn't completely closed.

Had she left it that way?

When was the last time she'd opened it?

She couldn't remember.

Oh, for God's sake, Jenna, the drawer's not completely shut—so what? Are you going to freak out over every little thing? Jake's right—you need drugs or something to calm yourself down! Disgusted with herself, she reached for the lamp, then decided to close the damned drawer. She walked to the bureau and looked into the box.

Every muscle in her body tensed. A tiny piece of lavender-colored tissue paper was visible.

What the hell?

She hadn't put anything wrapped in tissue in the box.

But Allie could have. She's always playing with your things. Maybe she found the missing bracelet and returned it, wrapped like a present.

Or . . .

Heart hammering, she carefully unfolded the thin paper and as she did, she thought she might be sick. Her eyes widened in horror and she screamed as she stared down at a severed, bloody finger.

CHAPTER 38

Jenna let out a shriek guaranteed to wake half the state. Trembling, she stared at the finger in horror. *Oh, God, oh, God, oh* . . . She heard footsteps and her kids calling her. "Mom! Mom!" Critter began to bark madly. "Mom, are you okay?"

Glancing over her shoulder, Jenna spied Allie in the doorway, her face pale, her chin trembling. Allie's little fingers were clutching the doorjamb, her nails digging into the wood casing. Cassie stood right behind Allie, her hands wrapped protectively over her younger sister's shoulders, her frightened eyes holding Jenna's. "What's going on?" she whispered, obviously terrified.

Don't lose it, Jenna, not in front of the girls. You have to be strong. Jenna took in a deep breath, glanced down into the box, and noticed that the blood looked fake . . . that there was no bit of bone visible in the flesh, that . . . what the hell? Her mind ran in circles and felt sick inside as she realized it wasn't a real finger, complete with wedding set, but a fake digit, the kind created by master craftsmen on a movie set. The kind of thing Shane Carter was talking about earlier.

"Mom?" Cassie prodded.

"I . . . I'm okay. It's just a sick joke," she said. "A sick, twisted, horrible prank." Still quivering inside, she forced a smile. "Someone left me a present."

"Let's see." Assured that things were okay, Cassie stepped around a horrified Allie and made her way across the room. "Sweet Jesus," she gasped. "What's that?"

"Fake."

"Where'd you find it?"

"My jewelry box."

"I wanna see." Allie, on bare feet, hurried to the dresser. "Oh, yuk!" she said, her little face scrunching in horror.

Cassie was shaking her head. "But who—"

A door creaked open downstairs.

Jenna's heart stopped. "Shh!" She wrapped her arms around both of her girls.

"Jenna!" Turnquist's voice boomed through the house. His boots pounded on the stairs. "Jenna!"

Relief flooded through her. "Up here! In my room! It's okay!"

He flew into the room, his weapon in his hand. "I heard a scream."

"Another visitor," she said, and hitched her chin toward her jewelry box.

Turnquist strode across the room. "Shit." He looked at the finger, but didn't touch it. "What the hell is this?"

"It's fake, someone's idea of a sick joke."

"Or worse. The rings look real."

"They are," she whispered, "or damned good fakes." Her stomach was in knots, and she felt the urge to throw up at the depths of depravity of the person who had done this. "They look like Lynnetta Swaggert's engagement and wedding ring."

"No!" Cassie cried, her already-pale face losing its last hint of color. "Not her real ones, right? These are just . . . kind of the same."

"I noticed them the other day when Lynnetta was altering a dress. If these aren't Lynnetta's rings, then they're a damned good copy."

Allie's eyes grew wide. She wrapped her arms around her mother and Jenna held her close. "I'm scared, Mom."

"Me, too, baby. Me, too." For the first time in her life, Jenna didn't know what to do. Her home had been violated and was obviously unsafe. Whoever had been terrorizing her came and went at will. Despite the alarm system. Despite her contacts with the police. Despite her damned body-guard.

She stared out the window to the snow falling, and she prayed the power wouldn't go out.

Where could she take her children? Where would there be a haven where her daughters wouldn't have to be in harm's way? And how would she get them out of here? The roads were nearly impassable and all the hotels in town were full. And the son of a bitch wanted her to run. That much was obvious. Why else try to scare her witless? Anger rode along the back of fear. Who the hell was this bastard? What was he trying to do? "We'll be okay," she said firmly, stroking Allie's hair.

Cassie stared at her mother, silently accusing her of the lie. For once there wasn't a trace of anger, disrespect, or sarcasm in her gaze. Just plain, naked fear. "I think we should all go to L.A. for the holidays."

Jenna didn't argue, but said, "I think that's what he wants."

"*He?* Who? The sicko who did this?" Cassie asked.

"Yeah."

"Too bad—I still think we should leave. Go somewhere else. Mom, this kind of thing *never* happened in California."

That much was true. It was almost as if the bastard wanted her to return. Why? Did he feel threatened that she was up here? Wanted her gone? Or was he trying to push her back to California because he wanted her there? Why? To make more movies?

Robert.

He wants the kids closer.

"I'm calling the sheriff," Turnquist said. "He'll send out

men, or get in touch with the Oregon State Police. I want this place gone over with a fine-tooth comb. Meanwhile, all of us, we stay together. In the den. When the police get here, I'm going to tear this place apart."

"Be my guest," Jenna said as he pulled his cell phone from his pocket and dialed. She didn't care if he pulled the walls down. She just wanted the son of a bitch nailed.

Carter pushed the speed limit through the snow. He planned to explain that he'd seen someone snooping around Wes's shop, had taken off after the guy, called BJ on his cell, and then, after losing the suspect in the snowstorm, had returned to the scene, where he would meet up with Wes. That would explain a lot. Cover his lies.

He pulled into town and saw Wes's truck parked on the street by his electrician's shop. It was a hole in the wall, not much more than an office and a repair room where he kept spare parts and tools. Wes was inside, the lights on, standing in the middle of the office.

Carter walked in the open door.

"What the hell's going on?" Wes demanded, his face furrowed and dark, the smell of beer and cigarette smoke clinging to him.

"I saw someone poking around."

"Who?"

"Couldn't tell."

"Nothing's missing. No window broken. Doors locked up tighter than a drum." Wes rested his hips on the old scarred desk.

"You were lucky."

"Was I?" Wes asked. "I've had this shop here for, oh, what? Nine years. Never a break-in, never anything stolen, and tonight you see someone you don't recognize, take off after him, lose him in the snow. That's what you're telling me?"

"That's what I'm telling you."

"You who had one dead body, three missing women, and all kinds of emergencies countywide were just cruising through town and saw someone poking around my place." He skewered Carter with a look that screamed *bullshit*.

"I was on my way home."

"You live in the other direction."

"I was on one last patrol, but hey, if you don't want my help, I'm outta here. Believe it or not, Wes, I've had a long day. I'm cold, tired, and don't need to take this crap from you or anyone else." Carter was angry now and saw no reason to mince words. "As you pointed out, there are more important cases than this."

Wes rubbed his jaw thoughtfully, didn't seem the least chastised.

"Took you a helluva long time to get back here."

Carter reached for the door. "I've got better things to do than listen to this. I thought you'd want to know that someone was hanging out at your shop. It seemed to me that he was intent on breaking in. Maybe I was wrong. See ya."

"Someone was at my house tonight."

"Who?" Carter asked calmly, every nerve ending alert.

"I'm not sure. But someone came in. I think I scared him off."

"How'd they enter? Break down a door? Through a window?"

Wes shook his head.

"No sign of forced entry?"

"Nope."

"Maybe you forgot to lock the place."

"Nope."

"Then what?"

Wes scowled darkly.

"Anything taken?" The pictures and videotape still in Carter's pocket felt like lead.

"Don't know yet."

"If you want, I could come out and look around. Go through the house. Find out what, if anything's, missing."

Wes blinked, then caught himself, but there was a trace of panic in his eyes that he quickly hid. "Maybe I was mistaken."

"You sure?"

"Hell, I'm not sure about anything anymore, Shane." His arms folded over his chest.

"Join the club. Now, unless you need me here, I'm leaving."

"I still think it's funny, you dragging me out in the middle of the night."

Carter lifted his eyebrows and played his trump card. "Maybe you shouldn't be driving."

"Why?"

"You smell like a brewery."

Wes's eyes narrowed. "You want to give me a sobriety test?" he asked, his voice low. "Your department fuckin' calls me down here on some bogus information and then you want to give me a goddamned sobriety test. What the hell is this, Shane? Some kind of setup?"

"I told you what happened."

"And I don't believe it."

Carter sighed and rubbed the back of his neck. "I don't want to have to—"

"You don't have to do anything, Shane. Not a damned thing. I'll just go home and we'll forget all about this." He stood away from the desk and snagged his keys from the desk.

Carter pretended to be thinking it over.

Wes eased his way to the door. "It's late."

"That it is." Carter rolled his lips in on themselves as if he was pondering the weight of the world; then he caught Wes's guarded gaze and stared him down.

"Let's call it a night."

Carter nodded slowly, still appearing to think things through. "Tell ya what. You lock up here, go home, check things out, and, if something's missing, let me know. I'll send out a deputy, or you can fill out a report down at the station."

"Great," Wes muttered as he opened the door and a gust of icy air swept into the office. Carter walked outside and made his way to his truck.

"Take it easy on the drive home," he warned, as if he really thought Wes might be inebriated. He knew better, could tell that Wes might have a slight buzz, but he was far from over the limit. But Wes was just paranoid enough that Carter could play on his worries.

Wes turned his collar to the wind. "I'll be fine," he said, stalking to his truck.

Not if I have anything to say about it, Carter thought, climbing into his own rig and watching Wes drive away in the rearview mirror. He smiled grimly as he noticed Wes's particular attention to signaling, stopping for the requisite number of seconds at the flashing light, and keeping his pickup under the speed limit.

Just to give Wes something to worry about, Carter followed him for six blocks before turning in the opposite direction and heading home. The streets were nearly empty and as he drove out of town, no vehicle was visible in his rearview mirror. Which was all the better.

Carter drove outside of town and caught I-84, heading west. The traffic was nil as the road was officially closed, but he ignored the barriers, driving around the iced barricades and, within a few miles, turning onto the Bridge of the Gods. He parked midspan. Leaving the truck to idle, he climbed out, walked to the side and pulled the videotape from his pocket. As he glanced down at the black case, he wondered what images of Carolyn had been caught on the damning video. Had she been naked? With Wes? In a compromising position? Or just a video of her fully clothed and smiling . . . who cared? He told himself he was better off not knowing and was surprised that so much of the old festering pain seemed to have disappeared. He really didn't give a damn what Carolyn had done, but he sure as hell didn't want it dredged up again.

Let sleeping dogs lie.

He wiped the tape case clean of any fingerprints and shivered in the cold. The wind blew harsh as a demon's breath, knifing through his clothes. Snow swirled wildly. Beneath the bridge, the inky waters of the swollen Columbia River raged.

Teeth chattering, Carter dropped the tape onto the slick asphalt of the bridge. He stomped on the casing with the heel of his boot, smashing the plastic and shattering it into sharp black shards.

Not good enough.

He ripped the tape, stripping it from its spools; then he picked up the debris and hurled the whole damned mess into the dark, icy depths of the Columbia below. "Adios," he said into the screaming wind and felt an unlikely sense of freedom.

He would burn the pictures in his pocket in the woodstove at his house. Nothing ceremonial about it. He'd just throw the betraying shots onto the fire and wouldn't even watch them curl and hiss as they incinerated.

They would be destroyed. Forever. When Wes Allen's house was searched, no pictures of Carolyn would surface to bring up the old scandal again. And Carter didn't believe Wes would be stupid enough to mention to the police that someone had taken his prints or his video of another man's wife—the sheriff's dead wife. Even if he did, so what? Wes Allen wasn't just his ex-best friend and wife's lover; he was now Jenna Hughes's stalker.

He was going down.

Big time.

Over the howl of the wind, he heard his cell phone. Slipping on the ice-slickened asphalt, he hurried to his Blazer and jumped into the driver's seat. He managed to pick up the phone as he closed the door with his other hand.

"Carter," he said into the handset.

"It's Turnquist." The bodyguard's voice was barely audible.

Carter's muscles clenched.

"We've got a problem here at the Hughes place. Everyone's safe now, but security's been breached."

Damn. "How?" Carter demanded.

"I think the guy was in here. Don't know when. Probably sometime tonight."

"What? While you were there?"

"I don't know for sure, but yeah, I think so."

"Son of a bitch!" Carter wanted to reach through the wires and strangle the bodyguard. "Jenna's okay?"

"Yeah. They all are."

"Both girls."

"Yes!" Turnquist snapped. "But I need some help. We're holed up in the den, and I don't want to leave Jenna or the girls in the house alone, but I need to search the place."

"Absolutely do not leave them alone!" Carter ordered, suddenly frantic. Why hadn't he followed Wes until he was home? But there was no way Wes could have gotten there in the past half-hour. *What about earlier, when you thought he was at the Lucky Seven?*

Carter stepped on the gas and pulled a quick one-eighty on the bridge. "Put Jenna on."

"She's all right."

"Put her on!" He gunned the engine and his tires spun.

"Hello?" Her voice was steady and touched him in a way he didn't think possible. The Blazer straightened.

"Are you all right?"

"All right? What do you think?" she said, and despite the angry tenor in her voice, there was more—an underlying current of panic.

"Stay with Turnquist." He drove off the bridge, his wipers fighting the ice accumulating on his windshield.

"Don't worry."

Something deep inside of him cracked. "I do."

There was a second's hesitation, then she said, "Carter?"

"Yeah?"

"Get the hell over here."

"Hang in there, Jenna." His voice felt suddenly rough. "I'm on my way."

CHAPTER 39

The seconds scraped by on the clock in the den, and Jenna was going quietly out of her mind. She, Cassie, Turnquist, and even Critter were sequestered in the small room. Every curtain and blind in the house was drawn tight and the lights and television flickered as winds, keening down the gorge, buffeted the house. The girls huddled together under a sleeping bag on the couch, and Jenna tried to keep her cool.

Impossible.

Get here, Carter, she silently thought, every muscle in her body tense.

Turnquist, too, was on edge, his weapon at his side.

Every ten minutes, he walked through the house, weapon in hand, eyes darting everywhere, stopping at the windows and opening the blinds a bit to catch a glimpse of the storm. Jenna listened to his footsteps creak on the stairs or pad lightly on the floors overhead.

She sat in a rocker, eyes fixed on the clock, one hand falling over the arm to scratch Critter behind his ears.

Finally, about the time Jenna was certain she was coming completely unhinged, the dog lifted his head and growled. Turnquist, who was just descending from the second story, walked into the darkened kitchen and squinted through the night. "It's Carter's Blazer," he said, and punched in the code to allow the sheriff to roll through the gates. But the gates didn't so much as budge. "Damned things. I'm going out," he called over his shoulder. "The gate's iced up." He threw on a down jacket and left the house, closing and locking the door behind him.

Allie was dozing, Cassie's eyes at half-mast. "Can you trust him, Mom?"

"Who? Jake Turnquist?"

"Yeah. It doesn't seem like he does much. Not if the guy still gets in. Maybe it's him."

"I checked him out."

"By talking to Mr. Brennan. Oh, wow."

"I called names on the list of references he gave me."

"Like he couldn't have set that up."

"Sheriff Carter recommended him."

"Maybe he's in on it, too."

"No."

"No?" Cassie lifted an eyebrow. "How do you *know,* Mom? This whole place could be some kind of weird community, everyone like an alien. They've got really odd stuff up here, Mom. Half the people believe in Bigfoot, and that Charley Perry, the man who found the body at Catwalk Point, he claims he was abducted by aliens for a while. What's freaky about that is that everyone in town just accepts it. He's 'a little eccentric.' Are they kidding? The guy's a full-blown nutcase and should be locked up. Just like half the townspeople. Don't you think it's strange that two of the men you've been seeing, Harrison Brennan and Travis Settler, have secret pasts—that they were involved in some kind of elite special forces military group or the CIA or something they can't talk about? And what about Rinda, your friend. Her brother and son are creeeeeepy. Something genetically wrong there, if you ask me."

"But Josh is normal."

"No. I didn't say that. His whole family is off! I'm starting to think that we—you, me, and Allie—are the normal ones. And that's crazy, too, cuz you're a Hollywood star, or were one, the family's divorced, Dad's remarried . . . but we still seem more sane than most of the people around here."

"You think?" Jenna asked as Cassie turned back to the television. Normal? With her distaste for winter? She doubted it as she peered through the slats at the white-out.

White Out. The unfinished movie. Where Jill had died.

Instead of you. You were supposed to be up on the mountain, not Jill.

She shuddered, remembered hearing the explosion, snow pluming hundreds of feet into the air, and then the horrendous rumbling, as if the earth itself was being painfully wrenched apart. From her spot on the Sno-cat, she'd watched in horror as a wall of snow and ice roared down the mountainside, to the very spot where the next scene was to be shot, where Jill was innocently waiting. Jenna had screamed and thrown herself off the vehicle, but was restrained by some of the crew.

They hadn't found Jill's body for hours, but Jenna had known the minute she'd died.

All because of you. You'd talked her into following your footsteps. You'd suggested to Robert that he hire her.

And look what happened.

The aftermath of the disaster had far-reaching repercussions. Investigators surmised that explosives intended to be used later in the filming had accidently been discharged early, causing the avalanche, that it had destroyed the set where they were to film. An unfortunate tragedy. No one at fault. Everyone associated with the film to blame. Jenna had been emotionally devastated, Robert nearly ruined financially. They had blamed each other, and Jenna had given up acting, refusing to finish a project that had cost Jill her life.

The press had gone nuts. Pictures of Jenna and her family splashed on newspapers across the country. The tabloids had promoted a conspiracy theory, promoting the idea that the financially troubled endeavor was so far over budget that the film had been sabotaged by one of the backers who wanted to get out and escape with the insurance money.

That time of her life had been an excruciating blur. She'd tried to hold herself together for the kids, but her career was a shambles, her already-strained marriage crumbling, her guilt eating her alive. Everyone she knew was angry and pointing fingers. One of the major backers, Paulo Roblez, had been particularly upset, as had Monty Fenderson, Jenna's agent, who, when she'd announced she was giving up acting, had lost his only star-caliber client. He'd threatened to sue her and Robert and anyone he could think of.

And so she'd ended up hating winter and Christmas.

So why did you move up here to the land of cold winters with the largest mountain in the state almost in your back yard? Why do you still take the girls skiing? To punish yourself, or to overcome your fears and grief?

A good question, one not answered in the year of counseling.

To this day, Jenna felt the guilt and pain at the loss of her sister. It had been Jenna who had gotten Jill into acting. Jenna, who by taking the role of Katrina in *Innocence Lost*, a part not unlike Brooke Shields's in *Pretty Baby*, had propelled herself to fame at an early age. From that point, she'd taken on roles of gritty, hard-as-nails heroines and had found some respect in a business that had little. Jill had willingly followed in Jenna's golden footsteps, only to lose her life.

It had been so pointless, and now, staring into the stormy night, she felt that same little niggle of doubt that had eaten at her since the accident. Not that it made any sense, but Jenna had always wondered if the tragedy was planned, if the accident on the set of *White Out* had somehow been cruelly orchestrated. Could someone have deliberately caused the avalanche? But why? A police probe into the accident had proved nothing, not even negligence, in her sister's death, and the entire catastrophe had been ruled accidental. But the rumors had abounded, and secretly there had been allegations that the movie had been sabotaged deliberately when explosives that were to be used in another scene had gone off prematurely, thereby putting an end to a movie that had already been hopelessly over budget. There had even been talk that the "accident" was a way of creating some buzz about the film, a macabre enticement to moviegoers.

But Jenna had pulled the plug on any expectation of profits made from her sister's death by quitting and letting the lawyers fight it out.

She watched as Jake managed to force the gates open and Carter drove his SUV through the drifts to the garage. A surge of relief swept through her, and she couldn't take her eyes off of him, a tall, rangy lawman to whom she was now affixing the unwanted role of personal hero. Which was ludicrous. Yet she couldn't stop herself from rushing into the kitchen and throwing open the door at his arrival. Silly as it was, she threw herself at him and his big arms crushed her to his body. "Thank God you're here," she said, perilously close to tears as the rush of bitter wind forced its way inside.

"Hey, calm down." His breath fanned her hair as he kicked the door shut, but Carter didn't let go of her, held her tight and hard against him. And she, damn it, was grateful for his strong body. His firm male presence. The feel of bone, gristle, flesh, and raw determination all wrapped in waterproofed down. "I'm not goin' anywhere."

Her knees nearly buckled and she clung to him. "Thank you." Her face was upturned, her lips touching the rim of his ear.

His jaw hardened. "Don't thank me yet. We've got a lunatic to locate."

"That we do." Reluctantly, she extracted herself from those oh-so-safe arms and blinked back tears that had no right to sting her eyes.

"By the way, have you ever met a poet named Leo Ruskin?"

She shook her head. "No."

"He lived in Southern California a few years back and it was his line, 'Today . . . Tomorrow . . . Endlessly,' that was going to be used in the promotion of *White Out*."

"I didn't know that," she said earnestly, "but there was a lot I didn't know back then, as Robert and I were barely speaking. I spent my days on the set, my evenings with the kids, and I left all of the financial matters—the promotion, development, all of it—with him. Have you talked to Ruskin?"

"Can't find him. Not yet. But we will." He paused. "I think we should ask your ex about him, the promo line, and whoever was contracted to do the makeup for the movie."

"The makeup?"

"Yeah. I assume a makeup artist or some company handled all the changes to your face."

Her eyes narrowed. "You think whoever did that could have had something to do with the finger we found."

"Don't you?"

"I don't know what to think, and I don't remember the name of the company, but I'll call Robert. He must have records."

"You'd think."

The back door opened again and Turnquist, stomping his boots and blowing on his gloved hands, strode in with another gust of frigid winter air. He glanced at the remains of Jenna and Carter's embrace and his thin mouth pulled down at the corners. "Why don't you stay here, and I'll search the place."

"I thought you did that already, when you first hired on."

"I mean I'm gonna rip up the floorboards. Somehow that son of a bitch knows what's happening in this house."

"Wait for the OSP. I called them on the way over."

Turnquist's already flushed face grew redder. "I can handle it."

"Can you? I haven't seen much evidence of that so far," Carter snapped. "I don't want any evidence compromised. Tell me exactly what went on here, then wait for the state guys."

"That could be hours."

"All we've got is time." Carter's cell phone beeped and he answered it as they all filed into the den. Critter yawned, stretched his legs, then walked stiffly over to sniff Carter's boots, but Allie's eyes didn't so much as flutter.

Cassie was slumped on the opposite end of the couch from her sister and she, too, had finally let exhaustion take its toll. Head cradled in one arm, she was snoring softly, dead to the world.

Jenna's heart twisted when she remembered her horrid dream. How had she and Cassie drifted so far apart? As a child, Cassie had been so effervescent, so happy, delighted with all new things from puppies to ice cream to airplanes, and then, as she'd headed into pubescence and her parents' marriage was falling apart, she'd lost that beautiful, whimsical *joie de vivre* that had been her essence as a child. Had it been a natural progression into adulthood or the slow erosion of happiness caused by her parents' inability to work through their problems after the accident?

Back to the tragedy.

Always the tragedy.

Carter clicked his phone off. "Larry Sparks is on his way," he said, "but the State Police are knocked flat with this storm. We'll all have to be patient. Looks like it's gonna be a long night."

"Already has been," Turnquist grumbled.

"Okay, so let's go into the kitchen there," Carter nodded to the open doorway, "and you two can tell me everything that went on here tonight."

CHAPTER 40

The next few hours seemed to go on forever. Larry Sparks and a detective from the Oregon State Police arrived and, with Turnquist, searched the house and grounds. Meanwhile, Jenna explained what happened in the last few days, naming everyone who had been on the grounds, when she had last noticed the jewelry box had been opened, when anyone could have possibly been in the house, what enemies she might have made who would want to do harm to her. The police searched her room again, dusted for prints again, removed the fake finger and were going to test its composition against alginate, the substance that had been found at the site where they discovered Mavis Gette's body. Sparks had already called Reverend Swaggert about the rings and would have the preacher verify if they had belonged to Lynnetta.

"So you think the person who's doing this killed that Gette woman and abducted the others," Jenna said, once the police were packing up to leave.

"Looks that way."

"But how? Why?" She shook her head and bit her lower lip in frustration and fear. "I don't understand why this is happening to me."

"Neither do I. You've got someone obsessed with you," Carter said. He was seated on the raised hearth of the fireplace, warming his back, his clasped hands hanging between his knees.

"A lunatic."

"Close enough." His eyes held hers. "A lunatic who's possessive. He thinks he owns you, that you're his. Remember the line 'My woman' in the poem?"

"Hard to forget." She rubbed one arm. "Damned hard."

"The FBI is working on a profile."

"And that will automatically point to whoever this monster is?"

"Unfortunately, no." He shook his head, stretched his back. "But we will get him, Jenna. We're closing in."

"God, I hope so." She sat next to Carter on the hearth, felt the heat of the crackling flames, felt a little stronger being close to him. "It seems like he's trying to force me to leave. Like he's trying to scare me out of my house. Why would he want that?"

"I don't know," he said. "Do you have any ideas?"

She shook her head, searched for answers she didn't have.

Lieutenant Sparks had squared his hat on his head and was pulling on thick gloves. "You staying?" he asked Carter.

"Yeah."

"And the bodyguard?"

"He'll be outside. He's out there already, got a bird's-eye view of the place and won't sleep until daylight. I'll be inside."

Sparks nodded, flashed his smile. "Good luck. I'll call you in the morning, let you know what the lab comes up with on the finger and if we've got a match on the rings."

"Thanks." Carter stood and shook the bigger man's hand. "And I want you to check on something for me."

"What?"

"Wes Allen. See what kind of an alibi he has for the nights the women were abducted."

"You think he's involved?"

"Wes?" Jenna asked, stunned. She shot to her feet. "Wait a minute. He's a friend of mine."

Carter ignored her. Held Sparks's stare. "Double-check, would you?"

"You got it."

"I said 'he's a friend of mine,'" she protested.

"Then he'll have nothing to hide."

As Sparks closed the door behind him, Carter locked it, turned on the alarm system, then watched through the curtain of snow as the state vehicle left and Turnquist forced the gate shut. It was nearly two in the morning.

"Why do you suspect Wes?"

"I suspect everyone."

"But you didn't have everyone's alibi checked."

He ran a tired hand around the back of his neck. "Jenna, there are things I can't discuss."

"This is *my life*, Carter. *My girls'* lives! You damned well better tell me what's going on."

"I will. Soon."

She wasn't about to be mollified. Stood toe-to-toe with the tall sheriff. "I have the right to know. What is it that makes you think Wes is involved? Wes is Rinda's brother!"

"And I've known him all my life. I'm just eliminating people."

"By what means?"

His lips tightened and his eyes glittered darkly. "I'll explain it all soon, okay? But I can't tell you anything that might compromise the investigation."

"Now, wait a minute, Carter—you can't just drop this kind of bomb and then ask me to be patient. Not after what's been going on. Why Wes?"

He hesitated, bit at the fringe of his moustache, and finally swore. "Oh, hell. You deserve to know."

"Damned straight!"

"But I can't tell you everything. I'm not going to compromise this investigation."

"Of course not, but give me a clue here."

A muscle worked overtime in his jaw. "For one thing, he's the person who has rented and bought more of your videos and DVDs than anyone in town."

"So?" she said, shaken nonetheless. The thought of Wes Allen viewing her in the privacy of his home over and over again made her uncomfortable, but it would with anyone she knew. Though she considered her roles on film, her career, work she was certainly not ashamed of, her art could easily be twisted into someone's particular form of depravity.

"And he visits all your fan sites. Often."

"A lot of people do." Again she had a sense of unease and remembered all the times Wes had tried to get close to her in the theater. "I would think since I moved here there's been a lot of interest in my work. Lots of copies rented and bought."

"But Wes Allen seems to be your biggest customer— number one fan. We're just ruling him out."

She thought about all the times she'd been around Wes Allen. How close he'd stood. How often he'd touched her shoulder, or arm. Friendly? Interested? Or obsessed? "I can't believe it," she whispered, but a part of her readily accepted what Carter had suggested, the part that caused the taste of bile to rise in the back of her throat.

"There's nothing to believe. Not yet. I'm just being cautious," he said, but she noticed the set of his jaw, the determined glint in his eyes. He was convinced that Wes was somehow involved. "You'd better sleep," Carter said, as if he'd noticed Jenna's weariness for the first time.

"What about you?"

"I'll be fine."

"Sure." She reached up and ran a finger down the beard-stubble on his cheek. "You already look dead on your feet."

"I'll take that as a compliment."

"Yeah. You should," she mocked.

Jenna knew she'd never sleep upstairs. She couldn't go back to her room with its fingerprint dust and haunting memories, so she shut the doors to all the rooms upstairs and after stopping at the closet, returned to the den with pillows and quilts. She tossed a pillow and hand-stitched coverlet to Carter. "Just in case." Then she walked through the French doors that led to the living room and settled onto the couch. Carter searched the house one last time—she heard his footsteps as he walked into every room and closet—then finally joined her, taking a seat in an overstuffed chair and resting a boot heel on an ottoman.

"Rest," he suggested.

Yawning, she said, "You should, too."

His mouth slashed into that irreverent smile she'd grown to love. White teeth showed beneath his moustache. "You know what they say about rest and the wicked."

"I thought it was 'the weary.'"

"Close enough," he said. "Tonight, believe me, I'm both."

"Me, too," she said, closing her eyes and refusing to think of Wes Allen. "Me, too."

In stocking feet, Carter walked through the house one last time. He'd been awake for over twenty-four hours. His nerves were jangled and he was rummy, but they were safe. At least for this night. The sun would be up in a couple of hours and the storm seemed to be winding down. It was still cold as all hell, but the wind had lessened and the snow had stopped falling. He sat at the kitchen table, where he could see into the den where the kids were dead to the world and had a peek-a-boo view of the living room couch, through to the fireplace, to watch Jenna as she slept.

Drinking coffee that had started to bother his stomach, he thought about the day to come and what he intended to do, starting with going over the evidence possibly linking the crimes, Wes Allen's alibis, his motives and getting the search warrant to go through his house and barns. Those huge buildings that had stood empty for years. Maybe there was more to be found than the shrine/video room tucked in the basement.

From the living room, he heard a moan.

Carter shot to his feet and hurried to the couch where Jenna thrashed, her features pinched in distress. "No!" she said, though her eyes didn't open. "No, please."

"Jenna," he whispered and noticed she was shaking. "Jenna. Wake up. It's okay. I'm with you."

"Don't. Oh, don't."

"Jenna," he said a little more loudly, his hands gently holding onto her trembling shoulders. "Wake up. You're dreaming."

Her eyes flew open.

Startled, she nearly screamed.

"Shh. Hush, darlin'. You're all right," he said, placing his face close to hers so that, in the half light from the fire, she would recognize him.

"Oh. Oh." She blinked and tears fell from her eyes. Her face was pale as death, and she was shivering as if cold to the bone.

"Everything's fine."

She sniffed and shook her head. He sat next to her on the couch, still holding her, and she burrowed her head into his shoulder. "It was Cassie again. He had her . . . that faceless bastard had her!"

"She's okay. Asleep in the den."

Jenna was inconsolable. Wrapped in a quilt, she walked to the den and peered inside where both her daughters were sleeping. Even the dog didn't move. Pushing her hair from her eyes, she seemed to calm a bit. "What time is it?"

"Too early."

"And?"

"Nothing out of the ordinary has happened since you dropped off."

"Thank God." She stretched, pulling the quilt up. It gaped open and her sweater slid up the flat wall of her abdomen. He felt his groin tighten. "I should get up."

"You should sleep."

"What about you?" she asked around a yawn, as she dropped her arms to her side.

"I'm fine."

"A man of steel?"

He laughed. "Maybe that's a little too strong. I'm probably more like a man of aluminum foil."

She smiled, and the hint of teeth he saw against her lips was tantalizing, made his thoughts run in unwanted, dangerous directions. "Steel or tinfoil, I don't really care," she admitted and stepped up to him, "I'm just glad you're here." Her green eyes found his. "Thanks, Carter. I guess I needed you last night." She said it as if it were a fact and he didn't argue.

Instead, though he knew he was being the worst kind of fool possible, he slipped his hands beneath the quilt, drew her close to him, and kissed her. Softly at first, feeling her warm, pliant lips respond, and then, not thinking of the consequences, his arms around her tightened, his mouth pressed harder against hers.

Parting her lips, she sighed into his open mouth and he was undone.

Lust fired his blood.

He didn't know how long it had been since he'd kissed a woman, but it was too damned long. And he'd been wanting this one ever since he'd pulled her over on the snowy highway. She wanted him, too. He felt it in the way she fit up against him, her breasts flattened against his chest, her arms circling his neck, holding him firmly to her, her legs parted as she stood on tiptoe. He pushed one leg between those legs, felt the zipper of her jeans rub against his thigh, heard a wanton groan escape her lips.

His hands splayed against her back, fingers rubbing her sweater, feeling the firm flesh beneath the soft angora, and he drowned in the scent and feel of her. His body screamed for release, muscles tight, mind weary, sex an easy and welcome antidote to all that was wrong in the world. She was so beautiful, so erotic, so damned sexy, and every nerve ending itched for the relief she could give.

Don't do this, Carter. Use your head. She's a victim, a woman you're supposed to protect, a Hollywood princess who has been wanted by every man she's ever met. Don't do this.

But her body was rubbing against him and her mouth opened so easily to his. He felt her nipples through her sweater and bra, hard buttons that he ached to touch, to kiss, to pull on with his teeth.

His heart was pounding crazily, his blood thundering through his brain, his erection at full mast. His lungs were so tight, he was breathing shallowly, his mind running in reckless circles. He imagined what it would feel like to make love to her, to feel her warm, moist body sheathing his, to look down upon her beneath him, black hair splayed around her face, her breasts full, her nipples dark and hard with want, a sheen of sweat glistening on her skin as he pushed into her and began to move. All night . . . it would take all night and more.

But he couldn't. Not here. Not like this.

He lifted his head and was nearly lost again when he stared into the slumberous, erotic eyes of Jenna Hughes. "I can't," he said, though his body was screaming that he was making the biggest mistake of his life.

"I know."

"The kids," he lifted a hand in the direction of the den.

"I know."

She was tugging on him, walking backward, leading him through the living room and down two steps to a guest room. Empty. Cold. Dark.

"We shouldn't," she said, but threw her arms around his neck again and kissed him feverishly.

His willpower fled and he shut the door behind her and twisted the dead bolt without lifting his head. He peeled off her sweater, his hands anxious for the weight of her breasts against his palms. She was gasping as the sweater hit the floor and he yanked a bra strap over her shoulder to expose her breast. Her fingers were fumbling with the hem of his shirt and he pulled it off, then lifted her onto his hips and took her breast in his mouth, anxiously. Hungrily. She moaned and held on with one arm, letting her head loll backwards as he suckled.

This is a mistake, his mind hammered at him, but he ignored it. *You'll mess everything up. If you do her, Carter, your career, your life, everything that you've worked for will be gone.*

He pulled off her bra as her fingers fumbled for his fly. He stripped her of her jeans and panties, and kicked his own away, then pulled her onto him, watched her gasp as he placed her over his erection. Sweet. Hot. Wet. He began to move, his tired muscles suddenly energized.

She held onto his shoulders, clung to him, their bodies straining. He held her around the waist with one arm, while the other tangled in her hair.

"Jenna," he whispered hoarsely, listening to the tempo of her breathing, watching her breasts rise and fall as she rode him, used him, let loose. Only when he felt her shudder, when he heard her moan, did he plunge deeper, harder, aware of the strain of the cords in his neck, hearing her breathing increase again, her sweet, short gasps as she caught his rhythm and moved with him. Faster, faster, faster, until he couldn't hold back a second longer and he threw back his head and released.

Both bodies jerked and she grasped him tighter. She let out a soft cry against his throat, burying her face into his neck as wave after wave ran through her body. "Oh, God," she finally said, her hair as damp as his own, her face flushed as he carried her to the daybed pushed against the wall and fell onto it with her. Wedged upon the small mattress, too many pillows surrounding them, he held her close and kissed her crown.

She glanced up at him and smiled naughtily. "Well, well, well, Carter . . . forget that man of tinfoil. You really are a man of steel."

"Ya think?"

"Mmm." She kissed his cheek, then nibbled at his earlobe. "I don't think, Sheriff, I know."

He laughed, a deep, throaty laugh, and it felt good to let go, if just for a few minutes. Soon, they would have to face the world again, but for a few more minutes . . . He turned his face to hers and began kissing her again. This time, he silently vowed as he felt her respond to him, he'd take it slow. Real slow.

* * *

"Slut!" He watched the vulgar display on his screen, compliments of a hidden camera he'd wired into her house, the electronics hidden deep in the insulation of the attic or wired alongside the ducts in the ceiling and floor vents. Everything she did, he witnessed as long as the equipment worked. As soon as he'd learned that she was moving into the old McReedy place, he'd set about wiring it for his special purposes, but some of the tiny cameras had failed and often he'd been forced to stand outside and stare down at her compound from his blind in the trees. Which he enjoyed. Especially with the snow caressing his skin.

But tonight, with the snow so heavy, he was forced inside to watch via monitor and as he did, he felt nausea attack. He was hot, itching from the inside out. Furious, he kicked a paint can and sent it reeling, red color splashing upon the walls. He barely noticed.

She was with another man.

Kissing.

Touching.

Fucking like a bitch in heat.

His pulse pounded, throbbed through his brain, and he felt betrayal of the worst kind as he viewed her getting off on another man. Pathetic. Couldn't she have waited? Didn't she know that only *he* could satisfy her? His shrine to her was nearly complete, and this was how she repaid him, by acting like a common tramp, spreading her legs eagerly for the sheriff.

Shane Carter, a man who had vowed to uphold the law, and there he was, stripping off her clothes, running his tongue and teeth over her skin, nipping at her breast. Pushing his cock deep inside her. And she let him.

His Jenna.

She let him!

Rage burned through him and he plotted out all kinds of satisfying revenge, but he could not abandon his plan. Not now. Precision was the key.

He watched them fornicate and his rage grew hot as the

night. He glanced over at the stage where most of the women were already positioned. How long had he worked for this? For years. Long before anyone would guess, and then the news about her move, he'd heard it long before she'd actually arrived in Falls Crossing. From the moment he'd heard a whisper of a rumor about her moving to this part of Oregon, he'd prepared, used the windfall of insurance money to buy this place and prepare it. He'd been lucky in that respect; the stars had aligned. Because it was fate. They were meant to be together. There were no coincidences. His life was meant to be entwined with hers, and everything he did was for Jenna.

Always for Jenna.

From the first time he'd met her face-to-face, he'd known. He'd prepared.

Taking a deep breath, he glanced at his stage. His shrine to her and her work.

Everything was set.

All the characters dressed and in position, painted faces near-perfect replicas of Jenna—Marnie Sylvane, Faye Tyler, Paris Knowlton, and Zoey Trammel, all ready except for the last two. They were waiting for Katrina Petrova and Anne Parks. Jenna Hughes's most famous starring roles. He'd considered creating Rebecca Lange, but as *White Out* had never been finished, he'd discarded the idea.

He relaxed. He was still in control. He would just have to make a minor adjustment, push things up a bit. But he was ready. Clicking off the monitor, he walked to his bathroom and began to dress. First the contacts, to tint the color of his eyes, then the hairpiece to add a new hairline and change his natural color, and finally a tight bodysuit to alter his physique and lifts in his shoes to add two inches. He was careful how he shaved.

When he was finished, he took a good, hard look in the mirror.

Even his mother wouldn't recognize him.

He smiled at that, then remembered caps. Slipped them on.

No, his mother would never recognize him.

Which was just as well.

His purpose in mind, he reached for his jacket.

It was time to hunt.

CHAPTER 41

She awoke to the smell of coffee and the feeling that something had shifted in her life. She moved, felt a tenderness between her legs, and smiled. She and Shane Carter had made love for hours and now . . . she glanced at the clock and groaned. It was barely seven, and he was already up, the first hint of morning light filtering through the closed blinds.

Rubbing a hand over her face, she thought about the events leading up to Carter's arrival and some of her fear returned. *Wes Allen. The police think Wes Allen has been terrorizing you.* She still couldn't believe it. Although she wouldn't discount Wes for some of the things, she couldn't see him as a murderer, and if her case was connected to the missing women, then whoever was behind it was a cruel killer.

Though no other bodies had been found, Mavis Gette's decomposing corpse led everyone to fear that Sonja Hatchell, Roxie Olmstead, and now even Lynnetta Swaggert had met the same horrid end.

Carter was on the telephone. She heard the soft, steady sound of his voice and, after throwing on her wrinkled clothes, she peeked into the den, saw that her girls were still sleeping soundly, then padded barefoot into the kitchen.

He took one look at her and, bless him, he seemed to blush.

"Morning, gorgeous," he said, setting down his cup. Before she could respond, he folded her into his arms, kissed her as if he never intended to stop, then lifted his head and with their noses nearly touching, winked at her.

Her silly heart fluttered out of control and her lips tingled where they'd touched his. Breathlessly, she placed a hand over her rapidly beating heart. "My goodness, Sheriff. You really know how to say 'Good morning' to a girl, don't you?"

A smile tugged at the corners of his mouth.

"That's the way I'd like to wake up every day," she admitted, and he chuckled, one thick eyebrow lifting as if he, too, were mentally picturing what had transpired between them the night before.

She felt a flush rise on the back of her neck as she, too, saw their entwined, panting bodies, the sinewy strands of his muscles straining, the way his hair fell over his eyes as he let out a last, violent gasp and clutched her as if he'd never let go. Ridiculously, she wondered what it would be like to live with Sheriff Shane Carter with his gruff, hard-to-crack demeanor, long hours, the danger that often came with his job. But the nights, Lord, the nights would be spectacular.

Dear God, what kind of fantasy was she conjuring up?

"Coffee?" he asked, eyeing her as if reading her thoughts, and she reined in her too-fertile imagination, swiftly closing her mind to such silly fantasies.

"Mmm. Sounds like heaven."

As he lifted the pot from its holder and poured a stream of coffee into a mug, she glanced down at the way his slacks hugged his tight rear end, remembered how her fingers had dug into those taut muscles as he'd made love to her. Her throat went dry and she glanced at the slope of his back, the way his shoulders stretched his jacket, and thought of the taut skin and muscle beneath the insulated fabric. They'd had one night together, she reminded herself. That was it. A few hours of sexual release, nothing more. *Don't do this to yourself, Jenna. You and Carter are trapped in an excruciatingly tense situation; you reached for each other last night. End of story.*

He handed her a cup, caught her eye, and as if he guessed what she was thinking, sensed the turn of her thoughts, he turned the conversation to the here and now. All business. "I've got to go in to the office, but I'll call you later."

"Do that," she said.

"And I'll let you know if we arrest Wes."

Shuddering, she took a sip of her coffee. "I can't imagine."

"I've talked to Larry Sparks. Someone's following Wes Allen until we can get a search warrant for his house. You and the girls should be safe here with Turnquist. I'll have patrols drive by and if anything bothers you, *anything* feels wrong, call me on my cell."

"I will," she said. "Promise."

He checked his watch. "Okay, I've got to run. I'll stop and talk to Turnquist on my way out."

She set down her cup and tugged on his hand, dragging him back to the guest room. Once there, she put her hands in the pockets of his jacket, pulled him close, and tilted her face up to kiss him again.

"Jenna," he protested.

"What, no kiss good-bye?"

"Maybe one." With a groan, he placed his arms around her and slanted his mouth over hers. She kissed him back, feeling a thrill race through her blood, desire bloom lightning-quick, her legs wanting to fold as she drew him to the floor.

"I really have to go," he said, and slowly released her.

"Spoilsport." As she withdrew her left hand, her fingertips brushed against the corner of something—cardboard?—in his pocket. Snapshots fluttered to the floor, and she felt his body freeze. He reached down and swept the photographs into his palm, but not before she saw the images of a woman—a beautiful, sexy, voluptuous woman, dressed scantily in a gold thong and holding her hands over her breasts as she visually made love to the camera. Another picture showed her on rumpled sheets, and this time she was completely nude, her hair mussed, her skin flushed as if from recent lovemaking.

Jenna took a step back. Her heart crumbled into a billion

painful pieces. *What in the world had she been thinking, with all her stupid fantasies about this man she barely knew? Dear God, what an idiot she was!* Her gaze found Shane's, and a spurt of hot fury surged through her bloodstream.

"Oops," she said.

"I can explain."

"You don't have to."

"They're pictures of my wife. My deceased wife."

"You carry snapshots of your naked wife around with you, in your pockets?" she snapped. "I hope to God that you're in counseling, Carter, because that's pretty damned weird. Maybe borderline obsessive."

He didn't respond, but his eyes narrowed.

She shoved her hair from her eyes with one hand, and from the corner of her eye glimpsed the daybed, the pillows tossed carelessly onto the floor, a quilt and sheets torn from the mattress. Again she thought of their hard, hot coupling, the fact that she'd never used any protection, and the cold realization that Shane Carter could have done what he'd done with her with dozens of women.

"There are things you don't know," he said, and winced as if it sounded lame, like something out of an ancient soap opera.

"Obviously."

"The pictures mean nothing."

She snorted. "Yeah, I run around with photographs of things that I really don't care about all the time." Before he could come up with another useless, see-through excuse, she began straightening the daybed, tearing off the sex-scented sheets and rearranging the pillows. "Listen, you don't owe me any explanations or apologies or anything." Gathering the sheets in her arms, she turned to him. "Just catch the damned stalker, okay? That's your job. That's why you're here."

She carried the sheets to the laundry room as the back door opened and Turnquist appeared. Carter stopped and talked with him for a few minutes as she stuffed the sheets into the washer, turned on the water and added soap. She didn't watch him leave, heard the back door open and close, and collapsed against the dryer.

Don't do this, Jenna. It was just sex. It happens all the time.

But not to her. She'd never let this kind of thing happen to her. Because she'd been guarded. Wary. Careful of her heart.

Until now.

Until she'd met that damned lawman.

Carter's back teeth ground so hard that his jaw ached. He'd blown everything. Now that someone had seen the pictures of Carolyn taken from Wes Allen's house, he'd jeopardized the investigation. "Damn, damn, damn!" he growled, pounding on the steering column as he drove home. The roads were still dicey, some plowed and graveled, others still covered with last night's snowfall. What had he been thinking, making love to Jenna Hughes?

He hadn't been. That was the problem. Blame his stupidity on too many months without a woman, too many hours without sleep, too many worries about the investigation, but it all boiled down to the sorry fact that he'd been horny as hell, half in love with the Hollywood princess anyway, and the opportunity had presented itself. What red-blooded American male would have done differently?

"Shit," he muttered as he pulled into his lane and the four wheels whined against the accumulation of snow. He made it home and burned the damned photographs, making sure, as he added more firewood, that every scrap of evidence had literally gone up in smoke. He checked his e-mail, searched the Web again for Leo Ruskin, and found several scant, old entries. More searching online for *White Out* did little to help him except to come up with the name of the company that did the makeup work on the unfinished movie. Why the hell did he think the movie was connected to the killings? Because of Jenna? Because of the damned cold weather? Or because he was sick to death of the snow? He couldn't find the makeup people listed anywhere in his first search and he didn't have any time to waste. In a dark mood, his tired brain still running over the information and trying to insert Wes Allen into everything he knew about the case, Carter fried bacon, eggs and frozen potatoes, ate the meal with one eye on the news before he dumped his plate into the sink and climbed the stairs to his loft.

Wes Allen never had anything to do with makeup. He wasn't directly or indirectly involved with any of Jenna's movies. It could be the lowlife is innocent.

"Son of a bitch," he muttered and stripped off his clothes. Nothing about this case was easy. None of it made sense. But someone, some bastard who had access to her house, was linked to her films. Her husband? No—they'd checked and he was still in L.A. An old boyfriend? As far as the police could determine, Jenna had none. Few dates and nothing serious. Not so much as a one-night stand.

Except for you.

What the hell did that mean?

While showering, he thought of Jenna and couldn't stop the erection that sprouted at the memory of making love to her. She'd been as beautiful as she'd been in all of her movies, maybe even more so. Eager. Supple. Hot.

"Jesus."

So you nailed a Hollywood actress, literally star-fucked, so what? You gonna brag about it? The fact that she chose you, over all the men drooling after her, to sleep with? And you messed that up, too, didn't you? Just like Dr. Randall predicted. Anything you really want, you screw up, don't you?

Ignoring the damning questions, he washed, rinsed, stepped out of the shower, and wrapped a towel around his hips. He scraped the stubble from his face with a razor and stared angrily at his image in the fogged-over mirror. He looked as tired and frustrated as he felt, but knew it was another day of powering up on caffeine and maybe some nicotine.

Because today was the day that Wes Allen was going down.

He felt another sharp niggle of doubt about the bust, but didn't examine it too closely.

Innocent until proven guilty, Carter—remember, innocent until proven guilty.

"Allen's alibi checks out," Sparks said from his end of the cell phone connection.

Driving through town, Carter passed by the theater and noticed there were no cars in the lot. Ice and snow had piled over the parking spaces, and no illumination streamed through the stained-glass windows. "The night Sonja Hatchell was abducted, Wes was at the Lucky Seven, sipping suds until well after midnight. The waitress remembers him because she has a thing for the guy."

"Jesus. Tell her to be careful." Carter cruised down the main street, saw a few familiar faces and vehicles collecting near the diner. Hans Dvorak, Charley Perry, Seth Whitaker, Harrison Brennan, and Blanche Johnson were migrating toward the door of the Canyon Café, as they did each and every morning. He spotted Dr. Dean Randall, paper coffee cup in hand, heading toward the library, and Travis Settler walked into the hardware store. But Wes Allen wasn't among those who were looking for a cup of coffee or pastry this morning. "What about the other women? Where was he when Roxie Olmstead and Lynnetta were abducted?"

"We're still working on it."

"Maybe he has an accomplice."

"And maybe we're barking up the wrong tree."

No way, Carter thought as he hung up. But the doubt was still there, and a voice inside his head accused him of going after the man who had stolen his wife from him. *Stolen? Or did you hand her to Wes Allen on a silver platter?*

He pulled into the courthouse parking lot and locked his Blazer.

Inside, the heat was sweltering, rising three stories to settle in the sheriff's department. He cracked a window and the cold air crackled inside, blowing on the wilting fronds of his Christmas cactus.

"Hey, are you out of your mind? What do you think you're doing?" BJ asked as she settled into a desk chair. "Jesus, Carter, what happened to you last night?"

"I look that good, huh?"

"Better," she said sarcastically.

"That's what a night without sleep will do. Did you find anything else? What about Ruskin? And the makeup people. Especially whoever did the makeup for *White Out*. That's the movie that connects everything. It's the one that ended Jenna Hughes's career, the one where the Ruskin phrase was supposed to be used for the promo, and the one with the musical score that she heard in the background of the crank call."

"I'll double-check. As far as the paper that the notes were written on, it's standard stock, could be bought anywhere from wholesale office-supply outlets to smaller stores. Same with the ink and printer. Dead end."

"So far."

"What about the alginate?"

"Most of the stuff ships to California. The particular type found on Mavis Gette comes from a firm in Canada, and I've got a list of their clients for the last five years."

His cell phone chirped and he reached into his pocket, tried to stop his galloping heart when he recognized Jenna's number on the digital display. "Carter."

"Hi, it's Jenna." Her voice was flat. Obviously she was still stung from her discovery of Carolyn's pictures. Damn. "I thought I'd let you know that I just called Robert and wonder of wonders, he was in. I asked him about Ruskin. He never met the man, but someone had left a leaflet with Ruskin's work on the set up at the ski resort."

"Someone who worked on the film?" He swung a legal pad around on the desk and grabbed a pen.

"Most likely," she said, and adrenaline rushed through Carter's bloodstream. "Robert had seen the poem and liked the wording."

"Did he get any legal releases to use the work?"

"It never got that far," she said, her words clipped and impersonal. "Because of the accident and the movie being scrapped. He did say that the company he hired for makeup and special effects was a firm named Hazzard Brothers, the same company Robert used in a lot of his horror films. It's a Burbank company owned by Del and Mack Hazzard and nearly went out of business after *White Out* because of the insurance claims. The families of the people who were killed and some of the workers who were injured sued the production company."

"And they paid?"

"The insurance company for Hazzard Brothers did."

"Thanks."

"Does this help?"

"Of course it does."

"Good."

"Jenna—"

Click. She hung up.

Carter sighed through his nose and looked up to find BJ observing him.

"So now it's 'Jenna,' is it?"

"No big deal."

BJ's lips pulled down at the corners. "If you say so."

He wasn't going to be lured into some woman-conversation about relationships. Especially since there *was* no relationship. "I want to find out everything we can on Hazzard Brothers, which is a company that does makeup and special effects, located in Burbank, California. See if they have any ex-employees who moved up here after working on *White Out.*"

His cell phone rang again and he answered. "Carter."

"Christ, Shane, what kind of witch hunt have you got going?" Wes Allen demanded. "Someone's got a tail on me and I want to fucking know why!"

"Maybe you should come in and we'll talk about it."

"Talk about what?" Wes demanded. "If I didn't know better, I'd think you were trying to pin the murders on me."

Carter tensed. "You mean abductions, right?"

"Oh, for Christ's sake, you know we all think those

women are dead. I hope to hell not, but come on . . . does it seem likely that the creep who's got 'em is keeping them all prisoners?"

"You tell me."

"Oh, fuck this! I'm calling my lawyer, Shane. I've got rights. I haven't done anything wrong and you've got someone watching me! This is a vendetta and I'm going to sue your ass from here until hell's gates if you don't let up."

"Sue to your heart's content."

"You sanctimonious, hypocritical bastard! I'll have your job."

"Go for it," he said, but Allen had already slammed down the phone.

"Your fan club?" BJ asked.

"Just the president of it."

"Why do I get the feeling that you're about to get yourself in real trouble?" BJ wasn't smiling. It wasn't a joke.

"Because you're a perceptive woman, BJ. Very perceptive."

"What's going on, Shane?"

"I think we're going to nail the son of a bitch who's behind all this, that's what. Call Hazzard Brothers and see how much alginate they use, if they're missing any, who their supplier is. Then ask them about their recent employees. Let's see if we can come up with a name that matches one of the names on this." He thumped two fingers on top of the printout of people who had rented or bought Jenna Hughes's movies. "I'll bet you a hundred to one, there's a match."

CHAPTER 42

"I'll be there," Jenna said, leaning a shoulder against the cupboard door as Rinda sniffled on the other end of the phone.

"I hate to ask. I know you're going through your own thing, but I really think I should attend the vigil. I could go with Scott, but he's kept to himself lately, always out, never around . . ." She sighed heavily. "Sometimes I don't think I know him anymore."

"I think that's the way it's supposed to be."

"When they're sixteen. Not when they're twenty-four. When I was his age, I was already married and a mother . . . okay, strike that thought. I'd hate for him to go through what I did."

"He'll find his way," Jenna said, cringing at the sound of her own platitudes. She didn't believe it for a minute, but right now, when Rinda was still feeling guilty about Lynnetta's disappearance, wasn't the time to remark that Jenna found Rinda's son a little offbeat, if not an out-and-out weirdo. No mother wants to hear that.

"I hope so . . . God, with all that's going on, I just wish he'd stay home. Close." That much Jenna did understand as she thought of her own two girls. "So anyway, where do you want to meet me?"

"I think I still owe you a cup of coffee, so let's hook up at the Java Bean at six-thirty. We can go to the vigil together. It's at seven, right?"

"I think so. I'll call back if I hear differently. Thanks, Jenna."

"No problem." And it wasn't. Not only did Jenna want to be a part of the candlelight vigil planned for the three women, she had to get out. She'd been cooped up in the house with the kids all day. Allie, coming down with a cold again, had been crabby, and Cassie had reverted to her normal brooding self. They were out of nearly everything grocery-wise, and Jenna, after the roller coaster of last night, was climbing the walls. One minute she was thinking about the horror of finding the damned fake finger, the next she remembered Shane's passionate lovemaking, then she would remember the pictures of Carolyn Carter fluttering onto her carpet. On top of all that, somehow, probably through a leak in one of the police departments or from Reverend Swaggert's camp, word had spread that she'd received a macabre gift in her home, a replica of a finger. She'd hung up on the reporter who'd called and was screening her messages. But she couldn't stay caged up another night. She needed to get out, even if Turnquist objected. Which he did.

"I don't think it's safe," he protested as they sat around the dinner table eating spaghetti.

"At a candlelight vigil in the church? It'll be fine. We'll all be together."

Allie's ears perked up. She'd been stirring her pasta listlessly with her fork. "I don't want to go."

"Why not?"

"Because . . ." She sighed loudly. "I don't know."

"Because it's morbid," Cassie said. "I don't want to go, either."

"Wait a minute. I promised Rinda."

"So go," Cassie said.

"And leave you guys here alone? After what happened last night?"

"You don't know that the finger was left last night," Cassie said. "That's when you found it. It could have been there for days."

"I would have noticed."

"Would you have?" Cassie rolled her eyes. "Memo to Mom—you haven't been yourself lately." She twined some spaghetti on her fork and took a bite.

"I promised Rinda I'd go. I'm meeting her at six-thirty."

"So go. I can't," Cassie said.

"Why not?"

She glanced at Turnquist, then whispered, "It's not a good time for me. I don't feel all that great."

"You, too?" What kind of conspiracy was this?

"No, I don't have a sore throat, but, you know, I feel . . ." Her face turned red. ". . . crampy."

"Oh." Jenna got it and felt like a fool for not understanding that her daughter was trying to tell her that she was on her period, and since Jenna kept track of this monthly event, she did a quick calculation and realized it wasn't a lie. This was definitely Cassie's "time of the month," which, considering her infatuation with Josh, was always a relief.

Cassie said, "Yeah, 'oh.'"

Jenna tossed her napkin onto the table. "Look, girls, I have to go in to town, but I'll be with Rinda, so I'll be all right."

"You're not going alone," Turnquist cut in.

"Someone has to stay with the girls."

He didn't so much as argue, just pulled out his phone, dialed quickly, and to Jenna's mortification, spoke to none other than the sheriff himself.

"Wait a minute!"

But it was too late. Turnquist snapped his phone shut. "Carter will pick you up. Six o'clock."

"No way." Not after last night and this morning. She wasn't ready to face Carter again, much less spend the night two inches from him.

"Absolutely. You hired me to do a job, Ms. Hughes, and now you seem determined to thwart me. I can't let that happen. Your life and my reputation are on the line. I'll stay with the girls. You go with the sheriff."

"I'm supposed to be the boss."

"You are. But we either do this my way or I walk. No compromises." His blue eyes were cold with determination, his lantern jaw set.

Jenna's blood was boiling, but she managed to hold her tongue. "All right. Tonight we'll do it this way, but in the future, we'll discuss any plans for outings until this thing is over."

"Fine with me."

The phone rang and Allie ran for it. "Wait. Don't answer," Jenna reminded her, and the message machine clicked on. There was giggling and then a naughty little voice saying, "Hey, Allie, I heard your mom got the finger!" *Click!*

Allie was stunned. "Who would do that?"

"Some little prick. Don't worry about it," Cassie said and scraped her chair back. "Whoever called has a brain the size of a pea and a dick that's even smaller. The only thing he's got that's big is his mouth!"

"Cassie!" Jenna said, but let out a laugh and Allie giggled.

Turnquist turned several shades of red and excused himself.

Jenna had no recourse but to accept a ride with the sheriff. She only hoped he had the good sense not to bring the snapshots of his wife along.

"Okay, let's get one thing straight," Jenna said as he held the door open for her and she hoisted herself into his Blazer. "This wasn't my idea. I could have driven myself into town but Jake wouldn't hear of it. So, whether we like it or not, we're stuck with each other for the next couple of hours."

"I'll try to survive," he said dryly and was rewarded with a stare meant to cut through steel. He slammed the door shut and walked through the cutting wind to the driver's side. Once he'd started the car and they were easing out of the gate that Turnquist had opened, he said, "You know, I think we should both lighten up. It'll make the night a lot more enjoyable."

"Okay." She nodded slowly as if to convince herself as he flipped on the wipers. "But I think I should explain about last night."

"Is there something to explain?"

"Yeah, I think there is. I know that you probably think everyone from L.A. is ultra-hip and sexually free and sleeps around."

"That's not what I think at all."

"And that's not what I do, either." She looked out the side window and scraped at the moisture collecting on the inside with a fingernail. Though her face was turned away from him, he caught a glimpse of her profile and noticed the corners of her mouth had pulled into a thoughtful frown. "I'm not all that sexually liberated and so . . . so last night . . . well, I should have insisted upon protection."

His hands tightened over the wheel. "Is that what you're worried about? Pregnancy?"

"Yeah, to begin with. I mean, I can't believe I lost my head like that. After all the lectures to Cassie and then I . . . I . . . oh, well, you know what happened. You were there."

"I was as much at fault as you."

"At fault. What a nice, romantic way of putting it."

"I didn't know there was romance involved," he said and noticed the little knot of wrinkles between her eyebrows.

"There wasn't. I just meant we should at least be kind to each other."

"I'd like that." He slowed for a corner and through the snow saw the lights of the town winking in the foothills. "Just for the record. I'm not hip and sexually free and I don't sleep around, either. At least not for a long, long time. As a horny teenager, I looked at things differently. So let's not worry too much about anything other than keeping you safe and catching the guy who's terrorizing you. One step at a time. Deal?"

She let out a long breath. "Deal."

"So the next problem is Rinda. She's not too happy with me right now. Thinks I'm harassing her brother and suspicious of her son."

"Are you?"

His lips pulled into a smile. "*I* wouldn't call it harassing. And I'm suspicious of everyone. Scott qualifies. But his mother thinks I'm overzealous."

They drove into town and he parked a couple of streets away from the coffee shop, but not before he noticed the television vans parked near the First Methodist Church and the crowd of townspeople collecting and milling near the church's steps. So much for his sleepy little town.

He hustled Jenna into the coffee shop, where the smell of brewing coffee wafted through the patrons. Over the whistle of the espresso machine and the notes of Christmas carols drifting from hidden speakers, conversation buzzed.

As predicted, Rinda, seated at a tall table and sprinkling cinnamon onto the foam of her latte with one hand while pressing her cell phone to her ear with the other, took one look at Carter, scowled, and aimed with both barrels. "Geez, Shane," she said, snapping her cell phone off while setting down the glass shaker so hard that cinnamon puffed up in a fragrant, rust-colored cloud. She didn't seem to notice. "You're the last person I expected to see tonight. Shouldn't you be out busting crime or at least persecuting innocent taxpayers?"

He grinned and tried to deflect. "Thought I'd take a break."

"Give *me* a break."

"Give me one, Rinda, okay? I'm just doing my job, and

tonight it's not about you or me or Wes or Scott. It's about the women who are missing."

She wanted to say more—he could see it in the flare of her nostrils, the pinched corners of her lips, the angry glare she bestowed upon him—but decided to avoid a scene. At least for the few minutes before the service, she held her tongue and there was an uneasy peace, one he couldn't think about for too long as he was watching the throng of people that had gathered in the coffee shop and spilled onto the street. He recognized many of the faces, though some were foreign to him—strangers. He stayed close to Jenna, his arm brushing hers, the scent of her perfume reaching his nostrils as he watched each and every person who filed toward the First Methodist Church.

Cassie checked her watch. Time to meet Josh. He'd called and said he'd be waiting on the other side of the fence. In the woods. Where they'd met before. There was an old logging road that abutted the property.

But she had to shake the bodyguard. Turnquist was more sticky than ever, though all her talk about "female problems" had been a brilliant stroke of genius and he'd left her alone in her room, staying downstairs with Allie.

Her attempts at making it look as if she was in the bed, lumpy pillows with a bit of doll's hair visible, were lame, but might work if she wasn't gone too long.

So . . . now . . . if she could just sneak out through her mother's bedroom and shimmy down the smooth wooden pole that supported the hot tub and deck, she'd have it made. She'd put extra clothes in a backpack and slipped through the rooms upstairs, her ears cued into any sounds out of the ordinary.

Assured that the big lug of a bodyguard wasn't climbing the stairs, she darted out the door to the deck, closed it softly, and eased her way down the pole.

She ignored the part of her mind that accused her of

being nuts, the part that reminded her that women were being abducted left and right, the part that mentioned the weirdo notes and icky finger her mother had received.

All it proved was that the house wasn't safe. Not even with Jake Turnquist, the ridiculous excuse for a bodyguard.

She slipped on her boots, hung close to the house, careful to duck beneath the windows, then sprinted across the breezeway and around the garage. She hazarded one last look over her shoulder and nearly tripped when she saw Allie standing in the window of Cassie's room.

What? No way!

Cassie looked up at the house again, but this time Allie's image was gone—almost as if what she'd seen had been a damned ghost. *Pull yourself together*, she thought, and zipping her coat to her neck, she dashed beneath the windmill and behind the barn, her boots slipping and leaving tracks that she hoped the snow would cover.

The air was so cold it burned her lungs, the wind wailing down the gorge and forcing the snow-laden branches of the fir trees to dance and sway.

This is stupid, she realized. It was too damned cold to be out here, too scary with the nutcase of an abductor on the loose, a royal pain in the butt. She'd meet Josh and tell him she'd changed her mind. No party was worth all the hassle. And then there was her mom. As mad as Cassie was with her, she couldn't risk scaring her out of her mind. If Jenna found Cassie gone, not only would Cassie be grounded for life, but Jenna would be frightened and the woman was already losing it. No . . . it wasn't worth it. And besides, truth to tell, Josh was boring her these days, but then, what wasn't?

Head ducked against the brutal wind, she made her way along the fence line, found the usual spot, and hoisted her backpack over the top rail. It hit the soft snow and was nearly buried. She climbed over, jumped to the ground, and grabbed the pack by its strap.

"Josh," she whispered. "Are you here?"

She heard nothing, glanced at her watch again, and silently

damned the big jerk if he was running late or had stood her
up. She flipped open her cell phone, dialed his number, and
waited as voice mail picked up. "Damn it, Josh, don't do
this." When it came time to record, she said, "I'm here where
I'm supposed to be. I'll wait five minutes and if you don't
show up, then I'm going back home. This is insane anyway.
It's freezing out here." She clicked the phone shut and eased
into the surrounding woods where she wouldn't be seen by
Allie.

*She wasn't looking out the window. That was your guilty
imagination working double time.*

The wind whistled wildly. Eerily. Cassie ducked behind
one tree, reached into her backpack, and after tearing off one
glove with her teeth, fumbled through the pockets until she
found her cigarettes and a lighter. She lit up with trembling
fingers, then shouldered the pack and walked toward the logging road. Maybe Josh was waiting for her in the warmth of
the truck. He probably had his music on so loud he couldn't
hear his damned phone ring.

But that didn't seem right. He was never without his phone.
Always answered. "First time for everything," she thought,
and spied a flash of light through the curtain of snow. She
drew hard on her cigarette and stared, saw the flash again.
Headlights! He was waiting for her. Well, the idiot. He was
going to get a piece of her mind! She marched through the
trees, heard the music from his CD player, saw him sitting
behind the wheel.

The son of a bitch wasn't even going to get out of the
truck to greet her. "Hey! I've been waiting over there where
we were supposed to meet!" she said, but he didn't move,
didn't act as if he could even see her. That was it. She had to
break up with him. She'd thought someone was better than
no one, but she'd been wrong.

"Cassie!"

She froze, turned toward the sound.

"Cassie!" Allie's voice rang through the trees.

What was the kid thinking? This was a nightmare. She

had to turn back. Tossing her cigarette into the snow, she walked to the passenger door of the pickup and yanked it open. "Look, I can't do this," she said, before she really looked at Josh. He still didn't turn in her direction. "Josh, did you hear me? I've got to go back to . . ."

Something moved behind her. Soft, stealthy footsteps in the snow.

Josh moved then—slid, really—his body falling across the seat of the pickup, his eyes staring up sightlessly, blood staining the front of his black shirt. A dark, oozing gash sliced across his throat.

Cassie screamed. Turned. Saw her attacker and felt him pin her against the car. Frantically, she kicked and clawed, slammed her fist into his nose. Beneath his ski mask, he yelped. She kicked upward, aiming for his groin, but, as if anticipating her attack, he shifted so that her knee hit him in the thigh. Over his shoulder she spied something, a movement. Her heart soared for an instant, thinking it might be help—and then she spied Allie.

"Run!" she shrieked, still fighting. "Run, run, run!!!!!"

Her attacker glanced over his shoulder. "Son of a bitch!" he growled in a familiar voice Cassie felt she should recognize.

"Run!" she yelled. "Get help!"

Allie took off through the trees, darting into the thicket.

"Shit!"

Cassie slid from his grasp, but he caught her again, his gloved hands catching her stocking cap. It came off and his fingers snagged in her hair. He pulled so roughly she was yanked backward, her feet slipping from beneath her. She fell into the snow and he was on top of her in an instant, strong legs straddling her, his crotch stretched beneath her breasts, one arm grabbing both her wrists and holding them over her head.

She flailed and bucked, but he didn't seem to notice as he reached into his pocket and pulled out a device that looked like the remote control to the television.

A second later he pressed it against her throat and Cassie's body jolted, electricity zapping through her tissues to leave her helpless as a lamb. She moaned, couldn't move, and just before she blacked out she sent up a prayer that Allie would be safe.

CHAPTER 43

The vigil fast became a media circus. Despite the bad weather, half the citizens of Falls Crossing gathered with candles in the square and walked into the church where Reverend Swaggert asked them all to pray, gave a short sermon, and seemed to turn on for the cameras. Jenna told herself that she was being overly suspicious, but she couldn't shake the feeling that something about the service seemed, if not phony, at least all for show. Oh, sure, the preacher cried a little, claimed that Lynnetta was his "personal angel sent from heaven," and prayed fiercely for the other women as well. Flowers decorated the altar, along with large posters of each woman's face, propped on easels and looking out at those in attendance. Jenna, head bowed, sneaked a glance at the display while Derwin Swaggert, his eyes closed, sweat beading on his red face, held onto the top of the pulpit in a white-knuckled death grip.

The lights flickered.

People looked up from their prayers while the reverend's voice, filled with supplication and reverence, droned on. Jenna tried to concentrate on his words, but the wind had picked up again, whooshing around the building.

Again the lights winked.

Carter's hand was on her elbow.

"You'd think God was listening," Rinda said, just as the lights went out. But the church wasn't in darkness, not with everyone holding candles.

Even the reverend's eyes opened and he held up his hands, quieting the crowd that had begun to whisper and shift. "The Father is with us," he proclaimed, "and we pray that He's with Sonja, Roxie, and my precious Lynnetta. Peace be with you and good night."

Slowly they filed out of the church, brushing up against other townspeople, whispering as they walked outside and moved slowly down the front steps of the church to the dark streets. Rinda paused, turning her back to the wind as she tried to call her son, then gave up in frustration. The windows of the surrounding businesses were dark, the streetlights out, the only illumination from candles, flashlights, and headlights of cars and trucks passing through the town.

Carter's cell phone rang and he paused, pulling the phone out of his pocket. "Carter . . . what? Great . . . the power's out in town here, too. Yeah . . ." His conversation became muffled.

"Jenna!"

She turned and spied Travis Settler making his way through the crowd to her. He had his daughter's gloved hand clasped tightly in his. In her free hand she carried a votive candle.

"Is Allie here?" Dani asked, her wiry brown hair poking out from beneath her ski cap in wild loops.

"She stayed home tonight. Didn't feel all that great."

"Bummer," Dani said.

"We were hoping she could come over and spend the night. Dani wants to go ice-skating on the pond we've got out back."

"Maybe tomorrow, if she feels better . . . and we have electricity," Jenna said and felt Shane step closer to her.

Travis glanced at Carter, then at Jenna. "Let's hope the power isn't out for the night."

"I think it's cool," Dani said, her hazel eyes alive in the faint glow of her candle. That was Dani, always ready for action.

"That's because you don't have to chop the wood, keep the fire going, or worry about the pipes freezing," her dad teased.

"No, it's because we play games instead of watch sports all the time."

Travis's mouth lifted into a half-smile. "She loves drubbing me at chess and poker."

Dani rolled her eyes but grinned, showing off a bit of an overlap in her front teeth. "I think he lets me win."

"No way! Come on, kiddo, I think we'd better go home. See ya," he said to Jenna, then nodded to Carter and Rinda. Carter snapped his phone shut and his jaw was suddenly rock-hard.

"Have Allie call me!" Dani said as Travis pulled her toward his pickup.

"Trouble?" Jenna asked.

"Lots of it. Not only is the power out here, but for miles. A car went off the Bridge of the Gods and there was a wreck on 84. Bad one. I've been called to it. Life Flight might not be able to get there with the storm." He motioned to the SUV. "I'd better take you home."

"That's the opposite direction," Rinda said. "I'll drive Jenna."

"I should have driven my Jeep."

Carter's phone blasted again. He answered it, swore, and had a short conversation. When he was finished, he said, "It just gets better and better. Another car slid out of control at the site of the wreck, slammed into a State Police cruiser, and killed an officer. I have to get out there."

"I'll call Turnquist to come and get me."

"Don't be nuts," Rinda said. She turned to Shane. "I'll run her home."

Carter hesitated.

"Oh, for God's sake, I've been driving in this crap all my life, except for those stupid 'I've-got-to-find-myself' years in California. My Subaru's got four-wheel drive. It's a dream in the snow."

His phone went off another time and he nodded. "Okay. But if anything goes wrong, if you smell any kind of trouble, call me. On second thought, call me when you get home. Let me know what's going on." He squeezed her arm, then brushed a kiss against her cheek and took off at a jog toward his Blazer.

"Oh, wow, a kiss? From tough-as-old-leather Sheriff I-don't-need-another-woman? That's something."

"Is it?" Jenna asked as they hurried, heads bent against the wind, to Rinda's little wagon. "I thought he was still hung up on his wife."

"She's gone, honey." They slid inside and Rinda fiddled with the heater and defrost. The crowd was thinning out, and without electricity, the town was nearly dark, only a few back-up generators illuminating shops. "Carolyn was my best friend . . ." she glanced over at Jenna. "Ironic, huh? Seems like Shane has a thing for people I like. Anyway, we all had a great time together, had known each other since high school. Wes and Shane and David Landis were really tight." Craning her neck to look over her shoulder, she pushed on the gas and did a quick U-turn, then headed out of town. "Anyway, David was killed when he tried to climb Pious Falls—Shane was with him. They were both sixteen and it was tough on Shane, but he eventually got together with Carolyn, at my urging, and they were pretty happy for a while."

"Just awhile?"

"A few years, and then . . ." She stared out the windshield, squinting against the snow piling on the glass. ". . . then I guess they did that old drifting apart thing. Shane was really into his work and Carolyn was bored and . . . well, to make a long story short, she had an affair with my brother."

"Wes?"

"Um-hmm. I think it about killed Shane. Worse yet, after a huge fight one night—a really cold, nasty night, kind of like this—Carolyn took off and lost control of her car and died." She stopped for a darkened traffic light, then eased through the empty streets. "If you ask me, Shane never forgave himself. Not only for David's death but Carolyn's as well."

Which explained a lot.

"You sure you want to get involved with him?" Rinda asked.

"I'm not sure of anything right now."

"You're hedging. Something big's going on between you two. I can tell. Shane isn't one for public shows of affection. In fact, I don't think I've ever seen him kiss a woman, except like, maybe on New Year's Eve."

She tapped her fingers on the steering wheel as her Subaru plowed on through the snowfall. "In fact, he really hasn't dated much since Carolyn's death. Believe me, I know. I've been trying to set him up for years, but, no, I don't think it's a torch he carries around for her, it's just plain old guilt."

They passed an abandoned car on the side of the road, snow piling over it, and Rinda turned on the radio. The weather report was grim—more of the same, with temperatures dropping. "I don't see how that's possible," Rinda said, and turned to a station playing Christmas music.

None of the houses they drove by had any lamps glowing in the windows. The dim illumination that escaped through blinds or cracks in the curtains seemed to come from candles, or a fire, or flashlights.

They met one snowplow, amber light flashing, fighting the onslaught from the heavens, pushing piles of snow onto the shoulder, and a dump truck spreading sand in the plow's wake. The road was treacherous, and they were held up nearly forty-five minutes by another accident on the main road—a farmer's truck had collided with a sedan and there was no way to drive around the accident. Jenna tried to reach the house and realized that the phones, all electricity-based, wouldn't work. She then called Turnquist, Cassie, and Allie, but no one answered.

"Why wouldn't they be picking up their cells?" she asked, worry creeping into her heart.

"That *is* weird. Weren't they staying home?"

"Supposed to."

"Maybe a cell tower's failed. That happens sometimes in remote areas. I was at the beach once, and I couldn't get through to anyone for two days—had to use a land line to get to the cell phone company."

"Or all the circuits are busy because of the storm."

"Oh, yeah, that's probably what it is. At least *try* to call Shane. Or the station," Rinda suggested, adjusting the heater. She had to keep the car running most of the time, as the minute she turned it off, the temperature inside the little Subaru plummeted.

"I will. If this doesn't clear up soon." She held onto her cell phone and tried to tamp down her worries.

"Good thing I have a big bladder," Rinda observed as a tow truck finally pulled the car blocking the road to one side and an officer from State Police waved traffic through. "And an excellent selection of CDs." They listened to Christmas songs while they waited and now, finally, drove past the weary officer. Rinda's little car crept along the icy road. The storm hadn't let up a bit and highway crews couldn't keep up with the snowfall. She flipped out the CD and turned on the radio and heard reports that most of the roads in Lewis County had been closed.

"Worst storm of the century," Rinda said, flipping off the radio. "Isn't that just the icing on the cake?"

"It has to let up," Jenna said, but wasn't as worried about the weather as she was about her family. Again she tried to call them, again she failed. She even punched out Carter's cell phone number, but he didn't pick up and she didn't leave a message. They were almost home, inching their way through the blizzard.

"This is pretty damned creepy," Rinda said, her lips folding over themselves as she nosed her car along the road that ran parallel to the river, the tires sliding, only to grab the frozen asphalt again. "I just hope Scott is at home and not out in this mess."

"Can't you call?"

"All of my phones are remotes, you know, with hand-held receivers. They need electricity to work, so I can't get through to the house. I've been meaning to get one that is just a regular, old-fashioned cord-to-the-handset type, but never think about it. Until the middle of the coldest friggin' storm in fifty years."

"What about his cell?"

"I've tried—three or four times. All I get is his voice mail, with a promise that he'll call me back. Yeah, right."

Fifteen minutes later, as the final notes of "Jingle Bell Rock" faded away, Rinda nosed her Subaru into the drive of Jenna's house.

The gate was open.

No lights visible.

A huge knot of dread tied up all of Jenna's insides. "This isn't right," she said as the little wagon slid to a stop near the garage. "Not at all." Jenna was out of the car in a second. Her boots slid as she ran to the back door and told herself to remain calm. Of course it looked dark. The power was out. No big deal. Everyone along the river was dealing with the same emergency.

So why hadn't her daughters answered their cells? Why hadn't Turnquist?

She tried to push her key into the lock but the door swung open and the dark house was cold. Lifeless. "Cassie!" she yelled, trying to keep the panic from her voice. "Allie! Hey, I'm home. Cassie! Jake!"

"What's going on?" Rinda asked, one step behind her.

"I don't know. Probably nothing." But Jenna's heart was pounding fearfully, the hairs on the back of her neck at attention. Something was wrong. Very wrong. She smelled it in the cold air, heard it in the silence.

A fire burned low in the grate and she fumbled in a kitchen drawer for a flashlight, flicked it on, and yelled again. "Cassie! Where are you? Allie!"

But the house was silent, aside from the sound of wind gusts buffeting the gables, the rattle of windows high in the attic. Only her own voice seeming to echo back to her. The interior was more than cold. It felt lifeless. As if no one were home.

A chill as frigid as death hissed down her spine. "He's got them," she whispered, a brutal fear grabbing hold of her throat. "He's got them."

"Who?"

Her cell phone jangled in her pocket.

"Thank God." For a second, her worries scurried back into the dark corners of her mind. Jake had probably taken the girls into town or somewhere safe when the power had failed, and he, too, was held up by impassable roads. That was it. That *had* to be it. "Hello?" she called into the phone, but no one answered. "Hello? Who is this? Jake? Carter?" She was nearly screaming when she heard something, not a voice, but the haunting notes from a movie . . . her first starring role, the theme song from *Innocence Lost*.

She nearly collapsed.

Him! He was taunting her. She looked wildly around, the yellowish beam of her flashlight sweeping over the chairs and counters in the kitchen. "Who is this?" she demanded. "Who the hell is this?" But the phone went dead in her hands. She sank against the kitchen counter because she knew it was true. Her worst fears were now reality: the madman, whoever the son of a bitch was, had her daughters.

CHAPTER 44

"Don't panic," Rinda said as Jenna tore the house apart. Searching, looking, calling for her kids. Denying what she knew in her heart.

"Where the hell are they? And the dog? Where's the damned dog?" she demanded. "Where did he take them?"

"I don't know, Jenna. But they're not here, and if you mess things up, clues or evidence for the police, it'll only make things worse."

Panic was shredding her insides and she was rambling, but she didn't care. "I have to do something!" She'd called Shane again, and couldn't get through.

"Then let's do this methodically, okay?" Rinda said. "Maybe then we'll figure out what happened here."

"Fine. Let's start at the top level and work our way down." They both had flashlights, but the house was big, a rambling behemoth that was dark as death.

Every muscle in her body tight, her nerves fraying, a headache beginning to form behind her eyes, Jenna worked her way down from the top story. With Rinda at her side, she searched through all the bedrooms and closets, the sauna, the bathrooms, checking every nook and cranny.

Nothing.

No sign of anyone, not even the damned dog.

With each step, dread tightened its grip on her lungs and she could hardly catch a breath.

Please let them be safe. Let me find them. Please—oh, God, let them be safe! "Allie," she called vainly. "Cassie! Girls!" Tears burned behind her eyes and her throat was thick and clogged. They weren't inside. Not anywhere.

Don't give up. You have to find them. You have to!

But her daughters weren't in the house. It was as if they'd vanished into the blizzard. Along with their bodyguard.

"I'm going to check the garage," she said, once the house had been searched. She tried and failed to keep the sheer panic from her voice. "Maybe Turnquist took them away. To somewhere safe. Used my car."

"Wouldn't he have called?"

"You'd think," she said, but the bodyguard had been marginal at best these past few days, his skills and judgment, in Jenna's opinion, sorely lacking. She headed outside where the wind lashed violently, slanting so that snow blew beneath the cover of the breezeway and caused the windmill to creak and moan as it spun.

"Cassie!" Jenna screamed over the rush of the wind. "Allie!"

Dear God, let them be safe!

How had he gotten in?

No sign of forced entry.

Why would they let a madman into the house?

What the hell had happened?

Don't go there. Do not let your worst nightmares get the better of you.

She searched the garage, inside and out. None of the vehicles were missing. Her Jeep, the old truck, and Jake Turnquist's pickup were parked in their usual spots, tools hanging from the walls, the lawn mower idle and dusty in its corner.

As if nothing was wrong. As if no dreadful acts had befallen her family.

Cassie's heart nose-dived, but she refused to give up. She spied a sickle hanging on the wall and grabbed it. Just in case. Then hurried outside to the exterior stairs leading to the loft over the garage, the quarters Jake Turnquist had claimed for his own. At the landing, she found the door unlocked. Just like all the others. Inside, Turnquist's suite of rooms were dark and cold and appeared just as she assumed he'd left them. She swung the flashlight's beam over the living quarters. Two soda cans, an empty beer bottle, and a couple of microwave dinner boxes littered the counter. Flannel pajama bottoms hung on a hook by his bedroom door. Beyond the door, his bed was unmade, the closet empty, a disposable razor lying by the bathroom sink.

In the living room his equipment—cameras, night goggles, and handgun—had been left behind on the coffee table. *He didn't have his gun with him?*

Something was very wrong here.

The more she saw, the more she was convinced that her children were unsafe. In danger. Who would do this? And why?

And how? How did someone—a single person, presumably—come in, overpower Turnquist, silence the dog, and kidnap the girls? Or was Turnquist in on the abduction?

Fear feeding her headache, she returned to the house where Rinda, back to the fire, was talking rapidly on her cell phone, her free hand gesturing wildly, as if whoever she was speaking to could see her actions. Spying Jenna, she cut herself short. "Just a minute. She's here now. Nothing, huh?"

"No."

"Damn." Rinda's face fell as she handed her phone to Jenna. "I finally got through to Shane. Talk to him."

Jenna nearly cried out in relief. As ridiculous as it seemed, just a connection to Carter gave her strength. "Hi."

"Rinda filled me in," he said, and his voice washed over her like balm. Tears sprang to her eyes. "Sorry I didn't answer earlier—too many calls at once. Some didn't get through. The circuits are on overload. Any sign of Turnquist?"

"No. There's no one here. No kids. No friggin' body-guard, no dog, no one," she said, her panic galloping unleashed, her voice cracking. It was all she could do to hang on to a thread of self-control.

"Okay. Listen. I want you to lock all the doors now. Keep Rinda there with you. Hole up in a room with only one entrance and lock and block the damned door. I'm sending someone over, an OSP unit that's not too far from you, and I'll be there in half an hour. Sit tight. Keep me on the phone if you want."

"I'm going out to check the stable and the barn."

"Wait until an officer gets there."

"I can't, Shane. I have to find them."

"A few more minutes won't make any difference."

"A few more minutes might make all the difference in the world. They could be outside in this damned blizzard, freezing to death. Every minute counts." She stared out the window to the snowy landscape, the drifts, the looming, dark buildings with their icy, black windows. "Or *he* could have them. Right now. I already got a weird phone call, so he's around."

"A call?"

"On my cell. He's taunting me, Shane."

"Stay put!"

"I'll be okay. I've got the shotgun."

"Keep it with you. In the house."

"I gotta go," she said.

"I'll be there soon."

Hanging up, she handed Rinda the phone.

"You're not going out again."

"Of course I am. You would, too. If it was Scott."

Since the cells were working again, she found her phone in her pocket and hit a speed-dial button.

Her first call was to Cassie's cell. No answer. Four rings and a quick transfer to voice mail, where Jenna left a quick message instructing Cassie to call home. Her second phone call was to Allie's cell. As she listened, she heard Allie's phone ringing and found it stuffed in the cushions of the couch in the den.

"Damn."

She met Rinda's eyes and then dialed Josh Sykes's cell phone. Once again, nothing. "Oh, pick up," she ordered, as if the kid could hear her. She was shaking inside, scared to death. When Josh's disembodied voice asked her to leave a message, she did. "Hi, this is Jenna, Cassie's mom. I'm worried about her. She's not here at the house and I thought, make that *I hoped,* she was with you. Please call me back as soon as you can." She rattled off her phone number before hanging up and dialing a final number.

A woman's rough voice answered. She sounded as if she'd just woken up. "Hello?"

"Mrs. Sykes? This is Jenna Hughes. I'm looking for my daughter. I was hoping to talk to Josh."

"He ain't here right now. Don't know when he'll be back, neither." She paused, and Jenna heard the click of a lighter, then the deep intake of breath. "I figured he was with your daughter," Wanda Sykes said, and the tone of her voice hinted that Cassie was the bad influence of the pair.

"I don't know where either one of them is."

"Don't that just figure." Another long drag of her cigarette. "You know, I been tryin' to rein him in, but he don't listen to me, 'specially when it comes to your daughter. I told him to keep his distance, that she ain't his kind, but would he listen? Hell, no. Never did have a lick of sense. Too much like his old man. Only interested in drinkin', smokin', and gettin' himself some."

Jenna was stunned. She'd never met this woman, and yet Wanda was more than willing to spill her guts. "Listen, when Josh comes in, or calls, would you have him phone me?"

A cackling, sarcastic laugh that ended with a coughing fit. "Oh, I'll tell him, if it'll do any good and if I'm awake. Sure, I'll tell him."

"Please, leave him a note if you're going to go to bed." How could Wanda not be worried sick?

"Didn't you say you left him a message on his cell

phone? He'll get back to you." She hung up as if Cassie's whereabouts was of no concern.

"Idiot woman. Doesn't she know there's a madman running around abducting women?" Jenna muttered. Without waiting for Rinda's response, Jenna raced up the stairs, taking the steps two at a time, the feeble light of her flashlight bobbing in front of her. She found the shotgun beneath her bed, the shells in her nightstand. She loaded the gun, clicked on the safety, and headed back to ground level where Rinda was adding wood to the dying fire. Red embers glowed and a few flames began to lick at the new chunks of fir.

"I'll come with you."

"No." Jenna glared at her friend. "Absolutely not. Stay here. I've got my cell. If I need you, I'll call."

"If it works."

"Yeah."

"Tell me you're not going to do anything foolish," Rinda said, spying the shotgun. She was sitting on the edge of the hearth, the embers in the fireplace behind her finally catching fire to crackle, hiss, and cast shifting golden shadows through the room. "Tell me you're going to take Shane's advice."

"I'm going to find my kids," Jenna said. "That's what I'm going to do."

Rinda's gaze slid to the shotgun. "With a gun?"

"For protection. Or if some creep's got the girls."

Rinda snorted. "Do you even know how to use that thing?"

"Well enough," Jenna said, and headed outside to the night where the wind blasted, the snow and sleet slanted from the sky, and somewhere, oh, God, somewhere, her children were.

"Sheriff Carter?" a male voice said over the crackle of static on the cell phone connection. Carter turned his back to the wind and the accident, a jackknifed semi and a small car smashed like a tin can. EMTs were working on the survivors, the M.E. had been called for the fatality. "This is Officer Craig, OSP. We were on our way out to the Hughes place, but we got caught up with an accident here on the highway. Two injured, one critical. A woman trying to have a baby. The EMTs are on their way, but we won't be able to get out of here for at least half an hour."

Damn! Carter checked his watch. The unit should have been at Jenna's by now.

"I've called for backup, but the department's stretched to the breaking point."

"I'll handle it," Carter said.

"We'll get there as soon as we can."

"I know."

Carter hung up and walked to the scene where Lieutenant Sparks was taking notes. "Do you need me for anything?" he asked, and Larry looked up, dark eyes assessing.

"What's up?"

Carter explained and Sparks nodded. "I can handle this. Go ahead and take off."

He didn't need any further impetus. He was in his Blazer and driving as fast as he dared, windshield wipers slapping off snow, police band crackling, his heart in his throat. *Hang in there, Jenna*, he thought, and planned to ream out and fire that useless piece of trash who called himself a bodyguard. What the hell was Turnquist thinking?

His cell phone rang and he answered, dreading a call that would pull him away from Jenna's place. "Carter."

"Hi, it's BJ. I've been called to an accident on 84, but I thought you should know that I got a match."

"A match?" he repeated, and his gloved hands tightened over the steering wheel.

"It's not much, but you were right. There was an employee who worked for Hazzard Brothers who left right after working on *White Out*. He was a makeup man who also did technical stuff and he was injured in the explosion, nearly lost a leg. Collected a hefty sum of cash, nearly a million dollars, and disappeared. They checked their forwarding addresses—one in, get this, Medford—but that was a while back."

"Mavis Gette was last seen in Medford," Carter said. "Okay, so what's his name?" He braced himself. Knew it could be anyone in town and probably not Wes Allen.

"Steven White," she said.

"Steven White? Never heard of him."

"Neither have I, and he's not in our local phone book. Of course, there are about twenty S. Whites in the Portland-Metro area and I'm looking into them. I'm also asking for all public records under that name.

"The Hazzard Brothers have a ton of employee information they're faxing me, including White's employee picture. If this guy's using an alias, we'll find him."

"And check any property bought since the accident. This guy has to live around here somewhere, and I bet he doesn't want a landlord snooping around, so get a list of people who've bought places in the time since the accident."

"There's one other thing," BJ said in a rush. "I don't know how this factors in, if at all. But Steven White was the name of a character in *Resurrection*. He was Anne Parks's, Jenna Hughes's character's, love interest."

"Oh, this factors in," he said, sure of it. "I just don't know how. I'll call Lieutenant Sparks and have him get in touch with the FBI, run Steven White's name through their database; and see if anyone with that name on the West Coast was ever incarcerated."

"You got it," BJ said, "as soon as I get back to the office."

"Keep me posted." Carter clicked off, dialed Sparks and made his request, then turned off the main road. Jenna's house was less than twenty minutes away.

Gripping the shotgun in one hand, Jenna directed the beam of her flashlight with the other. Icy snow pelted her as she tried to read the footprints that had collected around the house, garage, and sheds. Overhead, the windmill creaked and spun in the frigid wind, and though the night was alight with the blanket of snow, it seemed eerie, filled with an evil she couldn't touch or see, could only feel, as if it were breathing hard and cold against the back of her neck.

The tracks were half covered with fresh snow, but she noticed several sets leading to the stable, or the fence line, or the barn. Big footprints. Made by Turnquist as he perused the property.

A fine lotta good that did, she thought angrily, when she noticed the smaller prints, nearly buried, heading straight to the barn. Her heart galumphed. Allie . . . the footprints had to belong to Allie, and beside the girl's tracks, those belonging to some animal. The dog? There was also a larger set. Hopefully belonging to Turnquist.

Help me, she thought, and started following the footprints, the beam of her flashlight illuminating her path. Her heart was jackhammering with dread, adrenaline rushing through her bloodstream. What if the bastard had her daughters? She thought fleetingly of Sonja Hatchell, Lynnetta Swaggert, and Roxie Olmstead, all strong adults and probably up against the same sick son of a bitch that had taken her girls. Dread settled like lead in her heart. Her fingers clenched harder over the shotgun.

Would she be able to shoot the creep?

If he had her kids—no problem.

What if he used Allie as a shield?

She'd have to find a way to get her daughter free.

What if Allie and Cassie are already dead?

She wouldn't even go there. Setting her jaw, she trudged through the knee-deep snow to the window and peered carefully into the darkened barn. She used it only for storage now. She'd never owned cattle or sheep; her horses were housed in the stable.

She saw nothing but blackness through the icy panes, heard no sign of life. But the footsteps had ended at the barn door.

Drawing a deep breath, she clicked off her flashlight. There was no reason to draw any more attention to herself or make herself an easier target than she already was. If someone was waiting for her inside, she wanted to level the playing field a little.

And then she glanced at the snow near the door again and her hopes plummeted. A splatter of dark spots, partially covered by half an inch of white, oozing stains that had melted the snow and were now being covered by new flakes.

Bird droppings, she told herself but knew better. One quick burst of illumination from her flashlight confirmed it. *Blood. Deep red splotches of blood.*

Her insides curdled with fear. Images of her daughters came to mind, and she forced herself to push onward. Maybe they were only wounded . . . she could help them. Fear driving her forward, she pried open a side door and it creaked softly, the sound muted by the wind.

She slipped into the barn and wished she'd picked up Turnquist's night vision goggles, the ones she'd spied upon his coffee table. *Too late now.* The scent of dry hay and dust tickled her nostrils and over the sound of wind whistling through a crack in a window, she heard something . . . something quiet and steady and out of place.

Safety still locked, she hoisted her shotgun to her shoulder.

Inching her way around the old, empty mangers, she squinted into the darkness, spying shadows of tools and grain sacks and images that seemed ghostly in the gloom. Only pale light from the whiteness outside the small windows gave any visibility. The shotgun was heavy and the sound she couldn't identify, the noise that was out of place in this old barn seemed closer, still soft and muffled, but definitely human.

Her throat went dry.

She wasn't alone.

A low, frightening growl reverberated through the cavernous barn. Jenna almost dropped her gun as she spun to face the noise.

A dog barked loudly. Jenna's heart was in her throat as scrambling, frantic claws scraped against the floorboards.

"Critter, no!" Allie's panic-stricken voice shouted from the corner near the stairs to the hayloft.

"Allie?" Jenna nearly collapsed in relief. She headed toward the sound of her daughter's voice. "Allie? It's Mom. I'm here." She flicked on the beam of her flashlight, shining it on her own face before sweeping the weak illumination toward the wall.

"Mom?" Fear strangled her daughter's voice. "Oh, Mom!"

To hell with being a target—Jenna ran toward the sound, Critter nearly tripping her in his eagerness. Her flashlight swept one of the stalls and there was Allie, curled into a fetal position, rocking back and forth, tears running down her face. She jettisoned herself toward Jenna. The shotgun clattered to the floor as Jenna threw her arms around her child.

Gasping, sobbing, quivering head to toe, Allie clung to her.

"Shhh . . . baby . . ." Jenna said. "It's all right, I'm here."

"No . . . no . . ." Allie's voice was garbled, her face white, her eyes round in the darkness.

"Are you all right?" It was a ridiculous question. Allie, though showing no signs of physical wounds, was nearly hysterical.

"Where's Cassie?" Jenna whispered, holding her daughter close and remembering the blood.

"With . . . with . . . him." Hiccupping and sobbing, Allie seemed barely able to breathe.

"Shh, honey, calm down. We're okay. Now, who's Cassie with? Turnquist? Or Josh?"

Allie was shaking so violently, Jenna had to brace herself against a pillar supporting the haymow to stay upright. Critter, too, was anxious, whining and growling, pacing. The barn was cold as a meat locker and there was a smell that was out of place.

"No," Allie insisted hysterically. "Not with Josh, with *him*. With *him!*"

"Who?" Jenna asked, but her heart sank and icy blades of fear sliced deep into her soul. No . . . oh, God, no . . . not the pervert who had been stalking her. She glanced out one of

the small windows and prayed for headlights, some indication that the police were on their way. "Come on," she whispered. "Let's go back to the house."

"No!" Allie sniffed and clung harder. "He's there," she
whispered frantically. "He's waiting."

"He's where?" Jenna asked, her skin prickling.

"In the house."

Jenna's stomach twisted. *Rinda*. "But I was just there, I
searched it top to bottom. Listen, you have to be brave. Let
go of me for a second."

"No!"

"I need to call the house and get the shotgun. Come on,
Allie . . . I'm right here." Gently she peeled her daughter off
her and bent down to retrieve the shotgun. "You hold the
flashlight, okay?"

"Y-yeah."

Fumbling, Jenna extracted the phone from her pocket and
flipped it open. The battery was low, but she hit the speed-
dial number for her house.

One ring.

What was dripping? That sound. Now that Allie had qui-
eted, there was another noise. A plop, plop . . .

Two rings.

And the smell . . . what the devil was that smell? Copper?
Iron? Some kind of metallic tinge in the air?

Three rings. Why wasn't she answering? Panic assaulted
her. Was Allie right? Was the monster in her house, waiting?
Oh, no, please, not Rinda. "Answer, damn it."

Four rings and her own voice answered. "Rinda, pick
up!" she whispered over the recording. "Pick up the damned
phone!" Critter was whining, dancing beside her and she
gave up. Hung up and dialed Shane Carter's cell.

"Carter." He answered on the first ring.

"It's Jenna. Get out here. Cassie and Turnquist are missing. There's blood around the barn and . . ."

Plop!

"What? I'm five minutes away."

"That might be too long!" she said, and noticed the floor, where the flashlight shined on the boards, paw prints and footprints in a crazy pattern of red . . .

"Oh, God," she whispered, cradling the phone between her shoulder and ear as she took the flashlight from her daughter and focused its weak beam on the trail of bloody paw prints . . . backward toward the rear wall where a wide, dark pool was slowly spreading, oozing over the ancient floorboards.

Terror gripped her. She swallowed hard as she slowly moved the flashlight, raising the beam upward, and saw a body swinging from a crossbeam.

Her scream reverberated through the barn, her face twisted in horror as she recognized the victim. Stripped naked and eviscerated, Jake Turnquist had been gutted like a deer on a hunting trip. His body was white, drained, a vicious, gory slash running the length of his body. Entrails, still steaming, were piled on the floor in a slippery, grotesque mass.

Jenna dropped the phone. Allie, clinging to her, was screaming again, losing it.

Jenna's stomach convulsed.

She retched violently at the horrid, grisly sight.

Who was the butcher who had done this? Did he have Cassie? Breathing hard, fighting the mind-numbing horror, she scrabbled on the floor, into the wet puddle, her hands sticky with the bodyguard's blood. "Shane!" she cried, but the cell phone connection was lost. She managed to grab the slippery phone, the gun, the flashlight, and Allie's arm, smearing blood everywhere. "Let's get out of here." Propelling her daughter toward a rear cattle entrance, she started running. If they could get to the garage and the Jeep . . .

She slid open the big door and stepped outside to the quiet night. Pulling Allie with her, Jenna turned off the flashlight, then started running, plunging through the knee-deep snow. She had the phone in one hand and punched out 9-1-1. The more police she could get here, the better. Critter bounded behind, gasping, keeping up as the snow continued to fall.

Rinda! She couldn't leave Rinda!

But the creep had Cassie.

She didn't think he was in the house. She'd come from the house and there were no fresh footprints leading in that direction, no freshly broken path through the frigid white blanket. Jenna's gaze swept the ground and saw only her own trail, already softening with the onslaught of fresh snowflakes.

Get a grip, Jenna. Pull yourself together. You have to find a way to keep Allie safe while finding Cassie.

How? Oh, God, *how?* She needed help.

Shane Carter, get here, now!

Why the hell wasn't the phone connecting? Why was there no sound, no beep of life from the electronic contraption? Had the drop on the floor in the barn, the slide through a coagulating, warm pool of blood somehow short-circuited the damned thing? Or was it because thousands of calls were overloading the cell phone towers. *Maybe it's just an overload of the circuits. Keep trying!*

She was still dragging Allie, trudging through the snow, blinking against the icy crystals stinging her cheeks as the dog bounded ahead.

Come on, come on . . . where the hell are the police?

Carter said he'd send a unit.

The garage was only a few feet away and the keys were in the Jeep, weren't they? If not, there was a spare set hidden in a drawer in the garage.

Suddenly, Critter stopped dead in his tracks. The hackles on his back went up and he snarled, baring his teeth.

Jenna slid to a stop. Held fiercely onto her child. Through the viscous curtain, she thought she saw movement. Her heart stood still. Every nerve ending sprang to life and she squinted and decided it was only the dark silhouette of a tree, branches moving in the wind.

"Come on, Allie," she said, urging her daughter forward.

She didn't hear a sound, just felt a change in the air, a whisper of cold air against the back of her nape. From the corner of her eye, she saw movement again, a dark, leonine mass springing from behind the garage.

Allie screamed.

Jenna swung the shotgun upward, flicked off the safety as he landed upon her, a strong, heavy male whose weight forced her to the ground.

"Run!" she screamed at Allie. She attempted to stand, searching frantically in the drifts for her gun, facing her attacker as the dog barked and snapped. Dressed in camouflage that was visible in the snow, his head covered with a ski mask, he lunged at her again. She rolled to one side through the freezing drifts. "Run!"

She felt the barrel of the gun and reached for it, gloved fingers surrounding the cold steel. But he was upon her again. This time something cold pressed hard against her neck and then a jolt ripped through her body, thousands of volts of electricity that burned through her nerves. She let out a pathetic whimper and collapsed back to the ground.

CHAPTER 45

Carter was too late. He pulled through the open gates of Jenna's ranch and he knew it was over. He'd heard her terrified scream on her phone and then the still, damning silence that had followed. No matter how loud he'd yelled, she hadn't responded. When he'd tried to dial her again, he couldn't get through.

A lifetime had passed since the moment they'd been cut off, but if he checked his watch, it had been less than ten minutes. *Don't give up*, he told himself, but now that he was here at her house, he knew without stepping outside of his truck that he'd lost her. He put in a quick call for backup, but didn't wait. Time was too precious.

His gut clenched as he opened the Blazer's door and a blast of winter slapped him hard in the face. He ran through the thick snow to the house and noticed a glow in the windows. Maybe he'd been too hasty; there was a chance she'd survived. Drawing his weapon, he moved toward the breezeway and hurried to the house. The back door was unlocked. Not a good sign. He pushed it open and stepped quietly inside.

No one greeted him, not even the damned dog. "Jenna?" he called. "It's Shane."

From somewhere in the back of the house he heard a sob.

"Shane?" Rinda's voice. "Thank God." Footsteps clattered against the wood of the floors. "I thought you'd never get here!" A flashlight bobbed, the weak beam pointed at his face, and suddenly she was upon him, crying and sobbing, talking in gibberish, Jenna's youngest child at her side.

"Slow down and tell me exactly what happened. Where the hell's Turnquist?"

"Dead, I think, in the barn. I—I haven't been down there, but Allie was."

"You're sure he's dead?" Shane asked Allie, and she nodded mutely, her eyes round with terror.

A cold, certain fear twisted Carter's insides.

"It's worse," Rinda said. "Josh Sykes is dead, too. In his truck down on the other side of the fence, at the logging road. Allie followed Cassie after she snuck out to meet Josh there. She witnessed the killer attack Cassie. He'd already killed Josh. The poor kid's still in his truck. Dead."

"You checked?"

"No. But I took her word for it."

"He's dead. I saw," Allie whispered, her voice raw.

"And Cassie?"

Allie began to cry. "I shouldn't have left her. He had her. He had her!"

"He's got them, Shane," Rinda said, her face twisted in a deep, horrified fury. Her dark eyes flashed in the firelight. "That brutal monster, whoever he is, has Cassie and Jenna."

"You don't know who he is?"

"I never saw him, but Allie did."

Shane turned his attention on the young girl, who stared at him with wide, traumatized eyes. Her head was still moving up and down, not so much in confirmation, but because she couldn't stop it, an involuntary twitch that somehow soothed her. "Can you tell me what happened here?" he asked, and her lower lip began to quiver. "Allie, please." He touched her on her shoulder. "I won't be able to help your mother until you tell me what happened. Did you see the man who did this?"

She nodded. Tears filled her eyes.

"Did you recognize him?"

She hesitated. Shook her head.

"Think, Allie," he said, gently. "Do you know who he is?"

"No . . . but . . . but . . ." She bit her lip. "He knew my name. And his voice . . ." She swallowed hard. "I think I *should* know him."

"Can you describe him?"

Her chin wobbled and she glanced at Rinda. "Come on, honey, try."

"He was big."

"As tall as me?"

"But bigger . . . he wore a ski mask. Camouflage . . . It was dark and I was far away when he got Cassie and—" She was talking faster now, her voice pitching higher, nearly hyperventilating. "—and I ran back and I ran into the barn and that's when . . . that's when I saw Jake and I was so scared and I didn't know what to do, so I stayed in the barn, away . . . away from Jake, and Critter was with me and then my mom finally came." Sobbing hysterically, her face twisted in despair, she added, "And now she's gone!" Sniffing and swiping at her eyes with the back of her hand, she stared into his eyes. "You have to find them, Sheriff. You *have* to."

"I know. I will," he promised, his gaze flicking to Rinda's. What were the chances that Cassie was still alive? Or Jenna? Through the window, he saw flashing lights, strobing red and blue through the ever-falling snow. His backup had arrived.

But it was too damned late.

Cassie shivered, the cold permeating her skin. She ached all over and tried to move. Couldn't. Her eyes flew open and she panicked. Where the hell was she? Suspended in the air, six or eight feet above a huge vat of some clear liquid. What the hell?

Worse yet, she was naked. Completely nude . . . and what the hell had happened to her hair? The bastard had removed her clothes and then . . . what? Shaved her head. Strapped her onto this tiny little platform and tied her wrists over her head? To what end? Oh, God, this was crazy! Everything about it was so goddamned frightening. Through the thickness in her mind, she remembered seeing Josh in his truck, the lifeblood trickling out of him, and Allie running through the woods and that horrid jolt of electricity by the madman, a man she swore she knew, though she hadn't seen his face.

Quaking with a fear unlike any she'd ever known, she began to breathe in short, shallow breaths. She wanted to pass out, to close her eyes and fall into some deep sleep and wake up in her own bed, with Josh alive, her mother in the next room, her little sister bugging her . . . She let out a sob, then bit her tongue. She couldn't give in to the sheer panic overriding all of her rational thought.

No. She had to think. To find a way out of this ungodly terror. *Calm down, Cass. Figure this out. Don't panic. Do NOT panic.* She took a deep breath and surveyed her surroundings. The psycho wasn't around right now; at least she couldn't see him.

She had to get out of this spaced-out nightmare. So where was she?

Nearly immobile, she forced her gaze downward.

Dim lights glowed and she made out statues in various poses on a stage below, to one side, and a long recliner nearby with some kind of steel arm angled above it.

She squinted, tried to clear her head. The statues weren't random, nor were they just women, she realized, and a new weird fear skittered down her spine. All the statues looked like her mom. Or her mother dressed and made up for some of her most famous roles.

No, that couldn't be right, didn't make any sense.

What about this does make sense?

She had to be tripping or something . . . That was it. She tried hard to focus, and even though her brain was thick as mud, the lighting subdued, she recognized the characters . . . Paris Knowlton from *Beneath the Shadows,* Faye Tyler from *Bystander,* Zoey Trammel from *A Silent Snow,* Marnie Sylvane from *Summer's End*, all dressed as they had appeared in the movies, complete with jewelry and props, their hairstyles perfect replicas of each character's.

Weird.

And scary as hell.

Forcing back the fear, she angled her head and craned her neck to look upward. Above the beam supporting her, tacked onto the high ceiling, were posters, dozens and dozens of blown-up pictures of her mother in her most famous roles. The same characters that were posed on the stage below, except there were pictures of Jenna as Katrina Petrova from *Innocence Lost* and shots of her as Anne Parks in *Resurrection*.

This was all so eerie . . . She looked down again. Two statues . . . no, mannequins, that's what they were, life-sized dolls. Two were faceless, though one had a wig, long black curls reminiscent of Katrina . . . oh, shit, whoever this freak was, he hadn't finished his artwork . . .

Cassie's heart stood still. She remembered the women who had been abducted . . . Were they a part of this macabre scene?

Her heart turned to stone and she looked down to the stage where two mannequins stood with the others. Two that would surely become Katrina Petrova from *Innocence Lost* and Anne Parks from *Resurrection*.

When the artist got around to it.

But what the hell does all this have to do with me? She looked around frantically as her mind cleared and she remembered the abduction, the way the sicko had stunned her and Josh . . . dead . . . eyes rolled up in his head, throat slashed, blood all over his truck.

What was this all about?

Don't think about that. Don't think about anything but getting out of here. You have to escape now.

Her eyes swept the large warehouse of a room. There were doorways . . . not marked, but she saw them, and some kind of high-tech room with monitors. If she could find a way to cut herself down . . . How the hell was she suspended?

Her wrists were bound . . . but she wasn't exactly hanging—her feet were resting on some kind of bar and a cold pipe ran up her back . . . Why?

As her head cleared, she became more frantic, realized how dire her situation was. The creep, a man whose face she hadn't seen but thought she should recognize, was missing. But he'd return.

Somehow she had to be ready for him.

Groggily, Jenna opened an eye. Her entire body ached, and her brain wasn't working. Where the hell was she, and why were her thoughts painful and thick, as sluggish as if they were swimming through jelly in her brain?

Lying flat on her back, she was being jostled as she was transported in some rig—the bed of a pickup with a canopy, she guessed. Her hands and feet were bound and her entire body was strapped down, pressed against cold, corrugated metal. Tiny bits of memory cut through the sludge in her head. Cassie missing. Turnquist dangling and bleeding from a rafter. Allie scared out of her wits. What felt like a million volts of electricity zapping painfully into her body.

But that hadn't been the end of it, no . . . she'd been drugged, had witnessed a shiny needle being eased, almost gently, into her arm and a smooth male voice she should have recognized say, "Finally, you're coming home."

Coming home? What was that all about?

And now she was being unceremoniously hauled somewhere, tied into the back of a pickup, the cold seeping through the canopy, her body jostled by the rough ride. Her wrists were bound painfully in front of her, her ankles strapped as well.

She thought of her daughter. *Cassie . . . where in God's name was Cassie?* She hated to think that this madman had her. Jenna refused to think that her daughter might already be dead; that there had been plenty of time for this hideous beast who had captured Cassie to kill her.

Please, God, no, she silently prayed. *Give me the strength to find my daughter and save her.* She heard the pickup's big engine whine, felt the wheels sliding as the rig climbed, ever higher, bucking upward, sliding, spinning. As if they were driving up a sheer mountain.

The engine suddenly stopped and she braced herself. He must have arrived at his destination. This was her chance. Her moment for escape. *Think, Jenna, think.* She had so few options, but she had to get free. When he opened the tailgate, she'd throw all her force at him, kick her bound legs at his face as he leaned in to pull her out.

And then what? You'll still be tied up. No . . . you have to wait until he tries to move you. You can't do anything until you're untied from this truck.

But he'll use the stun gun on me again.

Not if you fake him out. Pretend that the drugs haven't worn off. Act as if you're completely feeble and out of it. You're an actress, for God's sake! Get ready for the performance of your life.

She mustered all her courage, prayed silently, and stared through the darkness to the point where she knew the back of the truck was. *Come on, you sick pervert,* she thought. *I'm ready.* But instead of the back of the truck opening, she heard a clanging of chains, close, from the area near the front of the truck, and then the whine of an engine. The entire truck shuddered, then jolted, and slowly the truck began to move, upward, inching at an impossible angle, creeping up the horrendously steep terrain.

What! No! She had to escape . . . now! Gravity pulled at her and Jenna would have slid to the back of the truck if she hadn't been secured, a cord around her body strapped to the sides of the truck. What was happening? Her thoughts raced and collided before she realized that the truck was being winched up the hillside. That had to be it.

Wherever he was taking her was remote. Hidden in the mountains. Away from the roads.

Any hope of being rescued disintegrated.

The police had no idea where she was.

In this blizzard, she would never be found.

* * *

He had her!

He had his Jenna.

He hummed to himself, the theme song from *Resurrection*. The haunting, nearly eerie melody reverberated through his mind like an anthem. His blood ran hot, the wanting a fever. Seeing her so close. Touching her . . . ahhhhh . . . Everything was almost in place, he thought, relishing the cold as the wind and snow raged through the trees. He watched as his truck was winched off the road, through a clearing to a plateau on the mountainside. He kept the winch for just this purpose, to hide his vehicle, and now, as the snow fell ever downward, kissing his skin and hiding his tracks, he knew all he'd hoped for, all he'd planned, was about to come to fruition.

He'd waited so long for this moment. He'd scouted out this property the moment he'd learned Jenna Hughes was buying in this part of Oregon, an area he'd been familiar with, a section of the country where his own pathetic excuse for a mother resided.

He smiled bitterly at the thought of the bitch who'd borne him and the father he'd never known, nor, he suspected, had she. Whoring slut! How many times had he been cast outside while she, in the warmth of the house, had entertained? Had his own father been like those he'd seen through the glass? A slick-haired musician with a cruel smile and smoldering eyes, the kind of man she'd attracted and brought home? How many nights had he been sent outside while she entertained?

Cold, cold mother.

Living nearby.

Some of his elation ebbed when he thought of her, a woman who didn't even recognize her own child. He'd seen her on the street and she hadn't so much as given him a second glance. A frozen-hearted bitch.

Ironic that Jenna had chosen this part of the Northwest to claim as her own. As if fate had drawn her to the Columbia Gorge and its frozen winters.

It had been perfect. He'd had no trouble finding a place close by, a private ski lodge that had been abandoned years earlier when the owner had gotten ill. After the owner had died, his heirs were anxious to get rid of what they'd considered an albatross. It hadn't been difficult to convert the lodge into his own private quarters. He'd done the work himself, and in the summer, when the roads were clear, had been able to haul up all of his building materials and supplies. Then, of course, there were the black-market sources who had supplied him with everything he needed for his artwork, including the alginate as well as the drugs and syringes, tiny cameras, anything he needed. His contact in Portland could get him anything, no questions asked.

The winch stopped and his truck was now twenty feet above the road, hidden by the trees. The only other access was around the mountain, a drive that would take forty minutes in normal conditions, and hours, if not longer, in a storm as fierce as this one.

Not that he was afraid of anyone finding him.

No one knew who he was.

And they would never know.

The answer was right in front of him. Carter was sure of it. While Rinda and Allie huddled in the den and officers from the OSP waited for the crime lab, he unrolled the printouts of the people who had visited Jenna's Web site, her fan Web sites, rented or bought movies, came into contact with her here at the house and through the theater, people who owned property within a twenty-mile radius . . . His mind was moving fast, but time was ticking by.

Merline Jacobosky and three associates from the State Crime Lab arrived after Shane had double-checked both the barn and the logging road to make sure that Jenna or Cassie weren't in either place. A deputy had been posted at each of the killing sites, waiting in the cold.

Carter had been on the phone with the OSP, asking for them to get in touch with the cell phone company that Jenna and her daughters used, hoping that the phones were still with the women and that the GPS chip would show their positions. He'd also asked for officers to check with Harrison Brennan, Travis Settler, Hans Dvorak, and Ron Falletti, two men who had dated her, her ranch hand and personal trainer, all of whom would know her routine. He'd discounted Wes Allen, who was, reported by a deputy, on his favorite stool at the Lucky Seven where the backup generator allowed the bar to remain open.

And time was ticking by.

"I wouldn't have gotten here so quickly," Jacobosky told Carter, "but we were working on the other side of Hood River. Looks like we won't be able to get back to Portland tonight. The road's impassable."

"I guess we got lucky."

"If that's what you want to call it. I think luck would be sitting around a fire at a lodge après ski and drinking mulled wine or hot toddies. But, of course, this would be my second choice, camping out in a town where most of the electricity is out and there are very few hotels," she said dryly. "So where's the first body?"

"In the barn." Carter filled her in and led the group to the crime scene in the barn.

"Jesus," Merline said under her breath as she ran the beam of her flashlight over the pool of blood, footprints and paw prints smeared on the worn plank flooring, then eyed what was left of Turnquist. "Looks like someone was waiting. Ready. Had the weapon with him. Probably slashed his throat, threw a rope around him and over the crossbeam, hauled him up, and gutted him. That's unofficial, mind you. The M.E. will make a determination." She ran the beam down Turnquist's torso. "Cut cleanly, probably a hunting or that type of knife, maybe even a surgical blade. By the way he gutted the body, he's done this before." She shined her light on the entrails piled near an old barrel used for feed. "Nice," she mocked. "Better scoop this up before the rats get to it."

"A hunter," Carter observed, eyeing the bloody mess. What kind of psychotic would do this?

"If he isn't, he should be," she said, her nose wrinkling in distaste beneath her rimless glasses. She looked pointedly at one of her assistants. "Maybe someone who's had military training. That would be my guess." She looked up. "Okay, guys, rope the entire area off . . . may as well keep everyone, including the damned dog, out of the barn at least until we sort out these prints and search for trace evidence." She made some notes on the papers on her clipboard.

"There's another body, right?" she asked.

"This way." Together, collars turned up, gloved hands plunged deep in their pockets, they slogged through the snow and along the fence line to a spot where some of the snow had been churned up and flattened, now covered with a fresh layer. They climbed over, made their way through a copse of iced-over trees, and saw the truck, door still open, interior light feeble, warning bell dinging softly and slowly, the only noise other than the ever-present wind.

Josh was lying on his back, his head lolled to one side and hanging off the edge of the seat. Snow and ice covered his face, but couldn't disguise the deep red slash beneath his chin. His thin goatee and hockey-stick sideburns were crusted with frozen blood, his skin a ghostly white.

Merline let out air between her teeth. "Just a kid. Anyone called his folks?"

"Not yet," Carter said, eyeing the pickup, his flashlight sweeping the ground where there were signs of a struggle, the snow disturbed, and Josh's blood seeping down the seat, over the running board and into the snow.

"As soon as the M.E.'s done, I'll send someone out to the Sykes place."

"Helluva job that'll be," she whispered, then bent down to get a closer view of the body. She ran the beam of her flashlight over Josh's throat. "Slit ear to ear. Doesn't look like much of a struggle. Again, I'd guess the guy was lying in wait, the victim not having time to defend himself."

Carter glanced at his watch, felt the urgency of the passing of time. Where was the murdering bastard who had Jenna? If the weather were better, there could be helicopters or planes searching the surrounding hills, but as it was, they were forced to the ground, and with the storm, a search would be nearly impossible.

The crime techs went to work, and Shane trudged through the snow toward the house. He was wired. Anxious. Felt that time was slipping away and with it, Jenna's chances of survival.

What did he know about this guy?

Lived in the area.

Obsessed with Jenna Hughes.

Considered himself some kind of poet.

A hunter, someone strong.

Someone who was connected to Hollywood and worked with alginate to make masks.

Someone who knew the layout of the grounds, understood Jenna's routine. Knew about Cassie's trysts with her boyfriend. About the logging road.

Someone close . . .

Someone who called himself Steven White, after a character in *Resurrection*.

By the time Carter returned to the house, Lieutenant Sparks and another officer from the OSP had arrived. Sparks was standing near the fire in the den, talking on the phone. Rinda, Allie, and the dog were hunkered on the couch, a quilt tossed over them, and another technician from the Oregon State Police was searching the place. "Haven't heard on the GPS chips," Sparks said after hanging up, "and Brennan, Settler, Falletti, and Dvorak are all accounted for. I had officers check."

"Can we leave now?" Rinda asked. "Allie can come with me. I'll take care of her. But I've got to find Scott."

"He's missing?" Carter asked and remembered that Rinda's son could recite lines from Jenna's movies, that he was near the top of the list for rental/purchase of every piece of film she'd made.

"He went into Portland, and Jesus, Carter, don't give me that look. Scott's not a part of this. Just like Wes wasn't." When he didn't respond, she threw the cover off. "Oh, for Christ's sake, Shane, get a grip. You're grasping at straws!"

"Hey!" the technician shouted from the stairs. "Up here!"

"Stay with her," Carter ordered Rinda as he and Sparks headed up the steps, passing the landing with its stained-glass window. The tech was standing in the doorway; he led them into Jenna's closet and a pull-down ladder that opened to an attic space above. Within the attic, beneath a thick layer of insulation, he pointed to a wire with a small, bulbous end. "A camera," he said, "not part of the normal wiring, back here." He showed them more of the same, hidden deep beneath the batting and run along a beam, barely noticeable, threading through the upper floor. "This is a professional job. Pretty high-tech, and he would have had to have time to do it. My guess, whoever wired this place did it before she moved in . . . like an inspector or someone hired to do work to bring it up to code. This insulation is pretty new, certainly added long after the house was built, probably before Ms. Hughes bought the place. So our guy, he does the legitimate electrical stuff, has the place inspected, then adds his own special little devices."

Shane thought about Scott Dalinsky. Yeah, the kid had some of the know-how, but not the opportunity. Wes Allen? Or someone else? Seth Whitaker came quickly to mind. And he was a transplant, wasn't he?

Shane whipped out his cell phone and called BJ. "Get to someone at city hall, find out who did the remodel work on Jenna Hughes's place, and where the hell Seth Whitaker lives . . . Isn't it up past Juniper?"

"I know that one. I've been checking," BJ said. "He bought the Farris property about two and a half years back. *Before* Jenna Hughes plunked down her money."

"But she might have already been looking. Where's Whitaker's place?"

"Remember the private ski resort project that was abandoned? That's the spot."

Carter felt that sense of awareness, the prickle of knowledge, a quick rush that accompanies cracking a particularly troublesome puzzle.

The acres surrounding the abandoned ski lodge overlooked this ranch. Located high upon a cliff, the very spot where Pious Falls started its furious descent, the acres set deep into the forest. The fact that some Arizona developer had actually thought about building a ski lodge up there had been considered folly by most of the locals. The access was nearly impossible, the permits unlikely, that side of the mountain ravaged by winter winds screaming down the gorge. The entire idea had fizzled before it had ever taken off. The man who'd dreamed up the crazy plan had died after some initial construction had been bogged down in red tape and red ink. His heirs had spent two or three years trying to unload the place.

Enter Seth Whitaker. The loner. A handyman. Electrician. Had he worked in L.A.? Was he connected to Jenna and her movies?

"You think Whitaker is involved?" BJ asked.

"I think he could be, yes. Check his alibis for the nights Sonja Hatchell, Roxie Olmstead, and Lynnetta Swaggert were abducted, then see if he was in Medford last year, around the time Mavis Gette was thumbing her way to Oregon. It may take some time, but there may be some credit card receipts indicating he was in Southern Oregon or Northern California. I need to know if this guy has changed his name legally, or illegally, for that matter, if he ever lived in the L.A. area, was associated with Hazzard Brothers or any other company that worked with Jenna Hughes's films. Find out everything you can about him."

"Tall order."

"In a short time. I need all this ASAP."

"I'll do what I can, but remember, you also thought Wes Allen was our man."

"Wishful thinking," he joked.

She didn't laugh.

"Dispatch a unit to Whitaker's place on the mountain, too."

"We don't have a unit, not so much as one deputy who isn't at another emergency," she said. "And wait a sec . . . the roads up on Wildcat Mountain are so steep, they're shut down. I just got the call. They're impassable up there, and a chopper won't work in this mess."

The mountain retreat was his lair . . . Carter felt it in his bones.

"Call the forest service. Get some of their equipment. Find a way to get up there and get back to me."

"Jesus, Carter, why not ask for the moon while you're at it?"

"Just do it, damn it, BJ," he said, impatient. Every minute wasted was a minute Jenna Hughes was with the psycho.

He clicked off his phone and turned to Sparks. "It's Seth Whitaker. He's our guy."

"You're sure?" Sparks was skeptical as they walked into the den.

"He's an electrician. Lives fairly close. Has only been in town two or three years."

Sparks was shaking his head. "That's still real thin."

"No reason not to go visit him." At the bottom of the steps, Carter turned into the den. Jenna's daughter was seated in a corner of the couch, a hand-held video game in her lap, but her eyes turned toward the window. "Hey, Allie," Carter said, careful not to lead her to a conclusion. "Does the man who took your mom have the same build of anyone you know, anyone who might have been at the house?"

"Maybe." She was still scared to death, regarded Shane with wary eyes.

"Like who?"

"Like the bodyguard, big like him."

"Tall and muscular?"

"Yeah . . ." She turned away, scratched at her cheek.

"But you didn't recognize him?"

Her face squeezed together. Tears slid from the corners of her eyes.

"Leave her alone," Rinda said. "Carter, enough!"

She was right.

The kid had done all she could.

He walked into the kitchen. "Can you stay with them?" he asked Sparks. "Until I get back."

"I've got to be here for the M.E. and the D.A. As long as the crime scene team is here." His cell phone jangled and Sparks answered. The conversation was short. His dark eyes narrowed and he snapped the phone off. "GPS found the location of the phones, along with Turnquist's. Looks like they were ditched along Wildcat Road, east of here."

"On the way to Whitaker's place."

"On the way to a lot of places, but yeah." Larry nodded. "You think he's our guy?"

"I'd bet on it. Call the feds. Send backup."

"You're going up there?"

"No other choice," Carter said and was out the door and into the freezing weather. "Get me a search warrant."

"Tonight?"

"That's right. Call Amanda Pratt with the D.A.'s office and let her know this is her big chance. She'll love it. Trust me, if there's a chance she can break this case open, she'll find a judge if she has to crawl into bed with one tonight. But I need to get into Seth Whitaker's property."

"I'll see what I can do, but how the hell you plan on getting to his place?" Sparks asked, his voice drowned by the wind.

"The only way I can," Carter said, and opened the door to his Blazer.

He'd have to climb the damned falls.

CHAPTER 46

The cold caressed him as he slid out of the pickup. Like a lover, it wrapped around him, sending icy thrills along his spine. He trudged to the back of the pickup and opened the tailgate. Jenna was lying as he'd left her, seemingly still unconscious, though she should be waking up.

Carefully, wary that she could be faking her state of unconsciousness, he touched her leg. She didn't budge. Then he raised a fist as if to strike her, slamming it toward her face, only to pull his hand back before he touched her. She didn't so much as flinch.

Satisfied that she was still out, he carefully untied the cord holding her in place from the pickup's grommets.

Her black hair tumbled over her face, her ebony lashes swept the crest of her sculpted cheeks, and he imagined what she'd look like as Anne Parks ... well, he knew. He'd watched *Resurrection* so many times that he could recite the dialogue from memory, knew every nuance of her gestures, anticipated her actions.

But before he created Anne, he had one more lifelike mannequin to create, compliments of the woman who looked so much like Jenna that she stole the breath from his lungs. Cassie Kramer, Jenna's firstborn, would be the perfect mold for Katrina in *Innocence Lost*. Her features were spot-on with her mother's, only her hair needed to be a darker color.

Once he'd finished with Cassie, he'd create his replication of Anne Parks by using Jenna, herself, as the mold. She would be immortalized, caught in her most beautiful role forever.

His shrine would be complete—the only character that would be missing would be Rebecca Lange of *White Out*. That part he'd reserved for Jenna's sister, Jill, but he'd fouled up years before and caused an accident he hadn't meant to. Not that the idea of an avalanche hadn't been an erotic fantasy, with snow and ice exploding down the hillside in a thunderous, rolling plume. But he hadn't meant to kill a woman who would have been ideal for the lifelike replica of Rebecca Lange from *White Out*, though of course, at that time, his shrine had only been a far-flung and half-formed plan. Only in the tragedy's aftermath, when he'd been injured and collected an insurance settlement, had he first thought of his special tribute to her. The movie had been scrapped and Jenna's marriage had broken up. She had pulled away from the glitter of Hollywood and had started talking about leaving L.A. Upon learning that she wanted to move north, he took it as an omen. Fate. That they were destined to be together. One. An incredibly perfect union of bodies and minds.

And now she was his.

Alone.

But he was running out of time. Could feel it. Had even altered his routine a bit, and that angered him. There had been no time to file down Cassie Kramer's teeth . . .

Not good. A bad sign. Things should be planned.

He gathered her gently from the truck and carried her, like a bridegroom lifting his new bride over a threshold, to the waiting snowmobile with its webbed stretcher behind, the same kind of stretcher used to transport the injured off a ski run.

As the wind whispered through the trees, he gently

placed her into the stretcher's cradle. "It won't be long now," he promised.

Jenna waited. It was all she could do not to hurl herself at the madman, but she knew that if she blew it now, she wouldn't be able to disarm him. Nor would she be able to locate Cassie.

Be patient, she told herself as she felt him strap her into a webbed canoe of sorts, fire up an engine, and take off. She didn't dare even chance the slit of an eye opening until she felt the sharp tug; the stretcher shuddered, then slid across the snow. A rush of cold air swept past her, and only then did she risk viewing the snow-crusted trees and brush flying by in a blur, old-growth timber rising high above her. She was strapped into some kind of sled that was anchored to a snowmobile, spraying snow.

Fear clawed its way through her, but she gritted her teeth. She would suffer through whatever he had planned.

Just take me to Cassie, you freak, then we'll see.

The equipment was old. Ropes and crampons and an ice pick that he hadn't used since the accident that had taken David Landis's life. Carter had never planned to use the ice-climbing gear again, but had kept it in the garage, never understanding the reason why. Tonight he piled everything in the back of his Blazer and headed to the logging road that intersected the falls about two hundred feet off the valley floor. He wore boots with cleats, gloves that were flexible yet warm, his body-fitting ski gear, and he never questioned his mission.

BJ was right—the road to Whitaker's land was closed, a back forest-service access road miles out of the way. Up the falls was dangerous as hell, but it was the quickest and stealthiest way to Whitaker's door.

He drove as far as he could up an abandoned logging

road, where his tires spun in the snow and his Blazer lurched and lunged, four-wheel drive forcing the SUV upward, the engine grinding. He nosed his rig along the ancient road, driving as fast as he dared, as quickly as the Blazer would go, past trees that knifed into the cloudy sky, and steep, sheer canyons that fell away from the narrow road.

He stared through the windshield, trying to make out where the road was stable and where the bluff, hidden by snow, gave way. His teeth ground together, his jaw aching, every minute anticipating a wheel sliding off the gravel, sending snow and rocks over the edge, his truck pitching into the darkness, but still he climbed. Upward. Lurching. Grinding. Clawing, the Blazer roared upward until the road ran out.

Carter didn't so much as think twice. He set the emergency brake and grabbed the gear from the back of his rig, then slogged through the snow. The hike was severe, ever upward through the deep snow, following a narrow trail that switched back and forth before it reached the falls and ended abruptly.

In the darkness, Carter shined his flashlight on the silvery sheen of thick ice—water frozen in time as it tumbled down the rocky cliffs to the gorge. In an instant he saw David Landis climbing up this very stretch of frozen water, heard his taunts as he'd scaled the sheer, slippery slope, the same taunts that had echoed through his head for so many years.

"Don't tell me you're afraid."

Hell, yes, I'm afraid.

"The ultimate chickenshit? Pussy-to-the-max?"

Carter's guts knotted as he remembered the fall . . . how he couldn't save David. And now, the wind whispered through the trees, seeming to echo David's jeers.

"Don't tell me you're afraid."

Carter set his jaw.

Strapped on his crampons and didn't look down.

He'd either save Jenna, or die trying.

* * *

They slowed and the snowmobile's engine died.

Jenna told herself to relax, to feign being unconscious, to keep up the act. So far, it had worked.

Oh, yeah, like a charm. Now you're a million miles away from anyone, trapped with a psycho.

She heard him stow the snowmobile, then felt him lift her again and it was all she could do not to recoil at the feel of him carrying her. She let her head loll back over his arm, felt her hair falling free and catching in the frigid wind.

He paused. Stopped dead in his tracks. As if he sensed something was wrong.

Breathe normally. Remain limp. You're Raggedy Ann. Don't shiver, don't look, don't so much as lift an eyebrow.

"Jesus, you're beautiful," he whispered, and she thought she recognized his voice. Inwardly, she cringed. Outwardly, she didn't react. "I've waited so long." He shifted, lifted her higher, and she felt his hot breath against her face.

Don't move, Jenna. Whatever he does, do NOT react.

"You are every woman . . . my woman . . ."

She thought she might get sick.

He brushed his lips across her neck, his warm flesh making her own chilled skin crawl. Still she didn't react, not even when his mouth nibbled at the corner of hers and he let the tip of his tongue press against the seam of her lips. She wanted to lock her jaw, but reminded herself of all the love scenes she'd played where the actor who was her love interest in the script was a nauseating, arrogant bastard.

You can do this, Jenna. You can.

She felt her abductor shudder with desire, and it was all she could do not to shrivel away from him.

Gratefully, he started moving again and she heard a door open, then slam shut with a heavy, metallic thud. His footsteps were steady and Jenna told herself she could do this . . . until she heard the voice—Cassie's voice. Relief mingled with fear.

"Hey! You! Let me down from here! Do you hear me? I said . . . oh . . . nooooooo. You have my mother? You bastard, you put her down, right now!"

Don't, Cassie! Don't taunt him.

"What the hell are you doing with her? Leave her the fuck alone!"

Her abductor stiffened.

"Shut up!"

"Let her go. You're never going to get away with this . . . this sick thing you've got going, whatever it is."

"Oh, no?" he tossed back, and Jenna's heart sank. *Don't push him, Cass, for God's sake!*

He set Jenna down on the floor—cold and smooth—cement, she guessed. It was so damned cold in here. She heard his footsteps moving away from her and risked the tiniest peek through her lashes.

Quickly, she saw that she was in a huge room. He'd left her in the middle of a stage with actresses posed across it. No, not actresses. Every one of them were replicas of herself in her movie roles. The clothes, jewelry, an umbrella hanging from Marnie Sylvane's arm, nerdy glasses propped on Zoey Trammel's nose, the missing faux pearl bracelet surrounding Paris Knowlton's wrist. All were props from her movies. Even the two mannequins without faces could be identified by the wigs they wore, Katrina's long, curling black tresses that fell over the shoulders of a sheer white teddy, the lace a perfect imitation of the costume Jenna wore in the role. The other faceless mannequin already wore a dog collar and held a butcher knife in one hand; no doubt she was soon to become a replica of Anne Parks.

Oh, this was sick . . .

A roiling nausea crept up her throat at the extent of this man's depravity. What was this, a weird shrine? A house of wax where she was the only display? Panic gripped her, and she had to force her eyelids to remain almost closed, to keep herself from trembling as she surveyed the stage. A dentist's chair was the only prop, a drill poised above it and dark stains . . . blood? . . . drizzled over the arm and headrest. What kind of sickness was this?

High overhead were pictures of her in her various roles or from magazines, blown up and stapled to the ceiling.

She took another quick look and located a computer room, lit by the glow of monitors, and from the hum, she guessed a generator was supplying energy.

But where was Cassie?

She chanced turning her head just a bit and when she did, she nearly screamed. In a far corner was a contraption that she couldn't fully understand. A huge glass tub, and above it her daughter was naked, her head shaved and propped on some kind of beam, her hands yanked high over her head, her feet balanced on a slim footing.

Jenna nearly cried out when she saw her daughter. Doom clenched its fist around her.

Jenna had no doubt in her mind that this psycho was going to kill them both.

Upward. One agonizing foothold at a time. Shane worked his way up, digging in, hugging the icy falls, using his rope, feeling the wind tear and shriek at his back. Snow tumbled from the sky and it was still dark—early morning but far from dawn.

Despite his insulated wear, his teeth were chattering from the cold, his body covered in sweat from the exertion. He was making progress—slow, steady, unnerving progress, his thoughts spurring him on.

Jenna could be dead already.

Another person he loved, a casualty of the winter cold and a madman.

Cassie, too, had probably already been killed.

"You crazy son of a bitch," he ground out, swinging his ice axe, making another niche in the frozen falls. He had less than twenty feet to climb—twenty agonizing feet.

Another gust of wind battered at his back, seemed to laugh at his futile attempts. He reached for the handhold. His fingers missed, his feet slipped. His body dropped, sliding along the icy wall.

"Shit!"

His rope grabbed.

Stopped his rapid descent.

Saved him from dangling or falling nearly three hundred feet to the icy ground below. For a second he thought of David. His heart pounded wildly as he eased back to the cliff face and the icy sheet that was his ladder.

Gritting his teeth, every muscle screaming, he forced himself against the face of frozen water and reached upward, making a handhold. "I'm coming, you son of a bitch," he said through the frozen bristles of his moustache. "I'm coming."

"Are you awake yet, Jenna?" he asked, and his voice seemed to come from everywhere, speakers hidden in the darkness. "This is my theater, dedicated to you. Wake up and see what I've done, the tribute I've made to you."

"Tribute?" Cassie yelled, and Jenna willed her to be quiet. *Don't antagonize him.*

"I know you're awake . . . pretending. No need. Not any longer. You're home with me. You know who I am, don't you?"

"Who cares, you dumb shit!"

Cassie, no!

Through the veil of her lashes, she watched as he slowly unlaced his boots and stepped out of them. Somehow he lost four inches. Then he peeled off his clothes, insulated camouflage jacket—the kind hunters wear to hide in the fall brush—matching pants, and beneath the outerwear, insulated thermal pants and shirt. Off came the ski mask and hat and she nearly gasped.

Seth Whitaker.

The man she'd trusted to set up her alarm system. How many times had he "checked the wiring"? Oh, God, what a fool she'd been.

"You creep!" Cassie yelled.

He looked up at her. "You don't even know who I really am," and his voice changed slightly, was a tad higher. He pulled off his wig to reveal that he was nearly bald, short,

blond fuzz over his head. Then he popped out contact lenses
to reveal darker eyes. Eyes she'd seen before.

"Who are you?" Cassie asked as he removed his teeth and
temporary implants along his jaw line so that he lost his
jowls.

Jenna had seen him before. She was sure of it. When?
California? He swung his face toward hers and she knew in
an instant. One of the technicians on the set of *White Out,*
one of the guys who'd been injured. The guy with the same
name as one of the characters in her films. Steven White—
that was it.

He tugged off his thermal wear and revealed a bodysuit.
As he stripped it off, his thick waist disappeared, revealing a
taut, corded body that looked honed by some kind of physical activity.

Seth Whitaker. Steven White. She wondered what his real
name was.

Naked, he looked up at Cassie. "Now, Katrina, it's time."

"Are you talking to me? I'm not Katrina. Just get me
down from here."

"Always the feisty one," he said, and walked into the
computer room and typed on the keyboard. Instantly, music
began to fill the room, music from *Innocence Lost,* the same
music that had been played during the phone call she'd received.

While he was still in the computer room, she frantically
tried to find a means of escape. She had to untie herself, but
her hands were bound so tightly, she could barely move.

With a clank and a deep whir, the bar on which Cassie
was suspended began to lower, slowly easing her toward the
vat of the clear fluid. What was it? It looked like water but it
could be anything horrible.

"Hey! No!" Cassie was screaming now, her bravado failing. "Let me down, please," she cried, her voice cracking.
"I've never done anything to you. Please, don't do this!"

He returned from the computer room and stared at her.
Didn't say a word, and to Jenna's horror, the closer Cassie

got to the vat, the lower she got, his reaction was just the opposite: his dick started to rise.

The pervert was really getting off on this, staring at Cassie. While his back was turned on Jenna, she scooted closer to the mannequin meant to be Anne Parks, to the knife that was suspended from the mannequin's hand. Only a few more inches, but she was running out of time; the pole on which Cassie was braced had reached the surface of the liquid. She saw Jenna move.

"Mom! No!"

He spun, eyes glittering.

It was now or never.

Jenna lunged for the mannequin, sending it toppling, the knife even farther from her. Anne's arm hit Paris, and in a domino effect, all of the strange, lifelike replicas of her fell, thudding, jewelry and props skittering across the floor. One mannequin's head twisted upward at an impossible angle.

"No!" he said, spinning, his eyes narrowing on the pile of crumpled mannequins. His hard-on shriveled. "Leave them alone!" He advanced toward Jenna and the pile of dummies. "Paris! Marnie! Faye!" he cried, his face twisting in pain before he glared furiously at Jenna. "Look what you've done! This was your shrine, you thankless bitch!"

Jenna moved as quickly as possible, keeping eye contact with the madman, seeing, in her peripheral vision, the long-bladed knife mere feet away.

Walking swiftly, he seemed to have forgotten Cassie, who, as her toe hit the surface of the liquid, let out a screeching howl that echoed to the rafters.

"Let her go!" Jenna ordered. "It's me you want. Obviously. So let her go."

"I need you both."

Cassie was inching into the liquid. Shivering. Her naked body trying to twist away. "Help!" she cried, then squealed in terror.

"Please, Seth," Jenna said. "Let her go!"

"I'm not Seth."

"Steven, then. Please!" She appeared to be moving closer
to him, meeting him, supplicating. "I'll do anything you
want. Anything. Just let my daughter go."

Oh, God, it was so cold, the water surrounding her felt
thick, like gelatin, and was so cold. Cassie tried to shrink
away, to shimmy backward up the pole, but it was no use.
She sank lower and lower, her gaze darting from the freezing
liquid to her mother and the monster and back to the tank.

Icy water—if that's what it was—crawled up her legs,
over her knees, up her thighs.

Carter pulled himself over the edge and rolled into the
snowbank. He gasped for air, ice crystals stinging the exposed parts of his face. Drenched in sweat and shivering, he
rolled to his feet, released his cleats, and slung his backpack
over his shoulder. Through the trees, the old lodge appeared,
a massive structure completely covered in snow. Only a few
small windows remained, the larger ones boarded over.

He approached with caution, an eerie feeling of dread
stealing through his blood as he surveyed the place. No
pickup or truck, but a snowmobile was parked near a door
and a rescue stretcher had been attached to it.

Grimly, he realized this was how Whitaker brought his
victims here. A few lights glowed from the inside through
the icy windows, and Carter's guts felt like lead. He reached
into his pocket, found his cell phone, and turned it on.
Nothing. No signal.

Shit.

From his backpack he dragged out his walkie-talkie and
hit the button. A crackle of noise erupted. "It's Carter—I'm
at the lodge, and I think Whitaker's here. Send backup!"

He didn't wait for a response, couldn't risk the time.
Stuffing his walkie-talkie into the pack again, he pulled out
his sidearm and held it in one hand.

The fingers of his other hand gripped the ice axe.

A scream tore through the woods, a terrified wail erupting from within the building.

Carter didn't think twice.

He kicked open the door, ducked inside, and with his weapon drawn, yelled, "Police! Freeze!"

What!

Whitaker heard the shout and turned. The lawman was standing in the doorway, gun drawn, aiming at him. Walking toward him as if he had the right.

Jenna let out a gasp of relief that curdled Whitaker's stomach. This couldn't be happening. Not now. Not when he was so close.

He lunged to one side and hit the ground, rolling over and grabbing Jenna, holding her against him like a human shield. He had no weapon, but grabbed her neck and twisted.

She cried out.

"I'll kill her, Carter," he said calmly. "And then you can shoot the hell out of this place, kill me. It won't matter—I'll be with her."

"Help!" Cassie cried, and Whitaker chanced a glance her way. She was almost submerged, gasping for breath, the freezing water slowing her reactions, hypothermia setting in.

"Shane, help her," Jenna cried. "The controls are in the computer room."

"Let her go."

Carter trained his gun on him, but Whitaker didn't care. He'd die with Jenna, take her with him, and he would have reached his goal. Here, with Jenna in his arms.

"I said 'let her go,' " Carter repeated.

"Fuck off," he growled, and while staring at Carter, held Jenna's head twisted with one arm while fondling her breast with the other. It was heaven.

Gurgling sounds came from the other side of the room. Cassie was drowning, and the lawman couldn't stop it.

Jenna bucked. All of her body convulsing, her tied hands flailing. Whitaker saw Carter shift, and he tightened his grip on Jenna, wrenching her neck.

The pain was excruciating, but Jenna didn't care. Cassie was drowning. In front of her eyes. And the knife was only inches from her hand. She threw herself up at her attacker, throwing all of her weight against him, her hands scraping the concrete, breaking nails. She found the hilt of the knife, picked it up in both hands, and turned, slashing wildly, her head feeling as if it would fall off.

Whitaker yelped. Cassie sputtered.

The harsh grip relaxed for an instant.

A shot blasted through the room, reverberating against the walls, and Whitaker fell away.

"Save Cassie!" Jenna cried, stumbling to her feet. With his ice axe, Carter unbound Jenna's wrists and ankles, and she ran blindly toward the computer room while Carter climbed the rigging.

Cassie was completely submerged, her body unmoving.

Carter didn't wait. He aimed his gun at the glass tank.

Jenna screamed.

He pulled the trigger.

The gun fired.

Glass shattered as the tank exploded. Water, in a huge, cascading rush, flooded the room, pouring over the equipment, skimming over the floor.

Cassie lay still as Carter pulled on the rigging and the beam swung to a platform. With keys he found on the ledge, he unlocked her and she collapsed onto the ledge. "Look for blankets," he yelled as he started mouth-to-mouth, forcing warm air into her lungs, then pressed on her chest. *Come on, Cassie, breathe.* He tried again. And again. *Don't do this, don't die. Come on, fight. Don't let that bastard win!*

He heard Jenna climbing the ladder to the landing. "Oh, God, is she—"

With a jolt, Cassie spluttered and coughed, water spewing from her mouth and nose as she turned to her side. She gasped, dragging air into her lungs, and coughed again.

"Oh, honey!" Jenna kneeled over her, wrapped her in a blanket, and cradled her head. "Oh, baby, baby, baby . . ."

Cassie was crying, shaking, trying to understand, and as she did, her eyes took in Shane Carter standing a few paces behind Jenna. Shivering, she looked down at her naked body, and groggily must've put two and two together. "Oh, gross . . ." She wrapped the blanket closer around her. "Yuk."

Carter, looking down at dummies of Jenna half-submerged in the icy water stained red from Whitaker's wounds, couldn't agree more. Jewelry and props, a broken umbrella and bracelets, floated in the murky red water that collected around the dentist's chair. A pair of plastic glasses, their lenses shattered, skimmed along the water's surface.

"I guess I'd better see if he's still alive," Carter said, but took his time getting to Whitaker, who stared up at the ceiling where posters of Jenna were tacked. Blood showed in the corners of his mouth and oozed from beneath his back.

Carter waded through the water, leaned down, and felt for a pulse at Whitaker's throat.

There was none.

Seth Whitaker, aka Steven White, was dead.

Jenna and Cassie were alive.

Things could have ended up worse.

A whole lot worse.

EPILOGUE

"I thought you were through with 'bullshit' sessions," Dr. Randall said nearly ten months later, when Carter arrived on his doorstep.

"I am." He stepped into the room where he'd spilled his guts for so many months and frowned at the soft leather couch, pastel seascapes, oak bookcase filled with tomes on every kind of psychosis, mental disease or syndrome in the world.

A fern, near the corner, catching the late summer light through the window, flourished, showing off new green fronds.

Randall seemed pleased, as if his prodigal son had finally returned. They both stood near the window overlooking the parking lot. "I don't have time to see you right now. I'm on my way out."

"That's fine, I won't need much of your time. I just want to remind you that I'll be watching, okay? I've heard rumors that you're writing a book."

"Everyone's dream."

"Not mine."

"Well, we can't all be authors," Randall said.

"I heard that it's loosely based on Seth Whitaker's obsession with Jenna Hughes."

Randall touched the edge of his goatee, turned a palm to-

ward the ceiling. "It's about an unbalanced person obsessed
with an ex-movie star."

"And you've had some bites, right? An agent and pub-
lisher interested, even Hollywood knocking on your door."

"Well . . . I don't know about that." Randall checked his
watch and Carter hitched his chin toward the parking lot,
suggesting the psychologist look through the window to the
parking space where Jenna, seated at the wheel of her Jeep
was waiting, the rig's engine idling in the hot afternoon air.

"Things are working out for you, I see," Randall observed
with the tiniest of smiles. "Maybe winter isn't so bad after
all."

"Maybe, and yeah, things are working out, but Jenna,
she's still got connections in L.A. and there are rumors that
her ex is going to try and produce a story that sounds a helluva lot like yours."

"Is that so?" Randall's humorless eyes met his gaze and
Carter noticed it then, that hint of superiority, the look of
soft disdain for those less intelligent than Dean M. Randall,
Ph.D. At least he hadn't lied and denied it.

"I just thought you should know that I suspect you might
have taped all my sessions with you."

Randall frowned. "I taped your sessions?"

Again the non-lie. "And if there is anything, just a whiff
of what I told you in confidence finding its way into your
book, I'll sue."

"I wouldn't—"

"Of course not," Carter said, allowing his mouth to stretch
into its most disarming country-boy smile. "But I just want
to forewarn you."

With that, Carter left. He walked through the door, down
the stairs and outside where late summer was giving way to
the first vestiges of autumn. The parking lot was dry, a few
dry leaves scattered over the pavement. Falls Crossing had
survived the coldest winter in nearly a century and though
there were some scars remaining, Randall was right, things
had worked out.

It had taken some time for the police to locate the bodies of the women Seth Whitaker had abducted. They'd been wrapped in tarps and hidden on his property, their frozen bodies naked and waiting for permanent disposal. Sonja Hatchell, Roxie Olmstead, and Lynnetta Swaggert, their heads shaved, their teeth filed down, had been located. The police had found Sonja's car hidden in an old shed and, locked in a drawer, dental appliances shaped from a mold stolen from the set of *White Out*. A way for Seth to give all of his mannequins Jenna's spectacular smile. The crime scene team, FBI psychologists, and of course, the press had all had a field day with the case.

Carter had been elevated to the status of local hero, a position he wasn't sure he deserved or wanted. He and Jenna had hardly left each other's side. They were talking about living together, perhaps getting married, though still taking things slowly.

Her kids, after spending last Christmas with their father, had returned to Falls Crossing. Allie had outwardly bounced back and puppy-dogged after Carter whenever he was at their house. He'd taken her and her friend Dani Settler riding, fishing and hiking in the woods before school started again. Allie seemed to be flourishing, coming out of her shell, though Cassie was still working through some of the trauma of her ordeal at Whitaker's hand.

Carter's jaw clenched when he thought of the bastard. In Carter's opinion, there wasn't a hell hot enough for Seth Whitaker.

Cassie's healing would take time. Probably years.

Her hair was growing out but she wasn't satisfied with it and, to make a point, she'd dyed the short strands a deep shade of magenta, which, surprisingly didn't look as bad as it sounded, until she used enough gel to make the short clumps stand out in weird spikes.

Despite her mother's counseling, Cassie was still struggling in school and hanging out with the wrong crowd, which, unfortunately, included BJ's daughter, Megan. However, Carter noticed progress in the girl . . . she was softening toward her mother, trying harder with her classes and, if somewhat warily, accepting Carter and Jenna's relationship.

"Get your message across to Randall?" Jenna asked as Carter slid into the passenger seat.

"Not quite."

"No?"

"Maybe I should add something for emphasis."

"Like what?"

Carter noticed Randall emerge from the building, adjust his tie, then hurry toward the parking lot. "Oh, like this," he said and wrapped his arms around her, dragging her hard against him. He pressed his mouth over hers and kissed her as if he didn't want to stop. Which, of course, he didn't. Her lips were warm and pliant, the little giggle and gasp that she had emitted when he'd grabbed her, melting away as the kiss intensified.

By the time he lifted his head, she was breathless and his crotch was definitely tight.

"Oh, my, Sheriff," she teased.

Smiling, he glanced over her shoulder, out the window, and observed Randall's look of surprise.

"What was that all about?" she asked.

"Just making a point." He winked at her.

"Did you make it?"

"Pretty sure. Let's go."

She snapped on her seat belt. "Your wish is my command."

"Yeah, right."

Flush-faced, she rammed the Jeep into gear and they drove through the town, past the old church with a marquee for a new production.

The storm had abated in mid-December, though lingering cold had ensured the ski resorts a fabulous season. But there had been a persisting gloom in the small town over the holidays. On January first, Carter threw away his ice-climbing gear.

He'd removed all pictures of Carolyn from his house and erased her from his mind, even bought Wes Allen a beer at the Lucky Seven; though when Allen had drunk the pilsner, he'd told Shane to "fuck off permanently" despite the fact that Rinda, ever the mother, had tried to help the two men patch things up. Scott had taken off for Portland, chasing down a girl, and Rinda had adopted two dogs and a turtle. In Carter's opinion, she needed a man, rather than the menagerie of pets she was collecting but figured she'd wake up to that fact soon enough.

Now, nine months later, Jenna drove to a section of town not far from the Junior High School, where a hundred-year-old Victorian home, complete with gingerbread accents, steep gables and a wide, sweeping front porch, stood behind a picket fence and small lawn where the grass was patchy and dry. Jenna checked her watch. "The lesson must be about over," she said as the Jeep idled near the driveway where Blanche Johnson's car was parked.

Allie was taking a piano lesson inside, though when Jenna rolled down the window, she didn't hear the usual musical notes escaping through the old, single-paned windows. Dani Settler was supposed to be with her as the girls had back-to-back lessons and had planned a sleepover at Jenna's place.

"My guess is she'll be out in a sec," Shane said.

Jenna checked her watch again just as Travis Settler drove up. He parked near the front walk and waved as he spied Jenna and Shane. His smile was still a bit tight, as if he hadn't quite forgiven Jenna for choosing Carter over him, but he seemed to be getting over it.

Swinging a small bag, he walked up to Jenna's rig. "Emergency call from Dani," he explained, holding up the small duffel. "She forgot her overnight bag when she went to school this morning and told me to drop it off here."

"We could have picked it up," Jenna said.

"Too late. I had to come into town anyway, and I wanted to talk to Dani before she took off for your place." He flashed a more amiable smile, then sniffed the air. "Do you smell smoke?" His gaze moved over the roof of the SUV toward Blanche's house.

"No . . ."

"I do," Shane said as he climbed out of the Jeep to stretch his legs. His gaze swept the area.

Jenna glanced at her watch again. The lesson was supposed to have been over nearly fifteen minutes ago and Allie wasn't one to hang out a second past the stated time. "I'll see what's going on." She was out of the Jeep and pushing open the gate as the acrid smell of smoke reached her nostrils. Not wood smoke. Something else.

"I'll come with you," Shane said as if he realized something wasn't right.

The first shiver of fear crawled across her skin as she rang the bell and heard chimes peal through the old house.

Then she noticed the door.

Ajar.

Probably one of the girls hadn't latched it properly as they ran inside. Right?

Jenna stepped inside and her heart began to knock. "Hi, Blanche!" she called, trying to calm herself. Nothing was wrong. Nothing could be. "It's Jenna." The foyer was empty. Dark. No sound inside except for the old timbers settling. "Blanche? Allie?"

She heard footsteps behind her. Travis and Shane had followed her inside. "What's going on?" Travis asked. "Where are the girls?"

"I don't know." She rounded the corner to the small parlor where the old upright piano stood. The bench was kicked out. Sheet music scattered upon the floor. A knot tightened in Jenna's gut. "Something's wrong," she whispered, her gaze flying around the room. Travis and Shane started searching. "Allie!" she screamed, and fear, the same mind-numbing fear she'd felt last winter, took a stranglehold of her. Not again, oh, please, *not again!*

"Jesus," Travis said as he looked behind the couch. His face turned white as death. "Call an ambulance!"

"What?" Panicked, Jenna was across the carpet in an instant, Shane already on his cell phone. Behind the couch, lying faceup, a pool of blood staining the carpet, lay Blanche Johnson. "No! Oh, God, no!"

Blanche, her skin a pasty white, her hair disheveled, blood pooled beneath her. Glassy, lifeless eyes stared upward.

Jenna's hand flew to her throat. "Not again," she whispered, fear grinding through her.

"Find the girls!" Travis ordered as he reached down to feel for Blanche's pulse. What seemed a lifetime later, he shook his head. "We're too late. She's dead."

Carter stepped over to the body. Held Jenna close. "I've called 911. Units are on the way." His eyes narrowed and he walked closer to the wall behind the piano. "What's this?"

For the first time Jenna noticed the mar in the wallpaper print, the angry words, scratched deeply, tearing the paper, smeared with a dark substance that trailed down the cabbage roses and vine print:

Payback Time.

"What the hell does that mean?" Travis asked, fear tightening his voice.

Allie? Where was Allie?

Turning, Jenna noticed the smoke. Thick and black, it curled in the hallway from the kitchen. "Fire!" she yelled. "Allie! Dani!" Oh, God, where were they? Frantically she ran to the front hall. They had to be safe. *Had* to. "Allie!" she yelled again. "Oh, God, where are they?"

In the distance, sirens screamed.

Travis grabbed a cloth arm protector from a side chair, held it over his mouth and nose and jogged toward the smoke. "Dani! For God's sake, are you here? Dani!"

Carter was already racing up the stairs. "Get out of the house, Jenna. Now!"

"No way."

"They're probably already outside!"

If only she dared believe it. Screaming her daughter's name, she threw open the door to the coat closet. Empty. She rushed into the living room. The dining room and butler's pantry. Nothing! She heard the crackle of flames and Carter's boots ringing overhead.

Travis, backing out of the kitchen, a fire extinguisher

spraying, called over his shoulder, "No one in the kitchen. Just a grease fire."

The house was empty.

As the police and fire crews arrived, a crowd gathered, and Shane shepherded Jenna outside to the Jeep. The cell phone! She climbed into the rig, found her phone and was about to dial when she noticed that she had two new messages. Both from Allie.

Insides churning, she listened and tears of relief flowed from her eyes at the sound of her daughter's voice. She blinked and swiped at her nose as she said to Travis, "She's at the school waiting for us there. Dani told her she'd gotten a call from Blanche. Piano lessons had been cancelled."

"So they're all right," Travis said, relief evident in the lines of his face. He pulled out his phone and dialed. Waited and frowned, then said, "Dani, this is Dad. Call me back." He clicked the phone shut. Stared at Shane. "She's not answering."

Jenna was already calling Allie and her daughter picked up immediately. "Hello?"

"Hi, honey." Relief flooded through her.

"Where are you?" Allie was angry. "I've been waiting forever!"

"I'm at Mrs. Johnson's. We must've gotten our wires crossed. I thought you were at your lesson, but stay put, I'm on my way to pick you up right now. I'll be there in five minutes. Is Dani with you?"

"No."

"No?" Jenna froze. Dread crystalized through her brain. Her eyes met Travis's. "Where is she?"

"I don't know," Allie grumbled. "She ditched me out."

"Ditched you out?" Jenna repeated. "That doesn't sound like Dani. What happened?"

"I said 'I don't know.' At lunch she told me that the piano lessons had been cancelled and that she'd meet me after last period and she's not here. *No* one's here." Jenna's heart nosedived. "Are you coming?"

"On my way. Wait near the office. Don't go anywhere. Do you hear me?"

"Yes! Geez."

A newfound worry clutching at her, Jenna looked into Travis Settler's eyes. "Dani's not with her," she said as the fire trucks, sirens screaming, rolled onto the street. Two police cruisers slid to a stop, spraying gravel. "I'm going to get Allie," she said to Shane. "We'll be right back."

"I'll come with you," Shane said.

"Don't you think you should tell them what's going on?" She hitched her chin toward the cops getting out of their cars. "I'll come back. With Allie."

Impatiently, Travis said, "Let's go. I'm right behind you."

Jenna sped away from the curb and noticed Travis's truck on her bumper. Three and a half minutes later, they pulled into the school's lot in tandem.

Allie, backpack slung over one slim shoulder, was waiting near the front doors of Harrington Junior High. Leaning on a post, arms crossed over her chest, she looked angry as all get out. Jenna didn't care. She threw herself out of the Jeep as Allie started walking to her.

The door to Travis's pickup burst open and slammed with a thud behind him as he crossed the parking lot.

"Where's Dani?" he asked, his expression military-hard.

"I already told Mom I don't have any idea," Allie said, some of her bravado slipping. "I haven't seen her since lunch."

"Has anyone?"

Allie shrugged and shook her head.

"Wait here," he ordered, then his tone softened. "Please."

Jenna's arms had surrounded her daughter. "We will," she promised as Travis left them standing outside and she, though it was over eighty degrees, shivered. Dear God, what was happening? Where was Dani? And Blanche? Why would anyone murder Blanche? *Payback Time?* What the hell did that mean?

Her cell phone chirped and seeing Shane's name on caller ID, she forced a smile. "Hi," she said, glancing around the deserted parking lot.

"Hi. Look, I thought you should know, my gut tells me this doesn't have anything to do with you or Allie. Whatever happened here is about Blanche."

"Then why is Dani missing?"

"Don't know yet. Maybe a coincidence, but—"

"But you don't believe in coincidence."

"Right. Listen, we'll figure it out," he assured her. "I already called the house. Cassie answered. She's fine."

"I was just about to do that." Jenna felt a new wave of relief that was tempered by her thoughts of Travis and his daughter. What the devil was going on with Dani. *She's all right. She's all right. She has to be. Calm down. This is all just a big mistake.*

Except that Blanche Johnson is dead.

Jenna squeezed Allie more tightly and was thankful for Shane. For his strength. For his love.

"Are you okay?" Worry edged his voice.

"Fine," she said, her throat thick with emotion.

"Good. Then, I'll see you at home. I'm going to be tied up for a couple of hours, so I'll catch a ride with someone."

"Or call me and I'll come get you." She was eager to be with him again. To feel him close.

"Either way," he said, then added, "I love you, you know."

"Yeah, I know. Me, too."

"The way it's supposed to be, darlin'," he said as Jenna heard the muffled sound of another voice vying for his attention. "Look, Jenna, I gotta go."

"Yeah." She blinked rapidly.

"See ya later."

"I'm counting on it, Sheriff," she teased, her eyes suddenly hot, tears of relief close to the surface as she clicked off, then pulled herself together. This wasn't the time to fall apart. Her girls were safe. Her life with Shane more secure and filled with more honest love than she'd ever thought possible.

Yet she couldn't help worrying about Dani Settler. Where the devil was she?

* * *

Travis felt as if something inside of him was about to explode. He jogged to the front doors of the school and swung them open. The halls were nearly deserted. No laughing children, no teachers, just a custodian wheeling a large garbage can down a hallway.

Inside the glassed-in office, a secretary was sitting behind her desk. Reading glasses were propped on the end of her nose, a phone was pressed to her ear and she was reading from a computer printout. She looked up at him as he approached. "Oh, Mr. Settler. I'm glad you're here." She offered him a forced smile. "Danielle didn't show up for physical education, the last period of the day. I was just making the call to your house. She'll need an excuse for—"

"What do you mean 'she didn't show up'?"

"Just that. Mr. Jamison had to mark her absent and . . ."

"Then where is she?" he demanded, his heart thudding in his ears.

"That's what I was going to ask you." Behind her reading glasses, the woman's eyes changed from taciturn to worried.

"The last time I saw her was when I dropped her off this morning," he said, a dark clawing fear scraping his insides. Images of Dani flashed, like ruffled cards in a deck, through his mind. Dani as a newborn, downy-haired and red-faced, Dani as a three-year-old with an impish smile and tumbling curls, Dani without her front teeth at Christmas when she was seven, Dani at her mother's funeral . . . Oh, God, where the hell was she?

"I think we'd better call the principal," the secretary said. She disconnected her phone and clicked a speed-dial button.

The principal, the police, the National Guard. Call whoever it took. In his peripheral vision Travis noticed Jenna and Allie walking toward the office. Both had strained expressions on their white faces and Travis Settler knew despair as deep and black as all hell itself.

Jenna and Allie stepped through the door, Jenna's hand protectively on her daughter's shoulder. "What did they say?" she asked.

The truth of it hit him like a sucker punch. "They don't

know where she is," he said, remembering Blanche Johnson's dead body, the weird bloodstained message scratched into the wall and the grease fire with its thick smoke. He swallowed hard and felt as if the very life had been squeezed out of him. All his darkest fears congealed. Life as he'd known it had stopped abruptly. "My daughter's missing," he said and knew, without a doubt, that his worst nightmare had just begun.

Dear Reader,

I hope you enjoyed Jenna and Shane's story. Boy, did I have a great time writing the book! The idea for *Deep Freeze* started when my editor said he wanted a book where the killer only kills in the winter. "Wow," I thought, "that's not much to go on. Why would he only kill with the snowfall? Where would the book be set? How would he do it?" But the idea for the story started to form just about the time my editor said, "And you know what? How about a companion book where the opposite is true: another serial killer, linked to the first, who kills either in or with intense heat."

I've always loved the idea of opposites or the yin and yang in life. I thought this was a fabulous idea. I ran with it.

So . . . the follow-up book that will be available in March 2006 is *Fatal Burn*. You'll meet old friends from *Deep Freeze* and meet some new ones as well.

Fatal Burn is Travis Settler's story. He's propelled into action as his only child, his adopted daughter, Dani, is missing, presumed abducted. He doesn't know how, where or why his daughter was stolen from him, but he intends to find her, and he'll use every method he's learned from his military/spy past to find her—with or without the cops.

Armed and dangerous, Travis follows a trail that leads straight to Shannon Carlyle's door in Northern California.

Shannon is Dani's birth mother as well as a beautiful woman with a dark past she'd hoped was put to rest forever, a woman who never thought she'd get the chance to again see the daughter she gave up as an infant.

Travis is giving her that chance and she leaps at it.

Neither trusting the other, Shannon and Travis have to work together. Time is running out. A serial arsonist has resumed his deadly fires and somehow, they fear, he's connected to Shannon.

And to Dani.

Don't forget to log on to *www.lisajackson.com* where you can learn more about *Deep Freeze* as well as my other books, play games, enter contests, take polls or participate in discussions online. At *www.themysterymansion.com*, you can log on and visit the mansion that has interactive rooms from some of my books.

Now, please turn the page, and get an exciting sneak peek at *Fatal Burn*.

Keep reading!

Best,
Lisa Jackson

Please turn the page for an
exciting sneak peek at
Lisa Jackson's
next new thriller
FATAL BURN
coming in March 2006!

He stood before the fire, feeling its heat, listening to the crackle of flames as they devoured the tinder-dry kindling. With all the shades drawn, he slowly unbuttoned his shirt, the crisp white cotton falling off his shoulders as moss ignited, hissing. Sparking.

Above the mantel was a mirror and he watched himself undress, looked at his perfectly honed body, muscles moving easily, flexing and sliding beneath the taut skin of an athlete.

He glanced at his eyes. Blue. Icy. Described by one woman as "bedroom eyes," by another as "cold eyes," by yet another unsuspecting woman as "eyes that had seen too much."

They'd all been right, he thought and flashed a smile.

A "killer smile" he'd heard.

Bingo.

The women had no idea how close to the truth they'd all been. He was handsome and he knew it. Not good-looking enough to turn heads on the street, but so interesting that women, once they noticed him, had trouble looking away.

There had been a time when he'd been so flattered that he'd rarely turned in the other direction, a time when he'd picked and chosen and rarely been denied.

He unbuckled his leather belt, let it fall to the hardwood

floor. His slacks slid easily off his butt, down his legs and pooled at his feet. He hadn't bothered with boxers or jockeys. Who cared? It was all about outward appearances.

Always.

His smile fell away as he walked closer to the mantel, feeling the heat already radiating from the old bricks. Pictures in frames stood at attention upon the smooth fir. Images he'd caught when his subject didn't realize he or she was on camera. People who knew him. Or of him. People who had to pay.

His eyes fixated on one photograph, slightly larger than the others, and he stared into her gorgeous face. He traced a finger along her hairline, his guts churning as he noticed her hazel eyes, slightly freckled nose, thick waves of unruly reddish curls. Her skin was pale, her eyes alive, her smile tenuous, as if she'd sensed him hiding in the shadowy trees, his lens poised at her heart-shaped face.

The dog, some kind of scraggly mutt, had appeared from the other side of the woods, lifted his nose in the air as he'd reached her, trembled, growled, and nearly given him away. Shannon had given the cur a short command and peered into the woods.

By that time, he'd been slipping away. Silently moving through the dark woods, putting distance between them, heading upwind. He'd gotten his snapshots. He'd needed nothing more.

Then.

Because the timing hadn't been right.

But now . . .

The fire glowed bright, seemed to pulse with life as it grew, giving the bare room a warm, rosy glow. He stared again at his image. So perfect in the mirror.

He turned, facing away from the reflection.

Looking over his shoulder, he gritted those perfect white teeth, gnashing them together as he saw the mirror's cruel image of his back, the skin scarred and shiny, looking as if it had melted from his body.

He remembered the fire.

The agony of his flesh being burned from his bones.

He'd never forget.

Not for as long as he drew a breath on this godforsaken planet.

And those who had done this to him would pay.

From the corner of his eye, he saw the picture of Shannon again. Beautiful and wary, as if she knew her life was about to change forever.

Look out, he thought, smiling evilly. *I'm coming, Shannon, oh, yes, I'm coming. And this time I'll have more than a camera with me.*

Contemporary Romance By
Kasey Michaels

__Can't Take My Eyes Off of You
  0-8217-6522-1 $6.50US/$8.50CAN

__Too Good to Be True
  0-8217-6774-7 $6.50US/$8.50CAN

__Love to Love You Baby
  0-8217-6844-1 $6.99US/$8.99CAN

__Be My Baby Tonight
  0-8217-7117-5 $6.99US/$9.99CAN

__This Must Be Love
  0-8217-7118-3 $6.99US/$9.99CAN

__This Can't Be Love
  0-8217-7119-1 $6.99US/$9.99CAN

Available Wherever Books Are Sold!

Visit our website at **www.kensingtonbooks.com**.

Discover the Romances of
Hannah Howell